Milk Fever

Milk Fever

a novel

LISSA M. COWAN

DEMETER PRESS, BRADFORD, ONTARIO

Canada Council   Conseil des Arts
for the Arts   du Canada

The publisher gratefully acknowledges the support of the Canada Council for
the Arts for its publishing program.

Demeter Press logo based on the sculpture "Demeter"
by Maria-Luise Bodirsky <www.keramik-atelier.bodirsky.de>

Printed and Bound in Canada

Library and Archives Canada Cataloguing in Publication

Cowan, Lissa–, author
   Milk fever / Lissa Cowan.

ISBN 978-1-927335-20-8 (pbk.)

   I. Title.

PS8605.O92528M54 2013   C813'.6   C2013-902295-3

Demeter Press
140 Holland Street West
P. O. Box 13022
Bradford, ON L3Z 2Y5
Tel: (905) 775-9089
Email: info@demeterpress.org
Website: www.demeterpress.org

MIX
Paper from
responsible sources
FSC® C004071

This is for my sister, Shannon

Contents

PROLOGUE
xiii

PART ONE

BOOKS
5

SOPHIE
9

KING'S LETTER
16

STRANGER
23

HANDKERCHIEF
31

LESSON
38

SIGN
45

JACQUES
55

DARKNESS
62

PAINTER
69

DIARY
76

PART TWO

DISAPPEARANCE
91

HUNT
97

PASSAGE
102

GRIEF
121

VISITOR
134

LIE
141

MILK
147

INVITATION
167

MILK FEVER

PART THREE

CLUE
177

HUMAN HEART
187

BEES
193

MANTUA-MAKER
201

PRISON
210

DOCTOR
216

DISCOVERY
220

PISTOL
228

RUMOURS
236

LOCKET
242

LISSA M. COWAN

PART FOUR

FATHER
251

GROWING
258

ACKNOWLEDGEMENTS
261

Man, are you capable of being just? It is a woman who poses the question; you will not deprive her of that right at least. Tell me, what gives you sovereign empire to oppress my sex? Your strength? Your talents? Observe the Creator in his wisdom; survey in all her grandeur that nature with whom you seem to want to be in harmony, and give me, if you dare, an example of this tyrannical empire. Go back to animals, consult the elements, study plants, finally glance at all the modifications of organic matter, and surrender to the evidence when I offer you the means; search, probe, and distinguish, if you can, the sexes in the administration of nature. Everywhere you will find them mingled; everywhere they cooperate in harmonious togetherness in this immortal masterpiece.

– Olympe de Gouges, Declaration of the Rights of Woman

Prologue, 1787

A PEDDLER WALKED TOWARDS ME with a bulging sack on his shoulders. He was tall, hunched, and his large, watery eyes rested in the folds of his eyelids like two fresh-cracked eggs in their half shells. He swayed from side to side as he trudged along the road, his wiry legs bent at the knee, his burden high on his back.

"What's your name?" he asked. Like a saucy sparrow, his eyes lit on my yellow hair, unwomanly waist and thighs.

"Céleste," I told him, feeling faint and barely able to speak for hunger pangs. I wondered what he might make me do for food, as it was rare to find a man who did not want something for his trouble.

"And what are you doing out here all alone?" He wore a three-cornered hat, had light-coloured hair and his red frock coat was worn at the shoulders.

"I am sixteen," I replied, thinking that was old enough to be walking by myself on a country road at midday.

Truth was, I wished my mother paid mind about where I was or what I would become, but she didn't and so I ran away and had wandered for days. My apron was soiled from sleeping on bare ground and my plain shawl in tatters. It was clear I was very poor, but my stomach hurt too much from lack of food to care about my appearance. I prayed the peddler would take pity on me. I did not know what he was selling yet reckoned there must be some food to be had in his oversized bundle of goods.

"Please sir, something to eat," I pleaded, waiting for him to strike a bargain with me.

Then, as if by magic, on top of his open sack, he laid out breads made with roots and exotic fruits, encrusted with wild white poppy seeds, anise and fennel. I had never seen breads like these before. Surely this must be the food of kings and princes from far-off lands. My eyes feasted on the sight, and I had to stop myself from grabbing one and stuffing it down my throat, not remembering the last time I had a proper meal. Yet the peddler soon showed me these weren't only fancy breads. He held one up in his bony fingers and broke it open. The yellow bread had a thick crust on one side that was adorned with fine gold lines and curlicues. The inside was made of delicate layers, like the finest pastry. I had never tasted such sweet delights, only desired after them in the village bakery. Like the other breads, it also had straight edges and looked as though it was baked in an oddly shaped pan.

"This contains a tragic tale of a country girl who goes to Paris and becomes a courtesan, a favourite among all manner of clergy and marquis," he said, his wide smile revealing a set of broken teeth.

What was this talk about stories told in breads one eats? Running my fingers over one that lay on his sack, I felt a tingling sensation run up my arm as if the bread held a special secret. It was unlike any bread I had come across, yet what else could it be? This one was nicely browned at the edges, and when I drew nearer, I saw that it had designs of birds, trees and hillsides carved into it. The peddler held the bread in his hands closer to me and I grabbed it from him, gnawing its edges. It tasted terrible.

He struck me on the back of the head causing me to spit out what was in my mouth. Then he took it from me and smoothed the edges with his fingers.

"These aren't food to eat," he said, sternly enough to give me a fright. "Do you wish to put me out of business?"

The peddler said there were tales inside, yet no tales came out of the thing in my hand. If they had, it would have been better buried in the ground, as it was a strange kind of magic to have a thing speak. He gave it back to me and said I could keep the object, as it was too scuffed for him to sell.

Opening it up, I saw that he had not lied about it being full of tales. Pictures of animals dressed in the clothes of gentlemen and gentlewomen spilled out of the bread and began whirling before my eyes. A princess slept in a very high bed while, from behind a tree a wolf watched a little girl who wore a red cape, a basket over one arm. The pictures delighted me and I could not stop gazing on them, the characters' expressions, voices and stories occupying my thoughts. Though somewhat afraid of it, I held the object close to me as I walked along the road.

Part 1

La Salle-les-Alpes, France

1789

Books

ARMANDE VIVANT HAD SOFT CHESTNUT EYES. I considered my own eyes to be cold looking. At least my mother told me that my green eyes were cold, and so I always envied women with a softer gaze. Women with eyes like that were prettier and people trusted them more. Since childhood Armande read many books, and I supposed that was why her eyes were gentler.

Margot the midwife had dark, yet pleasing eyes. She knew how to read but preferred to pen recipes for her tinctures or write in her diary about the stroll she took that afternoon and what floras she observed along the way. Our neighbour Nadine had eyes blue as a summer sky. I thought the woman's eyes were not gentle though, because she had never picked up a book. I read but had only learned when I was older. By that time my eyes had already taken on the character of a weak, unschooled girl that would define me for life. Though Armande did not agree with my views on this subject. She told me that any woman could become educated, and would appear that way to others, if she was determined enough and thought enough of herself. She taught me to read after I began living with her and her father Monsieur Vivant at their home in the mountains. I felt a growing inside my mind each time I read a book. Sometimes I didn't understand it all, but then whatever it was that entered me began to spring roots, and eventually become me.

I met Armande at a country estate where I worked as a servant shortly after meeting the peddler on the road. She was wet nurse for the Master's son. Her beauty struck me: dark curls piled atop her head, her eyes both stirring and comforting. Strangely to me, she spoke and walked like a gentle lady unlike most of her profession who were coarse as tree bark. When I asked the cook about her, she explained that while most wet nurses didn't know how to read or have a care for it, she read while giving suck to infants. Just as a gentlewoman gobbled sweet breads, pies and puddings, Armande devoured poetry, philosophy, history and botany. This, she said, made her refined, and also made the infants in her care different from other children. Everybody knows, the cook told me, her hands resting on her plump middle, when a child sucks at a woman's teats, the thoughts of that woman are impressed upon it. If a woman has vile thoughts and cusses morning until night, then any child she nurses will have the Devil for its friend. I realized then that books were a kind of food, and that reading was what made Armande's milk different from other women.

Determined to uncover the wet nurse's secrets, I would follow her skirts as she passed through an open door. Dusting porcelain figurines in the drawing room, I watched her as she sat by the fire brushing her long, dark curls with a shining silver hairbrush. She fastened the curls on top of her head, three or four strands washing over her cheeks. I hooked my gaze to her every gesture. At night I would repeat these pleasing images of her in my mind as I fell to sleep. She looked on me with tenderness as no one had before. Between chores, I tiptoed into the nursery while she slept in the rocking chair beside the resting baby boy. Just to be there. The cook told me she saw a change in the boy since he began taking her milk, curls now thick as sailor's rope, legs strong and wiry like a boy of six. Yet that wasn't all. The boy's eyes were pure and wise, the opposite of his father's. But just as I felt closer to knowing her, I learned that her time there was ending. The Master's child was weaned off Armande's milk and she would soon be leaving. I grew used to the wet nurse's kindness. Her singing, smiles in my direction, laughter, and her scent. I did not want it to end. Then a miracle came to pass. She asked the Master if she could take me with her.

"She has always been more of a curse than a blessing," he told her, speaking of me. And so it was settled.

Shortly after we arrived at her house in the mountainous village of La Salle-les-Alpes, she brought me to her father's library. Monsieur Vivant was away on business and bought and sold banned philosophical works in cities as far away as Bordeaux, Marseille and Lyon. Piles of books teetered on a table and replicas of Greek and Roman statues towered over me like giants from my wildest imaginings. Books covered the walls: brown spines with gold letters, green spines with red letters, dusty yellow with words surrounded by fanciful lines. A row of tall volumes rested on the first shelf behind an enormous oak table. These were encyclopedias and reference books, she told me. On the very top of the shelves were masks from Africa and beside that, a globe of the world.

Armande handed me a book that felt clumsy and stiff in my hands. I pressed it with all the strength I could bring to bear. She said the pages of books were made from cotton and linen rags stamped into pulp, then pressed into paper and hung to dry. I laughed at her for telling such a lie because I thought maybe she was just like my father who told tall tales to make me behave. Rows and rows of lines she called words looked odd to me. Many times I searched hard within every letter, every sound to find meaning. The letters cut my tongue as thorns on a rose bush, each one sticking to me. I could not speak the next letter until the one before it came unstuck. Soon after the word was finally spoken, my lazy tongue quit my mouth.

Months later, the wet nurse asked me to read a passage aloud. The first line was, *Bodies gliding on morning's cloak of dew, lit up as iridescent insect wings they flew.* When I came to the word iridescent, Armande said to say it slowly, one letter at a time. She told me it was from the word *iris* for the flower, and *escent* for colours of the rainbow that change as a dragonfly in the sun. Finally, when my tongue began working with me and worrying less, she asked me to say other words like deliquescent, effervescence, and florescence. These newfound words were as rare gems dug up by the wet nurse solely for me. She wrote them out with big stokes that filled a whole page. I rubbed my eyes to make the words go away, yet they only stayed there waiting for me to say them.

In the days and months that followed, I learned to read and write well, and I learned first-hand about the miraculous effects of Armande's milk on babies. Before, I was a mere servant watching from afar as the wet nurse suckled. Then I was part of her life, holding and changing babies, burping them, and rocking them to sleep. Armande cared for three babies during this period yet not all at once. She would also tend to others from time to time, reassuring worried mothers in soothing tones as gentle and sweet as the milk itself. First there was Jacques who she still cared for. His mother died in childbirth and Armande stepped up to nurse him without a thought about payment. Caroline came after, then Héloïse. The first time I watched from up close as Jacques drank her milk was in the drawing room.

Armande was on her favourite oak chair with the sagging blue leather seat and worn arms while I sat on the sofa. Suddenly Jacques stopped sucking, then gazed at me knowingly, his eyes full of light. In that instant, a slim ray of sun gleamed through a crack, lighting up the darkness inside me. My hands shook. Sweat ran down my cheeks and the back of my neck. Just as she said her father sometimes described it, we were entering a new age driven by light. And I, a peasant girl whose father and mother never held a book, would be there to witness the change.

Sophie

BABY NATHALIE WAS CRYING. I opened the curtain around my bed and wrapped myself in a blanket to fend off the winter chill. Floorboards creaked in the corridor as I stepped lightly on the cold wood floor. Armande's bedroom was at the end of the hall nearest the stairs. Nathalie lay in her basket at the foot of the bed. Her face was red and stained with tears, yet as soon as she saw me, and I drew her near, she calmed and was content. Downstairs Armande was in the kitchen, the fire blazing. Usually I lit fires in the drawing room and kitchen before the house woke up. That morning, although my mind wished to rise, my body had other ideas. I sat at the table by the frosted window rocking Nathalie and watching as Armande added turnips and carrots to the pot for soup. A dried bouquet of herbs hung over my head, crumbling mint and sage leaves collecting on the sill. I had picked the bouquet in the summer from our garden when all was blooming colours and sweet aromas. Yet that day, the snow was up to the window and looked as though it might creep inside.

"You slept long," she said with a gentle smile.

"The morning air was so cold," I replied. "My fingers are like icicles."

Her shining eyes laughed at me. She wore a deep red wool gown, the shade of roses in her garden. It cheered me to see a summery colour with the ground outside so thickly covered in snow. Jacques ran into the kitchen trailing a ball of yarn. His blonde hair was curly on top and straight at the sides just like his front teeth.

"Time to eat." She placed a bowl of boiled oatmeal on the table. He sat on his chair and didn't even notice the food in front of him as he proceeded to unwind all the yarn into a muddled heap.

9

"Jacques, put that away." She reached over his head and scooped up the yarn. "You can play after."

She mussed up the boy's hair and he grinned, picked up his spoon and began to shovel the food into his mouth. Nathalie was fidgeting and started to cry again as she was hungry. Soon Armande would nurse her and she would be content, yet until then it was my task to busy her. I began playing peek-a-boo using her knitted bonnet. Her eyes lit up, then she reached out to pull my nose. Next, she pulled my lower lip over to my ear. When she first came to us she would not swallow a single drop of Armande's milk, and instead wound her pink body into an angry knot. Then, suddenly, as if caressed by an angel, she began to draw the milk in, her tight fists slowly opening, wrinkled brow smoothing. The kitchen warmed and the windows steamed up as Armande added another log to the fire. Then she stood by the soup pot and nursed Nathalie who could barely contain her joy as she sucked greedily.

I hurried upstairs to change out of my bedgown and had just sat down to a plate of bread and stinky cheese when there was a loud knocking. That was often how it was at our house. Women came to ask Armande questions about their infants, or because they needed help with nursing. *Why does my child make a noise when he drinks? How can I get my infant to latch on? Why does she not sleep through the night? Can you take him?* There was never a moment's peace.

And, sure enough, there was a young woman at the front door holding a small bundle. She had freckles on her nose, cheeks and forehead, and her hair was the colour of butter.

"I wish to see the wet nurse." She entered the house and took the cloth from the baby's face. Its head was no bigger than a potato and wrinkles covered its forehead, cheeks and chin.

"He is two days old," she announced. "I arrived all the way from the village of Les Combes."

The shoulders of her cloak were covered in fresh snowflakes as was her grey-blue open gown and petticoat. She carried herself like a gentlewoman although she moved more slowly than one should for her age, which I supposed to be about eighteen. Her belly was still plump from being with child. Monsieur Vivant rushed down the corridor towards us. He was freshly shaven, his hair tied at the back with a ribbon and he wore his waistcoat with the gold buttons done up just right. Taking the young woman's hand, he kissed it and flashed a smile of the kind he saves to impress, and then continued to the library. She followed me into the drawing room where, by now, Armande was sitting in her armchair, Nathalie still tight to her chest.

"Madame Vivant," the woman said as she drew closer. "You must help me. My husband worked as an instructor at our new school where he developed a fever and died the very next day. Struck dead with a wintry chill, he didn't even see his newborn son. Villagers told me it was because he was teaching children to read and write, yet the old woman who sent me to you said that was nonsense."

"What is your opinion Mademoiselle?" Armande looked at her intently, the point of one of her sky-blue shoes peeking out from beneath her petticoat.

"He was a good husband to me, that's all I know." The woman's cheeks were shiny and red and she looked very tired, having walked a few hours in the snow.

"I've only just had my baby yet the milk hasn't come as milk should." She squatted on the floor. Her baby rested upon her lap. "I have no womanly way to feed him." Her desperate eyes searched Armande's face.

Nathalie finished nursing and was now fast asleep. I placed her in the basket with a flannel cover on top, and then began to bring the fire back to life.

"Besides the old woman, other villagers have spoken to me about your milk Madame Vivant. They say you have pots full with mother's milk hanging on hooks in the kitchen for babies to drink."

Her tired eyes lit up. Freckled nose shot up in the air. She imitated with bravado the gossiping women in her village, her voice soft, then high at times.

"With all that milk, the wet nurse will need to have more children to share in the abundance. Otherwise, the infants she suckles will be spoiled. They will believe that life is full of bounty and goodness instead of rot." She swished her infant to and fro, reciting a witches' charm to bring on the milk:

Hare's milke and mare's milk
An' all the beas' that bears milk
Come to me.

"Nicely done," Armande said, clapping her hands. "Even so, you won't draw out your milk by magic." She smiled, her eyes sizing up the woman.

"No I suppose not," Sophie replied. "Yet if it isn't magic then what could it be? You have no child, though I heard about the accident that...." I shushed her.

My face grew hot. Armande never spoke to me about her baby who died. I added a small piece of wood with flat sides to the fire, and watched until it lit, then added another. The woman had no business discussing Armande's past.

Sophie's face grew overcast and she started to cry. "How can I be a mother when I have no milk?" She held her child out to Armande as if showing off a basketful of fresh picked strawberries.

Armande smoothed a loose curl by her face and raised her thin brows.

"If you don't help me, my baby will starve. I fed him bread and water, which only made him sickly."

Little Jacques came in whining that he was hungry, and I stuck a morsel of cheese in his open mouth to quiet him.

Sophie took off her bonnet and cloak, and draped it over the sofa. By this time she was sobbing, her nose dripping onto her gown and on the thin ruffle of one chemise cuff. Her freckled cheeks reddened. She grabbed Armande's hand and brought it to the infant's fevered head. The wet nurse gazed into the mother's eyes.

"Watch." Armande untied her bodice and brought the infant to her bosom. She propped up her right elbow with cushions.

The infant opened its eyes, squirmed, bobbing his head. Sophie crossed herself three times, raising her eyes in prayer. At first the baby pushed the nipple away. Then he made lazy tries to catch her nipple in his jowls, losing it over and over to become a mouth sucking air.

"If the baby becomes agitated, you need to comfort him and try again." I thought how she was so good to these impatient women.

Finally, with several coaxes from Armande, the baby's little mouth opened, took the nipple and latched on. Its chops were like the mouth of a sea creature. In one of her father's natural history books were pictures of creatures slimy and long, sucking the water with their lips of jelly. All at once, Sophie lost her mask of worry.

"Tickle the baby's lower lip with your nipple," said Armande. "Caress its cheek if it turns its head. Bring the baby close to you so his nose touches your breast."

He drank peacefully, eyes closed. His hands were crumpled bits of leaf and veins in his head and neck pulsed. Slowly the baby came to life as he fed on her precious milk.

"Céleste, pray make Sophie some tea to warm herself as she shakes from the cold."

I came back with a blanket to find our visitor squatting down to look at her child feeding. After Sophie had the blanket I added water to heat the kettle. The infant's sleepy head rested on Armande's bosom like a king after a nightlong feast. His mouth was a dewy rosebud and his lids fluttered peacefully.

"Sit, sit," I said, bringing Sophie to the dish of tea I prepared. Her arms and legs trembled.

Jacques kept going to the fire, and I would pick him up and move him away from it. All the while, Sophie didn't budge from Armande's side rather she teetered on her tiptoes as if a mischievous spirit got hold of her.

"My child needs your milk," she said again, the blanket over her shoulders.

"Your milk will come, just wait and see," Armande said. "Put the nipple in the centre of his mouth above his tongue otherwise the baby can't suck."

"I've tried, but he won't even take it. An old woman in my village made me sniff, eat, and rub all kinds of runny, foul oils and leaves on my skin and I'm none the better for it."

"When was this?"

"Two days ago, right after my baby was born." Sophie finally plunked herself down and took a sip of tea.

"In time this will help. Remember, mothering teaches patience and listening. You must learn to listen to your infant."

Sophie sprung to her feet, almost knocking the tea from the table.

"Listen!" she exclaimed. "Je suis désolée Madame Vivant. I don't mean to be difficult." Her freckled nose pointed in the air again. "These are babies we're talking about. All they do is cry and fuss and soil their cots. Please tell me if I'm mistaken in this. What is there to listen to?"

She planted herself on the dormeuse, folding her arms across her chest. After the baby was full of milk, the wet nurse rocked him in her arms.

"He will tell you what he wants if only you listen." Armande caressed his cheeks and forehead. "See how he tells me he likes my gentle touches? His limbs are still, no wrinkles on his brow."

The baby's eyes opened as she held him up. He turned his tiny, wrinkled head to see who was there.

"You're so good with him. You see how he takes to you."

No truer words were ever spoken.

"Your emotions are all in a stir due to the loss of your husband and this has influenced the flow of milk coming in. Promise me you'll keep trying until the milk comes. Unlike what most believe about it, the first milk is the best."

The wet nurse looked squarely at the woman who nodded, forcing a smile.

"I will try, Madame Vivant," she said. Her eyes were tired. "You are gentle and wise, so naturally I shall do as you say." Sophie then scooped up her baby in her arms and quit the drawing room.

In the early afternoon I went about my chores in the house, stacking wood by the fires and mending. I was in the throes of darning one of Monsieur Vivant's socks when Armande came into the drawing room, a look of concern on her face.

"My father is most unsettled," she said. "He has locked himself in his library."

"What is it?" I had the highest regard for Monsieur Vivant. To me he had a big heart and a sharp mind filled with scientific facts and whole passages from books.

"He has just learned that Auguste, his dear friend was captured in Bordeaux during a hunger riot last month," she said. "He was in the city on business and had no part in what was going on, yet they imprisoned him. My father fears he is to blame for his friend's misfortune." She drew nearer to me and placed a warm hand on my shoulder. "Céleste could you please speak to him? I have tried but he is inconsolable."

I didn't know how I could help Monsieur Vivant.

"I've left a tray of food outside the door as he hasn't eaten all day," she said. "Perhaps if you bring it in to him...." She smiled at me and instantly my heart warmed, which gave me strength to do what she asked.

I went to the library and picked up the tray of food, then rapped lightly on the door. From the other side I heard Monsieur Vivant talking away to himself. After several knocks he finally opened the door to me. Although he wasn't cheerful in the least, the room was lit with the blaze of a warm fire which was inviting. I set the food on the table, and then all at once he opened his heart to me.

"Auguste's poor dear wife wrote to tell me that he has been charged with treason." His light brown hair speckled with grey was tousled. He wore no waistcoat, and his shirttails peeked from the top of his tan-coloured breeches. "Oh, my child, I have been the worst friend in the world to him." His breathing was laboured. "I gave him a book I wrote to take with him on his travels, which might have caused his arrest—merely a saucy tale of a scheming courtier and his unfaithful mistress. Yet because of that book the authorities might have suspected he conspired against the King. Any little thing will stir them these days."

"Do you really believe that you are to blame for his capture?" He was a learned man and had read many books, and yet he was talking nonsense.

"Most of the pamphlets I write or books I am having printed abroad are as harmful as a Sunday stroll in the Bois de Boulogne." He sat in an upholstered chair by the fire, his fingers nervously rubbing the arms. "Those in Versailles find ways to feast their eyes on all manner of erotic tales without fear of being reprimanded. The Duc de Praslin was found with six bales of forbidden books while it was rumoured that the King's youngest brother Artois was protecting hawkers. An aristocrat can hire private colporteurs to procure any erotic tidbit under the sun, while I cannot even qualify for simple tolerances from the King."

He stood up to get the bowl of chicken and barley soup, sat back down, and then dipped a crust of bread into the warm liquid as he drank up. Perched on the edge of the chair, my body soon settled into the warmth of his arm, and—as we watched the fire sputter and burn—I thought of how helpless I was to alter the destiny of a bookseller in the year 1789.

King's Letter

MONSIEUR VIVANT TOOK TO HIS LIBRARY again after hearing that his friend, imprisoned over a week ago for treason, was now dead. I was about to rap on the partly open door to console him when I heard him speaking in hushed tones about a wholly different matter.

"I received this letter two days ago and am too frightened to open it," he said.

"What is it?" Armande replied.

"A lettre de cachet addressed to me. Observe the royal seal."

"Why haven't you opened it? What do you think it could be?" Her voice quivered.

"It is an order for me to present myself to the authorities in Bordeaux where they will surely hang me just like poor dear Auguste."

"Open it, father," Armande insisted. There was rustling of paper and chairs scraping across the floor.

"What does it say?"

"I don't believe it," he gasped. "It's not what I expected at all."

"Tell me father," Armande pleaded.

"He summons you to Versailles...." His words trailed off.

"What do you mean?"

"His son the Dauphin is sick with consumption. It's right here," he raised his voice.

I thought they might open the door at any moment and so I quit the scene, my heart pounding throughout my body as I ran down the corridor.

Later that afternoon, seeing the letter on her desk in the drawing room, I knew there was no mistaking what I had heard. I hesitated a moment and then picked it up. The paper was of the finest quality. Like silk. I could not help myself and so touched it to my lips. The broken cachet or seal was the colour of blood. My first thought was that in my peasant's hands I held a letter signed by the King of France—the highest authority in the land. But what about Armande's safety should she go?

All of France knew the Dauphin was a weak child. Of course the boy had stopped nursing years before, but his father was desperately searching for an elixir to save his son's life. Now at the age of seven, his back was bent like Apollo's bow and he was in bed with fevers. Wet nurses were as common in France as mice in a root cellar. Rosy-cheeked peasants whose milk was healthy as the fresh country air they breathed. Yet somehow even the King and Queen, and perhaps all of Versailles, knew Armande was different.

Armande had just finished nursing Nathalie and brought her into the drawing room so I could get her to sleep. I began rocking the baby in hopes she would soon tire.

"The King wants me to nurse the Dauphin back to health," she said. Her eyes were distant and her corsage was partly undone from nursing.

"Will you go to Versailles?" My heart followed my words.

"How can I journey to Versailles when my conscience tells me that my duty is to those in my village? Does the King in his royal palace mull over the hardships of women here? He is more concerned with an innocent man like Auguste." She began to pace in front of the fire.

Above the hearth was a painting of a country scene, willow trees and river, two boys fishing knee high in water. A carpet covered the wide plank floors. The design was of orange and yellow autumn leaves.

"Perhaps, as my father believes, it all started from a harmless book."

I did not understand Armande's meaning until she told me of her first trip to Paris with her father, when she was six.

"We were in a church." She stopped pacing and stood by the fire. "My father was picking up a special package from a gentleman." Her chestnut eyes met my gaze.

"Did you know the man?" I asked, still rocking Nathalie to sleep.

"I came to know him later on." She gathered her hair at her shoulder and gave it a twist. "Monsieur Taranne. He towered over me, wore a yellow scarf and had a spindly nose and wide shoulders. The gentleman produced a small package, which my father quickly hid beneath his cloak. It was all very mysterious."

"What was the package?"

"A banned book, a series of stories that poked fun at the King. I remember that on leaving the church, my father bought me a bouquet of roses from one of the women on the boulevard. I stuck my nose into them, my senses filling instantly with their sweet aroma. Then, all at once, a boy reached out from a passing coach and pulled a flower from my bouquet, which sent the rest tumbling to the ground. When the pretty things were torn from my grasp, my eyes caught sight of children scattered in the streets like ants. Non-stop shiver of skin, heads split by the pain of hunger, bodies clutching ribs, broken, cut apart by pleurisy. As it sped away, my father looked after the gilded coach drawn by elegant horses in the finest trappings. His face suddenly turned overcast. 'How is it that the lord and lady and their handsome son can lie voluptuously in their coach while others line the streets with no shelter or food to eat? A time will come when people will become conscious of the tyrannies of kings and nobles. Then these despots will tremble before them.'"

She gazed into the blazing fire, a dark curl cascading over her brow. "It was a moment I will never forget. The uprisings happening in Paris and other cities around the country fill me with hope, yet still the future is uncertain." Her brow tightened.

"But how can you disobey the King's orders?" I asked her thinking how the King was appointed by almighty God to carry out his wishes.

"My father taught me to be brave and not recoil from speaking up against injustice and in favour of truth. My place is here, not in Versailles."

Monsieur Vivant came into the drawing room and sat on the sofa, his arms folded across his thin frame.

"Didn't you teach me that father?"

"Yes, my darling," he said. "Endeavour always to be brave." He had a scruffy face and sad eyes. "That's why we have to leave the village for Paris."

"What do you mean father?"

"The King addressed the letter to me," he said.

Armande met his gaze, her cheeks burning bright red. "I'm not leaving our home," she told him. "The King is like a spoiled child. His lettres de cachet are tantrums he takes to get his own way. These letters go against the parlement and have ruined the lives of far too many innocents."

Nathalie was finally asleep. I placed her in a basket with a flannel cover on top and began my daily lesson, which I missed doing that morning. Armande told me to get into the habit of reading well and understanding all the good in the mother tongue. For over two years I had taken her guidance to heart and practiced every day without fail. It was hard to concentrate though given their fiery discussion.

"I agree wholeheartedly and commend you on your steadfastness *not* to play by his rules, which are capricious at best."

"In any case, they asked for *me*," she told him. "Perhaps by staying I am putting you in danger?"

"It is a trap." Monsieur Vivant leapt up from the sofa. "He knows about my bookselling as I said. Why else would he have addressed the letter to me rather than you?" Monsieur Vivant's white shirt hung outside his breeches, his tails waving this way and that as he walked on the carpet before the fire.

"My father gave Auguste a book he wrote of libertine tales," she explained to me. "He thinks that might have caused his dear friend's arrest, and put my father in their sights once more."

I already knew about the book in Auguste's possession as Monsieur Vivant told me the day he received the letter about his imprisonment.

"Yes, they've heard about your milk and, yes, the King and Queen want you to nurse the dearly loved and sickly Dauphin, the next in line to be crowned," he continued. "Yet what is also clear to me on reading this letter is that the King doesn't know where I am, yet believes you will make his letter known to me. I will then accompany you to Versailles at which point I will be arrested. If you journey on your own they will demand you tell them of my whereabouts. It is possible that they will harm you if you don't obey their wishes. If we go together, all will be over for me. Yet should you refuse to go, eventually they would come looking for both of us."

"How can you be so sure they are after you as well?"

"My beloved daughter, remember when I went into hiding for several months and you mistook me for dead. Scoundrels sent by the King set the boat on fire that contained the books I was transporting down the Rhône River. I barely escaped with my life. As it happens, some time ago, Monsieur Taranne invited me to work with him in Paris just like old times. I told him I would give the matter serious consideration. With his connections to foreign publishers and go-betweens coupled with my good judgment about what to print, facility for printing pamphlets and finding authors, we are well-matched business partners. Just imagine that these various facets of our work are several springs, which, as La Mettrie writes, make up the man as machine, and you have the level of solidity and efficiency we embody."

"You are a very good match," said Armande. "That does not change the fact that you are the most obstinate man I know."

"Not quite the most obstinate man."

"You promised to never speak of him again." Armande's voice shrank to a whisper.

My ears perked up. Was her father talking about her estranged husband? I never met him, yet heard from villagers he fled the village saying she was a witch. She changed her name back after he left her. *What sort of woman would not take her husband's name to the grave?* Idle gossip was better to ignore.

"Can you ever forgive me? I am feeling the weight of what is before us and was thoughtless." He took her hand, brushing a hair from her face.

Armande's shoulders shook as she cried. I set my book to the side and ran over to comfort her.

"You mustn't go father. Not again," she said between sobs.

I held her for several moments, her wet cheek on my shoulder. I did not know what to say and so just kept her close to me until she pulled away.

"Now, now my darling daughter—you mean everything to me." He cupped her face with his hands. "You fear for my safety."

"There are more of the King's police roaming the streets in Paris, more chances that you'll be captured," she said, her eyes gazing on him with worry and adoration.

Little Jacques came running in at that moment. I quickly set out some blocks for him to play with so he wouldn't bother Armande. He sat on his heels, throwing a handful of colourful wooden shapes across the floor, then clapping his hands at the ear-splitting sound they made. His hair was messy and he wore one of Armande's scarves on his head like a turban. A green shiny necklace circled his wrist. "Please come with me to Paris. And of course Céleste should come too. I can protect you both there." He looked in my direction. "It is only a matter of time before they start looking for us."

"They may come for me if they wish father, yet my home is here and this is where I belong."

"Why is wet nursing your duty?" His tone was anxious. "I did not spend all that time with you in the library reading for you to care for other people's children." It was the first time I heard him raise his voice to her in anger.

"You have never understood father," Armande said to him. "Women seek my counsel and are lost without it. This is where we differ."

She hurried out of the drawing room, covering her face with her hands.

"Armande has enemies as you well know." He pointed a finger at me. "Ignorance is rampant here. She must stay out of harm's way."

"Yes Monsieur." I lowered my head, trying with every scrap of my being not to cry.

"Sometimes circumstances force us to stand up for what we know is right, no matter what the outcome. Auguste was a cherished friend." Two lines etched between his brows. "The other day I was on a jaunt through the forest when the woman who keeps bees passed by. She said something under her breath about my having a devil for a daughter. Peasants are becoming more restless as they have less and less to feed and clothe their children. They imagine things. Weave stories about people that aren't true. Soon they will be out for blood, not milk."

The hairs on the back of my neck stood up. His words sliced through me. I saw how some people looked at Armande as though she was a dark force, yet I also saw how villagers warmed to her and held her in high esteem.

"You will take care of my daughter won't you? See she doesn't come to any harm?"

"I will, Monsieur," I told him, not considering for a moment he might really leave us.

"You're a good girl, Céleste. Nobody is as sturdy and constant as you." His hair was tied back, a few strands trailing over his eyes. Beads of sweat collected on his brow and above his upper lip.

After supper, Armande and I sat side-by-side on the dormeuse. Her lavender and milk smells filled my nose when she hugged me closed and draped her shawl over my shoulders. She would put sprigs of the plant in her armoire to carry the scent with her throughout the day. The fire was almost out, the last log quickly melting into the embers. Armande's breath was light and steady. She pressed her body close to mine, a lock of her hair brushing against my cheek. One of my big toes peeked out of a hole in my stocking, and so it was colder than the rest. The drawing room suddenly became dark without the fire. A chill ran over my shoulders and the back of my neck when Armande got up and went to the window.

"Anything that encourages the fires of rebellion is viewed as a danger by those who hold power," she said. "My father is worried for us should we remain here. He is afraid that, like his friend, he too risks imprisonment, death, or being sent off in chains to row in the galleys."

Blue curtains surrounded her thin yet solid body on either side. Her gown was deep red like cherries and her chemise billowed at the arms midway down. I thought she could almost be a portrait hanging on a wall. She stood so still, her hair fastened on top of her head with a few locks around her face, just like a proper queen.

With her back to me, she said, "They have finally caught up to us Céleste."

Stranger

TWO DAYS AFTER MONSIEUR VIVANT received the lettre de cachet, a storm hit our village and a maple tree came crashing down, barely missing the house. I saw this as God's way of protecting Armande from malevolent forces and from stopping her father leaving us too soon. The wind knocked at the door like a desperate soul needing shelter. I rolled up an old carpet and placed it at the base to staunch the flow of cold air coming in. Monsieur Vivant dug snow from the front door. Then, axe in hand, he began cutting up the fallen tree for firewood. From the drawing room window I watched him hacking into the trunk as he cursed the storm for making him wait days to leave.

I put on my cloak and dashed outside. Our house had a red door with a letterbox beside it. Snowdrifts were high beside the narrow path and rooftops bent with snow. Like other houses in the village, ours was made of rough stone and sunken into the ground.

"It's as much as I can muster now," he said out of breath and pointing to the fresh pile of wood. "More trees fell in the woods during the storm so we'll have more to cut." His cheeks were red from the cold, his body wrapped in layers of clothing, and there was a sprinkling of snow on top of his greying hair.

"I'll chop." I took the axe from him.

He smiled at me, wiping his sweaty brow. His breath came out of his mouth in large clumps, hitting my face. The axe was hot where he gripped it. A leafless tree waved in the wind, the forest behind it was smudged white.

"As soon as the storm settles, I'll go," he told me, then grimaced and said, "Recently, inspecteurs de la librairie at Rouen confiscated copies I ordered from Brussels of *Nun in a Bedgown* and *One Thousand and One Memories* for the Comte de Pestels. In Paris my shipments will be less conspicuous. Besides, Monsieur Taranne will arrange everything for me there."

I tried to smile for his sake yet my face was tight from cold.

He added, "Don't forget what I told you about protecting Armande."

In the afternoon the wind died down. Armande's face showed grief as she stood by the window and watched the sun peeking through clouds. Good weather meant her father would soon go away. From where I sat by the fire, her eyes seemed hollow and her mouth was sunken a little into her face, like those on a mask from a Greek tragedy. There was a picture of one such mask in a book belonging to her father about the history of drama.

I was mending Jacques' coat and rather than play with his blocks he wanted to help me. He kept saying, "Let me, let me," and putting his hand on mine as I held the needle. This bothered me no end. I was behind on my mending and he was slowing me down. The collar was coming apart where he previously gnawed and pulled at it and the whole thing was almost off. I slowly pushed the needle into the cloth and pulled it out to show him how, then after a few moments, his attention turned elsewhere.

Monsieur Vivant crouched on the floor arranging his pens and inks. He had different size wooden boxes spread out in front of him. One had a faded label on the side that said *sauterelles*, and another, *papillons*. He collected grasshoppers and butterflies but his main love was bees. In his library was a wooden case with many small compartments that housed a hundred or more bees. Some were large and round with yellow and black markings, while others were much smaller, and had perfect wings.

"Céleste, father reminded me of the passages between our neighbours' houses," she said perking up.

"You used to clamber around down there as a child," he said.

"Our cellar has a passageway from it to Bertrand and Nadine's root cellar, and from there to the wool spinner Madame Jardin," she told me. "The passage then leads to the Gallants' house."

Monsieur Vivant glanced up at me, a box of butterflies in one hand. "It would be too cold to stay for very long. I've spoken to these neighbours and they told me they will keep you warm and fed."

"What if they come looking for us next door?" I asked.

"They will certainly call on the neighbours to trace you," he told me. "So you'll have to go between their houses depending on where the danger lies."

I imagined us scurrying back and forth between the neighbour's houses like a pair of frightened mice. Strangely though, Monsieur Vivant's plan made me feel more secure.

"Thank you," she whispered, clutching the gold pendant around her neck, which held a silhouette portrait of her mother and father. She curled up on the dormeuse, her dark hair streaming down the sides of her face and onto her delicate shoulders.

"We survived far worse," he said sensing her melancholy. Armande met his gaze. "Remember during the scourge when fever and chills gripped so many helpless souls?" He sat up, crossed his legs, his long shirt covering his knees.

She turned to me and continued her father's thought: "I comforted neighbours who lay in their beds crying out for God to have mercy on their souls. I applied a cold cloth to their heads, sometimes reading poetry or the Bible, to ease their suffering. Those who lived through the ordeal were badly disfigured."

I listened to their remembrances and watched Jacques proudly try on the coat I just finished mending for him.

"A villager circulated a story about the scourge that because our village was high in the mountains God was giving us a quicker way to experience Heaven," said Monsieur Vivant. "Another story went that we were being punished because a few people in the village were secretly involved in a ceremony in which an effigy was made of the King and then burned."

Armande laughed weakly.

"Do you remember what I said?" he asked her.

"Yes father, you called this talk absurd and told me not to heed words of superstition and fear because reason and science would save us from ignorance, eventually saving us from illness and disease altogether."

"Sophie was telling me about the cahiers," I said, eager to join the conversation. "She says a delegate was sent to her village by the King to collect grievances. Everybody from farmers to physicks fought to have their complaints recorded in these Royal cahiers. From what she told me, many are demanding a stop to the abuses of hunting rights."

"Why should a noble be free to hunt fox and wolf, keep pigeons and rabbits when peasants are punished for pulling a measly fish out of the river that runs through the estate they live on?" Monsieur Vivant stopped arranging his inks and pens on the floor.

"What do you make of this action by the King?" Armande asked.

"This is an astonishing gesture on his part, yet far too late to be of much use," he said dismissing it with a sweeping hand.

Armande ran upstairs to nurse the crying baby and her father tossed a log on the fire and quit the drawing room. Maybe he was right about it being too late for the King to mend his ways. I never had much faith in men, as most I met were scoundrels, except of course for Monsieur Vivant. Since living with them, I did not go hungry and was genuinely loved yet I had more questions. I called these questions my thoughts. When reading a passage from a great work or after watching an infant drink Armande's precious milk, something happened to make me wander around in these thoughts as if they were rooms. I asked: *What is life? Will I marry? When will I die? Will I ever be happy?* Now and then, I imagined they were the rooms of Armande or those of her father. I knew when they were his rooms because I recognized his brown books with gilded spines, his Greek and Roman statues, a favourite chair, heavy and carved with jungle creatures, like the one in his library, a walking stick, an old dressing gown. He often left it hanging on a hook in his bedroom. Her rooms were filled with plants, a red quill dyed from mountain berries, books of poetry, a sleeping baby, a clever baby, and a lock of dark wavy hair—though I cannot say from whose head it was plucked. When he left us would I only be wandering in her rooms or would traces of his presence remain in my mind and body?

Later that afternoon I went into the kitchen to find Armande chopping vegetables for the evening supper. Beside her, windowpanes were painted with hoarfrost in the shape of flowers. Nathalie lay on a blanket on the floor. I picked her up and she made a gurgling sound that told me she was content.

"He really is leaving us," I said, trying to convince myself it was true.

"He seems determined," she answered with a deep sigh. She wore a simple ivory robe with thick pleats at the back that brought out her curves, and a top petticoat in dark pink and white.

Jacques was at the table happily playing with an empty inkwell, round like the globe of the world. With book and paper in hand, I sat beside him and turned to a page from my reading the other day, about Jupiter and its moons as observed by the Tuscan astronomer through his self-made instrument. I began to write down a list of new words I learned—Jupiter, nebulous, Milky Way, orbit, when the front door flew open. A gust of wind entered followed by shrill laughter. I ran out of the kitchen to see who was there when a young woman scurried down the hallway, the puffed up backside of her gown slipping into the library.

She was laughing in that way women do when they want a man to kiss them. At first, I thought Monsieur Vivant was up to his tricks of seducing the ladies. Armande told me, as a young man he was to join the priesthood yet could not keep his nose out from under women's petticoats. I edged my way along the corridor to the library and heard muffled voices. Furniture scraped across the floor, then more laughter. "Yes, I saw the man you described to me," said the woman. "The house where he stays is two over from mine in Les Combes. There is little doubt it is he. Look, I found this in the snow by his front door."

The library door was thick and so I crouched firmly against it. My knees together, petticoat circling me, and my hands cupped to my ear.

"Yes, there is no doubt now, good girl Sophie. He must have dropped it."

There was more mumbling. It was almost dark in the corridor, only a sliver of day coming in from a small window at the end. Cold crept under my petticoat sending a chill up my back.

"Does he know about her reputation?" Sophie asked.

"Of course, yes he must know. That man makes a habit of knowing everything. I've heard he works undercover, spying on hapless citizens in Paris, since leaving the village. Keep watch on him each time he leaves the house. I need to know why he is here. I must leave, as it is no longer safe for me. I am counting on you Sophie. See that he doesn't come to our home."

"I will not seduce him Monsieur. You have been very kind to me and I am a poor widow, yet a girl has her virtue to uphold." Sophie's voice was feeble.

"There is no need for that. Here take this. Only present it to him if you think he means to come here. Once you show him this letter he will leave her be."

Suddenly the door flung open and I scrambled to the light at the end of the hallway. A black spider sat in a dusty cobweb between two beams in the wall. The tiny creature would be my salvation.

"What are you doing on the floor Céleste?"

Armande's father and Sophie loomed over me. She held the baby that she brought last week to Armande for help with her nursing. I thought she must have stashed the letter away in her pocket.

"Observing the spider perched in its web," I replied, my heart threatening to leave my rib cage.

"Spiders are wise creatures. Did you know they aren't insects at all but invertebrates?"

Still squatting on the floor, I shook my head at Monsieur Vivant's question. I took in a long, deep breath down to my toes. The shadows moved away from me into darkness, the echo of voices filling the corridor.

Sophie sat in the drawing room rocking her baby and was smiling from ear to ear. Her eyes looked tired, her skin paler than before.

"I'm here to report on progress with my milk," she said proudly. Armande wandered in at that moment. She wore a deep blue shawl over her shoulders and held Nathalie in her arms.

"I did just as you instructed Madame Vivant," she said. "Now he's the happiest baby in France." Her grey-blue cloak was open to reveal a lovely green robe the colour of pond moss. That shade made her blonde hair even more dazzling.

"I also began listening like you told me, even though I considered it strange to be so attentive to such a delicate, unknowing creature."

"Not unknowing Sophie," Armande corrected her. "All-knowing."

Sophie looked at her queerly, almost afraid.

"Don't forget you must be strict about your diet as it influences the quality of your milk. In summertime, eat soft foods like lettuce, spinach, clover flowers and pansies. In winter, eat foods that fix you to the earth—carrots, turnips and yams."

Maybe this was another reason people claimed her milk made babies more docile. Armande had a gentle way about her, which some said also penetrated the milk.

"That's a great distance for you to come Sophie, all the way from Les Combes," I said.

"My father escorted me," she replied anxiously. "He had some business to do in your village. I'm staying with my mother and father now that my husband is gone." Her eyes had tears in them. "Last spring and summer my father worked for a seigneur not far from here, and that is who he is visiting. He plowed the land using two of his horses, and helped sow the man's crops. When he returned to us after the summer, he was sunburned, almost black—the same colour as the earth." She forced a laugh, her freckled cheeks billowing.

I was desperate to speak to her alone. I did not like going behind Armande's back, yet I knew her father was being secretive for his daughter's sake, and it seemed only natural I should do the same. After all, as her father said, it was my job to keep her from harm's way. She was precious as was her milk. Both needed protecting.

"Why don't you stay and eat Sophie?" I said to her. "I'm going to make some cheese and honey on bread for Jacques, wherever he's hiding." Armande told me he was in the kitchen playing with some pots and pans.

"No, thank you, my father will be along any moment, and we must arrive back before dark." She stood up, curtseyed and left the drawing room.

"I am worried about Armande," I told her in a low voice as I walked her to the front door.

"So am I," she said.

"Oh, why is that?"

The young woman turned away from me, moving a hand in front of her face.

"Some villagers say she's cursed because she killed her own." Her lips were pressed together like the painted mouth of a porcelain doll. She hesitated a moment as if she wanted to tell me something more. Then she opened the front door to leave. She seemed honest at heart, yet not cunning like I was. Monsieur Vivant made a big mistake giving a task to Sophie whose only experience of thieves and killers was through fairy tales.

"Wait." I wanted desperately to get my hands on the letter Armande's father gave her, yet I could not ask her for it. Then she would know I had eavesdropped on her and Monsieur Vivant.

"I know you are looking out for the wet nurse, as am I. Of course, that's because she has helped you nurse your baby, and is so kind and gentle to you." Her eyes lit up.

"Maybe we could work together to protect Armande."

"Monsieur told me not to tell anyone," she said timidly. "I have told you too much already."

"I wouldn't want you to do anything against Armande's father. He is a father to me also, and I owe him every bit of my respect."

"I must go, my father's waiting for me."

Sophie's baby groped the air with his mouth. Then she curtsied awkwardly and was out the door, her darkly clothed shape bobbing amidst a sea of white. I gave chase with no coat or shoes.

"You must let me help you," I stammered, when I caught up to her. "Armande is in grave danger. You must promise not to tell a single living soul."

I told her about the lettre de cachet and Armande refusing to go to Versailles and nurse the sickly Dauphin. If I gave to her, she might give back. It was my only chance to learn more from her.

Finally, my words ignited something in the girl. "Come over and see me next Monday." She was breathless. "I'll be alone and we can talk then."

Handkerchief

I SUFFERED A STRING OF DISTURBING nightmares and awoke in a sweat to hear wolves howling. My bedchamber was dark and cold. Jacques was crying to himself as I walked by his room.

"Monsieur is going away." His face was beet red, his apple-sized cheeks streaming with tears. "No more horsey."

"Yes, he is leaving." I set the light on the bedside table. "I can play horsey with you. Why don't you climb on my back right now and I'll show you."

Jacques stood on his bed, a smile widening. He was two-and-a-half years old yet had the strength of a much older child. He jumped up and down and then tucked his nightshirt between his legs. I bent down, my back to him. I grabbed hold of his legs as he climbed on, whinnied like a horse and cantered round and round the cold bedchamber.

"Go horsey, go," he shouted, taking a clump of my thin hair in each hand. I took some clothes for him before we trotted down the stairs together. With each step my heart sunk as I thought about Armande's father leaving us. There would be no impromptu lessons about bees, the constellations, the machinelike qualities of the human body or any other scientific facts. He was the first man I knew who did not want something from me.

When I reached the kitchen, Monsieur Vivant was already dressed in his coat. The fire was roaring, the frost on the windows thawing in droplets. He wore a periwig, which he only dusted off for travelling and societal affairs.

I dressed Jacques in his heavy brown trousers with pockets at the sides, and a chemise with long arms and a plain round neck. The first I had fashioned from Armande's old cloak, and the second out

31

of a hemp scrap left over from a summer curtain.

Monsieur Vivant sat at the table eating porridge, his black felt hat on the table beside him. He raised his head to look at me as I entered the kitchen. "Dear Céleste, I know you will take care of things while I'm away."

"Yes Monsieur," I replied, my heart shrinking inside my chest. A chill went up my skirts all the way to my neck as I watched him spoon the thick liquid into his mouth.

"Unlike most young women of her station, Armande had no governess and never went to a convent," he explained. "She had no mother at her side, yet I raised her as best I could and encouraged her to spend much time in Nature. I have always worried that perhaps I raised her to be too independent. Sometimes when she needs a helping hand she doesn't ask for it."

"I understand. I will keep a watchful eye."

The lines in his forehead disappeared to show I had his confidence.

Moments later Armande came downstairs complaining of a headache. Her hair hung loose around her shoulders. Nathalie still slept upstairs.

The two spoke in solemn tones about her father's long journey ahead. How many days it would take given the new snow, how the poor horses would be made to plow through it, and where he might stay in the different towns and villages. He had friends throughout the countryside that would feed and lodge him. And if he stopped in a village where he was a stranger, then a peasant family would take him in.

"It would be most grand if I could hire a désobligeant in Grenoble," he perked up.

"Yes," replied Armande. "That way you could rest or write and not be *obliged* to speak to anybody," she mused. She wore a simple beige dress with black swirls of stitching at the hem and an off-white petticoat.

Monsieur Vivant's bags lay in a heap at the front door. Bertrand, a neighbour, arrived to accompany him on foot as far as the town of Briançon where he would then hire a coach to the city.

I pushed my feelings down when he hugged me close. I did not know when I would see him again.

"You have never done what you were told," he scolded his daughter. "You must have learned that from me." The two laughed and then wept as they held each other tightly. They pulled me into their circle so we were three. Warmth from their bodies filled me head to toe, and it was the first time I really understood the word family.

That afternoon, Armande was busy with Jacques. He had a new set of teeth at the back breaking the skin and was crying and fussing. After trying a few different things that bore no fruit, she consulted *Encyclopédie,* reading under the words enfants, nourrice, maladies d'enfants for a morsel of wisdom to help her. Yet she only became angry at the tome and those who wrote in it.

"Men of scientific methods using scholarly dissertations that are too stupid or inadequate to ever be applied," she mumbled then said, "The majority of these reasoners lack common sense and will cure me of reasoning altogether."

At her wits end, she quit the drawing room, leaving me with the screaming child. Since Monsieur Vivant left that morning she was more quick-tempered. I tried to hold Jacques to still him while I sang his favourite song, yet the child would have none of it. He broke free and headed for the sofa, jumping up and down on the cushions and screaming. I did not have the same skill with children that Armande did. They often squeezed out of my grip, their little mouths wailing and spitting until I delivered them back to Armande. Finally, I managed to lure the boy to the floor to play with some blocks. A few minutes later he said, "My blocks are gone. I lost them all." He had a dab of brown lentil on his chin from lunch. His forehead was bruised where he bumped it earlier in the day. I reached under the sofa to retrieve the blocks at which point he quieted down and began building a tower.

Armande returned with Madame Le Rebours' *Avis aux Mères qui veulent nourir leurs enfants.* Sitting at her escritoire, she flipped through the pages of the book and then read aloud what the good midwife counselled: "Rub whole clove over its gums to deaden the pain, and then rock the baby until it falls to sleep."

Armande went to the kitchen and came back with cloves. Though Jacques wasn't happy to have the strong taste of the spice in his mouth, he took what she gave him as per Madame's instruction. After, she brought him upstairs for a nap and gave him a cold carrot to chew on for the pain. She told the child a good yarn in his bed until his eyes closed.

When all was quiet, she wrote in her notebook. The lantern on her escritoire shook as her pen moved across the page. Maybe she recorded how the child would not even eat applesauce, his favourite, and how he kicked and waved his arms in the air when she tried to give him suck. An occasional treat, now that he was mostly eating solid foods. The flames greedily ate the wood scraps I threw into the pit and then clawed at the only log, partly burned away. Adding a bigger piece of cedar with some small branches attached, I poked the red embers to make it catch.

Now that Armande was busy, and Nathalie and Jacques were napping, it was my chance to go to her father's library. I had not had a moment to myself all day.

I tugged and pulled at the heavy curtains in the library to open them, then watched as dust particles floated on rays of light. Little glass windowpanes bent the image of a row of still-young cypress trees outside. I lit a lantern, as the winter light was dim outside. I looked around the room half expecting to see Monsieur Vivant correcting proofs for his next pamphlet. Thoughts of his booming voice, of his shining eyes, suddenly warmed me. I opened a drawer of his writing desk. Inside was a collection of ivory carved miniatures from the Orient. A mix-up of limbs, tongues and private parts. Where there was a buttock, there was a hand, a breast here, there a pair of lips. The sinful scene made me blush as it was just like I imagined her father to be with the women he frequented, twisted bodies groping, grunting, eyes gleaming.

On top of his desk were notes about bees' mating habits and their relationship to flowers. *Shortly after erupting from the pupae, the solitary female bee mates with a male counterpart and then carefully assembles a nest of her own making. After filling it with enough pollen for her progeny, she lays her eggs within each of the cells lined with wax, petals or tiny particles of leaf. The mother then leaves the nest, dying shortly after, perhaps while catching the final sip of nectar from her favourite flower.* The pages had his initials in each corner and were bent at the edges. *Solitary bees are very selective about what flowers they gather pollen from. Most frequent only a few species of flower and it is not apparent whether this is as a result of a preference for one colour of flower over another or whether it is the unique nectar that draws them.*

To smell wax and ink on these papers scattered over his writing desk and written in his hand made me feel how much I truly loved him as the father I never had. Yet, not finding any clues linking to his secret exchange with Sophie irritated me.

In a cupboard under the shelves was where Monsieur Vivant kept his writing books and published works, along with odds and ends such as special coloured inks, a gold ring with a red stone. Most of the papers that he did not take with him on his trip he burned for fear they would get into the wrong hands.

While crouching on the library floor to look in the cupboard, something caught my eye. It was a white handkerchief, dusty and smelling of honey and cedar. I shook it until it came clean, and then saw, inscribed in the corner in bright red the initials R.P.

Armande was calling me from the drawing room to fetch her some more dry wood. Quickly placing the handkerchief on the long table by the silver taperstick, I gathered wood from the small pile in the back room, then deposited some in the kitchen and drawing room. I thought the handkerchief must be what Sophie found in the snow and gave to Monsieur Vivant that day when the two met. Deeply ashamed for snooping through his things, I told Armande that I was going to chop wood, and then rushed outside. I didn't want her to catch the lie on my face, even though I had to admit I was content to have found something.

The grey stone wall circling the village was rough on my fingertips, and ice wet and cooled my skin. Our village was cradled in a valley, more like a saucer than a cup. It was so small and hidden against the mountains and tall trees above it that few people passing on the road from outside would have known it was even there. A shortcut through an old cow patch showed that neither man nor beast had come by there all winter long. When I put my feet down, the ground held onto me. Before placing my leg in front of me again, I had to pull my foot out of the hole every time I took a step. The snow was like feathers on top, broken and hard underneath. My bad leg pained me and grew poorer from walking. It was the leg that broke from the Master whipping me one time. I went a little further and stopped at a fallen tree. Sap was frozen in the wrinkles of bark, the branches clothed in fresh snow. Soft lumps of white fell on my hair and shoulders from trees overhead. A bird flew away, lighting on the branch of another leafless giant.

Feet steady, I began hacking the tree. Sounds of the axe ripping wood travelled into the still air that entered my mouth, stinging it at the back. The initials R.P., on the handkerchief in red stitching, flashed in my head as I chopped. A brown and white rabbit darted through trees and bushes, scared away by the noise. My body was warm, my hands and feet icy cold. I stopped to catch a breath, made a fist and blew on my fingers to warm them. A booming melody broke the stillness. The sound was coming from a nearby tree. A figure poked its head out and startled me. It was Pierre.

I straightened my chemise pulling the cloth to my neck. He was shorter than me, but with a wider frame. Once his mother asked me to take him for a walk, said he had trouble meeting girls. Probably because he didn't talk much and was sometimes rough. He reached out and rested a hand on my shoulder. His brown eyes shone, breath from his nose and mouth floating overhead. Before I could stop him, he pushed me to the ground. Not giving him the chance to kick snow in my face, I raised myself partway up, and pulled him on top of me. The two of us laughed as we hit each other. A bird called out as if to scold us for being childish. He looked at me funny and, for a moment, I thought he would kiss me. Instead he stood up and started singing again.

"Take your music elsewhere," I said.

He squinted and kicked snow at me. His brown hair was tied at the back. It swished to and fro like a horse's tail.

"I've work to do." I threw snow at him, a soft chunk landing in his eye.

"How is the good wet nurse?" He winked at me and tossed his head.

"Very well, thanks."

We stood there for a few moments, sensing the forest's quiet, our breath rising and mixing.

"I can write my own name," he said proudly. "I learned from an uncle who came to visit."

What did I care if he could write his own name? Lots of peasants could do only that. I wrote pages and pages of words every week for my lessons that I did not boast about.

"That's a start," I said. "Armande taught me to read and write."

"How is it she suckles and reads?" he asked. "No wet nurse before her ever needed instruction to care for babies." He was upsetting my work, making my thoughts scatter like little birds.

He caught me off guard just so he could push me again. This time I fell face-first into the snow with his force. I turned slowly over on my side. Sitting there on my back, knees bent, I hoped he would just go away.

"Her womb will dry up and she'll have no more children. That's what happens to women who become instructed like men, the *woman* in them goes away."

He reached his hand down to help me up. I hit it with my fist giving him the evil eye. Curse words stuck in my throat and if I let them out I might cry.

"Get back to it then," he said turning to walk away. He marched into the thick of the forest and was gone.

Once more, I heard him break into song, the words becoming nonsense as they hit the cold air. I brushed snow from my cheeks, hair and the front of my apron, and then picked up the axe. As I aimed for a weak spot on the trunk of the tree, I thought of Pierre standing right in front of me, a stupid grin on his face. He had not even kissed me, though he had the chance. When I lived with my mother and father, they would scold me for even talking to a boy because they said I would become with child.

As I made my way home, I wondered, would Armande judge me harshly if she found out I listened in on her father's private talk? That I snuck into the library like a crook to go through his private things? Yes, but I had something of his that might just help me protect her. Yet who was R.P.?

Lesson

THAT MORNING, I TENDED TO MY CHORES of keeping the fires lit, churning the cream and butter in the wooden ardoise and sweeping the kitchen and entrance. At times, when I was in the middle of this or that chore, I would see Armande in the kitchen preparing soup, or in the drawing room nursing Nathalie, and think our lives seemed almost the same as before the lettre de cachet, yet not quite. Armande did not tell me to turn mothers wanting her advice away at the door. She was too kindhearted for that, yet I knew anybody coming to call should be treated with suspicion. She had a good sum put away from her grandfather's inheritance and did not require other people's money. She need not know that already this week I sent two mothers away. One of them was a stranger to me, with grey, unfriendly eyes. The other saw the wet nurse once already that week and was not supposed to return for another few days. Besides, Armande was tired. Dark circles surrounded her chestnut eyes. She sang less when she nursed Nathalie and her stride was shorter, not as graceful. Part of that was missing her father, and part, I thought was her fear of what lay ahead.

I was preparing to leave for Les Combes to see Sophie the next day. I told Armande it was to bring her some of the soup for nursing mothers to improve the quality of her milk. It was Armande's special recipe and included boiling the leaves of fennel plants and seeds in barley water. Of course, she thought that was very good of me and did not consider it strange at all because once a week—along with other villagers—I brought soups and breads to those who were either very old or sick. Then, just as I was gathering dry wood for the fires, and thinking at the same time how good my story was, a cheeky woman slipped into the house of her own accord.

"Madame Vivant, Madame Vivant," she cried out.

I followed her calls until I spotted a stranger with a blue cloak standing in the entrance. Her hair was tucked under a bonnet and she wore black boots that were large and clumsy like a man's. She looked to be not more than fifteen years old.

"You'll wake the children," I scolded. Jacques napped upstairs and was sensitive to strange voices. Nathalie was also sleeping, a rare thing to have both of them in their beds. "Tell me your business?"

She held no baby in her arms nor did she look the sort to be a mother. Her fringe was too perfect, her cloak much too tidy at the neck. From the look of the boots she wore, her husband worked on the fishing docks of Nice or Perpignan before settling in the mountains.

"Name's Isabelle and I wish to see the wet nurse on a personal matter."

Armande was reading at the kitchen table. Dark curls fell over her face and onto the book, and her eyes were bright as though she just received a kiss. Without asking about the stranger, she proceeded to read a poem out loud. "Baise m'encor, rebaise moy et baise...."

As she went on reading, my face grew hot because it was a poem about a woman who asked to be kissed again and again by her love.

"Louise Labé, the femme du people from Lyon," she announced as though the poetess stood in our kitchen waiting to be introduced.

"Bonjour Madame Vivant, my name is Isabelle." The woman was a bit clumsy. Not like someone who spent any time in the company of gentlewomen. She did not look at Armande at all and, in fact, seemed frightened by her.

"Sit down, Mademoiselle." Armande gestured.

I did the same, yet the stranger turned her back to me.

"I wish to speak to Madame alone, s'il vous plaît." Her voice shook.

After leaving the kitchen, I stayed by the partly closed door as still as a mouse so they would not hear me.

"My parents are both dead. I've a brother who works in Nice on a fishing boat. He already provides for three children and a wife who has her sister living with them. I have an aunt in Grenoble who works for a goodly family. I mend breeches and shirts and can even sew petticoats from scraps of material if given half the chance. Yet to work, I need to know how to read and write. I can write my name and my brother's too. I know enough to read the Bible, the part about the burning bush and Lot's wife turning to salt I know by heart."

I watched through the keyhole as she took off her bonnet letting loose a stream of reddish blond hair. Her fine-looking mane took me by surprise and made me feel ugly. The baby started crying so I ran upstairs to calm her. Nathalie was on Armande's bed in a basket topped with a raccoon skin. Her little heart was beating fast as I brought her to my chest. This was a chance for me to disrupt their exchange. After all, babies needed to suckle, and I might just hear more of what they were saying if I brought her down to Armande without too much fuss.

"Would you teach me to read? I don't know how I will bear it if you don't."

I entered the kitchen just as the stranger said those words. Armande glanced over at her and smiled knowingly. When her father and she lived in the house just the two of them, Armande would tutor boys and girls in French and Latin. She also taught philosophy, rhetoric, poetry and literature. Last spring she tutored a farmer's wife thirsty for poetry. The woman read one poem at a time and committed it to memory so that she could recite it to herself while milking the goat each morning.

Armande reached out her arms to take the screaming baby from me. She lowered her torso, untying her corsage to give suck.

"It's a worthwhile pursuit to want to read, don't you agree Céleste?"

I nodded, ashamed I had not yet done my morning lesson. Armande might ask me why I missed two days already that week.

"To learn how to read is no carefree pastime, not like needlework or playing a cheerful ditty on the harpsichord, isn't that right Céleste?" She smoothed her buttercup-yellow skirt with one hand, her hips moving side to side as she nursed.

I nodded. By not doing my lessons I showed her how ungrateful I was.

The pretty girl stood up, rubbing her eyes. She opened her mouth to speak yet it was clear a cat had her tongue. Her cheeks were red and she pulled on her own hair as though her head was in the clouds.

"Céleste, please show Isabelle the library while I nurse Nathalie. I'll leave it for you to decide what book to start with."

"The wet nurse will teach me," said the girl merrily as we walked through the corridor. She reached out to take my arm, yet I pulled away.

"We need wood for the fire in the library," I said. "Stay where you are. I'll be back."

I returned with a bundle of wood in my arms. "There is no room for you here." I was worried she might want to live with us while she studied. If strangers were coming and going then I might lose track of Armande and I needed to keep her safe as I had promised Monsieur Vivant.

Isabelle smiled knowingly, as if she could see right through me, and said, "I don't mind. I am staying with a family friend until I go to Grenoble. That is if my aunt will take me."

The library was cold and breathed a sigh as we entered. Right away I looked and saw the stranger's handkerchief was no longer on the table by the taperstick. A sickly feeling planted itself in the pit of my stomach. As far as I knew, Armande did not go into the library, although maybe she went in one day while I was out chopping wood. My heart was beating fast and I could barely catch a breath. Then I noticed that Isabelle did not look well either. She stood in a corner of the library, her hands trembled, her body swayed as though her legs might give out.

"I must sit," she pleaded grabbing a chair at the table. "Never have I seen so many books." She laid her head on her arms, hiding her face with her reddish blonde hair.

"Do you think Armande expects you to read all these?" I laughed at her. "You can read something simple to start, a nursery rhyme perhaps."

"I don't wish to read after all." Her lower lip quivered.

She made me think of how I was when Armande first rescued me. Scared and uncertain as though words were an ogre waiting to eat me. Two years ago, I couldn't even write my name. I fumbled with the quill and the letters were messy, looking more like castles and bridges. I would pull my hair out, stamp on the ground and wring my fists. Even so, Armande told me she never saw a person with such a talent for learning. I studied morning and night until it finally came. The splinters of wood burned, and once the fire caught, I grabbed a child's book from the shelf and bid Isabelle sit by me at a spot closer to the window for light. The chairs in the library were like blocks of ice. I took off my shawl to sit on, wrapping it around my thighs. I opened the book, still thinking of the missing handkerchief. Isabelle read in a shaky voice. Twice she stopped to comment on the story saying, "If I were an ant I wouldn't crawl upon the ground," and "Only I know why rabbits have such long ears." Was she stopping out of nervousness? Maybe she thought I would forget the reading and engage in empty chitchat instead.

"Keep going." I was trying to encourage her just as Armande did with me though my mind was elsewhere. Isabelle read a little more. Then she fixed her eyes on the trees outside. Maybe she sensed how I too was distracted.

Armande came to join us. Jacques ran into the library ahead of her. He was playing dress-up and had stuck some feathers in Armande's hair. One of them fell to the ground. The baby in her arms tried to squirm out of her grip. She sat down in an upholstered chair while Nathalie began to crawl on the carpet over forests, gardens with red flowers, and scenes of men hunting deer. Jacques found a pile of small books, which he had hidden behind one of the mighty legs of the table. Some of them contained engravings that took his attention for a little while. Mostly he liked to pile the books up and build mountains or trees with them. Isabelle read the rest of the page.

"You did plenty for today," I said to her when she finished. "I'll give you the book to take home. Read some this evening before bed."

"But Madame…." She turned her head to Armande. "I only just began."

"Céleste knows best." Armande crossed her legs and placed her arm on the back of the chair. "My father taught me to read in this library when I was four years old. In fact, it was at that very table where the two of you are sitting now."

"How extraordinary!" said the young woman.

"I was always hungry to know what my father was doing," said Armande. "I thought that if only I could understand what he called reading, then I would be closer to knowing his mind. Every night after dinner, I would sit and read—or at least pretend to read—at his side. I was hungry to journey through the sky with books, to encounter the beasts and oceans of the world and to be dazzled by a poet's words." Her eyes lit up as they often did when she spoke of her father.

Armande scrambled behind the chair after Nathalie, and there was laughter and playful sounds. Moments later Armande came back holding the baby. In one of her little hands was a book while the other held a white handkerchief, a little corner of red peeking out. I leapt at Nathalie snatching the object from her before either Armande or Isabelle could see it.

"It's mine," I said. "I must have dropped it." My heart sank to where I swiftly stored the evidence far down in my bodice.

The baby was crying because of me, yet I had no choice in the matter. The handkerchief with the stranger's initials was now safely tucked away. Armande was spared and her father would be happy. I did not know whose handkerchief it was or why Monsieur Vivant wanted to keep it from her, but I knew that it was important. Armande stared at me, questioning. My breath was becoming normal again, yet I couldn't meet her gaze.

"Now let's see what else you found." She turned away from me to the baby who was now quiet, though still sniffling.

Armande examined the cover. "Why it's *Lettres persanes*. Exceptional choice little nut." She handed the book to Isabelle. "Nathalie has taken it upon herself to decide what you shall read. Would you like this one instead? Or, perhaps take both of them."

Seeming surprised, Isabelle took a quick look at the book. Not far away, Jacques tore a page from another book. I ran over and grabbed it from him.

"None of that," I scolded.

The sky was cloudy from snow falling. Light started to fade and soon dark would set in, which meant I had to wait until the sun rose the next day to gather more of the wood I chopped.

"Would you like the wet nurse to give you a lesson next week," I said to her when we were finally alone.

"Why yes, Mademoiselle."

She drew closer, the brim of her bonnet brushing my forehead. Her breath was warm on my cheek and smelled of mint. The blue cape she wore next to her milky skin made her look saintly. Perhaps she was as an angel sent by God to help me, an angel with clumsy black fisherman's boots.

"I will certainly do that, yet maybe you can also help me." Pulling the handkerchief from my bosom, I put it in her hand. "Keep this for me." My two hands clasped her one. My mind saw no reason to it, yet I felt that giving her the handkerchief would at least keep it safe and out of reach. I could not risk Armande seeing it. "Do not let anybody have it. When I ask for it back you are to bring it to me right away, you hear me."

Isabelle's eyes were fiery with excitement. She took a peak at the handkerchief. "Whose is it then?" She saw the initials R.P. "Are you to marry this gentleman? Is he your lover?"

"I can't tell you right now. Don't ask me any more questions. Just please go."

She stood at the entrance, folded the handkerchief and then placed it in her embroidered pocket.

"No one shall see it," she said. "It will be safe with me."

Sign

HAIL THE SIZE OF PEAS POUNDED DOWN on us as we entered the village square. I pulled the hood of my cloak over my head. The day I was to meet with Sophie in secret, we had received word she was ill with consumption. At once Armande decided that she must check on her and the baby. Sophie's village was almost half a day on foot. Before setting out, we had taken Nathalie and Jacques to a neighbour. We did not want them to get sick from Sophie, and besides, the trip was too hard for small children. As we walked along, my mind was caught up in the new turn of events. Sophie might now be too weak to tell me anything. Even so, while there, I aimed to find out the handkerchief's owner. I would sneak away while Armande was at Sophie's sickbed. Monsieur Vivant was gone only a few days, and already the morning he left seemed a lifetime away. The church in the square had a lion outside the door that guarded the village from harmful attacks or evil thoughts. On the other side of the door was a large stone bénitier with Holy Water for blessings. We came to the square, and as I passed the fountain, I noticed something red amidst the white.

Ice stones beat down onto the frozen water. I brushed them away to see a doll clothed in a black coat with gold buttons, caught under the ice. I squatted and placed my arms on the edge of the fountain, slippery and cold to the touch. The doll's shoes were black and on his head he wore a red hat. His eyes held an air of surprise. A small, round mouth made him look like he was about to ask a question. His eyebrows were half moons. I punched the ice with my fist until it eventually cracked, though not enough to break and set the doll free. My knuckles were stinging, and pain went all the way up my arm. It bothered me that such a perfect looking doll was not within my grasp. I never had a doll or a toy of any kind, as we were far too poor. The little man seemed to say, *let me out, let me out*. Soon Armande was at my side, her walking stick within my reach. I extended my hand to pull it to me, yet she yanked it away.

"Give it here. Please can't I have it?" I hoped to break the ice with the sharp edge of her fancy stick to set the doll free.

"Come now Céleste, we've no time to waste." She tugged my arm.

Then she looked into the frozen fountain and her face went pale. It didn't even look like she was breathing, and a sound came out of her, like a small, hurt child.

"It cannot be." Her eyes grew wide.

"What is it," I asked bewildered.

"My daughter, my little nut, used to play with a doll just like that. My husband Robert brought it back for her after one of his trips."

"We must rescue it," I said reaching once more for her stick.

"Leave it there," she told me. "I don't want it back."

We stood there looking helplessly at the bonhomme, his body encased in ice. She tugged at my arm once more; I took one last look and turned away.

She walked quickly this time as if to get further away from the little doll, further away, I thought, from her past. We went through a forest under branches laden with snow. The face of the bonhomme stayed in my head, his look of surprise, mouth open as if he wished to tell me something. We stayed close to the river then took a well-trodden path leading up the side of the mountain. Armande stopped by an oak tree that creaked in the wind. Her face was grim and the wind at her back made her look weak, not her usual self.

"After the accident I took my daughter's few playthings and laid them in the square for the village children, though it was my impression that I kept the doll with the funny expression as it was her favourite." She looked as though her heart would burst. "She would hold it in her little hands, stare at it for hours. It was the bright red hat and the gold buttons that entranced her." Her voice trembled. She grabbed hold of a low branch and leaned against the tree trunk for support.

I wanted to rush back and dig the doll out of the ice for her, thinking that might end her pain. No, she did not want to remember what the doll conjured up about her daughter. My head was spinning and my heart cried rivers of tears. We kept on our way, the image of the doll sticking in my mind, though I did not dare speak of it.

Sun melted snow on the mountain edge, streams trickling under rocks and ice, sign of an early spring. We walked in silence before she said to me, "I used to refer to Robert as l'homme des étoiles or l'homme de la rivière." He was always either star-gazing or performing mathematical calculations on our river's waters."

The sighting of the bonhomme in the ice had broken open the door to her past.

"Where did you meet him?" I asked her.

"I knew of him since I was a girl. One evening while strolling by the chapel on the hill after dark I saw him lying in the clover. We had not seen each other in a while and I was awestruck by his handsome appearance. He had large hands and very broad shoulders.

"'I am counting stars,' he said to me. 'By dividing the sky into sections I can calculate how many there are.' I lay down beside him and observed a mass of planets lining the heavens like bands of silk. The more stars I counted, the more my body quivered at the prospect that his shoulder might rub up against mine.

"I grew faint at the idea that the two of us could—paltry beings that we were before the immense firmament—give off some light of our own making. Stars danced before us like fireworks. One shot across the canvas and seemed almost to land at our feet. Brighter ones stood out. More digging made distant stars come to the surface, still more and I saw fused with all that blackness, clusters of them like masses of people with lanterns parading through a dense forest." Light returned to her eyes remembering the starry evening with him in the clover.

A shiver—that felt more like a tickle—went up my back as I became caught up in the romance of their stargazing. She loved him once I could tell. *He loves me, he loves me not, he loves me.* When Pierre touched me that time in the woods, his eyes told me he wanted to kiss me, yet instead he pushed me to the ground.

We reached the top of a hill and then came to a cemetery. After walking through the village gates, we passed an apple orchard. The house belonging to Sophie's family was white stone with a cheery blue door, steps leading to a small entrance. We walked through a corridor past three closed doors.

In a dimly lit room, Sophie lay on her sickbed. She was so small inside the large bed and her skin was greyish with traces of blue. She lay there, eyes closed, like a slab of marble sculpted into a girl's body. A young woman who resembled Sophie approached Armande. She wore a plain brown petticoat and had no lace on her chemise. An apron was tied around her waist.

"Will you please, the baby hasn't nursed all day and Sophie's been asking after you." Armande took the screaming child and found a spot at the back of the room to sit and nurse.

An old woman took a cup of pee from the bedside table then drew it to her nose. It was said the colour and smell of the liquid told a person what made the body sick. The woman's petticoat was stained with blood and a yellow substance like dandelion. She whispered in Armande's ear, and then returned to Sophie. Another woman, not as old as the first, stooped on a chair. She held a rosary, pressing and rubbing each bead as she prayed. The doctor came in and then with all of us there watching, Sophie suddenly sat up in her bed, looked at me and said the words as plain as day, "Don't let him come." Him? Who? What did she mean? As I struggled to understand, she vomited a reddish mixture that rained over the bed sheets, the floor and on the doctor as well as the old woman, sister, and me. My heart was in my throat, my body swaying.

"Menstrual blood mixed with urine," said the doctor after taking some on his finger and bringing it to his nose. The old woman put a precious stone near Sophie's heart so blood would cease to flow from her mouth. My fear of her dying grew as I watched her. Then just like that, she opened her mouth to take a last breath and fell back on the pillow. I stared at her still face and wept silently. The doctor grabbed her wrist and touched two of his fingers to it. He then folded both hands over her chest, gently but without emotion. Her mother ran over and began to howl. Sophie's face had streaks of red vomit on it and her bedgown was soiled. A sister quit the room to fetch the priest. Sophie's eyes stayed open until the priest arrived. The first thing he did was to cross himself three times, and then place a coin on each lid so her eyes stayed shut. After, he laid a wooden cross atop her chest.

Prayers around her began right away. Her mother wailed and stamped her feet on the floor. Her father prayed silently at the back of the room, the centre of his brow forming a letter V. There were two sisters; the older one came and went. I wandered outside not wanting the family to see my tears. Water dripped from the rooftop and the front garden was hidden under snow. Armande came out to join me and I saw the baby in her arms had colour in its cheeks. His hands pawed the air and his legs kicked, looking nothing like the frail infant I saw before.

Armande sat on a step then wrapped the orphan in her shawl rocking it to and fro. Her face was sullen, her usually bright eyes, lost-looking. Maybe she sensed Sophie's soul—or that of her own dead child—crying out from beyond. The sky was low and trees dragged branches on the ground. Even outside, I felt Sophie's presence. Her eyes had glazed over, her head turned in my direction when she spoke those words, *don't let him come.* She was gone now and so I had to rely on my own cleverness and my instinct as guides.

The old woman came outside and asked for my help with the body. The family quit the room where Sophie lay except for one of the sisters who relit the fire. Lanterns glowed at each bedpost. Another lantern sat by a basin of water on a table near a small window.

"I washed this child when she was born," the old woman murmured. "Now I am washing her dead body."

Sophie was the same age I was when I fled my mother and father's house. She was even weedy like me.

"Undress her," said the old woman. "While I ready the soap and water."

I was afraid to touch her, yet did what I was told, gradually pulling her arms out of her bloody bedgown. Her mouth was partly open. Someone had removed the two coins causing the skin of her eyelids to lift slightly as though she peered at me. My heart ached for the poor girl, and I wiped tears from my face with the back of my hand. It wasn't good, I thought, for her to see me crying. Sophie's buttery hair trailed upwards when the bedgown came over her head. Her nipples were the size of buttons on a gentleman's waistcoat, hips slender with no womanly beauty. The sister finished lighting the fire then stood by the bed for a moment, gazing with longing at her dead sister before she quit the room. There was so much coarse blood on Sophie that the bowl of water was soon as dark and thick as beet soup. Tiny golden hairs stood up on her leg tickling my wrist. Though her eyes were closed, I felt her watching me. She said, "We are the same, you and I, both of us dead inside."

One morning, when I lived with my mother and father, I had painted wooden spoons for my mother to sell at market—blue and yellow like shooting stars. My mother's spoons gave her just enough money to buy a chicken once a full moon, just enough to nab a cake at Christmas. Sometimes she even gave me a few coins from what she sold as long as I promised not to tell my father. He drank up much of his earnings while the rest he spent on girls. The graveyard was full of these careless maids who bent over the village's corpses, dead gentlewomen's robes on their backs and ne'er two sous to rub together. "Strong women they are," he'd say, "who undress the dead." He took money from corpses if any money could be found. Rings, earrings, charms and necklaces he did not dare touch. He reckoned those that gave it to them would come for him.

When finished, I tied a lengthy piece of cloth to the painted spoons, and was hanging them out my window to dry when my father came in.

"Look out the window, my pretty."

At the time, I thought my ears lied to me for he had not called me pretty before. Trumpeter swans flew and called overhead. My father clutched my waist from behind. I clutched the spoon I was holding, wet paint covering my hands.

"Look out the window." I did what he told me to do in hopes the loving words would keep on. He pulled me to him and lifted my petticoats. "My pretty, yes."

He propped me up with one hand as a puppeteer steadies a puppet. The swans called out again. Pain filled my body, legs shaking and caving in. Still, he held me up where I bounced lifeless, no longer hearing the swans, nor finding my breath. I am dying, I thought.

"My pretty, yes," cried my father once more.

Then suddenly my breath returned, and, standing up partway, I began to shout back at him. "My pretty, my pretty, oh yes, my pretty."

"Shut that mouth," yelled my father, but protests only made me shout louder.

"My pretty, my pretty," I said until my words ran together and my tongue went limp. He moved his hand from my waist to cover my mouth.

"There she is. That'll stop you."

That only made me bite his hand and shout more loudly. He picked me up dragging me to the window. I looked down from on high and saw a mix of trees and sky. The land was foggy to my eyes as if death was taking me away.

"You go out the window my pretty, you see?" These words were the last I heard.

Later that month, when blood ceased to flow from between my legs, my mother burst into my room, pulled away the covers, crying and shaking me as though she thought that would make the blood come. Though the child was never born. In its place a scraggy thing wrapped in a cloak of black filth came out of me just after arriving at the country estate where I had worked. I would be dead just like Sophie if I hadn't quit my father's house.

The old woman replaced the bloody bowl and brought over a fresh one. As I wiped the dead girl down with clean water, I thought for an instant it was me I was washing down. Somewhere deep inside me was a place that had not been touched before, a place that came alive. Thanks to Armande, all the blood and hurt was slowly coming off me, yet still there were some spots left to come clean.

When I got to Sophie's head, at first I saw no blood though her hair was a rat's nest. I parted it in the middle and began brushing the left side in long strokes. Her hair flowed over her shoulders like water. On the right side, strands of hair underneath were stuck together with dried blood. Under that was something thick, the size of a vest pocket. After prying the object from the strands of bloody hair, I saw it was a piece of paper folded several times. A letter. The date read 1783, which was six years ago, and it was addressed to Armande's father from his long-time business partner Monsieur Taranne. I read quickly for fear the words would vanish before my eyes.

I do not wish to cause a rift between us dear friend, as I know how much affection you have for your daughter's newly betrothed and how much his talents are greatly esteemed by you. Nevertheless, I feel it my duty to explain my actions, which at first glance may seem nonsensical. Sadly, I am unable to publish Monsieur Phlipon's pamphlet, which he sent me two months ago. In fact, it is my belief that it would be morally indefensible to do so and I shall explain why. Enclosed is a book, which will demonstrate better than I can how I came to my decision.

I stumbled upon the obscure little work in a bookshop that is owned by a customer of mine. I have since learned that it didn't sell many copies and in fact disappeared from sight directly following its publication. I was struck by the title of the book, The Cultivation of Alpine Plants, as the topic made me think of Monsieur Phlipon's pamphlet about plants in the High Alps. I purchased the book for my own amusement not realizing at the time what I was to uncover. As I began to read the little book with colourful illustrations I detected echoes of Monsieur Phlipon's shorter work. And so, placing the works next to each other, I began to read and compare them page-by-page. I was greatly alarmed to discover that whole passages by the posthumous author, best known as a village physick, were lifted by Monsieur Phlipon and planted into his essay. I suppose he thought it was a little known work and that nobody would find out what he had done. I know you honour originality above most other intellectual attributes and you would wish to be apprised of what the man is doing to make a name for himself. I also know that you prize your daughter's happiness above all.

Splotches of blood hid the last couple lines from view. My hands quivered as I placed the letter in my embroidered pocket for safe-keeping. Had he ever told his daughter that he knew about his son-in-law's thieving ways? The pieces fit together: the so-called stranger was Armande's husband. He had a reputation to uphold. If he knew Armande's father, a man with many friends in high-up places, was aware of his plagiarizing he would think twice before going near his wife. Then I remembered the handkerchief from the library that I gave to Isabelle for safekeeping. Stitched in red were the initials R.P.—Robert Phlipon.

I never dressed a dead body before, and touching her skin made me tremble yet for Sophie, I got on with it. I put the fresh chemise and gown on the body whose skin was still red from the blood, as there was no time to undress her and scrub her afresh. Sweat fell from my brow to my upper lip. What was Armande's husband doing coming back after all these years? When I tried to rub the redness from her hands and face that only made it worse and I started to cry once more.

The old woman saw me fussing and said, "Don't worry my child. Just arrange the cloth of her chemise so the skin is less visible."

I fluffed up the lace collar, pulling her dainty cuffs past her fingers.

The old woman then arranged Sophie's damp hair over her forehead and cheeks. Her tresses resembled a flowing stream of sunlight. The old woman turned her back for an instant, at which time I bent down and whispered in Sophie's ear, "Thank you for the letter. I promise to keep Armande safe."

Shortly after, the girl's mother came into the room and saw her daughter in her satin gown the colour of plums.

"She never looked so pretty," she moaned. She told me her daughter was between the world of the living and the dead when she said *don't let him come,* and could therefore see things others could not. She said her last words were about keeping the Lord Jesus Christ in our hearts to ward off evil. Then the mother's eyes turned angry. "We will have to guard her against those thieving bonesetters and pig-castrators." When she quit the room, the old woman told me what she meant.

"Dead bodies have gone missing in the village because of doctors wanting to use them for dissection." She held my hand and looked at me straight on. "The mother is afraid that if this occurs, her daughter's soul won't be able to leave her body." Her youthful blue eyes stood out to me over her wrinkled face marked with brown spots and veins.

Armande and I stayed with the family. That night I thought about Monsieur Vivant's letter that Sophie kept for me to find, and about the stranger who turned out to be Armande's husband. In the morning she gave suck to Sophie's baby for the last time as one of the sisters was nursing and said she would take the orphan.

The very same day we returned from Les Combes, I raced to the fountain to rescue the wee bonhomme in the ice. Once I had him in my hands I would forget about the recent troubles. I would give the doll a proper warm bath with water fresh from the well that I would heat up slowly in the pot. He did not look like he was stained when I saw him, but just in case I would rub a little fragrant soap in the water to get him nice and clean and smelling like fresh picked roses. His little mouth would surely open to say *thank-you.* I never had a doll before, not a toy of any sort. I would be sure to treat him well and take care of him as he belonged to Armande's little girl. I would set him by the fire, though not too close, just enough to dry and warm him. Of course, that night he would sleep nestled up next to me with his own little cover pulled to his ceramic chin. I would see he was safe and out of harm's way.

I did not wish to tell Armande what I was up to, as she would grow sad when she thought of the doll once more. Yet I vowed to fish it out no matter how long it took me or how much my fist might hurt if I had to punch the ice to get at it. After all, the doll was her daughter's and my heart told me nobody else should have it because of that. Armed with a stick this time, I circled the fountain poking the ice in search of the little face that previously looked with such longing for me to save it. It had rained since yesterday, but the ice was still clear enough to see the stones on the bottom of the fountain. At one side, the ice was broken up and so I stuck my stick in deep to pry a chunk of ice from the surface. Yet there was no splash of red. No little face of worry. The bonhomme was gone.

Jacques

FOUR DAYS HAD PASSED since Sophie's death. That Sunday I knelt down and prayed for her while the priest gave his sermon. After church Armande rushed home to suckle Nathalie. Pierre sat on the ground by the stone bénetier outside the church. He wore no hat and no coat, only a woollen scarf with holes.

"Why weren't you at church?" I asked him.

He shrugged his shoulders and flashed his eyes—green with grey and brown flecks—at me. He usually kept his lids partly closed, which made it hard to see how nice they were. He leapt up and grabbed my arm just as two young women strolled by whispering and giggling. One of them bumped into me, turned to her friend and mumbled, "slow-witted."

"Strumpet," said the other.

One had on a woollen bonnet and a dark blue gown, and her eyes bore into mine. The other wore a light beige cloak, yellow hair pinned on top of her head. They looked back and forth between Pierre and me. Did they think we were entwined? Armande frowned on idle chatter saying there were those who spent all their time discussing the lives of so-and-so as though these people were fireflies caught in a jar to amuse them. The women left the square, and when I turned to go, Pierre pulled me to him.

"I'm sorry for what I said about Armande." His breathing was unsteady and he dragged his feet. "It's just what I hear." Then he smiled adding, "Let's go to the chapel and catch snowflakes on our tongues."

"I can't."

I did not want to leave Armande alone by herself for too long. I promised her father and Sophie I would keep her safe. Now, with her husband not far away, I had even more troubles on my hands than before.

"I have something to show you," he said with a suspicious air.

"Show me and then I have to be on my way."

We descended into the valley and climbed the mountainside. The sky was grey and the snow hard and crisp underfoot. The big wooden cross next to the chapel stuck out from the hill before us as we made our way. I could make out the coq carved on top as well as a baby's shoe, a heavy cowbell, and a child's crutch that villagers had nailed to the cross. These objects belonged to souls and beasts the villagers prayed for. Wind from the north picked up and I edged my body closer to him. The bell on the hilltop rang in the wind like a blathering old man. Inside the chapel there was a picture of Mary on the wall above a wooden alter. Five candles were lit, which told me a body was praying in the chapel shortly before we got there. The ceiling was sloped and there were benches for sitting and kneeling.

"What is it then?" I said.

Pierre held his scarf close to his body then pulled out the very bonhomme with black coat, gold buttons and red cap I saw that day in the frozen fountain.

"What's the matter? Don't you like it?" He held the precious doll in his dirty hands.

"It's just that, it's not yours," I stammered. "It belongs to somebody else."

"But I found it. I never set my eyes on so fine a plaything."

"It's not yours," I said again. "Let me have it."

Pierre pulled the doll away, and at the same moment I lunged and fell, hitting my knee hard against the ground. My skin and bone smarted with pain and my skirt was ripped. He led me to a bench in front of the altar to sit down. My belly stirred with anger. I wanted to punch him between the eyes, not that I cared much that he hurt me but because he had no right to have that doll.

"Tell me who it belongs to and I'll give it back."

Candles flickered at the altar. The flames warmed the tips of my fingers as I cupped my hands around them. Mary looked down, gentle and loving. The blue of her gown matched her eyes. *Hail Mary, Full of Grace, The Lord is with thee. Blessed art thou among women, and blessed is the fruit of my womb, Jesus.* I bent forward to kiss the altar. Pierre shuffled on the floor behind me.

"It was her daughter's," he said. "After her child was taken by the Devil, she started gushing milk. It made the babies she suckled different from others," he added, an air of sureness in his voice. "My mom told me that."

"Your mother is a harlot."

"Say that again and your doll will burn." He held it over a candle flame.

Pierre fell as I pushed him then ran out of the chapel my breath quickening. He chased after me.

"I saw the boy sit down once on the front step of her house and look between the boards at a feather caught underneath." He took a few breaths of cold air. "He sat there for a very long time before he shoved a small stick with some honey on it through the crack to fish out the feather. How could a small child think of that? Something made him act that way. Her milk was what did it."

My mind was like a dog chasing its tail. It went to the village chitchat about the death of her baby giving her plentiful milk like Jesus with the loaves and the fishes. Then to stories about her milk making the little ones wise and sharp-witted. I knew these stories were true because the babies looked changed and acted different after drinking her milk. But the stories about her and the Devil were lies, I thought, because she was more like Mary in the portrait over the altar than an evil angel.

"Snowflakes." Pierre pointed to the sky.

We lay down by the tall wooden cross, where Armande and Robert lay a few years before. One by one, flakes of all sizes floated onto my tongue, my lips tingled and my throat grew cold. Pierre looked calm unlike when he had spoken of Armande and her milk. He repeated other people's gossip and was not smart enough to know for himself between lies and truth. The bonhomme's leg peaked out from his hole-ridden scarf. I thought if only I could get close enough to grab it.

Then Pierre planted a kiss on my lips and I found his mouth was warm as was his tongue. We lay on the cold ground kissing and hugging, my face and body becoming warmer. I didn't even open my eyes as just feeling the heat and firmness of his body was enough.

"You can have the doll," he whispered in my ear. "It's my gift to you."

Happily taking the bonhomme, I tucked him inside my cloak like a piece of Armande coming back to me. As long as Pierre held onto me and the doll was by me, my heart was filled with warmth. That feeling reached out and covered my whole body. What if we married? Where would we live? Yet Armande had a husband and he fled. Many men turned after they got married like my father who stuck my mother in an apple barrel when she became rotten. It was hard to know if Pierre was the kind of man who would turn. If he wished to keep kissing me, he would have to stop repeating lies about her. I needed to get back to Armande and waved goodbye to him.

A thin older woman greeted me when I entered the drawing room. At first I was angry with myself to see a stranger in the house, then I recognized her as Jacques' aunt. She wore a blue gown and a black cloak, and had the same eyes as Jacques. The older sister to his mother who died, Madame Lefèvre lived in Grenoble and was a woman of some means. She paid Armande a monthly stipend to nurse and care for the child, and agreed to take him as her own when he turned three.

She reached her hand out to me. "Madame Vivant tells me you are a great help to her in caring for my nephew, Jacques." The aunt had visited only once. Her face looked sad and worn.

"He's a good enough boy." I was out of breath from running.

The bonhomme was hidden inside my cloak. Armande suckled the baby on the dormeuse, a yellow handkerchief tucked in the front of her bodice, pulled down on one side for nursing. I threw a piece of wood on the fire and looked at the snow melting from the bottom of my dress, water collecting on the floor in a puddle by my shoes. I removed them and the stockings, emptying the shoes of snow. Hard white lumps sizzled, disappearing into a puddle on the hot stones.

"Yes indeed and so advanced for his age," the woman said. "He remembered my name even though we've barely met, and to be walking so steady and tall, my what an extraordinary thing. And his vocabulary! How could he possibly know so many words at his young age? If I was a religious woman I would call it a miracle." The tightness in her face melted into a smile.

"That's high praise Madame Lefèvre," said Armande. "The clever boy has done it by himself with little guidance from me."

"Is that a fact Madame Vivant?" Her eyes narrowed. She took off her cloak, placing it on the sofa before sitting down. "Why it sounds as though you have been reading our dear Jean-Jacques Rousseau who thinks children should run about willy-nilly with no discipline or formal instruction. He has caused such a stir with his book *Émile*. If we leave them to their own devices do we not risk our children becoming barbarians, half-human and half-animal?"

Armande drew back as though trying to avoid a nasty fly. "Allowing them to learn from Nature is not leaving them to their own devices."

She finished suckling and was now holding the baby over her shoulder, patting its back, her torso moving up and down. More, it seemed, to calm herself than the baby.

"I brought you some chocolates, Céleste," Madame Lefèvre said. "All polite people of an adult age are now consuming this food of the gods."

She handed me a gold box tied with a white lace bow—one of the most beautiful objects anybody ever gave me. I embraced her and then ran out of the drawing room to hide the doll in my bed covers.

On my way downstairs, I saw Jacques sitting on the steps, his eyes fixed on a wooden horse in his hands. He did not seem to notice I stood over him, did not even hear me ask him to move so I could get past as he pretend-galloped the horse up and down on the narrow steps. Nonsense sounds flowed from his lips mixed with the loud tapping of the horse's hooves on the steps. Then, amidst the noise, I swore I heard a song like one soldiers going into battle might sing. *Marching now, one, two, three, let's all fight together for our liberty.* The words and melody were so distinct I scooped up the child to see if he was indeed singing.

Madame Lefèvre came into the corridor from the drawing room.

"Look auntie, horse ... run," he said.

"Why, that's splendid. What a smart boy you are!" She clapped her hands.

After hearing the childish words I smiled to myself. How foolish to think a boy that age could sing a liberty song.

Back in the drawing room, I opened my beautiful gold box to sneak a chocolate, giving no more thought to the song I heard. The dark, rich sweetness filled my mouth, making me dizzy with pleasure. Never had I tasted such delicious flavours.

Armande and Madame Lefèvre were talking seriously.

"Madame Vivant, it was my intention to wait until after he was weaned, yet I see he is old enough now for me to begin to raise him as my own. I mean to say that, thanks to your guidance, he is quite a remarkable boy and just needs a mother's love."

Nathalie lay by the fire on her stomach, banging a wooden spoon on the floor.

Armande's eyes filled with tears as she watched Jacques frolic with the toy horse. "Madame Lefèvre," she said with a tremble in her voice. "The arrangement was for me to care for Jacques until he turned three, which is not for another six months."

"But I wish to take him this instant, to have him in my home and to begin raising him. I am quite alone you understand." She threw up her hands and started to sob. "My husband spends all his time at our textile factory outside Grenoble and I have no one to care for." She composed herself then took a handkerchief from her sleeve and dabbed her eyes. "Lately he has taken to sleeping there on a cot some nights to guard against thieves. Last month he was forced to let some workers go so he could cover the month's expenses. Three days later they broke into the factory and stole a dozen or so Indian calico prints. If it happens again with other workers, either those who believe they should be paid more or those he has let go, he might be forced to shut down the whole operations. Desperation is in the air, Madame Vivant, and I worry each day for my husband's safety. I will pay you for the months you would have spent caring for Jacques, if you're worried about that."

"I am very sorry about your husband's situation," said Armande. "It must be a tremendous burden on you, yet it is Jacques' well-being that concerns me, not my own." Armande's tone changed. "He is a bright and sensitive boy Madame Lefèvre. Like all children, he requires that we know his nature and help him at each stage of his growing."

"Of course, Madame Vivant. I don't wish to quash any possibility of intellectual advancement in the boy."

The discussion went back-and-forth until Armande's face softened. Maybe she felt it was a good sign the aunt was anxious to raise him, and that she should not stand in the way of that.

On Armande's request, Madame Lefèvre agreed to stay on a night or two so as not to cause the boy too much distress.

Armande went to her desk and wrote up a list of foods Jacques liked, games he enjoyed and details about his temperament. Her movements were stiff and her eyes filled with tears. Then she gathered together a pair of booties, a couple pairs of trousers, the precious coat I made for him and a bonnet, which he would soon outgrow. Until that moment, I did not think of Jacques as a son or even a brother. He was simply another body to clothe and feed, a plain nuisance when I was at my study or chores. Yet, seeing Armande arrange his little outfits in the basket, then looking at our dear boy who was now busy stacking blocks by the fire with such purpose, made me see just how much I cared for him. For all the time I had lived with Armande, he was there. A wave of sadness washed over me and I began to cry uncontrollably. Rushing out of the drawing room I sat on the steps leading upstairs where, only moments before I thought I heard him sing ... *let's all fight together for our liberty.*

Darkness

SHE MADE ME UNEASY shifting back and forth on her heels, her eyes flitting about. She had pale cheeks and a brown spot on her chin. Lines circled her eyes and mouth, her black hair tied away from her face. She looked like a woman of sixty, yet was probably twenty-five. Her clothes were ripped and her shoes were a couple pieces of leather stitched together. Her feet were red and blue from cold. My heart was sorry for her. Even so, I stood at the door, not letting her in. She said her name was Emilie.

"It won't eat much and I've not enough milk." Her baby lay limp in her arms. "When she does eat, she brings up green water like pea soup."

"I know little of babies," I told her. "I'm not a mother. Nor am I Armande, the wet nurse. Come later when she's back."

I tried closing the door, yet she pushed back with all her might.

"I've buried two children in one year." She was out of breath as though she just finished digging their graves. "My husband has a small parcel of land, a cow and a poorly horse, yet still we must pay the seigneur a fee of forty-two livres of wheat and three chickens. To another man we owe four livres of oats and a chicken. On top of this we are burdened with the heavy taxes. With seven children it's hard to live on the milk from one cow." Her small, dark eyes suddenly seemed less menacing and so I opened the door to her.

Armande would want me to, I thought, and in any case she would be back soon. Besides I had chores to attend to and did not have time to stand in the entranceway arguing with the woman. I brought Emilie into the drawing room, telling her to sit by the fire. Two weeks passed since Jacques went away. Still, I could not bring myself to pick up his wooden blocks scattered over the floor.

I rummaged through the kitchen cupboard and then unravelled a cloth containing a piece of sausage. After the pot was filled with water, I threw in the meat and cut up apples and carrots. When the soup was ready, I scooped some into a bowl and took it to the drawing room.

Emilie sat on the sofa clutching her baby. Not saying a word or taking the spoon, she placed the infant beside her. She then clutched the bowl with both hands, drinking the warm liquid with great attention until every drop was gone. Her eyes rested on my face and I was reminded of the man who owned the estate where I had first met Armande. He had those same small, dark eyes and that is why I called him Master Dogface.

I bent down and made a nest around Emilie's bruised and swollen feet from an old blanket used to carry wood for the fires. Nathalie was crying in an upper room and so I quit the woman and raced upstairs.

The baby's nose was gushing. After cleaning and changing her, I went to the kitchen to fetch Nathalie a wooden spoon to gnaw on. The dried herbs tied with string swayed back and forth over the table as though wind was coming in from somewhere. I looked outside, yet there was no wind, neither was there a door or window open. Another thing that was odd, the soup ladle was sitting out, not in the pot were I left it. Then a whiff of something hit me like the smell of a dead animal. Nathalie lifted her head right up. Her eyes were fixed on the soup pot. Armande came into the kitchen holding the stranger's baby.

"I just met Emilie in the drawing room," she said. "I wanted to fix up her baby's nasty cuts before nursing." The wet nurse's cheeks were still rosy from cold. Her thick woollen petticoat was wet at the bottom from melted snow. She lay the baby down on the table, mixed a spoonful of rose water and lard in a bowl, and then rubbed it on the child's cracked mouth and around its eyes. "There, there little nut." The baby clung to her. Head bobbing up and down in search of milk. Then she added, "I think I'll have some of that delicious soup you made Céleste. I need to warm myself after being outside."

I brought Nathalie with me into the drawing room and found Emilie sitting quietly on the sofa.

"Would you like more soup?" I asked her.

"No Mademoiselle." She clasped her hands tightly in her lap and did not look at me.

A few minutes later, Armande joined us with the sick baby. A sudden wind thrust a sprinkle of snow filled with the light of morning sun against the window. The whole room lit up, the dormeuse, the brass and porcelain ornaments on the table, the harpsichord, the writing desk, the sofa, the hearth and the vibrant carpet on the floor. I set Nathalie down on a blanket in the streaming light and planted a block and a spoon in each of her hands. When she's a bit older, I thought, I will bring her to my bedchamber and show her the bonhomme, now under my bedcovers for safekeeping.

"All the apothecaries in France could not prescribe a medicine to equal your milk," Emilie said looking warily around her. "I cannot lose another child, Madame."

Armande let down her bodice and brought the baby to her breast. Emilie cried as she watched her little one drink as if it was taking every drop of the wet nurse's milk. I passed Emilie a muslin handkerchief to dry her eyes.

"Have faith that you can produce more of your own milk," said Armande. "Please try to nurse your baby. Céleste will pack you a basket with some nourishing foods. That should make you grow stronger, and will help the flow better."

"Bless you." The woman bowed her head, but I thought I saw her dark eyes narrowing.

With quick movements, she took a small clock from a sack tied to her petticoat. Gold painted cherubs danced around a white face with black letters. Full of celebration, the object stood out against her tattered clothes and sullen face. Even I was moved by the kindness she showed in spite of her misery—though how did the poor woman come by such a nice clock?

"Please take this Madame Vivant. It's the only precious thing I own." She held the clock in the palm of her hand.

"You keep your treasure," said Armande moved by the woman's kindness. "I am happy to help. Remember to come back next week and we shall see how your milk is coming."

I walked her to the front door and noticed her frown as she looked down at her baby who slept in an apron folded to make a pouch around her middle. Where before the infant had a sickly green pallor, already its cheeks were beginning to redden because of Armande's milk. "I don't want my baby to die. If she lives past the age of two, she has a better chance. The wet nurse will make it stronger, won't she?" Her feet were patches of blue and red and two toes of one foot were missing. I ran upstairs and grabbed a pair of winter shoes from my room. Armande had given me four pairs of shoes, two for summer and two for winter.

"Try these," I handed them to the woman.

She clutched the shoes in her dirty hands and then set them down on the floor. They were robin's egg blue with two pearl buttons on the outside and a thick heel. Once again, she tried to give away her clock, yet I resisted. The shoes were exactly the right size for her. Yet her feet were so swollen and full of sores it took her a few tries to fit into them. She embraced me and a sickly sour smell entered my nose. It was the same smell that hit me in the kitchen earlier. The woman's small eyes stared at me as if digging into my thoughts.

I was about to say goodbye to Emilie when I heard Armande's distressed voice coming from the drawing room.

"Help me, Céleste. I can't see."

Lids drooped over her chestnut eyes and she swayed from side to side, gripping her skirt. Before I got to her, she fell to the ground. I helped Armande to her feet and guided her to her well-loved arm-chair. She was pale as could be; dark curls cascading over her face like strands of precious onyx.

"Can you see me now?" I crouched in front of her, hands resting on her knees.

"No." Her eyes were open yet her regard was vacant, searching. "Only a faint outline," she gasped. "I can't even see your eyes and nose."

She gripped her stomach and moaned. "The pain," she cried. "What is happening to me, Céleste?"

"Rest your eyes." I swallowed my fear.

After giving her a tonic to calm her stomach, I sent for a neighbour to fetch Margot, the midwife. Surely, she would know what to do? By the fire in the kitchen I saw black berries scattered over the floor.

The drawing room was aflutter on that late afternoon. Margot was applying a cold cloth to Armande's forehead as she lay on the dormeuse like a limp rose. Her eyes looked dead without their usual sparkle. The village doctor paced in front of the fire.

"Keep drinking the tea as it will clear the poison from your body." Margot had one eye turned in that made people afraid of her. White hair fell down her back. Her breasts were as fruit frozen on a branch during the month of December. She was Armande's wet nurse after her mother died, and was a midwife to many others.

"Herb of the beautiful lady indeed!" The doctor exclaimed. "Belladonna killed a neighbour's horse last year." He stopped pacing to examine the dried black berries in the palm of his hand. "We must rely on the old methods to rid the blood of poison, cut into the heart veins, the breast veins, and head veins, diverting the flow from the inflammations near the eyes and the stomach, thus relieving congestion in these parts."

Margot looked at him as though a lunatic just spoke.

"Do you remember, Armande, when you had milk fever and I gave you a very small amount of this plant to heal your inflamed nipples?"

Armande nodded, slowly turning her body toward her old midwife.

"You were so very ill. After taking only a small amount of this berry, your fever and your irritation subsided."

The doctor sat down on the dormeuse by Armande's feet, his elbows resting on his knees as he crouched forward.

"In his *Species Plantarum* Linnaeus writes that no fewer than ten of these berries can kill a woman." He held out his hand showing the dark specimens. "I am surprised you took a chance, Madame, treating her with such a deadly plant." His skin was cracked and dry like a reptile.

"Come now, doctor," Margot said in a light tone. "You often prescribe small amounts of poison for different ailments. If one understands what proportions to administer, then one can do much good."

The doctor stared blankly at Margot, stood up and grabbed his brown leather sack. "Since you seem to be oblivious to sound reasoning I think my work is done here." As he was leaving he said, "Babies must not drink from her bosom. Otherwise they too will be infected by the poison moving through her milk and into the chambers of her heart."

"Doctor, that's the most sensible thing you've said all day." The corners of Margot's mouth curled up ever so slightly.

The doctor pretended not to hear her. "I bid you ladies adieu. I will check in on you, Madame Vivant, later in the week."

While Margot took care of Armande, I was busy with a baby. Not Nathalie, as a neighbour with an infant of her own offered to nurse her until the wet nurse was well again. No, the baby I cared for was the sick one Emilie—if that truly was her name—had left us with when she ran off. After Armande took ill and was blinded, I found the screaming infant on the cold floor in the entrance, the woman nowhere in sight. My baser instincts told me to toss it outside where it would soon freeze to death. Yet in my sad and guilty state, instead of causing it harm, I took pity on the ugly creature.

I did not speak to Armande about the woman who added belladonna to the soup. She only knew someone tried to poison her. She was very tired—one of the effects of the berries—still had stomach pains and I did not wish to upset her further. I spoke to Nadine about it when the two of us were in the kitchen.

"That wicked Emilie came in here and poisoned my soup while I was upstairs changing Nathalie," I told her. "She was in our very drawing room. I even gave her a pair of my shoes because I felt sorry for her." The thought made me queasy; so gullible was I to have believed her story and let her in.

The stray infant liked the warm water streaming over her neck and shoulders as I bathed her in a basin on the kitchen table. After, I held a piece of cloth dipped in cow's milk at her lips for her to suck on. I tried to feed her bread dipped in milk yet she only spit it up. Nadine was boiling dried chamomile flowers on a pot over the fire for a compress to relieve tension and fatigue in Armande's eyes. She removed the flowers from the pot and folded a piece of muslin several times to make it good and thick. Then she put it in the pot and began stirring it, pushing it down into the fragrant, yellow water.

"You know what she looks like," she said to me. "She can't be too far away." Her wispy hair was light as dried corn husks and her skin had a rosy hue.

Now that Armande was sick and could not nurse, I had to find a mother to also take in the orphan. By the time I set about going from house to house to look for a family for her, night was fast approaching. I fastened my cloak and tied my bonnet tight to my chin. I then swaddled the baby, and secured her in the crook of my arm. I made it to the square just as night fell. After being rejected at two houses where mothers suckled their own, I went to the priest's house. The baby was crying for its dear life because it had not nursed all day.

"Please take her and find a home for her as she's an orphan," I said handing him the screaming baby.

He held the child away from him. A mother would not say no to our priest. If he took the baby it would soon find a home.

"Very well, I will see what can be done. We will have to find a family straight away." He was shorter than I was. Between words his top teeth rested on his bottom lip.

I nodded dumbly and was on my way.

The lantern made patterns of light on the ground and a mild wind brushed a sprinkling of snow over my cheeks. Waving the lantern to see better, I caught a glimpse of somebody cowering in the square by the fountain, and then I saw Emilie's face. I grabbed her by the shoulders, wrestling her to the ground. Wrapped around her neck was a shawl belonging to Armande, which she must have pinched while in our drawing room.

"You almost killed the wet nurse, you murderer." I pinned her arms over her head then sat on her stomach, turning her wrists until she cried out.

"I was only trying to slow her down so he could catch her more easily," she said trying to break free. "I didn't want to kill her."

"What? Who?" I pressed her hands to the ground.

"The man who gave me bread and some coins to watch her. I can feed my children for a whole week with what he gave me."

My hands still at her wrists, I tightened my legs on her small, yet solid frame. Then all at once she raised her body up and used all her strength to turn, knocking me off her. As I stood, a shoe that was once mine came straight for me. I felt a piercing blow to the eye and then a punch to the stomach. I lay on the ground shaking, an unbearable pain burning my eye and gut. By the time I crawled to my feet, she had disappeared.

Painter

ISABELLE SAT IN CHURCH, her shining red hair streamed out from her Sunday bonnet.

"I need the handkerchief back," I whispered and sat down beside her.

"I have kept it with me always, Céleste," she said, barely turning her head as she took it from her pocket and passed it to me.

Then she added, "Don't forget you promised me a reading lesson from Armande in exchange for this favour."

I nodded, clutching the handkerchief in my closed fist. I hoped it would give me a sign as to why her husband came back, yet all I felt on having it was a sense of dread, starting from the hand that held the handkerchief, and flowing to the rest of my body.

The wool spinner sat in front of us talking to the embroiderer. One sat behind the other with her four children and husband. The embroiderer was by herself, turning her thin body around to better hear. The wool spinner leaned forward, her hands clutching the bench in front. I caught the words *milk, God's punishment* and the phrase, *filling her head with ideas that impress upon the milk.* Isabelle shot me a nervous smile. Tears warmed my cheeks as I thought of how my thoughtlessness had led to Armande being poisoned. If I had not let the woman in the house, then the wet nurse would be as before.

Our priest came to see me after. "My child." He gently pinched my elbow, and brought me to a small-pane window at the back of the church. The gold cross delicately embroidered in brocade on the back of his priest's apron brushed against me. He told me that he found a goodly family for the orphan. Then he asked me, "How is Madame Vivant?"

"She is now able to nurse again as has regained her sight," I answered, "yet still complains of cloudy images passing before her

69

eyes. Hopefully the tea Margot gave her will soon make her well as she takes some every morning. And I prepare nourishing foods for her such as stew made of salt pork, squash and beans." I did not tell him about the chocolates I was also feeding her that Madame Lefèvre gave me, as I did not think he'd approve. Armande ate one every evening until the box was empty, and I'm certain that it helped to raise her spirits and improve her condition.

"Tell Madame Vivant to come and see me tomorrow. I will say a prayer to help rid her body of poison and make her well again."

I nodded wearily and quit the church. The melting snow in the square was like applesauce from all the feet trudging through it. A heavy grey sky added to my dark thoughts. Walking home, a song entered my head, *Black ink blood, white milk blood, what kind of blood does a bad woman have?* Armande was not a bad woman, it was that people talked for nothing. Some said blood was the seat of the soul. Well if it was, then Armande had airy blood running through her body. She was gentle as a summer wind, straight as the road to Heaven.

In the evening, Armande's fingers moved slowly across the keys of the harpsichord in the drawing room. Her gigue sounded to my ears more like a funeral march than a lively country dance. Armande told me she was still tired and that was why her playing was off. It had been two weeks since she was poisoned and she was still not herself. She seemed restless, yet her beauty shone through. The gown she wore brought out her eyes. It was green and shimmering like the leaves of the old oak in the garden after a summer rain.

Later, as she gave suck to Nathalie, I told her how Emilie had poisoned her, and what the vile woman said to me about being asked by a man to watch her. At first she was silent, and then her face turned sour. "It has been a while since receiving the King's lettre de cachet and he will be soon wonder why I have not presented myself at Versailles." Dark curls streamed down the sides of her face and onto her delicate shoulders. It was only when a log caught fire and a burst of light filled the room that I saw she was crying. I passed her a muslin handkerchief.

"I miss father and hope he arrived safely in Paris," she said dabbing her eyes. "He always knows just what to do, but it's now up to us Céleste."

I nodded and kept my worries to myself as I needed to be brave for her.

After the baby fell to sleep, she placed her in a basket by the fire, and covered her up. She sat in her oak chair, crossing one leg over the other and bringing one side of her petticoat on top of her knee where she placed her hand. The night wind howled over the rooftop, banging against the doors and windows.

I sat by the fire for more light and set about patching the chemise for a woman who lived nearby. As I tossed some branches and dried peels in the fire an aroma of cedar and apple filled the room. The fire changed from blue then to yellow and back to blue again. I drew the scent into my lungs and a calmness took over me. The next bit of mending that needed doing was a pair of wool stockings with a hole where both big toes would go. I squeezed together the two pieces of cloth to sew up one of the holes.

Armande lit another taper and fixed her hair atop her head with a piece of red ribbon. This spot of colour on a wintry night made me think of when, in the summer, she would pick a rose from the garden and place it behind her ear. Wild pink roses climbed the trellis in the garden. They grew in small clusters, and were the first roses to blossom each year. With the smaller ones, she arranged them through her soft curls, which made her look a queen. Rosebushes grew by the kitchen and drawing room windows. The scent of the flower was so strong that I always knew where she was in the house, by the terrace door, at her desk, in the kitchen.

She rested her elbows on the desk in front of her, her shoulders bending over something in her hands.

"Look at the lovely gift Madame Lefèvre gave to me." She pulled the letter she received from the envelope and out fell a comb carved from redwood and a shiny Louis d'or. She had not smiled like that for weeks.

"She writes that Jacques' favourite words are *cart, goose* and *rocking horse.*" She laughed softly, waving the letter over her face like a fan. Her skirt covered the chair where she sat, which made her resemble a flower bending over, its petals touching the ground. "He is curious about books and shrieks with delight each time Madame walks into the room." She returned the letter to the envelope. Although she had a pleasing look on her face as she inspected the new comb, her eyes were heavy with circles around them.

She strolled over to the green and light blue buffet edged in gold, and then opened the glass door, pulling out a bottle and two tall glasses. The label on the bottle showed a woman holding a lush plant that partly covered her face. Armande handed me a glass of gooseberry wine.

"Let's have a drink and raise our glasses to our beloved Jacques."

At first, my stomach turned with the fiery liquid, yet taking another couple of sips, I found it tasted better and warmed my insides. Armande's skirt clung to her thighs as she arranged herself, with glass in hand, on the dormeuse. She wore plain white stockings, the skin of her thigh barely visible past a blue ribbon tied below the knee. We had not celebrated in this fashion since Monsieur Vivant was with us and he had one of his pamphlets published.

Her eyes lit up and she clapped her hands together lifting her body off her seat. "I know.... Shall I tell you about the first time I snared a man?" She licked her lips after taking a sip of wine, smiling like a cat that just ate a fish.

I nodded eagerly as I crouched in front of the fire, happy to see Armande back to her old self again. It was a while since the two of us had a bit of fun. Heavy feelings of worry and sadness melted away as the liquid filled me.

"A group of gentlemen and gentlewomen were visiting us one spring from Paris and this young man, a son of one of my father's friends, came with them." She peered into the glass, turning it and watching as the nectar caught the sides.

Before long, I gulped it down and asked for another.

Passing me the bottle, she said, "You do it, Céleste. My eyes are tired."

I never poured liquid into such delicate glasses. Armande saw my hands shaking when she brought her glass over and placed it in front of me on the side table.

"Go on now," she said. "If they break, I promise I won't be angry." I did as she asked, yet then she started to laugh. "We don't need to drink that much all at once."

Without meaning to, I had filled the glass to the very top. Bending down, I sipped a little out so I could carry it without spilling. Once again, hot mixed with sweetness filled my mouth and throat. My belly grew hot also, but it was a pleasant feeling, not like when I was angry. Armande laid on the dormeuse with glass in hand. Eyes partly closed, the lines in her forehead softened, and she seemed at last to be at peace.

"I was all of fifteen at the time and I remember being at once transported by the distinguished attire of the women who to my mind resembled queens," she said. "Purples, yellows and greens filled the drawing room like a thousand jittery butterflies; silk flowers in their perfumed hair, pearls and iridescent trimmings, ribbons decorated wrists and necks. Alongside them were the men. Dressed like kings they wore powdered perruques; their boots and breeches adorned with gold buckles and jewelled tassels."

When I closed my eyes, the men and women from Armande's story appeared in my mind. They drank and carried on in the light of an evening fire in the very room where we sat. Scrubbed of any nasty odor, skin glowing with delicate and costly oils, the women shifted their skirts and eyed the men. My senses were caught up in the beauty of the spectacle Armande described for me.

"That first evening," Armande continued, "my father's friend introduced me to his son as a *budding painter*. I wore a lace-edged gown and high-heeled shoes, purple, I believe, with silk bows. My father gave them to me for my birthday. While the young man gazed on me intently, I couldn't help but fix my eyes upon the yellow crescent moons stitched into his stockings. The next day the party, led by my father, went out for a picnic and the two of us stayed back. The young man asked if he might make a portrait of me. I never had a portrait done before and thought what a splendid idea. Then his voice became affected, unnatural. He exclaimed that with his paintbrush he would seize the *essence* of me—Armande Vivant. To do that he wished to paint me clothed in shimmering silk, taffeta ribbons, embroidered bouquets of roses, lilacs and daffodils, with trailing rich shades of velvet the colour of blood, night, and sunsets." She shook her head in disbelief, a dark curl brushing her forehead.

"As you can imagine Céleste, this statement made me giddy with laughter—though I had the good breeding not to show it—for I knew from my father that the fellow was a novice painter and had not executed very many pictures at all in his brief career. I decided to play a little joke on him, teach the would-be painter a lesson in humility. After all, you must admit, he should get some comeuppance for his cheek."

The fire was blazing now, heating up my cheeks. Could I ever be as daring as she?

"When it came time for me to sit for him, I exited from behind the paravent without a stitch on; neither gown, nor chemise nor stockings. Unadorned as God intended. My heart was beating madly as I stood there before him. I was still young and inexperienced in the ways of love, but my desire to provoke him overcame my fear. I told him that his notion of concealing my body in mountains of luxurious fabric to capture my *essence* was from his own imagining and had nothing whatever to do with me. The man blushed like a maiden."

I too blushed as if I was the one naked before a man. She showed him how smart she was. Did he not know whom he was dealing with? My thoughts danced in and out of her words.

"What did he do?" I pleaded as I could wait no longer.

She gave me a wide smile. Her eyes lit up even more.

"His face turned pasty white, beads of perspiration settling in the wrinkles of his forehead. My naked self put the young man in such a frightful state that all he could do was to say a prayer. *Yahweh is my shepherd; I shall not want. He maketh me to lie down in green pastures: he leadeth me beside the still waters. He restoreth my soul: he leadeth me in the paths of righteousness for his name's sake.* Naturally, by this time I had lost all desire to be caressed and transported to the doors of Heaven by this sometime priest. Therefore, I did what any self-respecting believer would do. I recited my own prayer from the Holy Book. *Thy lips are like a thread of scarlet, and thy speech is comely: thy temples are like a piece of a pomegranate within thy locks.* I couldn't help myself Céleste." She snorted and laughed a long time from her belly, which then set me laughing.

"How can a man know God if he doesn't even know what he desires?"

"After that I kissed him on the lips and he leaned into me as though suddenly acquainted with his heart."

I pictured what came next, him touching her hips, her breasts. My face grew redder, yet hopefully she thought it was from the fire. I shifted a top log with the iron poker, which caused sparks to erupt as two pieces of wood rubbed together.

"It turned out he wasn't only a budding *painter*," she laughed and winked at me.

I joined her laughter, which woke up Nathalie. Her eyes opened and one hand toyed with the fur cover. What a wonderful evening it was, just the two of us drinking, telling stories and enjoying good memories. Armande had a life before sputtering, screaming babies, a life full of handsome gentlemen and pranks she played on them.

Diary

THE MORNING AFTER OUR DRINKING and merrymaking, I set out for some bread. Before I left, Armande handed me some coins she pulled from a pouch hanging under a shelf in the kitchen.

"Make sure you bar the door," I told her.

She nodded and gave me a half-hug while holding Nathalie.

The path was slippery and the dry, cold air stung my ears and nose. Snow buried the stones that, in springtime, made a walking path from the houses in the village to the square. I took the road instead of cutting through the sleeping gardens then crossed the street and entered a shop. Four loaves sat in a basket by the door. The man was not there sweeping or drawing bread out of the oven, just an old cat licking its paws in the corner. With two loaves in hand, I placed some coins in a bowl. There was a silver coin mixed in with the others that shone. It was new, unsoiled. The King's head was more distinct than I had ever seen. For a few moments I held it in my hand thinking to take it, wondering who might have left it. Then I stuck it back amongst the other coins and closed the door. The sack of bread warmed my hands as I walked.

I saw Armande standing outside our door, and I quickened my pace along the little path. She wore her winter cloak trimmed with fur and her dark curls were drawn together on top of her head. Her high cheeks, rosy and glowing, from the cold. She looked at me and then brought an arm over her head in a wave. In her other arm she held the baby. All bundled in a cap and blanket, Nathalie caught my eye and grinned.

"Bread." I opened my sack to show her the loaves.

Her eyes shone brightly as she passed the baby to me, then brushing hair from my face and kissing me above my eye, as it happened, right where the woman kicked me several days before.

"I am going to visit Margot for some medicine to help me sleep. Nathalie just nursed. If she fusses, give her some bread dipped in milk. I shall be gone only a short while, back before dark."

"Let me walk with you a stretch," I said, then set the bread inside the door.

We walked through the village, my hand clasped in hers. The other hand on the baby's bottom, as I held her close. When we strolled through the woods I kept looking around to make sure we were alone. Then as we reached the field, I saw the silent landscape with a handful of bushes poking out of the snow and felt at peace. She had not much farther to go before she would be at Margot's house. We said our good-byes and I headed back home.

In the afternoon, I played with Nathalie. She held onto my fingers and watched my hands floating in front of her eyes. While she slept, I went to the place in the forest where the wood was cut. I took a barrel with me, filled it and rolled it back home. I was soaping the linens when the blessed little crier started howling. When she saw me, she stopped crying and smiled as if content for making me rush to her side.

"What is it? I have no milk to give you." I sat beside her and jostled the basket.

My heart pounded and my bad leg was giving me trouble from pushing the barrel of wood. I looked outside for a glimpse of Armande. The curved lines of the mountain against the sky looked like a woman with her love. Just as Pierre and I in the snow by the chapel. I closed my eyes, taking deep breaths and then the calming image erupted with the baby crying into my ear. When I picked her up she stopped crying for a few moments as she sucked on a bit of stale bread dipped in goat's milk I gave her. She liked it at first, yet then cried again.

Though Armande promised she would soon be home, the dark arrived before she did. It came as I tried to make the baby take some milk from a cloth wound up tight at the end like a nipple. Nathalie sucked the cloth a while, yet then scratched my cheek with her nails and kicked my stomach. I rocked her back and forth, talking to her, as Armande would do.

"There you go, little nut. There, there."

That calmed her for a bit then she cried like the Devil. How in Heaven's name or in the name of the Devil could I make her stop? The fire went out earlier and cold wind was streaming in. I grabbed another woollen shawl from Armande's oak cupboard. The baby was wrapped up with all but her little nose and cheeks peeking out. I searched my head to think of something to sing that would make her stop crying. Unlike Armande, I was very bad at singing sweet songs, yet walking to and fro in the drawing room with her made her cry all the more.

She searched me with her mouth in hopes of finding milk. I tore off a chunk of fresh bread and wet it with milk again. The baby took every bit, eyes slowly closing. She pounded her fists to fight off sleep, yet lost in the end. After laying her down in her basket upstairs, I opened the front door, peering into the darkness. I thought of going to Margot's house and a strong wind shook the door as I held onto it.

The trip to Margot's house was difficult at night with no moon. One had to pass through dense forest then walk along a river before crossing to the other side. Snow was high and a person could easily become stuck or worse, drown. Though my mind imagined the worst that could happen to her, I calmed myself by thinking she must have stayed the night. She was tired after all, said she had not slept in days. Perhaps she became ill and Margot advised her to stay and be treated with her special medicines.

That evening, supper lay face down on the chopping block in the kitchen. Its reddish beak was bent as if burrowing a hole in the wood. Feathers came out of the bird's dimply skin with no trouble. Without its plumage and with dazed eyes, it looked like a weary old woman. Slicing the feet off I made a cut at the back of the neck to remove the skin. Next, the head came off, tossed outside for the village cats to fight over. The little heart was cold and soft between my fingers, the colour, like sweet plums. Lastly, I bathed the bird, picking off the smaller feathers. When the bird was cooked I was unable to eat any of it. Instead I sat there in the part-darkness watching the fire sputter and burn. If Armande came in just then, she would be happy to feast on the cooked bird. The wind tore over the rooftop making a sucking sound inside the kitchen chimney. I tossed a log into the flames, and the wood whistled and coughed. Sap spilled out of a hole, then bubbled and burned away.

I went back to the drawing room and prepared a big fire in case Armande returned before morning. It was good to leave the fire burning overnight in winter for the dead to warm themselves by. On her desk, I noticed the familiar red seal on the King's envelope. I knew the words in the letter by heart. She disobeyed the highest court in the land. How long would it take his men to come for her? My palms grew wet and my head pounded as if a body was taking a hammer to it. The back of her chair was hard, yet the seat had an old cushion on it, which my bottom sunk into with ease. Table legs curled, gold leaves climbing to the top. Flowers carved from the lightwood of fruit trees decorated the surface. A woody ribbon turned like a serpent around a garden. Armande wrote all her letters in that very spot, head down, strands of hair falling over her face. From time to time, she gazed outside. If the terrace were high with snow, she would observe how light made the ground glisten, before getting back to her words. In summer, she watched flowers and rosemary bobbing about or birds flying past. I picked up some quills on her desk, watching as they fell between my fingers. The smell of ink before it dried made me think of the first time I read a book aloud. *Bodies gliding on morning's cloak of dew, lit up as iridescent insect wings they flew.* She was so proud of me when I said these and other words. She pushed me to be brave and speak them even though my voice trembled, my hands damp from worry.

The desk drawer opened easily. It was her special spot for keepsakes. A stack of letters, tightly wound with a blue ribbon, her red quill that she used only to write about important matters, and a gleaming, white broach in the shape of a crescent moon. My knees shook together, the hair on the back of my neck standing to attention, the tips of my fingers damp. When Armande came home, she would find my dirty paw marks all over her possessions. Wiping my hands vigorously on my apron, I then tried to slow my breath and peered inside once more, not touching, just looking for something of hers to comfort me.

My eyes caught the corner of a book peeking out from under the stack of letters. Its red cover was made of the softest leather. Gently nudging the letters to the side, I picked up the object using only my thumb and index finger. Never did I see such a beautiful book. There were designs over it that I could feel with my fingers and see without using my eyes. It looked like a notebook for writing, not the sort bought from a bookseller. Yet it wasn't the one she usually wrote in.

Once opened, I saw her familiar hand. Letters were drawn out with spaces between them. Tall and shapely, they stood proud and pretty just like her. Each one planted on the page like flowers in a garden. At first, I turned the pages slowly, ashamed that I was reading her most private thoughts. Then I began to turn more quickly to reach the end. The dates at the top told me she wrote most of it before I knew her. When I looked through it, I saw places where she rested her hand. Letters were hard to read in these spots and there were many words I did not understand, yet heard her use before. Words like intolerable, illustrious, primping. The wind outside hummed like a monk tired from prayer. I turned to the very first page, cradling the diary and rocking it to and fro as I read.

March 2, 1784

For anyone who chances upon this faithful diary of mine, I have a secret. Not the foolish kind a woman tells another over English tea and profiteroles. My secret is about a little nut inside me who I can almost hear speaking my thoughts will only settle down. I am not quite myself. Grow is all I do. Swell her belly, yes, warm and watery inside her.

My husband is gone six months now and I am with child. The young rogue doesn't even know that he caused a seed to grow inside me, must have skipped over that lesson. Though after all, as a Man of Science he should know these things are possible. Furthermore, being at the same time a Man of Plants, he should be doubly aware that little nuts grow in human places. That is, when amorous alliances are formed, or shall we say entwined.

"How can I leave such bliss?" he said before going off to Paris to research plant specimens. It was a rhetorical question clearly.

I uttered a gushy reply as though following an operatic script. "I don't want you to go." Of course, I didn't want him to, but life is cruel and separates us from those we love. Robert will come back to me, yet what good is longing when my bed grows cold and I have no inkling of when his body will again warm mine?

Perhaps I should give some background about him, as my diary writing appears to have skipped over our entire courtship. First love encounters are rarely as piquant as the imagination makes them out to be. Ours went pretty much like this. I was giving him a lesson by the river when I asked if he could read me some Petrarch—Love sends me messenger of gentle thought. Earlier attempts to seduce him with my wit proved fruitless. The Italian love poet was a deliberate choice on my part. I believed that this poetry would gradually steer us toward our first heart-led encounter—and it did. After I read the sonnet aloud, Robert said out of the blue, "I've never seen a woman's body before as I had only brothers in my house and my mother died when I was very small."

"We women aren't that different from men," I said. "One of the principal elements that separate us is that we have less hair on our bodies, which is why we feel things more." I teased him while my heart madly raced beneath my ribcage.

"I am being honest with you, Armande, and all you can do is mock me."

Since he was such a serious man, I decided to treat our encounter as a lesson, as though I were his teacher, and he, my pupil. Perhaps then, he would be at ease with me and entertain the thought of us being as one. I sat very close to him, our bodies touching. I then instructed him to move his hand gently along my arm, my neck. A cool wind caressed my shoulder and my body came alive. The sun played peek-a-boo behind a tree that swayed its leaves back and forth like a lively stallion. I reached for his other hand and planted it on my shoulder. He looked at me with the impishness of a child and began to kiss my back. I turned toward him and his lips met mine, hands swimming over my body until they dove beneath my skirts at which point a sprinkling of red rose petals fell out. I place the petals amongst my skirts and stockings in my drawer to keep them smelling fresh and sweet.

And, so, began my amorous alliance with the Man of Science who I also call River Man due to his habit of spending time on its watery banks.

The baby kicks inside me now. I imagine gurgles that sound like words. She writes about father. Love growing, her and him. Just like me, though I am not yet born.

A *few months after that first encounter, I hardly recognized the man I wed. His attention shifted to exploring new subject matter. Nipples, shoulders, thighs, the curve of my neck and hair replaced his alpine flowers. It was as though his former self, which was shy, not at all interested in the fairer sex, suddenly became reincarnated into a physick with a fondness for the female anatomy. Where before, he spent hours examining the planets; stars became my nipples, his plants—my sex.*

I would be immersed in a good book or writing a letter when he commanded me to lift my skirts and, although I didn't always wish to disrobe on the spot, as both his teacher and subject his intolerable thirst to learn from my anatomy was hard for me to resist. As were his thick almost-black hair, dark brows, and blue eyes, a constant reminder to me of the river he adores. He unfurled my crimson petals, and toyed with the lacy edges uttering exclamatory phrases such as, "I can't get over it" and "Remarkable how a woman is made."

While exploring my nether regions he often drew pictures of his findings in his notebook. They were very detailed and as well drawn as the flowers he recorded on the pages of his botany books. What was I doing—legs akimbo—all this time? I was usually reading a book by Diderot, Crébillon or my beloved Rousseau to steady my mind. It wasn't easy to be pulled and prodded for such long periods. At times, while he was working my fleshy blossoms and entering his fingers into my vessel, my body began to jiggle. The book fell to the ground and I grabbed hold of the Science Man's wrist at which point he usually asked me to stop my bodily delights so he could focus on the experiment at hand. Ah, the pleasures I lived through in the name of science.

My monthlies were his favourite time. When they came, I found myself making a formal declaration as an attendant declares the King's arrival. Robert dropped what he was doing and fetched the notebook used to record the flows of my moon cycle. He washed my soiled rags and hung them out to dry. Writing feverishly, he recorded each day the flow of blood from my body, the texture and scent. He sometimes asked me to perch over a bowl and let the blood flow down so he could examine its thickness. During this time, he was like a boy who found veins of gold in a stone.

"It is like being in a foreign land," he said to me once about my monthlies. "Strange fruits, languages and perfumes are not the same as a man is used to in his own country."

His new hobby concerning my womanly state did not slow his romantic impulses. He rapidly transformed from a Man of Science to an experienced lover whose hunger for sensual pleasure could barely be satiated. He wanted me before each lesson. As his tutor, I not only found this distracting, but I feared my father could enter the library and catch us in the act.

"My lessons will take place at the same time every week," I explained. "Other plans will have to be made for our lovemaking."

Then he whimpered: "Don't you see that the lesson and the lovemaking are one and the same?"

Protestations like this made me love him even more. My admiration for him grew stronger each day, my heart's desire being revealed to me in wondrous ways. At my insistence, the young man was finally agreeable to conducting our lovemaking sessions at a time when wet ink on the page of a notebook lying open on the desk, wouldn't be smudged by a hot backside nudging against it.

We were married a year after our first love encounter, precisely four months ago in the village church. It was a simple but joyous wedding, villagers crowded into the cold and thinly adorned place of worship while most camped outside in the snow. Even those who despise my father for his carrying on with women, and for not going to church, attended. The miracle of that is explained by the fact that after the ceremony, we had a gigantic cream cake and all the wine one could swallow. With these kinds of trappings even one's enemies will come.

My monthlies stopped after hours, days, and weeks entwined in an embrace befitting a Roman orgy. Sun came and we laughed off its advances, pinning shut the curtains. Nightly winds made us rattle our bed even more. Barely a word was spoken between us: language of bodies sometimes demands we listen and not speak. Hand in hand, lips on lips, on ears, toes. Arms and legs twisted into a spidery jumble. Cool of his rings trailing along my spine and taste of his kisses. Our honeymoon. Love is a fruit, isn't it? Our sex, at least the womanly kind, is like the inside of a melon or apple, the delicate softness, the shape of it. He tells me this and I believe him only because when he touches me there the sensations I feel are fruit-like. I am an apple being tasted and tasting a man with my sex, vibrations of this delectable flavour resonating deep within my womb.

"Please me," I repeated to him until my throat crackled and hissed like the vocal chords of Eve's serpent. "You shall not surely die."

I expect the child around the festival of midsummer. Robert will have returned from Paris with a keener understanding of plant nomenclature. Before going into the fields to work, peasants will tie kerchiefs around their heads to soak up the heat. But what does that matter to me as I'll be doing some heating up of my own, lying on a swampy bed, nightdress sticking to my thighs, a head between my legs. Pain will split me in pieces as an arrow through an apple. I have seen babies come, yes, how women struggle, pushing and heaving as though trying to shake the earth from its axis. Women around the childbed watch and seem with their wills to push also. It is as though their stone-hard intent makes the baby come faster. When the head comes into the world first, that is a good sign. I am not the superstitious kind, but a small part of me thinks that means the child will be clear-headed. What if the feet come first? Well then, they will run as far away from home as they can and never return. All this talk of childbirth is causing me to yearn even more for my Robert. I must write him a letter telling him of our little nut approaching. It has been far too long since I've heard from him.

Could it be that while pouring through stacks of books in libraries and examining plant specimens with his scientific cohorts, he is all the while taking in other sights of Paris such as those of the female variety? No, I cannot allow my imagination to sway me in this fashion. If I listen very closely, I am almost certain to hear these words coming from the baby cradled between my hips. Gossip with oneself is as foolish as gossip with others. I happen to believe that learned women make far better lovers than the non-learned kind for we look upon love as one would a seashell offered selflessly up by the tide and not as an unavoidable procedure carried out between man and woman just as a rotting tooth has want of being pulled. Fleeting encounters fail to satisfy me if they are only a test of physical dexterity—a leg up here, knee over the shoulder. I hope that he doesn't plan to stay away much longer from his pretty and learned wife than a husband should.

My neighbour Nadine came by asking if I would care for her two children while she peddled eggs in the square? She is rosy-cheeked and tall and has all the simple charms of a country girl. She held a baby in her arms, which she proceeded to suckle as she spoke to me. I asked her whose little one she had, as I knew her to have only a boy who was four years old and a girl of two. She told me that she began wet-nursing as a way to supplement her family's income and that she was given an allowance of nine livres per month by the Bureau des Nourrices. She proceeded to tell me that the poor infant she now nursed was female and that when she went to see her she was sucking her fingers in a room far away from her mother. It seems the mother was afraid of giving birth, and of having the child be a girl, as the couple desperately wanted a boy.

"Since the woman gave birth she's not seen the husband and as a result wants nothing to do with her offspring," Nadine said with a deep sigh.

I watched her for a moment, the baby's eyes moving back and forth beneath the lids as it ingested the warm liquid. Although the child belonged to another, I soon saw that she bestowed upon it as much tenderness as if it were her very own.

May 3, 1784

My bedgown sticks to me as I write this; my skin is covered in sweat and my mind all in a whirl. In the nightmare I just had I was a little girl again. It is difficult for me to pick up the pieces as I'm still trying to make sense of it. We were playing Colin-maillard in the garden and it was my turn to wear the blindfold. I loved the game, but feared shutting out the sun would cause bad things to happen to someone close to me. Yet it was a nonsensical belief, so I put on the blindfold nonetheless. After all, why should I be afraid of such a simple gesture? My playmates stirred on the grass, laughing and brushing up against each other. I stepped forward, already wishing the game would end. Reaching out my arms, I caught hold of an object, pulsing like the heart of a frightened animal. It seemed I had quit the circle and was at my mother's side, my hand resting on her pregnant belly. The children broke up and ran away, which meant that there was no one left but the two of us. The flesh between my mother's hips was warm and tingling as though something was waking up inside her.

I remember that next my mind peeled back layers of her skin, each layer drawing me closer to a pulsing strangeness. At last, I reached the end of veins, blood, tissue and the being inside her spilled fiery light all over the lawn. Then it came to me: this thing inside my mother was I. As I quickly but ever so gently replaced the layers of her skin I began to weep. "You will die if you give birth to me," I said using the language of my hands moving across her belly. A wave of warmth coddled me and steadied my fast beating heart. "Don't let me live mother. For if I live you will die. I don't want you to die." She caressed my cheek wiping away tears. The garden was hotter than Hades. Birds sang and the sun's heat scorched the petals of flowers that sent a sickly sweet fragrance into the air. There was no wind and the incessant heat of August stung my skin. When I took off the blindfold, I saw my mother dead on the manicured grass, her summer skin turned to winter.

I awoke very troubled and went to the window. I opened my diary and sat there for a moment to collect my thoughts. Dreams are powerful forces that can make one forget one's head sometimes. I feel numbness at the temples and a sense of needing to be cautious or feeling afraid. The dream has left me yearning for my mother, wishing for her to observe me as a mother also. That is if I live through the torment of childbirth and my infant doesn't die. If I hadn't removed the blindfold, perhaps the dream wouldn't have ended with my mother dead? At least that's how it appeared to me in the strange place of the dream. It doesn't matter how it ended anyway as I know all about what really came to pass: how Margot tried to save my mother by vigorously rubbing her abdomen, hips and flanks with oil of violets. She gave her sugar and vinegar to drink, mint and a dram of absinthe. Her eyelids grew heavy; she took quick breaths and clutched the sides of her childbed. Margot bathed her with water from chickpeas, flaxseed and barley, but this did little good for life was quickly draining from her. Every cloth in the house was soaked with her blood. She breathed her last on her childbed, clutching an amulet to her chest.

The surgeon came and lifted my infant body from the belly of my dying mother. Margot said I was first seen crying tears of blood. Along with a simple linen cloth, aspen leaves were gathered to wrap me in so I would sweat out my mother's toxins and take in the virtue from the leaves. My father claimed that I looked like a freshly bound book. "Perhaps that is why you found your nature in books," he said.

Never did he express in words how beside himself he was that his clever and pretty wife bled to death. Nor did he tell me that a piece of him shrivelled up and blew away along with her, though I saw that it had. That is why, after her passing, he burned all the embroidered landscapes that she had sewed on cushions, quilts, gowns and wall hangings. The only thing I have of hers is a gold locket, now the amulet I wear around my neck—my mother's and father's portrait.

The moon peeks through cloud. I place my free hand on the infant growing inside me. The lump the boy or girl makes in my belly is shaped just like the moon. I've heard it said that if a pregnant woman looks at the moon, her child will turn into a lunatic or sleepwalker, but my father taught me not to be swayed by superstition. Contrary to popular belief, sinister beings don't take the form of old women, black dogs, wolves, or monks. It is all just folk legend, a way of scaring peasants to keep them in their ignorance and misery so they can be taxed to death and remain the King's humble servants. The angle at which bread rises in the oven means this or that and the pattern of clouds in the sky. To attribute meaning to these accidental things and base one's decisions in life on them is nothing short of lunacy, a condition that cannot be blamed on the moon or anything else.

One silly superstition that some scientists try to explain using flawed logic is that women—because of their moon cycles—are unable to reason or decipher mathematical equations. I recall a picture in one of my astronomy books that shows women dancing. Ribbons of light connect them to the moon as though they have no power over their own minds. Yet there is no evidence to suggest these moon dances exist, that maidens leave their marriage beds in the dead of night to go whirling around like disturbed hens with no rooster in the chicken coop. My father tells me we are entering a time where reason will prevail over superstition, yet many so-called reasoners use formulas as nonsensical as any village gossip.

Margot taught me that the moon is the first mother of all things. As a child, I used to wave goodnight to her before sleeping. She governs the waters of oceans and rivers. Seeds germinate and plants grow wondrously of her influence. Women's monthlies flow in accordance with the rhythms of the moon and babies are born under her watchful eye. Her light stirs the humours of trees and guides the smallest insect crawling upon the earth. Humans are so enamoured of their own handiwork, yet they do not always regard Nature so highly. Landscape planners are devoted to the mathematical organization of gardens, fields and hothouses. They shape Nature according to their own visions. Pastry chefs who fancy themselves more architects than creators of sweets construct temples with sugar paste. They add life-like flowers and colours to their buildings that one can barely dream. Some of us applaud the man who makes a tower from sugar, but then are blind to the truth that the moon above us has a hand in manufacturing the ocean's tides, the seed's growth. What one might see as superstition, another sees as wisdom. How can we tell the two apart?

In the midst of this moon gazing and musing the dream of my mother suddenly revisits. It is the same garden and the same unbearable summer heat. Where before I saw my dead mother on the grass, I now see an infant before me. No, it's a little girl. Why does my mind torment me this way? Pieces of her are scattered upon the earth: an arm like a tree branch snapped off in a storm, a leg as small as a stick of bread. Pray thee moon, make the unspeakable picture go away.

Part 2

Disappearance

THE SUN HAD BARELY RISEN when I dressed, opened the shutters and looked outside. I knew Armande did not come home in the night because I got no sleep for worry, and so I would have heard her. Besides, the storm made it impossible. I arranged Nathalie in a sack of rabbit fur as she cried and fussed, while on her head, I placed a woollen cap. The top of her skull poked out so all that showed were her eyes and nose. A fierce north wind cast hazy white bands of snow like ribbons across the hills. My legs were not visible to me, neither were the nearby trees or houses. I walked about ten steps in the direction of Margot's house before turning back. Inside, Nathalie took the scraps I gave her, yet cries told me she wanted Armande's milk. I was all thumbs. I smelled different; my skin and voice were not like hers. I thought about what I read in her diary the night before. What would she say when she found out I saw her most private thoughts? How shameful my actions were. Yet I only did it to be close to her. Anyway, she would never know as I put the diary back in the drawer under the stack of letters just as I found it.

In the afternoon I set out again with Nathalie as the wind had died down. There was a way we went each time to see Margot. That way was different in winter and different summer to spring, as the river was higher then. I took the familiar path through the forest and then hugged the river. Armande's tracks from yesterday were long erased. Cold air pinched my cheeks. Fingers burned with cold. I reached in to pat the baby's soft head and felt her quick breath on my hand. Nathalie made a squeaking sound like a mouse and quieted. I tried to walk faster but almost fell as my bad leg was sore and snow was thick on the ground. I stopped on the bridge that crossed the river.

Ice broke into tiny shapes at the edge. Snow made the place where I stood wet and frosted like sugar on the tongue. Dead grasses twisted and danced like snakes. All was still. No wind, no current of water, not even a drop from snow melting on trees. I looked down into the frigid water as questions crowded my head: What if she went away for good? Whose petticoats would I mend? Whose kindling would I carry? How would I eat?

The snow deepened, making it hard for me to walk. Only when I arrived at the forest on the other side of the field was I able to go faster. I bent my body to stay clear of cedar branches thick with snow.

Before long, I arrived at Margot's village. As I walked past the houses I felt eyes looking out at me from every window. Nathalie found her tongue and let out a noisy cry.

A man darted out from one of the houses. Dressed thinly for the cold, he approached, looking me square in the eyes. "Where do you go, wench?" His eyes shone between layers of saggy skin.

He saw my gaze fall on his hands, which were split apart like crusts of bread. "I fell trees, strip the bark and smooth them down to make boards for houses," he said. "I carry stones from the mountain and chip away at them, carving to make blocks for walls. My hands are those of an honest builder."

When I tried to get past him he insisted I run my fingers over his palms. They should have been rough like a round of cheese or a mule's backside, but my hands were too cold to feel them.

"I know not only who lives in these houses, I know how they are made down to the smallest bit of wood, the tiniest piece of stone wedged in a crack to stop mice from entering."

"I'm going to see Margot, the midwife," I told him.

"She lives in the old monk's house beside the dead tree." His gaze was steady. "What will you do there?"

Unable to hold it in and impatient to reach her, I replied with a burst, "Armande the wet nurse was there yesterday but she didn't come back home." My heart beat faster as I watched the man's face change.

He bobbed back and forth, his breath a cloud around him. His brows curled up and the skin on his forehead wrinkled.

"I wouldn't trust the woman with any child of mine."

His hair moved as if it wasn't part of his body—alive like Medusa's head of snakes. Before I could get a word in, he turned, entered a door and was gone.

Gently resting a hand on my shoulder, Margot pulled me into a small sitting room with a couple of upholstered chairs and a table. A red carpet covered the floor and pictures lined the walls. She wore a bodice tied loosely in a bow, and had only one tooth at the front that hugged her bottom lip. She glanced at the bulge in my coat, now fussing and crying. I undid the buttons, lifting out Nathalie. She promptly shut up, looked at me and at Margot then wrinkled her mouth and yowled.

"You have come about your limp." The old woman lifted my skirts to see my leg. "It is from the falling of the womb." She put her hand behind my knee, poking the skin of my calf. "Your womb is starved. How is your appetite for sex? Do you have a suitor? You must be close to twenty by now."

I tried to speak, but the cold walk over made words stick in my throat. Not able to talk, I began to sob.

"Mon cher enfant, what is wrong?"

"It's not my leg that is the trouble, but Armande. She didn't come home yesterday."

"She is not here, ma petite." The skin on her face pressed together as a moneybag pulled tight. "She came by for some medicine to help her sleep, gulped down a morsel of lardy cake and was out the door. She seemed eager to return home, saying she needed to nurse Nathalie and then rest."

Bile from my stomach was rising in my throat.

"The infant needs a mother's milk," said Margot as she took the screaming Nathalie from me, gently rocking her to and fro. "I'll ask the neighbour two houses over to see if she will help out. She has a young one still nursing and is a goodly soul."

If I opened my mouth to answer I would surely be sick all over her nice carpet.

Margot returned not long after and said her neighbour would nurse Nathalie for now. She passed her fingers through her long, white hair and looked deep in thought. She told me about the conversation she and Armande had. "I asked her, how was the baby she suckled? Was the milk flowing? Did it feed often? Armande told me that the infant was eager to nurse like all the rest, but took only what was needed then slept like she would never wake up. She said her milk flow was fine, but that she had soreness at the nipple and needed more rest. She looked sturdy enough, though her face was strained. Airs of distress circling her eyes."

She crossed the room, picked up two brown flasks from the table and poured liquid from one to the other. Dried lavender, heather and sedges stuck out from her bony fingers as she added some springs to her mixture.

"I fixed her some medicine with a bit of something I gave her before for milk fever as she felt a little warm, and I prescribed chickweed tea for her cracked nipples. After that she quit me."

The old woman ripped up dried petals, crushed them in a bowl with the flat end of a stick, then bringing it up to her nose, she walked toward me carrying a large bowl of hot liquid. Her eyes were sad, searching.

"Since you're here now, I'll treat your limp," she said. "Pull up your skirts nice and high. The flowery vapours will help the restlessness of your womb."

"But what are we to do?" I asked her trying to stand up.

"Keep sitting," she instructed. "You'll need strength to find her."

I fell back in the chair and spread my legs. She placed the bowl on the floor between my feet. The liquid smelled of rose water and oil of violet. Heat climbed up my legs and grew in warmth as it reached my thighs. Eyes closed, my stomach calmed somewhat as I took the sweet mist into my nose. My skirts dampened, water dripping off my legs and landing in the bowl at my feet.

"Do you feel the womb fall into place?" Her eyes were intent. "When it does your limp will improve, you'll see."

I only felt my womb twice before and knew little about the mysteries of the body. When Pierre kissed me by the chapel, I was sure it tingled and pulled as if waking me from a deep sleep. Another time was at Master Dogface's estate just before the scraggy thing wrapped in a cloak of black filth came pouring out of me. A tightening was felt along with soreness lasting for hours. Armande told me the womb was like a stove where a baby grew. This stove could give or take life just as a real stove made bread rise or burned hairs off a dead bird. My mind drifted back to the sensation of heat on my legs. The scent from the bowl of water beneath me filled my nostrils. My knees started knocking together and my head grew weak. Everything in the room was clothed in thick whiteness then pictures, walls, lamps, chairs and table started spinning.

Moments later, I opened my eyes.

"You fell, Céleste," said Margot standing over me. "The vapours were too much for you. Let me help you to your feet."

I looked around and saw the bowl upside down beside me, a puddle of water on the floor. My head hurt and was cloudy. I sat up, pulled myself onto the chair and she handed me a cup of elderberry juice.

"This will wake you up."

Margot's remedy made my head feel clearer, yet it did nothing for the fires burning inside that told me Armande was in danger. Not like having an anxious womb or stomach-ache, conditions that might be rid of through vomiting or having oneself bled at the arm. After wiping my legs, I pulled my skirts down to where gentlewomen wore them, nice and low. I took a couple of steps and noticed my leg had indeed improved.

"Armande is not an open book, ma petite," Margot said. "You might think so, yet there are things she doesn't speak of."

Things she did not speak of? Of course, I knew what those things were. At least I thought I did. Anyway, what did this have to do with her disappearing?

"Her heart was forever broken after her child's death," she told me. "Nursing brought her back to the rest of the world—back to us." She was teary-eyed.

I pulled my coat over my shoulders and sat beside the wood stove, the heat soothing my tired bones.

"It is near dark. Tomorrow I'll round up some people to look for her."

Then I remembered the lettre de cachet that I tucked inside my embroidered pocket to show her. I thought maybe Armande had mentioned it to Margot, but no, she was clearly learning about it for the first time.

She fanned the letter over her face, lightly brushing her cheeks with it. "If she has been taken against her will to Versailles then she is in great danger of losing the magic and wisdom of her milk." Her eyes grew wide and she drew a hand to her temple. It was the first time she ever voiced such thoughts to me about Armande's milk.

"I have been worried something like this would happen." Her shoulders caved in as though her body was collapsing under the weight of what the letter told her. "Over the past couple of years, rumours about her milk have spread to towns and villages. Now that the Dauphin is ailing and the King is in desperate circumstances, he hopes against all hope that his son will be saved by the wet nurse."

She searched my face, her restless eyes causing me to feel more alone than ever before, then she said, "Wisdom in the wrong hands can drain magic from those who possess it."

Hunt

THERE WAS INSISTENT KNOCKING and shouting outside. Margot waited at the front of the house with a dozen or so villagers. Though their heads were covered, the way they stood, their size, I knew them all. Who among them had not called Armande witch or harlot? Big snowflakes fell to the ground, slowly like feathers. Nadine smiled at me, though her eyes were sad. Tufts of hair stuck out from her bonnet. Her husband Bertrand was close by, shorter than she was and had wide shoulders and a bent back. Others lingered at the door, heads down. Children swayed to and fro with the wind and a woman sang to herself. A man coughed and spit looking like he would murder for a handful of coins.

"My child, we must move quickly," said Margot. "Very soon it will become impossible to see with the snow."

I rushed back in the house to slip on my coat and woollen bonnet. I then placed her diary in the embroidered pocket at my waist and was pleased to see it fit perfectly. If I kept it with me while we searched for her today, it would surely give me luck. Margot fixed her eyes on us, one at a time. Her voice was loud and carried far.

"Armande went missing a day-and-a-half ago. Let's follow the route she took to visit me. If you see any articles of clothing or notice something out of the ordinary, please alert us to stop."

Margot did not say anything to the villagers about the lettre de cachet, which was wise of her, as that would start all kinds of rumours.

The group started down the path to the square. Horses scratched the frozen ground and whinnied beside a house. Tied to a fence, an overstuffed swine with black speckles on its back started squealing. Villagers poured out of their houses to watch us go by. Most wore no coats as they stood at their doors, arms hugging themselves for warmth or hugging their sleepy-eyed children. Some cheered while some muttered nasty curses. A woman poked her head from a high window. She was stout and wore a man's bed shirt.

"I hope you find her," she paused and then said, "drowned in the river."

At that, she wailed and tossed a bucket of dirty water at me, yet missed and hit a small child who fell to the ground from the force. His mother picked him up, took the mantelet off her shoulders and dried him as best she could. She then pulled him by the arm to start walking, the child in tears.

A woman stood in the square chanting, "The kind and learned wet nurse is gone. Damn us all."

She did embroideries, made jams with currants and wild cherries and was mother to eleven children. Three of them, all close in age, stood by her watching. A small child, barely two years old, singled me out. Armande nursed her one summer while her mother picked cherries in the valley. The child's blue eyes sparkled. She smiled strangely at me and then took my hand while the others trudged ahead. Then in a small child's voice, I heard words so perfect as to be coming from the mouth of a scholar or poet. "The flames of revolt are catching, little by little." I let go of her hand, backing away and tripping over a mound of snow behind me.

"What is it?" The mother saw the look on my face. "You're all pale."

The child looked at me once more as though to make sure our secret was safe, and then ran to join her mother.

"Nothing," I shouted. "I lost my footing is all."

I caught up to the others. The child's words echoing in my head. My body was tingling from head to toe. There was no mistaking what I heard, yet my head kept trying to convince my heart I made it up.

We entered the field on the other side of the village then crept into the forest. Every so often I heard a grunt or caught the sound of the man who coughed and spit. Now at the back of the group, I watched as they hunted for tracks, a piece of clothing such as a scarf or glove, the body of a woman. They were like crows scavenging for food. When one stopped to dig, the others stopped and did the same, even if they saw nothing.

"She skipped off with her lover," said a man to a woman beside him who sold yarn coloured from onionskins. "A woman whose husband left her cannot be trusted."

"She did no such thing." Margot stopped in her tracks. She pressed a finger to the man's shoulder to push him back. "You should feel shame for what you said."

The man lowered his head and walked on. He was lost in a coat too big for his small frame and he carried a stick with a shredded rag tied to the top. Armande helped him write a letter one time to an uncle in Paris, and yet he had no care for her well-being.

"Maybe she took her own life," another woman said to the man. "No better way for a godless woman to end her days."

"Egypt of old had fewer locusts," I whispered to myself.

"Don't mind them," said Nadine, a blue scarf wrapped around her head showing only her eyes. She drew me close. In spite of our layers of clothing, her body warmed me.

Walking faster to pass the group, I heard more angry words.

"We'll find her tied to a tree, wilted and hanging like last year's fruit." The man said this as though telling a joke. He drove the stick he held into the ground at each step.

"We'll find her, we will," murmured a petite woman who lived on a hill just outside the village. She sewed petticoats and bonnets and always had a bit of ribbon or scrap of cloth to offer me. Her red hair was very short. Every three years or so she sold her lovely locks to a wigmaker in Grenoble to pay for the fabric she bought.

The river was in the distance. A man shouted at me to slow my pace yet I kept on. I wanted to find some evidence she passed by there before anybody else did. Lit by the sun, tiny flakes of white filled the air like fairies. The cold muffled a trickle of stream, silenced the wind. In springtime, these waters were part of the village apothecary's treatments for cleaning the insides. The diary was in my embroidered pocket. I sensed it was there to protect me. Its shape and thickness pressed down on my thigh. I imagined the diary's deep, red colour, its softness, and the way it felt in my hands. Behind me were breathing sounds and feet scratching and crunching on snow.

The flames of revolt are catching, little by little. What could it possibly mean? And why tell only me? The words gave me strength and a sense of purpose as I walked. Their wisdom came from Armande's milk and therefore must not be ignored. A man was at my side, tugging my arm and reminding me once again that malice was rampant in the world.

"A Devil with breasts is who took her away." He let go of me and pulled open his shirt for all to see. Making believe he was a Devil, he said in a shrill voice, "I seduced her with blood for her milk. She had a philosopher's tongue, sharp and godless. No-one but a she-devil would take blood for milk."

Others laughed at the man who bared his chest and paraded like a peacock in the snow. Another man raised his hands to his head for horns. He put his lips together, pretending to suck at the other man's teats like a baby. The group howled and begged for more. Some tossed snow at the would-be beast in protest. My belly churned at the cruel spectacle, a bitter taste rising in my throat.

Hours passed and the group was tiring. Men shouted at their wives to hurry. Mothers dragged tired, hungry children along behind them like rag dolls. We stopped in our tracks when a block of icy snow broke off and crashed into the water, clapping sounds echoed through the valley. All heads turned toward the river where a boy came too close to the edge. He ran trying to catch up to the others, and then stopped midway, pointing and shouting.

"Look, look up there." His eyebrows and lashes were frosted, spittle collecting at the sides of his mouth. Heads bending up to see a strange object caught in the branches. "It's a crow frozen to a tree."

Skinny feet were twisted round the bough. A gasp rose from the group as they looked up at the bird that hung upside down and swung in the wind like a timepiece.

"The bird's beak points down," said a woman. A cloak covered her face so just her eyes peeked out. "The wench must be buried here in the snow."

"I once found a snake in the well and the next day we had no water," said a young woman.

"Stand not directly under it," yelled a man, snow on his beard, and a nose with purple spots. He was a farmer who had his own land and animals.

His pronouncement caused villagers to scatter in fear like little birds, a deathly cry running through the group.

"If it points to you there is no telling what evil may come to pass."

Everyone stared at the man and then moved their gaze to the

crow that dangled high up. Wind sent a chill down my back. The crow's head seemed to wave at me as if it were alive, yet no bird could swing like that if it wasn't already dead. The beak was long and sharp as a witch's fingernail. Feathers came away from its body. Wind that moved through the valley sounded like laughter. Was it Death laughing at me, Death that took Armande, fingernails just like that ripping into her flesh? He kissed her mouth with marionette-like jaws, dancing with her across the fields, taking her far from home, from me. But no, her diary was safe in my hidden pocket. It cradled me, kept me unbroken.

Four men were digging. Snow floated in the air landing on their dark wool coats and scarves wrapped around their heads. Breath made a cloud overtop of them as they worked to get rid of the snow and layers of ice, and soon met the frozen earth.

"Nothing here but a couple of stones," said one of them pointing. The rest of the group approached to look in the hole made of snow.

"This crow may be an omen, but the wet nurse isn't under it," said the boy who first saw the dead bird hanging. His nose gushed, his eyelashes stuck together with ice.

"When we find her, she'll be stiff as a loaf of bread in a house where all the children have died," said an older woman who puffed her cheeks, coughed up bile and spit it in the hole. She wore no coat just an old shawl with pieces of sackcloth sewn into it.

"Let's follow the river, then return," Margot signalled to the others. She looked my way, her goodly eyes consoling me.

At the tree line, I turned to leave. My nose was frozen and my fingers and toes burned from the cold. Everything became foggy, the snow, the sky, the hill in the distance. I thought about what the man said about her being a she-devil and the odd song entered my head once more, *Black ink blood, white milk blood, what kind of blood does a bad woman have?* Although this time, mixed with those words, was the faint yet persistent cry of freedom.

Passage

THE FRONT DOOR WAS OPEN. My heart beat like crashes of thunder inside my chest as I crept inside with great care and made my way to the kitchen. Two men were talking as they shuffled down the corridor in my direction. I grabbed two tapers and the tinderbox and ran down the rickety wooden steps to the root cellar. A few moments later they were in the kitchen. The room where I stood was small and had a little window high up and full of cobwebs. Shelves of preserve jars and baskets of carrots, turnips and other vegetables lined the dirt walls. I looked around for the passageway Armande and her father talked about, the place where she used to play as a child. Then the door to the root cellar swung open, and there I stood in a stream of light. I bolted into the darkness, feeling with my hands until coming upon a small wooden door. The latch lifted easily, and I squeezed myself through the narrow opening and stood up, though stooped. Cold and dark enveloped me, the air smelling of damp earth. After catching my breath I opened the tinderbox and blew on the tinder until a flame arose. Then, lighting one of the tapers with it, I edged along the passage just big enough for me. The ground was uneven, scattered with stones and crevices. I walked for a long time before thinking I made a mistake and had taken the wrong passage. Perhaps I missed the door to Nadine's house and was on my way to the neighbour's further away, or to somewhere else entirely. I went over in my mind what Monsieur Vivant had said. *There's a passageway to Bertrand and Nadine's root cellar, and from there, to the wool spinner Madame Jardin. The passage then leads to the Gallants' house.*

My taper burnt out and I fumbled for a few moments trying to light the second one, then decided to keep walking for a bit in the dark so as not to waste the light. My fingers were frozen and so I stuck them inside my cloak for warmth. Voices in my head told me I was going to die, that the strangers in our home would hunt me down. I closed my eyes trying not to listen. If I let my mind wander to dark thoughts while in the narrow passage with no light and little air, I would lose my senses. My head hit something solid in front of me. It was a door, again with a latch. After pushing it open I came upon the neighbour's root cellar: a little bigger than ours and with shelves full of preserves, and tools for digging and planting. I rapped loudly on the door that was bolted.

"It's me Céleste," I shouted. "Let me in."

I was sobbing, begging for Nadine and Bertrand to rescue me from the cold and damp, from the men who I felt were trying to capture me just as they captured Armande. I hit the door with my fist until it was numb, yet it was no use, as they could not hear me. Then I remembered Monsieur Vivant telling me the root cellar was in their garden, not under the house like ours. I sat on the steps, leaning my back against the door and then lifted my under petticoat and felt for the embroidered pocket at my waist. The cover of her diary was cold, yet soft as before. I pressed my fingers down on it then kissed the spine, hugging the object to me. A little window gave me just enough light to read.

July 16, 1784

It would be odd to some in the village if they knew that merely two days after sweating, straining and bleeding on my childbed I am now sitting up in bed to record the events of the past few days in my diary. A handful of women in the village came by earlier with cakes for me, and bonnets, and blankets for the baby. All I could think of—as they were spouting aphorisms of motherhood—was writing about the birth. Many mothers have come before me, yet their experiences and thoughts about labour have scarcely been transcribed. Must hurry before another inquisitive lady should enter with yet another morsel of too-sweet cake.

Exactly two days ago, I was in the meadow by the house. Margot was right that dwelling on my troubling dream was no way to pass the time before for labour. Surrounded by clover, I ate wild strawberries, eavesdropping on the banter of bees. As the sun played behind a dusty cloud and droplets of rain danced across the pages of my diary, drinking in Nature's magnificence soon steadied my mind, clearing away dark thoughts. I sensed that the summer wind pleased the baby inside me as I thought I heard her murmur, soft and gentle, rocking to and fro.

When all at once Nature's riches were replaced by twinges of such proportion and strength that they became crashing waves. I stood up and a rush of womb water soaked my skirt, trickling down my legs and into my shoes as I crossed the field where pigs were fenced in at the far end. Grasshoppers snapped against my arms and tiny insects emerged.

Bertrand, Nadine's husband was tying a length of rope around a fence when he saw me struggling and called out to his wife. The two pulled me along arm-in-arm to the door of my house, up the stairs and to my bed.

"Margot," I shouted. "My baby will soon be here."

Bertrand dashed off to find the midwife while Nadine prayed at my side as I thought of my mother and of how she died on her childbed. By the time Margot entered the room, the air was filled with women's voices, praying, laughing and chatting at my childbed. They eyed me, making enough noise to cause Lucifer to plug his ears.

"It will all turn out right," said a tiny woman with bouncy red locks and a cream complexion.

"You are so strong. You'll drive that baby out from sheer will," said another, her voice breaking up. She kept bees and extracted honey and wax from their hives. Two of her children died shortly after they were born.

Nadine crouched down next to me and whispered, "Patience and prayer for the pain."

My eyes met hers. She repeated the refrain over a few times until a chorus was playing in my head. Patience and prayer for the pain, p and p and p.

"If you keep in mind this simple song, you will pull through," she said.

The little nut moved inside me, my body was heating up, my loins tightening. Margot pulled up my skirt and placed her hands on my

belly, moving her head downward, ear perched on the quivering within.
The pressure inside me turned to gnashing aches. Margot rubbed
my temples with poplar ointment and applied a generous amount to
my roundness and to my thighs. Then another violent wave crashed
over my body, and the scream that came out of me was so loud that
I surprised even myself.
"Yes, soon, very soon." Margot wiped me down with cool rags.
She did this several times already, yet still my head was on fire.
A spasm consumed me like someone yanking my innards, trying
to pull them past my loins.
Beside myself with fatigue, I just wanted the spasms in my belly,
my groin and back to leave me, for the child to be born and for
sleep to take over. As though in a dream or in death, I floated up to
the ceiling. The chorus of women ceased their banter. Faces became
pale, expressions wistful and for a moment, I thought I was dying.
Women's hands gestured in my direction as majestic statues in a
garden. There was blood on the sheets though less than I imagined
there would be. I could see myself from above, my legs plum red.
My skirt, pulled up to reveal my sex.
"Blessed be God," said Nadine.
An awful violence brought me back to my body and my thighs felt
like they had been picked raw by crows. I convulsed.
"The head," one of them shouted. "It looks at us."
"Next time will be the last," said Margot.
I pushed once more with all my might, and then collapsed on the bed.
"A rich jewel in the cabinet of God," said Nadine.
Tiny puckered face and eyes as two little nuts.

August 1, 1784

The long sickness that has shaken me has come to an end. It was
always my wish to follow Nature and nurse my child, even though
many women of my station have no care for it. Margot told me I
needed to nurse the baby right away as the milk that came at the very
beginning would provide much goodness for her and would keep her
well. She said to nurse about ten times a day to prevent engorgement
and assist the milk's flow. After the fifth day, I noticed that the milk

was thinner and lighter in colour and my breasts gave me a sensation as if to burst. Once again Margot said to keep feeding often as the soreness would eventually subside. I did as she instructed yet began to feel increased pain and swelling around the nipple. Rose-Marie sensed that I was ill at ease with nursing. She nursed infrequently and began to cry more, sometimes for hours.

After three days of this pain and frustration, Margot applied a cabbage leaf compress to my chest for two hours. Then she removed the drooping leaves and added fresh ones. She did this all day until some of the swelling dissipated.

The next day, a feeling of foreboding drifted over me. Margot said this sometimes happens to new mothers. As an antidote to my melancholia, she instructed me to walk in the garden and meditate on God. These quiet times only caused me to be prey to my own distressing chatter. Robert still hasn't returned even though I wrote him in March to tell him I was with child. So much time has passed without a single letter from him after I wrote him several times. Perhaps my worry of him being enamoured by another was not unfounded after all. Could it be he took up with a lusty Parisian actress and forgot his educated mountain girl? Then there was my father who always counselled me to remain childless. From the time I was a little girl, he told me mothering could only bring sorrow when the child dies, and distraction from the important issues of life such as rallying against the King's tyranny. These thoughts weakened my spirit and threatened to draw me further from my own self.

I pulled the curtains, retired to bed and handed off the baby to Margot to care for.

One never knows how experience will pull at our heartstrings. I longed to care for my own child and refused, whatever my weakened and melancholic state, to send her away. I thought that I would be blissful about the motherly duties presented to me. Yet where before, I could spend hours in my father's library reading or laze about watching clouds change from sea beasts into towers of silk, now I was bound to the simple needs of this little being who was reliant on me for everything. That woman is naturally committed to her offspring, that motherhood is a gift from the gods who bestow upon the fairer sex the most delightful experiences, is a philosopher's flight of fancy. The fact is, though I would not admit it to a living soul, a part of me longed to be relieved of my shrieking and odorous destiny. I washed the child and no sooner did I replace the napkin with ties at the side than she soiled herself again. I held as truths Rousseau's ideas about motherhood being the equivalent to bliss, yet I now felt that my existence was an illustration of despair. I know I am not the only mother who feels this way.

Let the truth be known: sometimes we mothers are sad, worse even. Sometimes we are nothing at all and are told we have no earthly reason to be thus. You're a woman. And woman must bear fruit and be glad for it. How could I express sentiments of sadness at being a mother? I've nobody to turn to but the extension of myself that I rock back and forth, this bit of breath that clings to me for survival. Never having had a mother to care for me, I grew up clinging to the myth of her wonderfully embroidered quilts that my father set fire to before I was of age to look on them. Margot told me she was also a gifted singer who showed her talent only to her husband and to a few trusted friends. Why must women be so unbearably modest? In the past, I have taken comfort in writings by some of our respected philosophers and thinkers though, as a mother, have neither time for study or for reflection. Although I love my father dearly, if it was up to him I would be neither wife nor mother. Spinster scholar is more in line for what he wished for me.

After days of loneliness and despair a morsel of hope has edged its way into my life. After months of waiting, I have finally received a letter from Robert. The poor dear has been laid up with both his legs broken from an accident in which he fell from a horse during a dreadful storm. On his way home, he was visiting his cousin Gaston and went to look for a precious lily observed in those parts. Gaston searched the countryside when the storm calmed and found Robert crumpled against a tree, the horse no doubt scared off as the beast never returned. He summoned a doctor. Splints were applied to both legs and Gaston's wife Françoise and their daughter Claudette are tending to him until he is up and on his feet once more. When I read the letter, I thought, poor dear and poor me for being alone with a child to care for.

Claudette has eyes like a Spanish dancer and a head of thick black hair. The two came to visit last year and I recall what a vision she was. I am certain her beauty alone will help him to be well again.

Yet what if, when he is better, he falls for her and never returns to my side? I responded to him without delay telling him of our dear baby girl, and wrote a few words of love and so forth. There was no point in pouring out my sentiments of despair, as he would discover soon enough what was in my heart.

A day later I was cheered to receive a letter from my father who was in Paris. He continues to distribute books and travel throughout the country, occasionally journeying to England. He was writing a fair bit and said he missed everything about me—my wit, views, tears, cooking, and even my temper. I would write him when my body grew stronger. I hoped he would delight in hearing that I was a mother in spite of his warning me against it.

I wasn't able to rest much that week. I forced my eyelids open and dragged out of bed with nary an ounce of vigour. To allow me reprieve, Margot applied rancid oil on Rose-Marie's temples so she would sleep longer. The old woman looked on me sadly. No doubt disappointed by my failure to mother, as I should. Rousseau instructs that a mother needs rest at the time of childbirth, a soft and sedentary life to nurse her children, patience and gentleness from those around her, zeal and an affection that nothing can rebuff in order to raise her children. Yet most rarely have the occasion to rest and hold their infants when they are thrust back into their duties such as cooking, soaping the linens, chopping wood, mending, and on and on. Where is the time for rest?

Margot was right that I did know better than most what a child required and embraced my motherly duties with almost completely open arms, yet still I couldn't shake the melancholic feelings. I wasn't sure how such sadness produced in me. My child was born healthy and had a calm temperament. Her little mouth opened to let out the sweetest and most joyous sounds and her eyes radiated warmth.

"With patience, a taste for living will return," said Margot.

Could it be that joyous thoughts would ease their way back into my life? Each time Rose-Marie awakened my melancholia grew fiercer. Why didn't Margot come and take her from me so I could sleep or read? Then, just as I was pondering my fate and feeling shame over what a wretched mother I was, my bodily condition grew worse.

What I am about to write will be of great service to mothers and that the great service to me is in the telling of it. The swelling came back the second week. Not only that, the milk was begging to come out yet something was stopping it. I'm still trying to arrange it all in my mind. The sickness, if I can name it thus, started with redness around my nipples, cracked skin and a burning pain that felt as though tiny knives sliced into my flesh. Nursing Rose-Marie caused me discomfort and I had trouble sleeping because of a constant throbbing. My face grew hot and my whole body was aflame.

"You are too full of milk," Margot said when she saw the milk mixed with blood seeping from my breasts and soaking my shirts. "The milk needs to come out. It has stopped up and is causing swelling."

My fever worsened. I don't recall all who came to assist me on my sickbed during those few days of torment, but I know the village doctor was there for a time, along with a travelling barber-surgeon, an apothecary and a healer of the stone evil. One advised bleeding and another clysters. Still another insisted on purgatives in the way of small spoonfuls of cinnamon water. Margot applied compresses and told me to continue suckling even though the doctors warned against it.

"Eventually your body will rid itself of milk fever," she said.

Heat consumed every part of me, setting my skin on fire. One night I didn't sleep and hallucinated instead. In my half-mad vision, all the saints were there before me—Augustine, Teresa, Sebastian, Thomas, Francis, Cecilia—and many mortal beings who were now absent to me. Although I lay in bed amidst damp sheets, I saw my dear mother who died bringing me into the world, childhood play-mates of mine who fell during the scourge and were buried together in one solitary grave. A neighbour who didn't survive the birth of her second child, and yet another woman crying out as her son lay on his deathbed—all of them scaling the exterior walls of my house like red-eyed lepers seeking a crypt to hide their half-deadness. At first, I didn't want to let these lost souls into my life. They were, after all, echoes of the past, wreckage from a sea-bound ship that never made it home. Although I am afraid of what they showed me, I was compelled to let them in.

I awakened in a pool of water, nightshirt clinging to my hot, wet body. My child was no longer beside me. Did the lost souls take her, I wondered. Perhaps the flames licked her all away. Just when I had given up hope of ever seeing my darling baby again, Margot walked into the room. She passed a cool cloth over my forehead and cheeks. Its freshness soothed me.

"Where is Rose-Marie? What happened to her?" I asked deliriously.

"She is asleep in a basket by your bed. There, you see?"

I raised my head and glimpsed her round face peeking out from the covers. She batted the air with her fists, emitting rapid cries. Margot sat on the bed and looked upon me as a mother does a daughter. "You were burning up."

"Yes. I have spent the night watching saints and others battle the fires of Hades."

"Take the child. She needs your milk." Margot handed her to me and I brought her to the spot of all my woes.

Amazed to find that feeding her soothed the pain in my bosom, I felt my fever much less than before. A sensation that I cannot put my finger on took hold of me when my milk fever subsided and I became bright-eyed and shiny as a new coin.

I am no more able to understand my transformation than I am able to blame Rose-Marie for taking me from intellectual pursuits. My melancholia vanished with the morning mist.

My baby's little mouth curled and eyelids like pea pods opened and closed. When she looked up at me with knowing eyes, I couldn't help but think it was my milk that produced such a state. My heart was suddenly joyful and I reasoned that there was no better place to be. Her gurgles and chirps told me she was happy in my arms and I now sensed the same emotion holding her. Ten little fingers and ten little toes, she was built of the stuff that made a body unstoppable. I held her always, all day, bestowing kisses upon her downy head. I couldn't believe that this little nut, this sleeping angel, was mine. I cried and laughed as I rocked her. My words were caresses for her, flowing and erupting. She drank in my sweet hums and coos, her mouth lingering at my every syllable.

After feeding, I wrapped Rose-Marie and myself in a blanket and madly raced down the stairs toward the door. As I combed the garden for a bit of wind to quell what was left of my fever, I sensed my present life slipping away. My head and heart informed me that mothering wasn't contrary to learning, yet instead part of it. I can write and reflect and talk philosophy just as I can suckle a child. No one can tell me—not even my own father—that it is not a woman's privilege to do both.

October 7, 1784

Last week my flow suddenly diminished. I wanted so desperately to nurse my baby that I hired a poor woman to let me give suck to her infant. Margot told me that Rose-Marie alone would help the milk flow resume, yet I wanted to do everything I could to keep nursing. When two neighbours heard of my motherly problems, they told me not to bother nursing as the government paid wet nurses and I need only sustain minimal costs. They are so very wrong to think I would hire a woman to nurse my own child. After nursing Rose-Marie and the other infant for a little over a week, I am overjoyed to write that my milk came back stronger and with greater consistency.

This afternoon I cradled Rose-Marie in my arms, swishing her around the room in a dancing motion. She uttered gurgling sounds, and I found that her language was close to being decipherable although I admit that I was at a loss to repeat it. Every day there is some change in her body and mind. Where before, she had no hair, my little girl now has golden curls sprouting on top of her head. Her eyes chase me around the room and she listens intently to me. I feel that my mother's milk makes her head quicker. It gives her the nutrients she requires to develop and grow, as she should.

Yet many gentlewomen who become mothers prefer to send their babies off to the country to be cared for by a wet nurse rather than experience this miraculous stage of life. With Margot's help and the latest edition of Avis aux Mères, I vow to do it all myself with no help from either wet nurse or physick. In Madame Le Rebours' book she states that nursing mothers must get ample rest and eat soft foods such as lettuce, while eating squash and carrots is also good for them. This may turn the milk yellow in colour, yet not to worry says the midwife, as the milk is only taking the colour of the nourishing foods. To nurse an infant is a course in morals. Margot told me to stay away from sweets so as not to communicate my fancies to my daughter. She also said not to take my eyes off the child for they are such delicate creatures. I have moved everything into my one room so I can watch her day and night.

Two days ago, I had a strange request from a young woman named Gabrielle. She cradled a baby in her arms while a little boy stood by her side lifting his legs one by one like a soldier in a marching band. It looked as though he hadn't walked very long because he stumbled each time a leg came up. Gabrielle was short, wore a blue shawl and her hair was pulled on top of her head. Her fringe cascaded over her brow and eyes. The bottom of her skirt was thick with mud.

"Can you nurse the baby?" She asked, her hazy green eyes imploring.

"I am not a wet nurse," I said in a way that I thought would end the discussion.

She then went on to share a surprising bit of gossip about me.

"I heard from villagers you have too much milk," she said, and then added, "I will reward you for your efforts."

"What are you talking about?"

Gabrielle let go of her little boy's hand and hugged the baby to her chest. Swaying back and forth, the dirty edge of her skirt made a swishing sound on the front doorstep. I soon learned, when I led her and her little boy into the drawing room, that the baby wasn't hers.

"I very much need the money that the baby's mother, Madame Blausen, pays me to nurse her. Even if you give me half of what you earn it will be enough."

Her sullen face tugged at my heartstrings though her story confused me.

"The milk has all but dried up and I have no way to feed my boy until my husband works again." She explained to me that he went away to find work in the next town.

Her son stood at my escritoire and hugged the seat cushion. Gabrielle then began crying uncontrollably. I reached for the baby who was clearly upset by the wet nurse's state. I rocked the baby softly back and forth, which soon quieted her. Her little eyes shone in spite of the fact that she cried and was hungry.

"This milk fever gave you more than one woman need have. Margot the midwife said so. Please, Madame."

While I was bedridden and feverish, the midwife said I had too much milk and that it needed to come out. She didn't mean I had more milk than most women. Gabrielle clearly misunderstood.

She proceeded to add layers to her story.

"Villagers say your milk fever is as a result of a spell gone wrong."

For many weeks I was consumed by my melancholia and not visible to anybody. I had no knowledge of any rumours developing about me. As she sat in the drawing room, she on the sofa and me on the dormeuse with the infant, she told me a random tale of superstition that I supposed had stirred her imagination to believe the gossip she heard about me.

"A housewife in another village used a spell to make her cow give milk. After her husband filled all the containers in the house, the milk kept coming. The husband and wife were forced to bring in a witch to stop the flow. The old woman burned a rope and told her and her husband that no cow in the neighbourhood would give milk that night."

Gabrielle folded her hands across her chest as though she just told me a great mystical secret of the ages. She pulled her mantelet that fell down her back, onto her shoulders and to her neck.

"Many women can be ill with milk fever," I said hoping to talk some sense into her.

In spite of the woman being superstitious, I undid my bodice to nurse the baby, assuring myself that it was to placate the woman and sustain the child, thinly and pale from lack of nourishment. The downy head sunk into my nipple, and a flood of memories came pouring back to me about my dark reveries brought on by milk fever.

After seeing the saints and those who were plucked early from life, I stumbled from my bed and opened the window. My house was a burning cinderblock teeming with bodies, mothers, daughters—all of them women. I reached down to take hold of a groping hand and flames as long and wide as a river threatened me. Fire attacked my arms, licking away particles of skin. I bent my body inside and shut the window. Back in bed, I could hear the incessant struggles and moans. Dreadful noises were embedded in the floorboards. They were part of the house, a part of me.

As the baby's little bud of a mouth intently sucked, eyes fluttering beneath closed lids I began to sense my spirit lifting to yet another height. The joyous sensation that filled me was not unlike teaching someone to read. Young or old, their eyes showed a spark of life because of what they were taking in. "To nurse is like teaching, but in a subtler, fluid form," I said laughing at this discovery of mine. Had my years of formal instruction led me to this? The wet nurse gazed on me as though I lost my senses.

"I will try again Madame Vivant," she said with a little cheer in

her voice. "I'll do as you advised and visit Margot for some elixir to make the milk come back."

She took the child and said, "There's a bit of rose to her cheeks."

Then she smiled. "This is the first time I've seen any life in her for days."

I resigned myself to go with the motherly sensations moving through me, whatever form they took. To completely abandon myself to the wonder and to my fear of what would happen if I let go. The women in my fevered dream kept surfacing in my mind. Sad, hopeless faces, hands clawing towards me. How could I refuse to open the window to my bedchamber—to my heart?

October 16, 1784

My lover arrived yesterday. After being separated for many months his appearance stumped me at first. All decked out he was in Parisian dress, skin smelling of Indian cinnamon and hair tucked beneath an absurd powdered perruque. He wore a pair of black silk breeches, satin shirt and pointed shoes on his feet. When we saw each other, we both erupted with laughter.

"I mistook you for one of the King's courtiers," I said to him.

He bowed to me as though I was his queen. His attire was meant to delude me into thinking he was now a man with refined tastes and a bag of tricks with which to woo me. Then when I saw that he brought me no ladies' gloves, no perfume, and no feather purse, I knew he was still the same country boy.

He took one look at our precious Rose-Marie, gave me a wet, fiery kiss and then rhymed off a multitude of incoherent sounds just for the amusement of our little nut. The instant bond he clearly had with her, warmed my heart and gave me the impression that we would be a family at long last. He gently placed Rose-Marie on the sofa in the drawing room and surrounded her with cushions. She just fed and was soon sleeping soundly.

"This is for you." he handed me a Latin dictionary. "It is a new edition that I have been using to teach my students."

Although not the kind of gift gentlemen typically buy their ladies, he understands what attracts me. How wonderful of him to remember that mine is old and tattered and good only for the fire.

"*And here my love is something of a lighter, saucier variety.*"

It was Aretino's little book on sexual positions, a book I had heard of, yet not read.

"*I vow to commit to memory this little book as I am certain that my body will rejoice in this newfound knowledge.*" *I leafed through the sonnets and erotic drawings before setting it down.*

We had not embraced since last winter. While he was away, I wondered whether our minds and bodies would be as they once were. I began to undress the man and his secret scent told me that, yes, it was still my Robert, the same young man who measured the river's quickness, who counted stars at night next to the chapel. The very one who touched my heart in such a way the organ began to improvise its own melody. I tossed his girlish perruque in the air, nudging his precious shoes off his precious feet.

When I got past his waistcoat, satin shirt and breeches, our smiles caressed and his hands washed over my face, neck and shoulders. His fingers were softer than before, cool and feathery as Chinese silk, perhaps from all those days and nights turning pages in the library. He swiftly moved around me on the small rug in the drawing room decorated with dancing peacocks and olive trees, gently stroking my skin with a silk handkerchief straight from a Paris boutique. With each touch, my body lit up.

"*What a heavenly body you are,*" *he said as he licked away a line of milk running down my ribs. His tongue danced around my nipple, until finally he was in the throes of sucking. This act of whimsy aroused within me an intensity of feeling that took me back to our first love encounter beside the river. Yet then he abruptly pulled away from me and sat up.*

"*What is this I hear about you nursing our baby? Is that not the work of peasant women? You must rest more. You are looking pale and fatigued. Hiring a wet nurse will help restore your health.*"

"*Margot is a godsend,*" *I replied defensively. How dare he call me pale? My cheeks are rosy as any twenty-year-old's are. "I consult l'Encyclopédie and Madame Le Rebours' Avis aux Mères qui veulent nourir leurs enfants when a problem arises that I cannot solve myself. So you see my dearest, I am not entirely alone in my mothering.*"

My husband has no idea that I not only nursed Rose-Marie with no assistance from a wet nurse, but that I also agreed to nurse an-

other baby for a short while. The decision came when Gabrielle, the wet nurse, who visited me more than one week ago, returned to see me a couple days later after Margot gave her herbs to bring on her milk. I told her there was nothing I could do and that she would have no choice but to let Madame Blausen feed her own child. She then explained to me that Madame Blausen does not care to nurse her own as she's afraid of becoming predisposed to diseases of the nipple, and prefers to feed her baby cow's milk or worse, sugar water. I admired the young woman's conviction to do what she thought was right for the child, and so I agreed to help her until she and the baby regained their strength, and her milk began to flow as before.

I did not wish to explain this to Robert just then. He was already annoyed with me for nursing Rose-Marie. I was angry with him for interrupting our lovemaking.

"Now my dearest, if you were to offer your milk to the likes of me, Petrarch's verses would surely flow from my lips as honey from an upset hive."

He took one of my breasts in his hand as if measuring the weight to judge how much milk was there.

"What a true scientist you are."

"It is not the quantity of milk that counts," he said, further lowering my bodice, "but the quality."

He crept under my skirts, his breath ignited my lower quarters, biting and licking the soft skin of my thigh and scratching and kneading my buttocks. His hands worked my flesh and heart into a whirl and his tongue found the spot where, over a year prior, its Master toyed for hours. When he came up for air, he nudged my neck with his wet mouth and nose and I applied love bites to his shoulders, back and the skin of his loins. To measure these nibbles was a lesson in control for my impulse was to devour the man whole and have him for my secret supper. There would be many courses to this ritual. Oh, yes, and the dessert would be one that no pastry chef in France could dream up.

His member was persistent; I thought it would slice through me! Who was the Master of whom? For the hard, blushing flower of strangeness before me was clearly in charge of the scientist at that moment. I rode the Master, turning my back to the man who was at this point of no interest to me, except for his hands, which pinched and prodded my buttocks. A tidal wave of delight shot through me, filling my head with colours and shapes. The alignment of his Master with my Mistress gave me such bliss. These two led us to a heavenly fountain where Robert and I were mere spectators.

October 20, 1784

Robert found out that I was helping the wet nurse with the infant in her care. How could he not, as the young woman was over every day seeking my guidance. In only two weeks of me nursing the little nut, her cheeks reddened, her eyes, fingers, and legs were livelier, and she spoke using her own secret language of goos and gaws. As I gave suck to the infant, I went over with Gabrielle the importance of eating nourishing foods, managing a good rest, and nursing continuously until her milk grew stronger. I told Robert that I would only help her a short while. He insisted I forget her altogether, take to my bed when I felt myself fatigued, and tend to my own daughter the rest of the time, as he reminded me, had been my wish to do all along.

Can I help it that I have a heart to see the suffering around me: the pauper who scrounges in the ditch for a bit of food or the poor woman who has no inkling how to nurse her infant, and who has already lost two children in one year? Since I was ill with milk fever, the desire to reach out to others grows deeper. While a tyrannical empire ruins France and peasants grow poorer with fewer means to help themselves, let people say that Armande Vivant did what she could. I mean to continue recording my thoughts on mothering in this diary and to submit some essays to the Encyclopédie to be published. The essays are for gentlewomen like myself who see only the good in nursing one's own children no matter what others may say against it.

Today, Robert scolded me for writing in this diary and not rushing to calm my child who, only a few moments before, began to cry.

"You told me you wished to care for Rose-Marie and not hire a wet nurse, yet your mind is elsewhere and doesn't heed her incessant cries." He stood there, a crooked frown on his face, pointing a finger at me as though I was his misbehaving student.

"*I will be along in an instant,*" *I replied.* "*Rose-Marie knows that I am never far away.*"

Robert said nothing in response and went back to the library to continue his study of plant anatomy.

It is strange that women must be one thing or the other. Perhaps it is because we are both sharp and givers of life that men and unthinking women debase us. Bloated by science, men of the enlightenment talk of equal rights yet oppress the very sex that gave them life. My husband means well, has a gentle disposition most of the time and is honest and considerate. He is tasty between the sheets, and adores our little nut, yet sometimes I think he fears things he cannot measure or count. His greatest joy, like many reasoners before him, is taking a thing and plucking the life from it in order to see it clearly and classify it. I do not wish for an instant to take this away from him. Only, there is a rawness to the experience of being alive when you take what good comes your way with your hands open. My father always told me to follow my head, not my heart, yet I have learned that some possibilities may be gleaned over entirely if your mind is the only one mixed up in the decision.

Margot told me that little ones are delicate and need a mother's constant attention. During the night, I always have one ear and one eye open. When Rose-Marie fusses in her cot, I bolt from bed to make sure she is dry; that she isn't hungry, and that she's warm enough. Robert moved temporarily to my father's room so he could get some rest. I spend hours reading all I can about mothering, and then make my own decisions based on a combination of sound judgment, observation, and motherly intuition. How then could Robert possibly believe that my mind is elsewhere?

Just before dark, I wrapped Rose-Marie in a blanket and covered her head with one of my velvet caps before going outside. The air rubbed against my warm cheeks, and invigorated my blood. Clouds filtered the sun making a funnel of light, which shifted from rose to orange to violet. I am a good mother, I thought, as I watched Rose-Marie's eyes widen at the play of light upon the apple trees. Nobody can say otherwise.

My head was numb, fingers and toes frozen and aching. I made my way back along the passage thinking two or more hours must have passed and maybe the men had gone. When I finally reached our root cellar I saw that the door into the kitchen was still open, light pouring down. I crawled up the steps and poked my head around the corner into the corridor.

Then I heard someone say, "Céleste, where are you?" It was Pierre.

"What are you doing here?" I couldn't believe my eyes.

He stood in the corridor. "The door was open. I brought you some soup."

His shabby scarf was wrapped around his neck. His coat undone and his face blotched from the cold. Then he added, "You need taking care of."

I was so happy to see him that I burst into tears. After that, I told him about the men, and we began to search the house. In the library were rows of empty bookshelves, their books upended on the floor. Papers were scattered along with objects such as marble statues, wooden boxes containing dead insects, framed pictures and cushions. One of the heavy curtains was torn away from where it was attached over the window. It hung like a flag at half-mast. The sight of Monsieur Vivant's library in total disorder left me feeling ill. Her father would be grief-stricken to find his precious refuge sullied in this way.

I stoked the embers in the kitchen and raised the pot above the flame to heat the soup. The thick salty liquid soothed and warmed my throat flowing down to satisfy the rest of me.

"You think she was kidnapped by the men who ransacked the house? Or she ran off with a man?"

"Armande would never desert a suckling baby," I told him. "Besides, if she went willingly she would taken me with her."

He knelt down at my feet and grabbed my hand, kissing my fingers one by one. This made me smile even though my belly was upset. His hair was messy as always. He stretched his neck up, his lips puckering for a kiss.

On the table, he spun an object like a pinwheel. It was Aretino's little book of sexual positions; the very one Armande wrote about in her diary that Robert had brought back from Paris for her. Pierre picked up the book and began to flip through it, then stopped suddenly and raised it to his eyes; the look on his face was of shock. Heat came into my cheeks. Would he think me a harlot for having a book like that? It's true he could not read, yet he had no need, as a dirty picture of a naked man and woman went with each of the poet's sonnets. It reminded me of Monsieur Vivant's ivory figures from the Orient, a jumble of buttocks, breasts, limbs and lips.

"It's not mine," I blurted out. After I said it, I regretted it.

"I never understood what these things were for." He tossed the book on the table. "I heard they were the work of the Devil. Now I know for sure."

A rush of bitter liquid filled my throat. Opening my mouth, the pea soup came out all at once. He ran to my side, cleaned off my mouth and then helped me upstairs to my bedchamber.

I crawled into bed feeling too poorly even to remove my petticoats and stockings. He lit some twigs and then placed a big log on the fire in my bedchamber. Pulling the covers up to my chin, he covered my face with soft kisses.

"You have a fever." He stroked my forehead and temples. "You must have caught cold in the root cellar."

The fact I was in a weakened state made him at ease with me. He talked more and was not shy about getting close.

"Don't leave me," I said pleading, afraid the men might return.

He pulled back the covers. The bed sagged a little when he climbed in next to me. As he placed his hand on my warm chest, I thought of what Armande wrote about following one's heart over one's head. Some possibilities would be gleaned over entirely if your mind was the only one mixed up in the decision. Though sick, I sensed a tingling between my legs that made me press my body into his. Was that how Armande felt when she lay next to Robert that evening under the stars by the chapel? Then I remembered the diary was in my embroidered pocket hidden beneath my petticoats. I turned, afraid he might feel its shape. His smell was a mix of cedar pitch and chicken feathers. His breath on my cheek and his warm body pressed next to mine gave me a sudden rush to the head. Except for some light kissing and hugging nothing much happened. When I could be sure he was asleep, I stuck my hand inside the pocket to touch her diary. The pages were rough against the soft leather cover surrounding them. Not having her diary to read would be bad for me. Yes, I knew what I could do: I would protect the diary and it would protect me.

Grief

GREY WINTER LIGHT EDGED its way into my sleep. Under the bed sheets, Pierre's body was warm against mine. My belly was better than the night before, though still unsettled as I rose to go downstairs. From the kitchen window I saw Nadine and Bertrand standing by the back door.

"Winter is hard and you'll need this for the long nights," she said, holding up a bottle of blackberry wine. Her infant peeked out from the top of her coat. Still in my bedgown and with nothing on my feet, I trembled from the cold. Bertrand handed me a sack that jumped and screeched. Sure enough, the orangey head of a rooster was visible when I peered inside.

"Thanks." I blushed at their generosity.

It stopped snowing and a sliver of sunlight broke through low clouds. The two sat down at the kitchen table. "Only a few months back my girl was delicate and wanting in the noises infants make," she said, arranging the child in her arms. "Armande gave her suck and soon made her quick of body and mind."

"Here," she said passing the child to me. "I remember she likes you." She had a wide mouth and small nose, and it was hard to see where it got its looks, from the mother or father.

I told them I heard two men in the house the day before, and that they had pulled apart Monsieur Vivant's library as though looking for something. Their faces showed fear and worry.

"People talk about Armande being seen with a man on a horse," said Nadine.

Bertrand cut in. "The day she went missing I saw a figure on his horse just outside the village. He was dressed in black, and I didn't recognize the horse. I was loading our horse with blankets for a family whose son froze while fetching water at the river. So he would live the father cut off four of his toes that were dark as stewed plums."

My mind was troubled by news of the stranger, yet then I remembered that Pierre lay sleeping upstairs. I did not wish to explain his presence in the house, even to my goodly neighbours. I excused myself to see if he still slept, telling them I needed to fetch a warmer shawl. The baby was content in my arms so I carried her upstairs with me. I found Pierre sprawled out in my bed, his mouth partly open. Happy he still slept and would not come downstairs while they were there, I picked up the shawl and quit my bedchamber.

I was walking down the hallway to the stairs when the little one made a sound as if something was caught in her throat. Her eyes moved from side to side, her bottom lip quivering. Then she said, "If I were a gentlewoman with stockings of silk, I would ask the servant to bathe me in milk. But as I'm just a washerwoman, plain as dirty water, I'll dream up a way to help me go farther." I stood there unable to move, watching the baby's face and hoping with every morsel of my being that more words would follow.

When Bertrand and Nadine saw me come back into the kitchen, they thought I'd seen a ghost.

"You're very pale," said Nadine. "Whatever is the matter?"

"I'm cold that's all." I handed her the baby, my mind consumed by the strange poem the little one had just recited. My hands shook and I hid them behind my back. I was trying to make sense of it on my own and did not want them to find out.

The three of us spoke about the stranger on the horse, and Bertrand vowed to find him. "He must have had a hand in Armande's disappearance." His eyes were weary and his shoulders sunken.

Shortly after they left, Pierre woke up and I told him about the sighting. He said he would look out for the stranger and visit me to make sure I was safe. While it warmed my heart that he wished to protect me, somehow I knew that her leaving had set off a chain of events that the villagers, and perhaps even myself, would be powerless to stop.

A couple days later, the doctor came to call. "I found this where the dead crow hangs," he said, a shiny, speckled box resting in the palm of his hand. "I passed by the maple on the hill the same morning you set out to find the wet nurse. I was on the way to visit a woman whose husband was doing very poorly. When I heard you were digging at that very place, I found it curious as I happened on this by chance before anybody even looked there." He raised his brows and scratched his forehead in a nervous way causing specks of his skin to fall to the floor.

"What is it?" I never saw anything like it before.

"What a peasant you are, my child! It is a snuffbox of course! It is made of tortoise shell, obviously belonging to some very distinguished gentleman by the looks of it."

How funny, I thought, that a tortoise man should bring me an object made from his own skin. The doctor saw me grinning at him.

"Did I say something to amuse you? I'm attempting to guide you to the dark truth about Armande and all you can do is poke fun!"

My eyes lowered and I fixed my mouth to a frown instead of an almost-smile. The word snuffbox was familiar to me though I had no idea what it was used for. I must have looked confused for he opened the box, took a pinch of the yellowish brown powder inside and drew it to his nose. Then as if on cue, he sneezed.

"There you see it's very refreshing at any hour of the day, especially before a fire in the evening."

The man smiled, his thin lips like two earthworms stretching across his face. Taller than him, I stared at the bald patch on the top of his head. Like other parts of his body, it was flaking off, yet in smaller bits. Looking more closely at the snuffbox I then saw the initials R.P. carved into it.

"Monsieur, these letters say nothing to me," I lied tightening my jaw.

He shot me a strange look and then proceeded to scold me. "Well, think again. For why would a woman keep a man's snuffbox except to one day relive a bawdy affair, the likes of which she most certainly kept from the likes of you?"

The rooster was screeching in the pantry, and so I threw a few breadcrumbs into the cold, dark room and shut the door.

"I haven't laid eyes on this object before." I went back to the drawing room. The doctor reached over and grabbed me by the chin.

"No surprise to me, Mademoiselle. Women such as the wet nurse often keep secrets from those most close to them." He circled the room. "There must be some trace of this gentleman in the house."

His nostrils opened wide, cheeks puffed up and turned a light shade of pink.

"What is it you're looking for?" I followed along behind as he pulled himself up the stairs with the slowness of a tortoise.

"A letter, kerchief, lock of hair, anything that will confirm for me that she's fled with this R.P."

Nobody, not even a physick could convince me Armande would voluntarily go anywhere with her estranged husband Robert Phlipon, the source of much of her melancholy. Must not let him see her diary, scratch his tortoise claws over it as if it was a piece of skin to be flicked away. No, he could not do that, as it was safe inside my pocket. I ran ahead of him up the stairs to block Armande's door, yet he overtook me and marched right into her bedroom. He slid his hand along the bed covers then lifted the pillow and brought it to his nose. He sniffed the corners, diving headfirst into the cloth, both back and front. To my disgust, he left flakes of his skin where, only a few days ago, Armande laid her sweet head. He ran his hand over the clothes in her wardrobe then he stopped, bending down to pick up a silk stocking folded in a basket. He waved it in the air as if this act would start the object speaking to him about the naughty habits of its owner. Then with a flick of his wrist, he tossed it under the clothes and slammed shut the wardrobe. I wanted to slap him across the face, yet the thought of touching his scaly skin stopped me.

Next, he was rummaging through the porcelain box on her dresser. Finely painted gold lines and flowers adorned the lid. His small fingers picked up a string of Italian glass beads. He stared at them with passing fondness just as he stared at the piece of skin he took from his forehead moments earlier. He picked up a small dried rose that was from Armande's garden, and then threw it back in the box. How could he fondle her precious things as though they were bits of his own skin falling away?

"When you find your dear wet nurse I'm sure you'll catch her *in flagrante delicti*. It is her heated condition causing her to flee. She has gone to the man whose initials are scratched into the box. That's what women do who are driven by desire."

What was the doctor talking about? He found nothing and yet he invented an ending to fit his idea of her. I grabbed the object from him. It was cold and fit perfectly into the palm of my hand. My heart leapt as if I too thought this object would lead me closer to where she was.

"Give it back to me," he shouted, his hands groping the air.

"Sir, if this object belongs to her lover, then shouldn't he have it back?"

I was tired of his lies and just wanted him to go away and stop taunting me with the snuffbox.

"Keep it then," he said out of breath. "I have no use for it. I won't be at all surprised if you find a love letter confirming what I've told you."

After seeing the doctor out, I sat at the fire rubbing the box as though it were an amulet and could show me hidden truths. With my thumb, I traced the initials R.P. The tortoise doctor tried to plant in my head a thought of Armande going away with the snuffbox's owner. Her husband. It was a ridiculous notion because I knew that, if the two were in fact together, it was only because he had captured her. The child and baby speaking to me was a sign. No matter what danger came my way, I had to see she was safe. Yet how could I do that if I did not even know where she was?

The last bit of day went to the edge of the forest and vanished. Wind brushed snow from nearby hills, tossing it at the windows of the drawing room. Upstairs, the lantern sat crooked on a chair beside my bed. Once under the covers, I thought of what the doctor said about women like her keeping secrets from those most close to them. It's true she did not talk to me about her past, yet that was because it was too painful for her. Margot said there were things she didn't speak of, yet surely if she were planning to go away I would be the first to hear of it? I opened the diary to where I left off, words, Armande's, spilled into my head and I could not read them fast enough. I sensed her through them as if she was right there with me. I wanted the new feeling to come back, the one where I was safe, unbroken. I never knew such a thing before meeting Armande and coming here. Several pages on, I read softly to myself while other times mouthing certain words aloud.

March 1, 1785

My child is dead and my heart pains as if begging to be torn from my body. She was asleep in a basket in the kitchen and Robert was outside chopping wood. Yes, I am sure that he was outside. I looked in on my baby, kissed her sweet cheek, nudging the blanket up to her chin. I was fifteen minutes—no more than that—in the drawing room at my escritoire writing in my diary when an awful clamour erupted from the kitchen.

A pig had come in through the open door and was thrashing around the room. It flung its head from side to side knocking over the table, chairs, kicking cupboards, and walls with its hind legs. Blood covered the floor and was slippery and wet on my feet. The basket where Rose-Marie slept was empty, then I found her crumpled beside an upended chair. She was not the same as before. Robert came in and struck the beast with his axe, blood from the pig raining down upon us, entrails stretching over the ground and organ still pounding. Scooping up my little nut, I collapsed on the floor.

I awoke hours or maybe days later to a baby's cries. For a moment, I thought it was my own Rose-Marie and that the previous horror was just a nightmare. I felt a tingling in my nipples from the crying that came from the other room and half-convinced myself it was my own child. I turned my body to rise from bed and follow the sound.

"Where was my Rose-Marie?"

My mind abruptly dredged up the image of the pig, my dead child, and the blood. The sorrow I felt was unbearable. The child's cries came not from her, but from another who I cared for.

While I was sleeping, Robert fed the child soggy bread dipped in bouillon and butter after Margot's advice. Then he tried to feed her some applesauce and mashed up carrot. At first, the little one took the food, but then she choked and refused to eat. A few nights ago, Robert woke me.

"She will die if you do not help," he said. "Please try. I have sent a letter to the Blausens, yet have not heard from them."

The child was propped up between two cushions. Her two-tone eyes framed a wrinkled face that begged me to nurse her.

March 11, 1785

Robert let the village doctor into my bedchamber even though I told him that I didn't want anyone examining me. I think it was early in the day when he came. I was sleeping day and night, drawing the curtains when the sun tried to force its way into my room. His business was to prescribe a diet of guinea fowl and apricots, to provoke vomits, and apply several empiric courses of herbal balms and ointments to the place where he said my heart bled. He held out a stinking concoction and asked me to remove my bedgown. I flatly refused, yet listened to his nonsense because I had no energy to fight off the revelations of his quackery.

"You will die of a broken heart if you don't follow my counsel," he said. "I have seen it all before. The heart pains more when it's a child."

He had a strange skin condition that made it appear as though he was peeling away bit by bit like a delicate fruit. When he finally left me alone, my mind wandered to the picture of my child on the kitchen floor. A neighbour said the pig belonging to a farmer down the road jumped a broken fence and was missing for days. It burst through the door of another neighbour's barn, trampled chickens and ate young chicks and rabbits. A boy tried to stop it by hitting it with a rock, which struck the animal's head. In any case, I didn't care to hear any of it because it wouldn't bring back my darling girl.

Later that morning I rose from bed and pulled the curtains back. The sky was pure blue, snow almost blinding, crisp and still like a Dutch winter scene. The beauty of the frozen landscape made me weep uncontrollably. I was beside myself with sorrow and longing for my child, and to think of how she must have suffered. Then to add to my grief, my husband shares with me his true sentiments. Standing at my bedside and weeping, his voice is a whisper.

"How could you be so careless?" His face is streaked with tears, his eyes red and swollen.

"What do you mean?"

"You didn't attend to her," he responds.

"How can you say such a thing? It was you who left the kitchen door open for the pig to enter."

The two of us break down, he sitting down beside me, the bed shaking as he howls from grief. I reach out to him and clasp his hand before he goes away. From an another room, the Blausen's child cried producing an awful pain in my heart that threatened to overtake me. Rose-Marie was dead, my breasts were full of milk, and the other *one wanted me to nurse her. I started to eat again, yet couldn't see the shape of things beyond that.*

"Fetch me some lettuce in broth with poppy seeds," I called out to whoever was within earshot.

Robert came into the room with a pot of soup in one hand and the child in the other. My first thought was to ask him to take her away, yet then I looked on her and sensed her sorrow merging with my own. Her eyes of light and darkness seemed to say, "Nurse me. Only you can fill me up." After helping myself to a small bowl of the soup, I guided the little one to my nipple and held it there until she latched on. I could almost hear her sigh as she ingested my warm milk. This little show of being soothed as she nursed made me sob. I didn't hold back but kept on crying for my Rose-Marie as the child who wasn't mine drank and drank.

It is very late as I write this. Monsieur and Madame Blausen arrived in the afternoon to console me over my dead child, or so I thought. Gabrielle, the wet nurse who originally brought me their infant in October accompanied them. Her son stood at her side looking around the room. She wore a violet robe with a bit of blue at the collar. Shortly after they arrived, Madame Blausen's questions shed a different light on their visit. I walked into the drawing room with their now-contented daughter in my arms. As soon as he saw me, Monsieur Blausen stood up. He removed his coat and hat, proceeding to straighten his vest and breeches. His hair was light brown with distinguished flecks of grey.

"Hello, Madame Vivant," said his wife. She reached out her arms and took my hand. Her fingers were icy. "Such a frightful thing to have happened."

The room itself was very cold, as Robert had not lit the fire since that fateful day. The windows were frosted, logs and piles of branches strewn before the hearth as though he intended to start a fire and gave way to sorrow. Madame Blausen stood there looking at me inquisitively, clearing her throat and swaying back and forth.

"Can we be certain which baby is dead?" She eyed her child suspiciously. "We pay you a healthy sum to care for our infant and need to know for certain." Her voice was soft, yet insistent.

"Your child is right here." My voice trembled and my temper threatened to erupt.

"Madame Vivant," she said. "Do you not suppose that I know my own child?"

"There, there," added Monsieur Blausen. "The doctor said that part of the child's head was preserved. We shall examine it to clear up the mystery."

"Mademoiselle, tell me that this is the child you brought to me to nurse in October," I said presenting the squirming baby to Gabrielle, the wet nurse.

She stepped forward and gazed longingly at the child. "It is, Madame Blausen," she said looking at her shyly. "Madame Vivant took over her feeding in January when it was plain I had no more milk."

Gabrielle looked at me through the long fringe that fell over her brow and into her eyes. "She has done the best job that ever a wet nurse could do." Tears rolled down one cheek as she hugged her son to her.

"You see Madame, no mystery exists." I was trying to keep my composure. "Do you not recall the colour of your daughter's eyes? Or, colours, I should say."

"Don't be absurd. Of course, I know the colour of my own child's eyes. How can a mother forget such a thing?"

"Apparently you did forget because her eyes have always been both blue and black."

"Positively absurd," she replied batting her arms at me.

"You've not seen your child since last autumn. It seems there are many things you've forgotten," Robert said.

It warmed my heart that he spoke up in my favour. I realized that when he blamed me earlier it was because he was overcome by grief.

"Look, this child does not even know me. Wouldn't she know me a little if I were her true mother?"

I could not believe the woman didn't even know her own child, and here was I with my Rose-Marie dead. The thought occurred to me that she didn't deserve her infant. How could such a woman adequately attend to the complicated needs of a delicate being?

"When did you last visit the child?" I asked.

"I have no idea and don't appreciate such accusing questions."

"It was eight months ago," Gabrielle piped up. "You brought me some gowns for the infant and a couple of wooden toys, a goat and a pig." Then she shot a look at me and said, "I am so very sorry

Madame Vivant," and promptly burst into tears.

I too felt myself on the verge of tears, yet could not give Madame Blausen the satisfaction of seeing me break down. The harsh look on her face refused to soften.

"When you came home, I recall you saying that the infant was a strange colour, a greeny white," said Monsieur Blausen. "You considered hiring another wet nurse."

"Then a few months later an acquaintance of mine was passing through here with her husband and daughter," said Madame Blausen. "I asked her to pay Gabrielle a visit. She reported that my infant was rosy cheeked and as happy as could be so I assumed the woman I hired was taking good care of her and that perhaps my baby was merely sick and had recovered. I didn't know until later that the wet nurse had little milk all along and had hired another woman, Madame Vivant, to care for my infant." The woman's lips stiffened.

"If I may say so, you are not at all how I pictured you." She cleared her throat, emitting a low cough, and then her tone changed as if trying to repair the damage she had done. "I was told that you were educated unlike other wet nurses, yet having met you in person, I must confess that you are far too much a gentlewoman to be given the humble title of wet nurse."

The village doctor entered and began pacing back and forth. "There is no way of knowing what caused the creature such distress," he said. "The swine hadn't eaten for days and, even when it was safely locked in its pen, grain supply was low in the family household so it wasn't getting its share."

The doctor rubbed his eyes and looked at Monsieur and Madame Blausen. "Perhaps it was the hit on its head by the rock that caused it to become wild and lose all control. Typically pigs are obedient creatures, even as they are about to be slaughtered."

He stopped for a moment, looked at the cold hearth, rubbed his upper arms to warm himself up, and then continued pacing. "Mothers should be more careful," he said disapprovingly. "Accidents happen all the time with children because of such neglect."

My grief took all my energy and left me with nothing to defend myself. Robert was also at a loss for words. He just sat on the dormeuse staring out the window, a mournful and vacant look in his eyes.

"In all my years I have not encountered a thing like this before. I heard about a hog that burst into a house during a storm last winter, knocking over a child and killing it, but nothing of the kind that happened in this house," Monsieur Blausen said. "I understand you have kept the child's head."

"Kept it, yes to be examined by myself and a fellow physick for tooth marks, saliva," said the doctor. "We were hoping to determine whether the creature had some sort of disease, but alas, we've uncovered nothing at all."

I hadn't seen Rose-Marie's broken body since that dreadful day.

"I would never have let such a thing occur," said Madame Blausen. "I pay women to watch my children at all times. Never do they let them out of their sight."

I ran from the drawing room and upstairs to my room, the soup I had for lunch churning in my stomach. Without warning, a thin, bitter liquid came flowing from my mouth onto my clothes and the rug by the bed. Minutes later Robert came in and saw me sitting on the bed naked, using my jupe as a rag to wipe my mouth.

"I am sorry Armande," he said. His shirttail was outside his trousers, which were soiled. His blue eyes showed sadness and regret.

"Tell them to take their child from this house." I wept unable to stop myself. "I want nothing to do with them or their offspring." He nodded and left the room.

Robert sent Gabrielle in to help me clean myself, and change into fresh undergarments. After taking a short rest, I got dressed and returned to the drawing room to fetch my diary from the little drawer of my desk. Writing was the only activity that kept my grief at bay. I was surprised to see Madame Blausen sitting on the sofa. She was holding her throat, emitting dull moans; her body slumped to the side. I expected that by that time they would both be gone.

"Madame Vivant." Her husband stood by the now-roaring fire. "We don't wish to cause you more distress. From what Gabrielle tells me, you have cared for our child in a loving manner, taking her in when she was no longer able, showering much attention upon her. Though I fail to recall her appearance fully, I am certain that you do indeed speak the truth."

His wife nodded in agreement. "Better to leave wet nursing to simple folk, don't you think, Madame Vivant."

She did not mean this as a question, but as an assertion.

I looked at her curiously and was about to reply when Monsieur Blausen smiled and said, "My wife has not been well, Madame Vivant." He told me she was recently bedridden with quinsy and her throat was inflamed with an abscess that would not subside.

I vowed not to engage with her so they would soon leave. After they quit our home with their child, Gabrielle and her boy, I retreated to my bedchamber. I went to bed early that night, my heart thudding against my ribcage and my head full of all manner of images that revealed to me my inner torment.

In the early morning, the room in partial darkness, I am imagining the sun lighting wisps of hair on top of her head: a sea creature with a halo. It was as though she came from the deep waters of the sea as even her skin glistened. I consider the dream I had before she was even born. Pieces of a child's body scattered upon the earth; an arm like a tree branch snapped off in a storm, a leg as small as a stick of bread. Where has my Rose-Marie gone now? How can I possibly put her back together?

March 28, 1785

Since our little nut died, Robert has become distanced from me. Everything before her birth is as if it had never even happened. He adored Rose-Marie, yet instead of joining me in my grief he carries on as though he is the only one in pain. I carried her inside me for nine months, listened for her whisperings, felt her tugs at my loins. I brought her into the world and nursed her for hours every day. He knows I hurt as much as he does and yet pushes me away.

Snow covers the ground outside. Garden, path, stone gate, and field have all combined to make a sweeping canvas of white. The only things my eyes can see of green are the tufts of sickly carrots poking out of the soil. Winter has put to rest the scents of rose, lavender and clover and stifled the sounds of women at market or children playing horse-and-cart. Lately the cold tries to have its way with me. I bundle up and spend hours at the fire warming my feet, hands, legs and face. I consider reciting a prayer, not a scandalous one to poke fun at the clergy, but one to console me.

Today Robert told me he was leaving for Paris to take up his study of botany. I know he can no longer witness my anguish, probably because it mirrors his. Last evening while walking past my father's bedroom where Robert now sleeps, I heard him call out Rose-Marie's name in his sleep, not the names of precious alpine flowers.

"When will you go?" I asked.

"Early April."

"And how do you expect me to manage here on my own."

"You always do," he said unfeelingly.

"Do you still blame me?" He didn't answer my question. "You no longer want to make a life with me," I said, searching his face for a sign that he was still my lover. "That is what you are saying, isn't it? This hasn't a thing to do with the need to go to Paris."

I understood his silence to mean that I wouldn't see him again. He's wrong to think that things will be better elsewhere. When you leave a place that doesn't erase the pain of loss but simply hides it away more deeply. My father was no longer with me, my child dead, and now Robert was leaving me.

Since my father quit our village almost two years ago, I received a handful of diverting letters wherein he recounted details about his adventures as a bouquiniste journeying through England. He said the English were hungry for French books especially those of the piquant variety and had little care whether our King banned certain ones or not. My father wrote that the English were too busy with their steam-powered mills and coal gas experiments for lighting to worry about such trifles. One afternoon while journeying outside of London, a cotton factory owner sat him down in a tavern on the banks of the River Great Ouse and said with a most serious comportment, "If the Americans could overthrow Britain and form their own republic, then why couldn't France overthrow its King?"

I sent a letter to Monsieur Taranne to give to my father when he sees him. In it, I told him about Rose-Marie's death. Even though he didn't want me to be a mother, I knew he would have accepted his granddaughter into his heart, maybe even loved her as much as I. How could he have done any different?

Visitor

A FIGURE MOVED ACROSS A FIELD and then disappeared into the woods. Nose pressed to the bedroom window, my eyes studied the frozen landscape. The sun tried to break through clouds and a raven's broken song filled the morning sky. Rose-Marie. What a pretty name. Armande's fondness for roses must be why she called her that. My head hurt from crying and tapping it with my knuckles. Even the prettiest roses in the world could not make up for the loss of a baby, a little nut. Mine was not a baby at all but rather a tangle of blood and filth, a stinking awful mess, dark like blood pudding sausage. Armande's was alive. Wisps of hair caught the sun as she played in the garden. She was a *sea creature with a halo*.

I took out my blue gown and laid it on the bed. Wearing it on a wintry day would be foolish, yet something prodded me to try it on. She had it sewn for me by a woman who kept a fancy shop in Grenoble. It was made of Chinese silk and very costly. When she gave it to me, I said I did not deserve such a fine garment. She told me that was nonsense and made me wear it, yet I only wore it twice since. After putting on my stockings, I tied the pocket around my waist, placing the diary inside so it was close at hand. The weight of it nudged against my hip. Some might have thought I had a thimble, a pincushion, or a pair of scissors in my pocket. Little did they know it was a book full of words protecting me, keeping me safe. Even though the last pages I read were filled with sorrow, the fact they were Armande's comforted me. I pulled on my under petticoat and put on the gown. Fetching my handkerchief, I tucked it into my chemise. Though it was clearly too light for winter, wearing the gown lifted my spirits. Then, two booming knocks came at the front door. I stuck my nose outside to see who it was.

"Forgive me for troubling you, Mademoiselle."

It was the man I saw walking across the field only moments ago. He held a cane and his open frock coat framed a blue waistcoat and breeches, a cravat tied at his neck. I cautiously stepped out and closed the door behind me. He had raven-dark hair flowing in a single stream over one shoulder. His face was perfectly drawn like a painting one might see in a gallery. Armande told me about some she visited while in Paris. He fixed his gaze on my gown. His eyes shone as though an angel peered from each one. Was I dreaming? My knees knocked together under my skirt. The skin beneath my lace collar grew hot. Then I warned myself to be careful as devils sometimes took pleasing disguises.

"I have been told that a woman, une certaine Madame Vivant disappeared from your village." His misty breath rose and melted away.

"Do you know her?"

"By reputation only." He drew closer. Then bending down, his breath brushed against my cheeks. "People say that her milk is more abundant than that of other women and that its quality is likewise superior."

His long, manly nose had a slight point to it, which made him look even more distinguished. His dark brows were arched and the hair over his forehead was curled in such a way that it looked like he wore an expensive wig, though it was his own hair. From what I read in her diary, Robert wore a periwig when he made social calls. When he came back from Paris she had tossed it as she found it girlish.

"My name is Monsieur d'Agenais." The man bowed gracefully. "I recently became aware of the disappearance of the celebrated wet nurse and it distressed me greatly to consider that someone possessing such an exceptional character would simply vanish."

I clutched the door and stepped back. Armande spoke of her Robert smelling like Indian cinnamon. The perfume on this man, lily with a touch of pepper, roused my senses. I had no idea a man could smell so sweet.

"She is said to have the purest of hearts, generously sharing her education with all who seek to go beyond their stations. Pray thee welcome my presence as an angel here to show you that kindness still does exist in the world."

His eyes had no specks in them, pure like a mountain river or summer sky. That was surely a good sign. The last visit I had was from the doctor who spouted lies about Armande. Clearly this person was a gentleman—an angel—come, at long last, to help me. Opening the door, I bid him come in. To my shame, the drawing room was not welcoming in the least. A rush of freezing air came in through the chimney. The curtains were drawn to block out the wind, which meant the room was both cold and dark. The gown I put on that morning suddenly felt stiff and cold like ice.

When he saw me crouched to light a fire, he ran to my side and said, "No, you mustn't Mademoiselle. Please allow me."

He bent down on one knee and lit a match to the sticks.

"It would be an awful shame for you to soil your lovely blue gown." He brushed a ruffle at my elbow, which sent a rush of blood through me.

My cheeks warmed. My heart jumped nervously. What flattery from such a handsome gentleman.

We sat in the drawing room. He told me he grew up in Villeneuve, the next village over, and that his father had just died. "I came back to assist, along with my two brothers, in settling my old man's affairs." He sat on the yellow and blue striped dormeuse, his eyes on the fire. "Do you have any idea what might have happened to her?"

I rubbed the worn arms of Armande's leather chair. My knuckles had turned white from cold and nerves. He seemed to be a sentimental man as he plainly saw how distressed I was by her leaving. The stranger's singsong voice and penetrating blue eyes put me in a kind of trance. Before I knew it, my mouth took over. I had no time to stop it.

"I think, Monsieur, she was taken against her will from this very village."

"Taken? Now why would any good body want to capture such a gentle soul as she?"

"Not *good* body. There aren't only kindly people in these parts." Ever since she went away I wanted to tell somebody how angry I was over how others treated her. "Many believe knowledge leads us astray. Good folks exist, but they see the wet nurse for who she is, a woman with heart enough for all. No, Monsieur d'Agenais, it's the jealous ones, the ones who don't grasp her purpose."

The presence of the gentleman wound my emotions like a top. I felt foolish for thinking for one moment that this man could be Armande's husband Robert. He was a kind-hearted gentleman come to help me find her.

"And what exactly is her purpose?" he asked.

"To care for infants who require her virtuous milk," I replied.

He clutched his cocked hat, moving his fingers along the rim. He then stoked the fire, his dark wavy hair coming loose and flowing down his back. He was tall, wide-shouldered, and had a slender frame. Any woman would be lucky to have a man like that. He walked over to the harpsichord as if to sit down and play. Instead, he skimmed the keys with the tips of his fingers. Armande sometimes played the harpsichord while I made supper or did my lessons. An infant's cooing or crying joined her soft yet mighty voice in the throes of a song.

"Peasants wonder why the rich pay less tax than the poor," I blurted out.

"We are in difficult times," said Monsieur d'Agenais.

"She helps the very people who need it the most, imparting cleverness and wisdom to those who, tomorrow, will be of age."

"These times call for severe measures. You must be in great distress over her absence."

"She left me no sign she was leaving … said she would be back before dark and that was eight days ago. It's not like her."

"All is not lost." His blue eyes twinkled at me. "I can make some enquiries. The process of settling my father's estate is tedious and my brothers are under a misapprehension that they have larger shares than I do." He removed his frock coat and laid it beside him. "Although there is very little that is left to us if truth be told," he laughed, sucking in a breath. "It will refresh my heart and head to do a good deed whilst immersed in this somewhat dreary family affair."

"That is very kind of you Monsieur."

He went on to tell me that he worked as a schoolmaster in Paris.

"I teach students during the day and study in the library at night in preparation for a book. In effect, I shall return here in the spring to collect further specimens for my research."

"What is your book about?" I asked him.

"It's of a scientific nature," he told me. "Much too dull for you Mademoiselle."

What an ambitious man Monsieur d'Agenais was. His shining hair and blue eyes caused a fire to ignite in my heart and between my thighs. His eyes followed the lines of my body and a pleasing shiver passed over me. I gazed down between my feet, an ugly big toe poked out of my stocking. Afraid he would see I quickly hid it with my other foot. When I looked up, the man's eyes caught my glance. Rosy warmth filled my cheeks. He was a scientific man just like Armande's father.

"How do you bide your time Mademoiselle, uh…?" His pause suggested he wanted me to tell him my family name, one belonging to my father. I had renounced that name, and so told him it was Vivant.

"I was an orphan and Madame Vivant took me in," I added.

My face reddened. A wave of shame passed over me. He must now consider me distasteful. His eyes opened partway, and then he smiled.

"I have my lessons Monsieur. Armande teaches me and I in turn teach myself. There are ever so many things to learn in this world, don't you find?"

We talked away most of the morning, just as learned men and women do when they have not a care for time passing or a need to complete a household chore such as mending or chopping wood. He made me feel a true gentlewoman and did not seem to judge me for being an orphan. Before I knew it, the sun was over the rooftop, melting snow falling in clumps outside the window. When he bid me adieu, my body was warm from head to toe. It was the first time I ever conducted myself with a man, as would a true gentlewoman. Yet before I let my heart run away with me completely I needed to find out whether he truly was a gentleman.

Two days later, children laughed, pushed each other and tattle tailed in the square. Mothers shushed little ones and fathers shifted and eyed each other. We were filing into the church when Pierre's mother approached me.

"Where's your wet nurse?" she said. "Gone to the Devil?"

Her words buzzed around my head like a noisy pair of flies playing chase. Catching up to Pierre, I nudged him as we entered the church, yet he did not greet me. I nudged him again, this time with more force, but he kept walking ahead as though I was invisible. Did he see the stranger enter Armande's house? Monsieur d'Agenais had not come on horseback when he visited me and it was early in the day, so I thought nobody saw. His mother pushed me to the side. When I watched how they looked at each other I realized he was tied to her apron strings, and we would never be close. My belly churned. I looked around and saw other people looking my way, eyes judging, tongues mocking, fingers pointing. I took a seat. There was chatter and laughter behind me.

"She's dull-witted, has no idea, poor thing."

"Reading puts loose thoughts into women's heads."

When the priest asked us to kneel, I dropped to my knees praying to Almighty God to keep Armande safe. My head pounded. Eyes closed, I let myself slip into a foggy state where neither nasty stares nor laughter could find me. Armande's diary was tucked safely inside my pocket, its cover pressing on my thigh.

The woman next to me snored while her child crawled under my seat, poking my legs, shrieking. I shushed it and it crawled away. The priest's voice echoed in the cold, damp church...*Kyrie eleison* (Lord have mercy on us)...*Dominus uobiscum* (May the Lord be with thee). There was burning in my belly and a taste in my mouth like rotten fruit. The group rose, kneeled and sat back down. My eyes opened just enough to follow along. *Sed libera nos a malo* (But deliver us from evil). Pierre turned his head to look at me. His eyes seemed lost and sad. Would he ever make up his own mind without his mother telling him what to do? His kisses made an impression on me even if he could not read. Tears collected in my eyes, rolling down my cheeks in spite of my will to stop them. Please do not let them see me cry Almighty God. Give me strength. *Sanctus, sanctus, sanctus Dominus Deus Sabaoth* (Holy, holy, Lord God of Hosts). Tears spilled onto the front of my cloak. So nobody would hear me, I sniffled at the same time the woman snored.

After church I sat on the edge of the fountain in the square not wanting to go back to my empty home. Pierre passed by me and turned his head.

"My mother doesn't want me talking to you." He was hunched over, watching as the group broke up and left the square.

"Go away then," I told him.

He nudged some snow with his shoe, looking down so I would not see he cried.

"What can I do?" he pleaded.

"You know what you saw that time," I told him.

I was thinking of what he said about Jacques putting honey on a stick to capture a feather stuck under the front steps of the house.

He looked at me wide-eyed, his eyes full of tears.

"You told me it was her milk that made the child act that way," I said to him.

"I still believe it." He stamped his feet on the ground, a piece of hair coming undone from where it was tied at the back.

"Is that a bad thing, an evil thing?"

"It must be," he stammered. "Most children aren't that way and if God wanted us all to be like that then he would have made us so without her milk."

Snowflakes drifted into the square. The sky was grey, the air damp and sticky. A chill went from my spine to the top of my head as I thought about the children's prophetic words. How nobody, only me, had heard them.

"The lack of bread and all the hunger is not the will of God," I told him. "Surely he would want us to better our lives."

"Like the riots over bread," he replied. "People are tired of not having enough, of all the riches going to those who have everything."

Pierre understood more than he showed. He reached down just then, grabbed my hand and walked me home, looking over his shoulder should his mother be watching.

Lie

THAT EVENING, I OPENED THE DOOR and looked around to make sure nobody saw Monsieur d'Agenais enter the house. It was not proper for a lady to let a strange man in with no female companion to watch over her. He wore a periwig, tilted on his head like a hat and his regard was mischievous as a boy about to put a frog down a girl's chemise.

As we sat down to dinner, his eyes lighted on my hair, shoulders, and the pleats of my chemise. It pleased me that he looked me over and clearly liked what he saw. His dancing eyes shimmered and his face beamed at me, which caused my heart to quicken. Margot told me that taking a lover would help the uterus fall back into place. I was no foolish virgin but nor had I begun to master the ways of love. Sweat collected on my brow, my hands fidgeting from nervousness.

As he ate the bread and cheese, Monsieur d'Agenais took little bits at a time instead of filling his mouth in one go. He touched a finger to his chin, sniffing the ale before drinking. The kitchen was cold, yet the measly broth pinched from a pork bone warmed my insides. Armande knew how to make good soup, even with few ingredients. Mine always lacked taste.

"I have news that two men were sent here by the King to request Armande's presence in Versailles." He poured ale into a glass and took a sip.

"But Monsieur, whatever for?" I pretended to know nothing about it and did not dare mention the lettre de cachet until I knew him better.

"Gossipers told me the ailing Dauphin is in need of the wet nurse's milk, and since she has the finest milk in the land, they requested she come with them to assist the King and Queen." Then he added, "I am told she went without much fuss."

"She would never quit the village without first alerting me." I roared these words surprising even myself.

Monsieur d'Agenais seemed like an honest man who would not repeat falsehoods, yet I refused to believe what he was saying. Even so, a wave of sadness hit me as I pondered for a moment whether it might be true.

"There, there, Mademoiselle, let your tears flow." He gave me his handkerchief.

The lantern's soft glow fluttered on the table. Stopping for a moment, I glanced at the piece of cloth, casually turning it over in my hand without even thinking. Just as I caught a glimpse of a letter stitched in blue, the man yanked it from my grasp.

"How thoughtless of me, that one is soiled."

I did not need to see the initials, R.P. inscribed on the handkerchief. In an instant that one gesture told me I was wrong about his identity. My body shook as the truth got hold of me, a trickle of sweat rolling down my back. I was a fool to be taken by his pleasing appearance and kindness toward me.

"My apologies," he said, his voice trembling. He gazed not at me but out the window. "It is my only one."

Finally, his eyes came back to me and once again he played the perfect gentleman. "Your hair is lovely in this light, Céleste."

He reached his hand out, letting a single strand of my hair fall between his fingers. I held my breath, heart racing, eyes closed as though the Devil himself caressed me.

"The colour and texture of honey," he mused, bringing the hair to his face for a closer look.

Nodding my head, I choked back tears. He poured the jug of ale into his glass, and in a couple gulps, it was empty.

In the drawing room, Monsieur Phlipon—not Monsieur d'Agenais—took off his embroidered waistcoat and boots. He sat on the dormeuse, his elbow resting on the upholstery, his body leaning to one side.

"I am told that Armande's father, an author and bookseller, now lives in Paris." He raised an eyebrow. "Maybe he advised them on where to find his daughter."

"That's impossible Monsieur," I said, my voice strained with emotion. "Her father would never do that."

"Yet I am told she went willingly, and, why wouldn't he want the King to find his beloved daughter? Does he not look upon his Majesty as the highest authority in the country?"

He already knew about Monsieur Vivant's political views, his forbidden bookselling, his scandalous writings, yet he acted as though he did not. Did he consider me a fool? Earlier I was taken by his charms, yet now that I'd come to my senses, there was no way he would fool me again.

Searching to fill the silence and slow my beating heart, I said, "How will your mother get on now your father's departed?"

"My mother died when I was very small," he answered.

"It is unfortunate not to have known her."

"From what my father told me she wasn't maternal in the least," he said absently. "In fact, I would be surprised if she cared about us at all." His eyes closed for a moment and his face showed anger and regret.

"Come sit by me," he said nudging over to make room on the dormeuse.

I moved slowly as if in a dream. It seemed to take forever to walk there. My body pointed away from him and to the fire so I would not meet his gaze. Even so I could feel him next to me, his warmth coming through my silk sleeves to my skin. He rested a hand on my knee. Feelings of desire for the younger man of her diary—mixed with hatred for him—filled me. I thought about the first time she and Robert kissed. The first time he touched her, and she touched him. His eyes were just as she described them: *a constant reminder to me of the river he adores.*

"In a few days I shall be fixed with a post-chaise and coachman and will travel with an older couple, a doctor and his wife from Grenoble, first to Orléans and then on to Paris," he told me. "I've not met the duo before; however, a mutual friend assured me they are enjoyable travel companions." His hands made sweeping movements, his eyes lighting once more on my body. "I detest travelling alone and it is a stroke of good fortune that his dear friends welcome a third party. His poor wife is quite ill and must undergo a special treatment available only in Paris."

My heart kept saying *hold me*, and I saw him kissing my neck while I stroked his shiny dark hair. How could I think such things, now that I knew who he was? Had he bewitched me? Could he hear me, see my thoughts? In the dim firelight I saw he had fixed his gaze on me. He moved closer, his head next to mine. I turned away and felt his warm breath on the back of my head. Then I jumped up, adding another log to the fire.

"Monsieur, I am awfully tired so will say goodnight now." I did not look at him for fear he would charm me some more. Just as I was about to accompany him to the door, he rested his legs on the dormeuse and stretched out like a cat. He then removed his periwig and placed his hands comfortably on his chest as though he was in his very own drawing room. I could feel my heart beating faster, my cheeks turning red.

"It is too far away on foot for me to leave now," he said closing his eyes. "If you are agreeable I think I shall sleep here tonight."

"Very well," I said, tossing a blanket over him. Neighbours would not like it if they caught sight of a man leaving our home late at night. I could sneak him out before the sun came up. It would be safer that way, I thought, and so I let him sleep. Even so, feelings of intense disquiet crept into my thoughts as I ascended the steps to bed.

The moon was full and shone through my window. Light streamed across the floorboards. Close to sleep, I thought of what Monsieur Phlipon said about Armande going with the King's men willingly. How her father had told them where to find her. She promised me I would be with her always, never to worry, as she would not leave me. Yet could he be telling the truth? Could she really be the same as every other person I knew in this rotten dunghill of a world? I was so tired and confused I felt I did not know whom to trust. The light in her eyes when she taught me to read and write, and the way her beauty calmed me. These things could not be lies I thought.

At first, when I woke in the night I considered the noise I heard was, Armande come back. There was a sound on the stairs and a rustle at my door.

"Madame, you left me sleeping tout seul. The fire is out in the drawing room and I am cold as a corpse. Je déteste le froid." I was startled to hear Monsieur Phlipon in my bedchamber. He flung open my bed curtain and stood over me.

"What are you...?" I was barely able to spit the words out when he lay down next to me. Lifting my nightdress, he began to chase after the small curves of my hips and waist.

"You will soon warm me won't you, ma petite?"

I grabbed his cold hands to push them away.

"Come now, why so shy?"

"Monsieur you must leave my bedchamber this instant." I turned away waiting for him to go.

"If that is what you desire."

He bent over to give me a kiss on the lips, when all at once, every limb of mine started shaking as though the Devil was in me and would not let go. His embrace was warm and sweet as honey fresh from the beehive. My head was unable to control my heart's vicious tugging. As if in a dream, I guided his hands to my body's warmest spot. The man growled with pleasure.

"What lovely thighs you have," he said caressing them with the tip of his ice-cold nose. "The scent of your body is sweeter than the Queen's perfume. Why is it that nobles should be dressed in the finest silks when country folk are just as handsome and worthy of riches."

He held my hands in his, nudging me onto my back. I looked and was stilled by a flash of his icy blue eyes, lit by the moon. I tried to speak yet he kissed my words away, then touched his lips to my nipples.

"Your flesh is a continent, your navel, an ocean glistening in the sun. Why, you are worth ten of the Queen." His loving words filled my head and heart to the brim.

He lit a candle by the bedside, strands of hair falling over his face, beads of sweat on his upper lip.

"My, what a divine specimen of natural beauty my eyes behold! The harmony of your curves fills the soul."

Ah, what a man to fancy me. He's a poet and scientist all in one who finds me beautiful, a sight to behold. I was with a couple of men in the past, though they were more boys. It was not the same as being with a gentleman who was educated and dressed nice and made fires for a girl. No man ever did that for me before. His large hands showed strength, his body pressing down told me of his longing. My tongue tasted his salty lips stained with my tears. Yet just as he was kissing me on the cheeks, eyes and forehead, a pang of shame hit me and I grabbed my nightdress, trying to hide from his gaze. Here I was giving way to my bodily impulses and forgetting all about Armande, my beloved sister and mother who had been wronged by the very scoundrel.

"We'll find her, don't you worry," he whispered as if he read my thoughts. He drew the candle closer. "Ah yes, your belly, how delicious.... I'd surely give up a twenty course meal prepared by the King's cook for such a feast as you."

"She helped me speak words I never knew," I babbled, giving the man a half-hearted push. "These words fell off my tongue like wine. I am now so sensitive I even weep at the sound of some words to my ears." I could not stop myself talking.

"Hmm, yes, it is very good to cry tears of joy and sadness, the mark of a true gentlewoman to be sure."

He held the candle over my belly letting a single bit of wax drop into my navel, which made me cried out. As he washed my face with kisses, my body felt like it was falling into a deep ravine. In the blink of an eye, the ground shifted under me.

The next morning when I awoke, the bed sheets were rumpled and I had not a stitch on. A trail of wax led from the table to the bed covers; a souvenir of him anointing me. All dressed in my bedgown, I then ran a brush though my hair, covered my shoulders with a shawl and headed downstairs. There was a note on Armande's desk, which he wrote with one of her special quills.

Last evening's kisses from thee were sweet as the finest honey. Away until nightfall.

Faithfully yours, M. d'Agenais

Milk

WHAT HAD I DONE? He is not Monsieur d'Agenais, yet neither is he the man in her diary. At least not the first one she loved and who loved her. Armande would never forgive me. Even if she was able to, I would be too humbled to show my face to her. Sun pushed through thin clouds and a bird stood on the hard snow pulling at a piece of grass with its beak. I had chores to do, the chimney needed cleaning and more wood had to come in so we would have some dry to burn later in the week. After changing into my old skirt stained with the spit-up of babies, I used a rough brush with a long handle to clean the bricks on the inside. It smoked the night before and Monsieur Phlipon had produced a slight cough. Clumps of soot fixed to the stone broke off landing on my face and shoulders. I went outside to gather wood. Two women leered at me as I passed them on the path, then I heard one of them say in a very loud voice, "That orphan was drinking ale with a man last evening. I hear he's known in these parts. I went over for a bit of cream and saw them in the candlelight. She was rosy-cheeked and smiling, bending over to give him a better view."

The other replied, "Then did she take it up the backside."

The women's howls scared off birds in the trees and I too scooted away like a scared creature. A black cloud wrapped around me making it hard to breathe. When I came to the pile of wood, I sat down on a tree stump. The women's lies filled my head joined by thoughts of his hands on my skin, his desire for me. Yet I hated him for all he did to Armande and hated myself for wanting him. I had nobody to talk to or confide in, so I took her diary from my pocket, passing over a handful of entries until my eyes caught the words *milk fever*.

147

April 12, 1785

Last week, Bertrand and Nadine came to see me and insisted I visit a man in the village whose wife just died. At first, I considered perhaps they pitied me for being husband-less and thought we might fancy each other. This notion of mine quickly vanished when he answered the door. I realized then that my goodly neighbours thought I might end my grief had I another baby to care for. And they were not far wrong.

"Are you the wet nurse?" he asked, a squirming bundle in his arms.

"My wife's skirt caught fire while cooking. I tried to save her, but the burns...." He paused, fingering the wrinkles around his eyes. "I am at my wit's end." He passed the baby to me and the poor being started to wail.

His four children rushed to his side and hugged him, his chest caving into his lap. The baby struggled in my arms, his pure blue eyes catching mine. The dream I had when ill with milk fever about the desperate souls crying out for mercy rose to the surface, and I knew I had to help the family.

In a few short days, I have developed a daily rhythm and ease of being with the infant that makes me recall instances of my past life with Rose-Marie. He loves it when I tickle his feet, and often smiles, turning his head back and forth when I kiss him on the neck and behind the ears, as though he has invented his own game. The little one lifts my spirits and I sense that my milk is giving him everything he needs to become strong once more.

Despite this, my heart still aches for mine own child. Now it is summer and I can lie in the grass day or night next to the rosemary and rosebushes and cry my heart out, the birds and crickets comforting me with their sweet songs. If I stayed here another winter, snow and ice would fix me in the ground just as they would a measly, forgotten carrot. Cold is more bothersome when one sleeps alone. In the dark at night, I live in a place of half-sleep where the pig that killed Rose-Marie crashes through my bedroom door. The creature has left a cavernous trench in my mind from running back and forth. It is not dying that I am afraid of, but rather seeing my child ripped apart by that creature each time I try to rest, and thinking of what she suffered before she was taken from me.

Six months later, her cries continue to steal into my sleep at night.

Two weeks ago, I poured out my grieving heart in a lengthy correspondence to my father. Although I haven't seen him for two years, sometimes when I read a philosophy book or wander through the fields and come upon a bee nudging its way into a flower in search of nectar, I sense his presence. At times, I even feel that he inhabits me, as though he and I share one soul, one skin. He is and always will be my father, my teacher, and the man who shaped me. Yet the absence of letters from him after my daughter's death is akin to a second death. As a child whenever I was melancholic over not knowing my mother or sad for those in our village who became sick or hungry, my father would hold me tightly in his arms and read to me. What mattered more than the words was the gentle, yet sturdy timbre of his voice.

July 10, 1785

Finally, a letter arrived today giving me some hints about my father's whereabouts. Monsieur Taranne wrote to tell me that my father has been travelling. Am I to take from this that he is therefore too busy to pick up the growing stack of letters that awaits him in Paris from his beloved daughter? The last letter my father wrote to me was about how beautiful he considered the women in London to be and how he enjoyed tea with Lord and Lady So-and-So, who spoke of their trip over the River Severn on the world's first cast iron bridge. He expressed excitement at going to visit the bridge, and he was planning a return to France when he thought it was safe for him. In spite of not hearing from him since early this year, I have made up my mind to travel to Paris once the infant that I began nursing in April is weaned. If it happens that he is in Toulouse or, for that matter, back in London, I shall stay in Paris with Madame Rousset, a cherished friend whose name he gave me as a contact. I am aware that seeking him out could be dangerous for me given his illegal activities. Yet, as I have already lost a child and a husband, what more do I have to lose?

The help that I am bestowing upon some mothers in the village further tempers the motherly grief that threatens everyday to consume me. This afternoon, I was in the village square and the sun was beating down on me. Emmanuel, the boy I care for was snuggled up to my chest. I stopped by the fountain to splash water on my face, and it was refreshing to feel the coolness on my cheeks. Then a woman approached me. She wore a white bonnet, a bluish grey gown, and was visibly with child. She was the daughter of an older man, one of many labourers paying through wheat, chicken and oats to tend a seigneur's land.

"Madame, can I have a word?" she asked me with a bashful air. We stood under the arched entrance to the church as a light summer rain danced over the square.

"I have two children and one soon to come," she told me. "Tell me how I can make my milk like yours? Should I eat soft foods like lettuce? What about bathing in water from the mountain, thinking pure thoughts or reading poetry?"

Her hands fussed at the skirt pleats that fanned out around her bulging stomach. Her shape was slender yet pleasing. Her eyes watched my every gesture, and then fixed on my mouth so as not to miss a word.

"The same quality?" The question stumped me.

I was well acquainted with the idea that a mother passes her thoughts on to a child through the milk. My father would call this an absurd superstition. To him, if something cannot be explained in scientific terms, then it is no better than a fairy story. Yet a woman's ability to influence a child for the better through her own understanding and education was indisputable, as were the nourishing qualities of her milk. I decided to explain what I knew in simple terms so that the woman would see my meaning and act in the best interests of her offspring.

"I digest a tasty assortment of philosophy, poetry, history and botany by way of my mind," I told her, spinning the best yarn imaginable. "This learning impresses itself on the milk." I could feel myself pulled into my own fanciful stories of the milk, which lifted my spirits at the same time, and was no more able to stop my tongue than a pregnant woman can stop her baby exiting her womb.

The woman's eyes lit up. "Eating poetry? How is this done?"

"The mind takes in sensations provoked by the words," I continued as would a misbehaving child. "And if the poetry is worthy, *one won't develop stomach troubles."*

"How do these sensations enter the milk?"

"By way of the mind." I felt the passion for my words rise within me. "Their union is what makes the child both robust and clever."

Yes, I was my father's daughter, I thought, yet on this point we differed. The age-old story about the milk revealed a greater truth that science could not easily capture like a bee or butterfly to fix with a pin for study.

"Please teach me some poetry, Madame Vivant. I wish to be a good mother to my child." Her eyes looked on me helplessly as she rested a hand on mine own.

February 24, 1786

As the carriage moves through the streets of Paris, there is just enough light from the lantern hanging above me to write. Only moments ago came the screeching and clamouring of fireworks mixed with shouting and laughter: Mardi Gras is being celebrated in the early morning hours.

Milk wets my skin and chemise giving me a sudden chill. Only a week ago, I was nursing Emmanuel, the infant whose mother died after her skirt caught fire. These past months many mothers have come to see me, sometimes with questions about their nursing, while other times wanting me to suckle their infants. I put away my ideas of leaving and was content to assist them for as long as was needed. Yet then I received a letter from my father and my decision to leave for Paris became clear. He wrote that he would be journeying to Lyon, but foresaw a speedy return to Paris in early March. In his lengthy letter he addressed the contents of each of my previous letters to him. Naturally, the news of Rose-Marie's death caused him profound sadness and made him even more eager he said to console me as he used to.

Just now, outside the carriage window, a blast of light took over the night sky, cascading onto the river, buildings, church towers, roads and bridges, everything soaked in a milky whiteness. At first, there was shouting and then a flood of bodies encircled our post chaise. Arms, torsos, mouths, capes, breasts, hats, and perruques danced by. A woman with a frog mask reared her head while eyes peered from an amphibious smile. A rat face stick of a man thrust his staff at the wheels jolting the vehicle to one side. Two men seized our post chaise. The coachman yelled and struck at them with his crop until they leapt off. Creatures from forests such as rabbits and foxes, and those from the jungles of Africa such as elephants and hyenas, spilled into the street. We had to wait until the crowd passed before we could forge ahead. A handful of people held up a giant straw man that the crowd proceeded to strip of all his clothes. Minstrel singers floated past, hedge-like wigs and satin waistcoats, faces powdered up as dolls, muslin encircling wrists. One donned a pair of garters, ruby coloured lipstick, and a lily flower on one cheek. For a brief moment, I thought I saw Robert, my husband who left me after Rose-Marie died, then the body vanished into the crowd.

"Shall we drown him, hang him, toast him or roast him," shouted a person who wore the mask of an old man with a hooknose. He held a torch to the effigy's feet.

The masked humans clamoured, "Roast him, roast him, roast him." Their roars grew louder as they chanted.

The man lit the straw figure, which soon blazed in human form. As it burned high on the pole over their heads, the crowd marched toward the river, songs and shouts lifting into the night. Although the event was light-hearted, there was an air of cruelty about it that brought a chill to me.

We pass an iron gate with dagger-like pinnacles rising up. The post chaise rumbles and shakes on the cobbled streets. Beyond the gate are more churches and a cathedral.

"Almost there," the coachman shouts at me when I open the window, rap on the roof, and stick my head outside. Several moments later, he says, "rue des Capucines."

The carriage turns onto a street draped in darkness save for a lamp hanging outside a house. The very paper on which I write is being jostled out of my hands. At the only house that is lit, there is an iron staircase framed by a pair of stone horses, just as Madame Rousset described to me in her letter. Through the window, I glimpse an older woman sleeping in a chair. I secret the diary away in my bags, and resolve to continue after my arrival.

It is the next day. The evening I arrived, Madame Rousset led me into her drawing room filled with vibrant draperies, carpets, and a hearth that warmed my cold cheeks. Then she proceeded to tell me how she met my father.

"You were four years old," she recounted. "My husband and I were travelling through your charming village." She tilted her head as though trying to nudge memories out. "My husband's feet were swollen from the gout and he was in much pain. I've never forgotten how your father cared for my husband and let us stay there until his feet were better." She raised one leg, tapped it with her hand and sighed. "Five long years now I've worn only black. It has been the perpetual state of my heart since his passing." Her gown was meticulously cared for. Lace of the same colour atop the heavy silk of her skirt showed refined whimsy amidst the sorrow. Her story made me think of my father and how my longing to see him had grown more intense these past few months. It was extraordinary to me that in a few days we would be reunited at last. Then came the disapproving comments from her about my wet-nursing.

"I was struck by what you said in your letter about nursing another woman's child." Her head swayed back and forth as if the very thought sickened her. "It saddens me that a woman of your station should resort to such dreary ways of making a living not to mention open yourself to the possibility of contracting diseases of the nipple."

"Oh, Madame Rousset it is not for money that I assist mothers with their infants." The conversation fatigued me, yet I was content to sit at the fire and warm myself after the lengthy trip. "My father has provided for me sufficiently in that regard."

As I mouthed these words, it occurred to me that my money was in actual fact running out. If I continued to live in a modest fashion, I could make it last no more than a few months.

"There is much poverty and disease in our village. If I can ease the suffering of one...."

"There is no harm acting from a sense of what is just and good Madame Vivant," she interrupted. "But really, this is highly irregular for a woman of your education and breeding."

Her superior tone angered me. I was exhausted, my nipples ached and my calves were seized up from the long ride in the post chaise.

"Madame Vivant, I had a wet nurse for my son. Why, it was in-

tolerable to me to be tied down to a screaming, groping infant, and unable to circulate more freely in society. She was a plain woman from Nantes, didn't read or write, but what did that matter as her profession did not require it?"

My body was sinking into the leather chair, the crackling sounds of the fire lulling me to sleep.

"What about remarrying? You're a widow like me, aren't you? You are handsome. A moneyed man with character and influence would go to great lengths to have you at his side with your education and refinement."

Her eyes grew overcast. I could tell she thought of herself and her loss, rather than me when she said, "You must be very lonely without a husband."

It was shortly after that I met Monsieur Paradis. A plump man with fish eyes, he sported no waistcoat and no shoes, only socks with holes that exposed chubby toes. His face was red and ruddy and his perruque sat crooked on his head. His complexion caused me to think that he was a gout sufferer and had a bilious temperament.

"Monsieur Paradis, there you are," she said to him as he entered the drawing room. "I expect you've been waiting to meet Madame Vivant." She looked at me. "I told him you were coming and he could hardly contain his rapture. He was at my salon this evening where I invite the brightest minds to partake in social and literary alchemy."

I sent Madame Rousset a questioning look at which point she said, "Monsieur Paradis is director of the Bureau des Nourrices."

The man approached me with an anxious half-grin then reached for my hand to kiss it. His lips were moist and he had a small mouth. I remember my neighbour Nadine telling me about the Bureau des Nourrices where women found babies to suckle.

"I heard some gossip about a wet nurse who had more milk than any woman should. I was told this woman had no child of her own and that her milk was as plentiful as the Lord's loaves and fishes. At long last, I finally have the occasion to meet her." He smiled, tugging nervously at his chemise.

"Are you a man of science Monsieur Paradis?" I was tired and irritated by the man's tales about me. "For if you are, then why would you pay heed to the chatters of a few peasants."

"*A highly distinguished gentleman told me about the miracles occurring with certain infants in your village, infants who as you might gather, had tasted the sweet nectar of your bosom.*"

What he said was astonishing. I wondered if he was not in fact jesting with me.

"*I was just telling Madame Vivant that she should withdraw from such a thankless profession. I am pleased to hear that it is her intention to do so,*" *the old woman said with a look of victory.*

"*My word!*" *bellowed the man.* "*What would we do without the extraordinary milk of Madame Vivant? Two wet nurses living in the same mountainous region as yourself have spoken to me about you. They have taken it upon themselves to learn to read and write to impress virtuous and quick-witted thoughts upon the milk. It is not for me to judge from where others derive inspiration, as there is so little of it to be had these days. Everybody is far too serious and driven to melancholy at the slightest hint of a sad tale.*"

Monsieur Paradis took a seat on the armchair by the fire. He then propped his legs onto a quilted stool. Madame Rousset and I sat on the blue plush sofa with gold cushions. I longed for her to cut short the visit and show me to my room so I could sleep.

"*Of course, each of us sees what we wish depending on our particular hobbyhorse. Did Madame Rousset tell you she welcomes all manner of priest and poet to her salon every month to discuss the essential topics of the day? Each of her guests has a notion in his head, which propels him forward. Why just this evening I spoke for an hour with an English pastor on the new rotary steam engine that is now being used to power looms in factories and paper mills. James Watt, the man who invented it calculated the number of horses it would take to power each engine and so he came up with one horsepower as equal to 33,000 pounds per one foot over a period of one minute. You see, there I go again....*" *He pulled a gold watch from his vest pocket and turned to the door.* "*Almost three o'clock in the morning. I have to leave at once as my wife will have my head.*"

He guided my hand to his lips a second time, bowing to Madame Rousset and myself.

"*Pray do visit me, Madame Vivant, at the Bureau des Nourrices,*" *he whispered in my ear.* "*I've a handsome proposition for you that*

I believe you will find most agreeable." He then turned and was out the door. At long last, my cue to retire for the night.

March 6, 1786

At the Bureau des Nourrices women huddled on the steps, reaching into the circle, prodding, pushing and burrowing into the warm bodies of other wet nurses to escape the crisp morning air. They wore bonnets, shawls, their skirts thick and heavy. Many held babies in their beefy arms, rocking the bundles, others with infants hanging from their breasts. These little ones sucked nipples, deep red as raspberries, pressing up against the milky bosoms of their wet nurses. Most of the women came from the country, as mothers sent their babies there for the superior quality of the air and for the abundance of fresh cream, eggs, fruits and vegetables. Amidst the lunar formation that quivered and danced was the buzz of chatter, a chorus of voices singing at different ranges: everything from bellowing to cackling to screeching to whispering. They touched hands, shoulders, breasts, faces and backs. Muffled slightly by the talk were the sounds of infants crying.

I was totally captivated by the women, yet at the same time it seemed impossible to me that, like them, I was also a wet nurse. I wanted desperately to speak to them, be among them, and so, drawing closer to a woman on the outside, I tapped her on the shoulder and said, "What are you doing here?"

Her voice was clear, her grey-blue eyes shining. "I came from Toulouse to find a baby to care for because they say women are paid a fair price." She brushed a strand of brown hair from her cheek. "The doctor will make sure I've no diseases. You must be eating good before they let you nurse."

A woman who heard us talking broke from the circle and came over. She looked to be about fifteen years old, had blonde hair, long, delicate fingers and a doll's nose. Her hair was combed perfectly over her ears as though her mother had combed it for her.

"What about you? Are you a wet nurse?" I asked.

"Yes, but some women shouldn't be wet nurses, as they've not enough milk. They say they do because they need the wage. They

are not soft and gentle. They don't eat lettuce and eggs." She coughed a lot and spoke in a low voice as though her throat was made of sand. "I'm being checked for diseases of the nipple. My mother pushed me to nurse. I even helped suckle my own sister. After that, I took on another for pay. I have a child of my own, yet the father ran off when he saw my fat belly. Having my child at thirteen and being a wet nurse made the family a little money for all the trouble I caused."

A horse carriage stopped in front of the building. The door opened and Monsieur Paradis, the man I met the night before at Madame Rousset's, stepped out. Like Moses parting the red sea, he approached the steps and the women scattered. A few moments later they took up their chatter once more, the door opened, and the human circle formed a thick line that pushed through the narrow entrance. I tagged on to the last of them, chasing the echo of voices and shrill laughter down the corridor. Entering a room I saw several women standing while a few rushed over to sit on the remaining chairs.

Two plump women, one with curly red hair, the other with shimmering black hair, crouched in a corner murmuring and pointing to another who was seated, fingers sifting through her long hair. The woman's brow was tense with wrinkles, and, from time to time, she shook her head. Her skin was grey in colour and bones protruded from her face, legs and back, which I saw as she hunched over. She emitted a dull moan, and, as I approached she looked at me through a web of thick strands; however, it was not her eyes, but rather holes in the earth that stared back at me.

"How to live?" Her voice was like the faint noise a tree makes when it creaks in the wind. "I shall shrivel away to a pea. I have waited four days and still no nursling in sight. I've gone on only bread, water and bad fruit and they expect me to wait some more." My heart went out to her.

I asked the two who tittered away in the corner why this poor woman wasn't given a chance to nurse when she was clearly so helpless. The raven-haired one said she was no more a wet nurse than her grandmother. She added that it was her own fault for having diseases of the milk and for letting a baby die. The one with the curly hair told me there were three orphans to every wet nurse so there wasn't much a doctor could do to stop women suckling for pay.

"*They will probably send her to the Maison de la Couche, as there are thousands of abandoned infants to choose from there,*" *she said. "Only the poor and sickly wet nurses suckle these ones, as the pay by the royal government is very poor for orphans.*"

I naively asked them why there were so many motherless children hoping the women might share their stories with me.

"*Mothers haven't the means to care for them. Many women work in the city alongside their husbands. They've already enough mouths to feed and little time to spend with babies that do them no good in the end if they die,*" *said the dark-haired woman.*

Death called out to children as colic, congestions, scurvy, chilblains, coughs, lice, and ringworm. It lurked behind every step the child took and every day the child breathed. The sickly woman crossed her legs, arranging her cotton skirt, much too light for the weather. A few women sat on the floor between those with chairs. Some women left that morning to visit the Maison de la Couche as it was thought there would be more than one orphan for them to take home. Others stayed on with the prospect of having a healthy child from a good merchant-class family that would allow them nine livres a month or more.

"*Even so, she'll surely leave here with an infant.*" *The curly haired woman motioned to the female creature propped up like a doll.*

The other woman peeled back her shirt to reveal the slight bulge of her bosom. "I've lots of milk," *she said using all the force she could muster. She told me she was old and frail before her time, struck by an illness that left her bones bent out of shape.*

I had some mutton that Madame Rousset packed away for me to eat. The woman's holes-for-eyes gazed at the offering. I peered into the crevices of her face thinking that I saw in them a glimmer, a distant light. She took the mutton and, without removing it from the cloth, began to gnaw away at it. She kept up until the bone was meatless, wrapped the remains and tied it to her waistband, fluffing the cloth of her skirt. I went over to the woman with the curly hair and asked her if she was waiting for an infant to care for. She told me she had lots of milk so nursing two would suit her fine.

Then I asked her, "What about the infants?" "Do you like caring for them?"

"*Do I like the babies I suckle?*" *She looked at me strangely. "Well,* some of them I do. They are soft, smell good, and don't cry much. Others are stinky; they cry all the time and have temperaments like imps." When she laughed I saw that her front teeth were green. "Skin is soft, their smell different, one a scent of cinnamon, another of rose petals or sage, even gosling feathers." She added that this difference in smell helps her know the child before all others and without seeing it by sight.

Monsieur Paradis came to the door just then and invited me into a small room decorated with a painting of two women, bathing nude by a river. There was a half-filled bookshelf and an examination table.

"Tell me Madame Vivant, you seemed surprised the other night when I told you of those who spoke to me of your wondrous milk?" His lids drooped and his complexion appeared ruddier in the daylight.

"Indeed I was," I replied, pulling up a chair on the other side of an enormous oak desk while he sat behind it. "Simple folk have a way of letting their imaginations get the best of them and gentlefolk have a habit of repeating them just as children tell tales."

"So you do as you wish to prove them wrong?" His eyes moved to my face, then darted to different points in the room.

"I am simply exercising my rights and helping those less fortunate than me," I answered.

"Speaking of rights, I notice by our records that you have not been contacted by a meneur in your hamlet or by your local priest. The royal declaration states that the care of infants by wet nurses be regulated by governing bodies."

"I am aware of the meneurs Monsieur Paradis. Yet the parents who come to me have heard about my wet-nursing through channels other than the Bureau des Nourrices. Adding to this, most of the time I have not accepted payment for my services."

"Well, your case is highly irregular." He cleared his throat and adjusted himself in his chair. "Nevertheless, specific guidelines have been put in place regarding wet-nursing. Tell me Madame Vivant, why we should change a system that has worked for hundreds of years simply because an educated woman decides to play by her own rules?"

"I am not asking you to alter the way you conduct your business Monsieur Paradis."

He smiled knowingly, looking on me not as a man who just scolded a woman, rather as one from whom he was about to request a dance.

"Since you have told me that you are no different than other wet nurses and that your milk is also no different, I will try to convince myself of it. Although, the more I know you Madame, the more I grow certain that your milk is not merely the superstitions of some peasants." His hands fidgeted with paper on his desk. "Come to Madame Rousset's salon next month and we'll converse on whatever topic you fancy, the hobbyhorse of your choosing." His tone changed and he said, "In truth, there's another reason I asked you here." He glanced at a letter on his desk. "I know a gentleman, a wealthy landowner who lives a day's journey from Paris. He wrote me two weeks ago to see whether I was acquainted with a nurse he heard about, a certain Madame Vivant who was both learned and motherly. He thought perhaps you were made-up, un conte like the kind told by labourers in his fields. At the time I did not know you, however when Madame Rousset told me you would be coming to stay with her in Paris, I could not believe the incredible twist of fate. He heard about you through a wet nurse I sent him to care for his son."

Shrill voices came and went on the other side of the door mixed with the sounds of chairs rumbling.

"He will pay you a healthy sum to nurse his infant. His son was sent away to nurse after the mother died tragically by falling into a vat of wine and drowning. The child did not fare well with the wet nurse and the poor boy soon became thin and weak. At a loss to save him, the nurse returned the infant to his father. Then there was the other woman sent by me, another dreadful failure. As you can imagine, the infant became sicklier still and the man is now beside himself with grief and worry, having no wife and a son who might not live to carry on his name. There would of course be a small stipend given to the Bureau for placing you, yet I assure you that your reward from him would be most generous."

I didn't need any time to consider his offer and so told him straight away that I couldn't help him. "I have not seen my father in a long time and he is soon to return from Lyon," I explained.

His face twisted into a knot. "How saddened I am to hear that Madame Vivant. However, I understand that you must proceed according to your own better judgment."

In truth, I sensed my wet-nursing days ending as a desire rose within me to devote my time to teaching women the basics of reading and writing, and to compile the nursing notes in this diary into a much-needed book for new mothers. Perhaps those who read it might begin to trust more in their own instincts and less in what so-called reasoners said and thought on the subject.

March 9, 1786

A pimple-faced boy arrived at Madame Rousset's door holding a small, crudely drawn map. The time and place to meet Monsieur Taranne, a dear friend of my father's, was written above. A red X designated a tavern called Corinthe. To my left was a woman pouring ale into glasses. A young woman sat by herself listening to a table of drunken men as she sipped her ale. By the fire I spotted Monsieur Taranne's wiry frame. He rose from his chair and took me in his arms. After a few moments holding me, he reached his head down, kissing me on both cheeks. His mouth was large, his eyes two perfect ovals. His hair was dishevelled, wavy in spots just as I remembered it.

We sat down and he stared at the blazing fire in front of us. His big, watery eyes glanced at me and I thought I might drown in them.

"What is it?" I pleaded.

"It is so very nice to see you Armande. You are quite a lady now."

"Please Monsieur Taranne, whatever is the matter?"

He pulled a handkerchief from his pocket and blew his nose, a trumpet blast echoing through the cavernous room.

"I recently returned from the banks of the Rhône River where two weeks ago a boat caught fire." He gulped his ale. "It was carrying a shipment of my books. I believe the fire was set by somebody, that it wasn't an accident. You can imagine how many enemies we have printing the books we do."

"I'm sorry to hear about the loss of your books. I hope it will not ruin you."

He cleared his throat and gazed at me, his face full of worry. "Armande, I haven't asked you here to speak about the turbulent state of my business." His eyes grew wider, and then filling with tears. "I

*am not quite sure how to tell you this." The deep wrinkles on his
brow formed an upside V over his nose. "Your father is missing."
"What are you saying?" I asked, my voice breaking.
The men at the table beside us stopped their wild chatter to look
in our direction.
"He didn't have to be on the boat," he continued. "Sometimes
he went along to make sure the books were safely delivered even
though I pay someone to do that. He was to leave Lyon as soon
as he finished his business there. Yet so far I have had no word
from him."
I began to tell Monsieur Taranne that I expected my father in early
March when it hit me that I might never see him again. The fire,
candlelight and those seated around me became a sweeping haze of
colour and distorted sounds, and I was unable to speak.
"There is a chance that he might have quit Lyon and not yet arrived in Paris." He wiped his face of tears and cleared his throat. My
mind went in and out of his words as I tried not to think the worst.
Monsieur Taranne invited me to his house, only a stone's throw
from the tavern and the river. In the corner of one of his rooms was
a desk, and next to it, three cabinets with little drawers, then bigger
ones lower down.
"I live alone but from time to time my daughter comes to stay,"
he said. "She helps me with my accounts."
There was a series of large-scale botanical drawings sprawled out
on the floor in the corner of the room, which reminded me of Robert's
plant drawings. He was surely still in Paris though I wished not to
see him. Rumour had it that he became a police inspector.
"I'll contact these customers to see whether your father mentioned
to any of them that he would travel on that boat." His head was
burrowed in the open ledger. "I was in touch with one of them while
there last week; however he told me that your father only counselled
him on what books he should add to his illustrious collection."
I sat on a sofa next to a heavily curtained window and a table piled
high with papers. Monsieur Taranne served me some gooseberry
wine, the same wine he used to bring to gatherings arranged by my
father at our mountain home. He had a strong, yet resilient body,
which he said he maintained through his daily two-hour promenades
by the river.*

"I admire your father's fortitude and intelligence, especially when it comes to discovering what pamphlets will sell and which authors to pursue. Armande, you must know that I would be at a loss without him."

His kind words and the thoughtful way he looked at me put me at ease and caused me to recall my father's own nature, his firm yet tender voice. How he would listen intently to me as though nobody and nothing else mattered in the world to him.

"Where is the boat now?" I asked him.

"A burned out hollow shell." He didn't look up from his ledger.

My father was a strong swimmer. Surely, he could have made it to shore.

"What of the man driving the boat? Did he not make it?"

"Too cold," he mumbled. "That river is freezing, even a strong swimmer…." He stopped himself, closed the ledger and came to sit beside me on the sofa.

"When the craft floated to shore most of it had either already sunk or burned. She was still smouldering when I came to her. I couldn't climb onto the boat, but did catch a glimpse of a wooden box, some tools and a mass of scorched, wet pages."

"Did they find the boatman's body?" Tears crept down my cheeks.

"Not while I was there."

He lowered his head, his bony frame trembling. I reached over to kiss him on the forehead as I used to do with my father when he was distressed. I would interlace our hands as though we were one and the same person, then hold the palms of his hands up to my face. Monsieur Taranne gazed into my eyes, smiling the way an older man does who is still affected by feminine charms. When I opened his arms, he pressed my body close. This simple act was one of consoling me, his strength making me feel protected.

"Monsieur Taranne." I let go and moved deeper into his body.

It did not feel like seduction at first. After all, we were only sharing our joint sorrow and concern for someone we both deeply loved. Then at once, the scent of the man's hair, his breath on my neck, his arms cradling me, ignited a flame that Robert stamped out when he had refused to sleep in our bed after Rose-Marie died. With an unmatched sense of rhythm and purpose, Monsieur Taranne was unfastening my stomacher, removing my gown and sliding his hands under my petticoat. His hands instantly warmed my thighs, his kisses soft and sweet. I slipped off his breeches, washing my long hair over his body. All the while, he spoke few words. Robert used to chatter away during lovemaking and so I was not used to silence in these matters. Monsieur Taranne was a solemn man and very dignified, which showed itself in his caresses. The way he ran his hand along the pleats of my skirt, smoothed my hair, said "please" and "thank you" suggested a properly raised boy being handed a tasty pudding. Robert was at times a selfish man who demanded love, though in the end he gave little. This would prove to be an essential part of his overall character. How did I not see this plain fact before?

My love encounter with Monsieur Taranne happened so quickly. When it was over, I realized that I was crying the whole time, pleasure and pain intersecting throughout. Crying over the loss of my first love, the death of my baby, and the idea that my father too might be lost to me forever.

March 13, 1786

Two boys were skimming rocks outside a town called Viviers-sur-Rhône when they found the boatman's swollen body on the banks of the river. He had tied a rope around his waist and to a piece of his boat that was strong enough to keep him above water. That is until the stronger current took him. I heard the news from Monsieur Taranne who came over this afternoon. Did my father encounter the same end, I wondered? My mind went from one horrible possibility to another. Perhaps he drowned and they hadn't yet found his body, or, he escaped only to be captured by those that set the boat on fire. His dear friend was fatigued; his head drooping like a tired workhorse. It was the first time I saw him since our heart-led encounter. Although the event had lifted my spirits that evening, and caused a shut door to open inside me, I knew it wouldn't be repeated.

"The day the boat caught fire a silk workshop burned to the ground by the Saône River and somebody untied all the horses in Place Bellecour." His grey hair and long eyebrows prominent in the

light of day made me see him as a family friend once more, rather than a tender lover.

"Did they catch who was responsible?" I asked.

"No, yet the authorities believe the incidents are related."

A feeling of helplessness overtook me, yet I knew I had only myself to rely on. As my funds would soon disappear, I decided to once again visit Monsieur Paradis at the Bureau des Nourrices to see if he still wished to hire me.

I had not nursed since leaving my mountain village for Paris in the middle of February, yet my breasts were still plump with milk. Despite that, he asked me to discharge some milk into a cup.

"It is a good thing you will be nursing again as your milk is on the thin side," he said. "Come by here tomorrow and a carriage will take you to meet the widower Monsieur Bluche and his ailing infant son." Then he added, "I am very pleased Madame Vivant that you have had a change of heart."

After leaving Monsieur Paradis, I sat on the steps of the Bureau des Nourrices and cried as the sun slid behind the rooftops. Would I ever see my father again?

With an armful of wood, I arrived home to find Margot at my door. My hands were numb from cold as I was outside at the woodpile reading Armande's diary, and my head and heart were still humming from her story. I added a log to the fire in the drawing room and sat in her oak chair. Margot settled firmly on the dormeuse, her arms crossed and her probing eyes on me.

"On the day Armande disappeared there were tracks in the snow made by two horses," she said. "They led through the forest to the other side of the river."

"Did you see them?"

"No, but the priest was going back to the church from being at an old man's deathbed the day Armande disappeared. After, he took a shortcut through the forest, and, by the light of his lantern made out the tracks of two horses."

I told her about Armande's husband who visited the house a few days before using a made-up name and about the found snuffbox with his initials engraved on it. The handkerchief he briskly pulled away from me so I wouldn't discover his true identity.

"Why didn't you tell me this before my child?"

Ashamed of succumbing to my desire and his advances, I had kept our meetings secret. I knew at that moment I had made a grave mistake. "He left her after their baby was killed by the swine," she told me. My limbs felt heavy like I was the dead boatman Armande wrote about in her diary, a great wave threatening to wash me under. Margot looked as if she knew my secret, as if she could see Armande's husband and me tangled in a sinful embrace.

"He told me she went willingly with them to Versailles," I said. "I won't believe it," she gasped. "Oh, they were a lovely couple at first. Yet I always sensed he was wrong for her. Don't let him near you again, Céleste. No good ever came of Armande and that man being together."

As Margot talked, my mind was inventing a scheme for how to hurt Monsieur Phlipon. He was so seductive, played the part of a lover so well. And now hearing Margot speak about him with such distaste I was flooded with even more guilt that I had welcomed his advances. I would need to punish him for tricking me and betraying Armande. First, I would let him take me just as he did the night before. Then, while he slept, I would tie his arms and legs to the bedposts. He would then wake up, think it was a lover's prank and play along, most likely sweet-talking me until I blushed. At which time I would reach for the candle by the bedside, pouring hot wax, not into his navel but all over his handsome face and eyes, scarring the look of a gentleman so others would see his true nature. To me, he was even worse than Master Dogface, and the same sort of no-good as my father.

"It cannot be mere chance that he should show up and she vanish," Margot said.

I knew she was right about that. Then I thought, to punish him would mean no chance of him telling me what he knew. My heart beat faster, sweat collecting at my temples and the palms of my hands as I thought about how to trick him.

Invitation

SHORTLY AFTER MARGOT LEFT, I hurried to Armande's closet to pick out a dress. Monsieur Phlipon sent me a note that he would come for dinner and I had no time to waste. I wanted to make him think I was falling for him, and then I found just the thing to help that along. Instantly my eyes fell on a gown of pink silk with white flowers, pale green and white braided rope at the back. She must have worn this before she had Rose-Marie, as it would be too small for her now. Maybe she bought it to wear for her beloved Robert. The thought made me shiver. I pulled a pair of stockings over my knees, binding them with buckles. I even put my shoes on with buckles done up. My underskirt and stays went next. Tying the pocket to my waist, I then fixed the panier. After arranging my petticoat, I pinned the stomacher to the stays, pulled on the gown and looked at myself in the mirror. All lovely, but for the rat's nest of hair on my head. With her brush, I pulled and strained until finally rid of the knots. A piece of green ribbon tied round my head kept the strands in place. To finish off the look I tied a lace choker around my dainty neck. I was not as lovely as Armande, yet pretty all the same. To stave off gossip I told Nadine and Bertrand to circulate a story that my brother was visiting. Many did not know Robert Phlipon's appearance as he spent little time in the village as a grown man, yet I knew eventually the truth would come out, and so I had to work quickly.

For dinner, I prepared a small chicken and some apple cake for dessert. I lit lavender-scented candles and added more wood to the fire. He was Monsieur d'Agenais, not Monsieur Phlipon, a name I had to forget for the time being.

After stepping inside, he kissed me on the cheek. "How very lovely you are, Céleste." His eyes danced across my special gown, and he said, "Springtime came early this year."

I was very nervous about my plan to snare him, yet tried not to show it. We sat at the kitchen table across from each other. He was full of compliments, each one a trap to avoid.

"Very nice how you've prepared the bird, flavourful herbs and just the right cuisson."

It was her recipe and I wondered if he had eaten this meal with her before. He held a chicken leg in one hand, never two, as someone who learned from books how to do these polite things. He did not talk about plants, stars, or women, maybe because he thought Armande had told me about her husband's interests and he did not want me to become suspicious. He took only a drop or two of ale and raised his hand to stop me filling his glass. His gesture put me off because I wanted him drunk so he might let slip the truth about how she was captured and where he hid her. I snuck some more in his glass when he was not looking.

Later he sat on a chair by the fire and then patted his thigh for me to come to him.

"I'm a gentlewoman. Pray, Monsieur d'Agenais, treat me as such."

At that, he started to laugh. His cheek made me want to slap him.

"What do you call the other night, Céleste? I trust you remember what heavenly law of attraction brought us together."

He opened his waistcoat as before, keeping his boots on this time.

Margot spoke the truth about him, yet to find out what he knew about Armande I had to pretend I was falling for him. His eyes would be all I looked for, his touch my only medicine. Now standing before him, I lowered myself onto his lap, fanning my skirt out.

"Yes, I remember. I was in a weak state, sick with worry for Armande who is both mother and sister to me. You were very kind."

I almost choked on the words that I said so sweetly.

"I am very fond of you, Céleste. You underestimate the effect you have on the opposite sex. Your light grey eyes are as those in a painting I once saw in Paris that reflected the landscape. You are very lovely to me and, yes, of course, I consider you a gentlewoman and pay you the respect you deserve, utterly." His compliments would not reach my heart.

"Tell me then, what is it like to live with such a celebrated woman?"

"She has only ever been Armande to me." That was not entirely true, yet I didn't want to tell him my feelings about her. I rose from his lap and rooted around for some mending to tame my nerves.

"Tell me your thoughts Céleste?" He sat beside me on the sofa, one arm resting by my chest, the other stroking my hair.

I put down the shawl I was mending and touched my lips to his palm. He kissed me softly and I returned the embrace, adding spirit to the act so he would not doubt my growing affection for him. As I did that, words entered my head ... *traitor, bad woman, liar*. With eyes closed I almost forgot whom I was kissing. On the outside, I was eager and loving while inside, a tangle of loathing for him, and other feelings I could not patch together.

He hummed a little song as he lifted my petticoat. Armande wrote in her diary that his hands were large like fishes. The sensation of them on my thighs was more like a smooth stone rubbing up and down my body. My skin was warm, burning to his touch. *Soft as a duckling's downy chest*, he said. He wrapped my legs around his neck and grinned like a schoolboy.

"I leave for Paris in three days. The doctor and his wife will join me in Grenoble."

He pinched the flesh of my thighs just enough to cause me to cry out with pleasure. My plan to make him think I was falling for him was finally working.

"Céleste, why don't you accompany me?" His pure blue eyes pierced through me. Then he planted a kiss on my lips and added, "Follow your heart and see where it leads you."

The next morning, the woman who was doing me a favour by nursing Nathalie asked me to care for the infant while she delivered soup to some needy families. Nathalie's eyes grew large when I held her and her head tilted into mine as if to kiss me. My heart warmed to be with her once more, even though she smelled of hay at harvest time instead of the lavender or rose scents she gave off when Armande suckled her. I brought her into the drawing room, emptying yarn onto the floor for her to play with. Nathalie crawled towards it, nudging the coloured balls with her fingers. In the bottom of the knitting basket was a half-knit shawl of blue wool started by me. Armande had taught me to knit pretty patterns. I had wanted to repay the kindness by presenting her with a gift of my own making, yet never finished my creation.

I first learned how to knit at Master Dogface's estate. It was just after I spied on Armande suckling the baby in the garden. She was singing to him in the gentlest, sweetest voice I ever heard. I thought the boy did not deserve such love. The Master saw me spying on her and chased me with a stick. He was mad at me for not being in the kitchen cutting curds to make cheese. I ran screaming until the two of us came to Armande who told a lie for my sake. Her kindness surprised me so much that, at the time, I thought she might turn on me. One day, not long after I spied on her in the garden, I locked myself in an empty stall in the livery. It was my way of hiding from her so I would not be caught by her spell.

"She's a witch," I told the Master's daughter. "She makes me not who I is."

The daughter shoved a mirror into the stall for me to see myself.

"Take a look at yourself, idiot girl. Why would a kindly wet nurse put a spell on you? You're no more than a pocketful of dirt." I looked in the mirror at a sad figure with a crooked nose and chin.

"Homely as Master Dogface," I said under my breath.

I bent the mirror to view my torso. While my portrait looked frightened and weary, my neck and shoulders were lily-white and soft like the flesh of my thighs. I untied my bodice to marvel at my cherry red nipples. It was the first time I saw them as pretty to my eyes, and so I caressed my body again and again until I felt lovely all over.

That same night Armande arrived at the door to my bedchamber holding a ball of yarn and two knitting needles. Sitting beside me on the bed she showed me how to cast on and how to make a garter stitch. With her help I made my first square. One of many squares I would knit to form a vibrant wool quilt for the Master's beady-eyed infant.

Now I scooped the shawl from the basket and picked up the knitting where I last ended. Maybe my concentrated work would stir Armande, wherever she was, to think of me?

A little later, Nathalie stopped playing with the balls of yarn and crawled over to me. She was making soft sounds with her tongue against the top of her mouth, which sounded almost like words. I bent down and put an ear to her head as if it was a seashell or nest of nearly hatched bird's eggs. Then, in a small yet distinct voice, I heard her say, "The King's people are dying of hunger. They are without hope, yet will rise up to take what's theirs."

My knitting fell to the floor and I picked up the baby, holding her to me.

"How are we to do this?" I looked deep into her eyes. My knees trembled and my voice along with it.

"Tell me." Tears rolled down my cheeks. "I beg you."

Her eyes could see my thoughts, and in that instant all my fears were laid bare. Then just as it came to pass with other children, her visage suddenly changed to its original look. Baby Nathalie's words flowed from her mouth as if they were not coming from her mind at all, but from a deeper wisdom contained in the milk. And Armande was in danger of being drained of this magic. Yet if, for her sake, I went with him to Paris, what was I hoping to find once I got there? With Nathalie to my chest, I knelt on the floor to pray. I begged the Good Lord to keep Armande safe and lead me to her.

My last full day in Armande's home, I set aside the gown I wore to please Monsieur Phlipon. That and a winter one Armande had a woman in the village sew for me. I had no ribbons or fancy shoes, yet while looking through a box in her room, I found some pearls for my hair, a bracelet made from feathers and a pair of pink shoes with embroidered blue flowers. Somebody might even mistake me for a gentlewoman. Spring was on its way and so I arranged some lighter gowns, petticoats, a bonnet, hairbrush, and a couple of books in a porte-manteau bag belonging to Armande's father. Behind a dusty row of books was a soft leather pouch. I grabbed some silver coins from it, a handful of deniers and sous and took more than one demi-louis d'or, crossing myself and swearing, with God looking down on me, to return every last one.

Armande told me Paris was a city where poetry, music, and theatre were more important than the colour and thickness of leaves in the field, the quality and scent of sheep's wool. Poets, actors and artists went to that city to be among their kind. Her father went there to write and sell forbidden books. Women hosted literary salons frequented by well-known philosophers. Armande went to one, showing herself to be as sharp as any man. Yet she also said the poor lined Paris streets. They went because it was thought the loaves of bread were bigger there. Winter in that city was especially cruel. Desperate folk burned their bedsteads, chairs, benches, hampers, baskets, and cases to escape the cold. They pawned cloaks, rings, carpets and cupboards in exchange for a day's food. Mothers rocked and shushed babies, reciting spells against their lot. *Poverty, go to sea and drown yourself.*

Before sleeping, I said goodbye to the neighbours Nadine, Bertrand, and others, goodbye to the house, then closing up the chimneys, shutting the curtains, and finally rolling carpets snug against the doors to keep out the winds. I thought of how I would miss gathering wild plants in the summer with the other villagers for eating, such as dandelion and clover, yet would probably be back for the harvest of oats, wheat and barley before wintertime. That night, the wind banged at the shutters and there was a soft tapping sound no louder than a knuckle at a door. It was the last night in my bed, the last night in the comfort and quiet of my own familiar home. Almost morning and I woke to the noise of myself crying in the dark. I needed to believe I would find her, that because of me she would be safe. Once in Paris I would journey to Versailles where I would certainly find her held against her will. I imagined her at the foot of my bed, arms outstretched. With an arm out to her, I believed it would be possible.

"Mon enfant, you must rise." Monsieur Phlipon stood at my bedchamber door, his face aglow from the lantern in his hand. "We are to be at Grenoble before dark."

He wore his frock coat, cravat and boots, and tapped his staff on the ground. I stumbled from my bed, got dressed and passed a comb through my hair, as there was little time for fussing to pretty myself. A rider and his horses were making an awful noise outside.

I put on my winter cloak trimmed with fur. Armande's diary was in my pocket beneath my heavy wool skirt. It pressed against my thigh. A hazy blue light, like the colour of a woman's hair ribbon, outlined the fields. A coach with a leather roof was parked in front of the house. Two horses pawed the snow. Steam rose from their fur, noses thick with clouds of breath. The rider sat at the front of the carriage tugging on the reins to still the beasts.

"Come Mademoiselle." He helped me into the coach.

The seats were upholstered with a dazzling blue and yellow flower pattern. I had never been inside a fancy carriage like this before. Sitting down, I felt like a gentle lady. Monsieur Phlipon shouted at the rider and climbed in across from where I sat. He rubbed his hands, blew on them and pinched my cheeks.

"Ma petite, my hands are so cold. Could you find it in your heart to warm me?"

I reached over and grabbed his hands, which he quickly directed to my waist. In spite of my woollen layers, he chilled me. I didn't understand his motives for asking me along, yet I had no choice but to go with him.

"You're so warm my lovely," he said, a sly look in his eyes. "Look how you brought life into them."

When he held his hands up and moved his fingers before my eyes, a sensation of panic overtook me. What if he found out that I knew his true identity? What would the King do to her if she refused to suckle the Dauphin? I wasn't even sure she was taken there. The rider shouted at the horses and the carriage moved backwards and turned. As we sped up, I gave a feeble wave. Armande's house looked tiny from the coach window. A picture hanging on a wall. The babies she suckled spoke of a revolt. Through the milk, their voices proclaimed the truth of what was to come.

Part 3

Clue

WE ARRIVED IN GRENOBLE before nightfall and took a room in a hotel with chipped yellow paint and blue shutters. At the desk, a small woman with hair past her waist handed Monsieur Phlipon the key. Her fat eyebrows joined in the middle of her face like mating caterpillars. Our room had a small bed with a curtain to draw across and another bigger bed near the fire.

"This is ours," he said flopping on the bigger bed and lying lengthways upon it. On the outside, Monsieur Phlipon was as gentlemanly as any other man of his station. Yet I could see past the silk breeches and periwig to his true nature. It scared me to play this game of impassioned lovers with him, yet I knew that for me to find Armande there was no other way. Whether I liked it or not, we were soon entangled.

The next morning, we were in the carriage once more. Monsieur Phlipon told the couple, the Jolycoeurs, who joined us, that we were married. A woman voyaging by herself was looked down upon. I was no gentlewoman yet I wanted others to see me that way. Being polite and having a thing or two to say made me good enough to most. The doctor's wife looked at me the way older women look at those younger than themselves. She studied the fabric of my skirt, how I held my hands. She was taller than her husband and dressed plainly—a brown gown, white bonnet, a fichu at her neck, and gloves. Instead of sitting beside me as a woman might do, she sat with her husband. I saw why when, as soon as we were away, she closed her eyes, left cheek pressed against his shoulder. While she slept, my eyes took in her face. She had a large head, manly features but for her small and delicate nose.

"Paris is a city of possibility," said the doctor whose eyes were large and bright. "All sorts of men of genius reside there and have in their minds the most astounding inventions. In time, these wondrous creations will be seen to enhance our lives. Why, our dear Monsieur Montgolfier is such a physician. He manufactured an immense balloon from taffeta propelled by nothing but hot air. Imaginez-vous! Perfectly composed during the performance he was, as though he knew the experiment would be a success."

He looked tenderly at the ostrich fringe on his hat, petting it as if it were a small dog. His movements were slow, his voice a high whisper so he would not wake his sleeping wife.

"His first apparatus was azure blue with gold fleur-de-lis painted on its body. Its flight from the Royal Palace was to transport a sheep, duck and rooster."

His story made me picture in my mind's eye a great blue gown with farm animals attached by golden threads flying through the air to the sea.

"The balloon man's imagination knows no bounds," said Madame Jolycoeur, her eyes now open. She licked the tips of her fingers and ran them over the folds of her skirt.

"The French can fly with the birds."

"'Tis true mon ami. We are entering a time where the impossible is now occurring. Did you know that there is a new Musée des Sciences in Paris where learned men give lectures on topics of great scientific importance? That is right. Merchant, fop and artisan go there to listen alongside cordon bleu."

The doctor reached into his pocket, pulled out a handkerchief and blew his nose.

"At this Musée one can view a suit for submerging oneself in water. This watertight apparatus will keep the wearer perfectly dry. Another of these inventions is a hat with a built-in lamp, perfect for night time excursions."

"Incroyable," said his wife.

"So, I gather you're well-acquainted with Paris?" Monsieur Phlipon asked.

"No, I wouldn't say that. Alas, I have not been there before, but I have met many a worldly man who has. What about yourself, Monsieur d'Agenais?"

"The past couple of years we've lived in a mountain village not far from Briançon," he lied, gazing at me as a husband to his wife. "I did live in Paris though while studying theology at the Sorbonne and am returning there to visit Comte Buffon. That is if he will receive me. I am writing a book on alpine plants and it is my deepest wish that the Count take interest. I am a staunch admirer of his work and very eager to share my botanical findings with him."

His botanical findings? I thought of the letter Monsieur Vivant gave Sophie in secret. It was to Monsieur Taranne detailing how Monsieur Phlipon stole ideas from an obscure plant book. The letter I found stuck to Sophie's bloodied hair was now tucked away in my embroidered pocket for safekeeping.

"Ah yes, I read his *Histoire Naturelle*," said the doctor arranging his cravat and smiling.

"The Jardin des Plantes is unparalleled," remarked Monsieur Phlipon. "Winding paths and geometric forms lead each time to a new scene that renews the spirit: a trickling stream with a lamb grazing before an ancient ruin, and what a world of scents. It makes one half-drunk with pleasure to see man improving on Nature."

"Do you share your husband's passion for plants, Madame d'Agenais?"

The name he called me meant nothing. On top of that he was not even using his real name. Monsieur Phlipon, the no-good, elbowed me in the ribs.

"I like Nature and all it has to offer," I stumbled over my words.

"We love the city yet prefer the quality of air found in our mountain village." He cleared his throat and looked over at me to add to his tall tale.

"Yes," I replied, trying to appear calm. "Mountain meadows provide us with many grasses and flowers, yet the past winter was nasty. The harvests were bad, the price of flour too high."

Could they possibly believe we were married? My palms were wet so I hid them at my sides.

"Yes, I read that 1788 was a particularly bad year and that production fell by half," said the doctor. "I know all about the attacks of peasants on granaries, but how can these people be as hungry as they say given they have many fields in which to grow crops? In our city...."

"It is true, doctor," I cut in. "These families give up most of their earnings to taxes and the rest goes to rent a plot of land from the *seigneur.*" Nathalie's words gave me the courage to speak. *They are without hope, but will rise up to take what's theirs.* My heart was racing yet I did not stop.

"Many families had to make bread from plant stems. Children became bloated and sick. The field grass made their poor stomachs swell like balloons. You should have seen them. Each one looked as if it were big with child."

When I spoke in short bouts, my voice was like a gentlewoman, yet when I rambled on did the doctor and his wife see through me? Words rose in my throat like hills of mossy rocks and tree roots. I was from a line of no-goods, line of dead children, line of disease, line of chestnut gruel, line of water soup, line of farm workers, line of beggars, line of knife, scar, child, worm. Monsieur Phlipon's disapproving eyes burned a hole in my skull. Yet I spoke the truth after all, and so what did I care if they thought me ignorant?

"I have just the remedy for a child who imagines he's a goat and grazes all day in the fields." The doctor's voice that time was loud, no hint of a whisper. "There is a plant called burdock that is so abundant it grows in ditches and highways all over this land. Why, little boys even play with it. They toss the burrs off and throw them at one another. The children may eat grass if that is their wish, but then they must bring the roots of this plant home for their mothers to prepare. I have used burdock for years now and can attest to its healing properties. The root must be beaten with a pinch of salt and laid on the swollen belly." The doctor patted his stomach. "That will soon ease the pain and it even helps those bitten by mad dogs. There are other uses too, yet I will surely bore you if I persist."

"We are very fortunate to be in the company of someone so generous with his knowledge," said Monsieur Phlipon.

He startled me. I half-forgot he was beside me, forgot I was supposed to be his wife. Sweat collected on my upper lip as the corner of Armande's diary dug into my thigh, giving me a sudden pang of missing her.

"He didn't discover the many uses of this plant," the doctor's wife piped up. "Oh, my husband is a good enough doctor, but it was a midwife in our neighbourhood who first told him of it. She knows many things about herbs and their medicinal properties. She was the one who taught us about burdock soothing the belly."

"Yes, my wife is right, but she forgets one thing." The doctor raised his hand, pointing a finger. "The midwife is dull-witted, as are most women when it comes to the ways of science. She has not the cleverness to use the roots as I do with a pinch of salt. She applies the leaves of the burdock with the white of an egg to wounds by fire. She knows not that the roots carry all the plant's goodness. I have no idea why she wastes her time with the leaves."

The road became bumpy and the rider shouted at his horses, pulling on the reins to slow them down. Each shake of the coach brought me closer to Monsieur Phlipon. I wanted to pounce on him and then smash his head open with my heels for all he did to Armande. Similar to when my father got mad and cursed the seigneur and his prize doves. He wished he could hunt yet it was not allowed for peasants, and so instead he would shout to force out his anger. *Pull the heads off hares! Smash the eggs of every woodcock, pheasant and snipe!*

Hours passed and the road narrowed. I awoke to hear wheels crushing bits of sand and rock, and far-off birdsongs. Low hanging branches slapped against the roof as we drove swiftly by. The doctor and his wife shifted, their eyes closing and opening. By the time we reached the mountains, the sun was melting the snow, rivers overflowed and some roads were washed out. Cool air smelled of mud as the coach climbed the bumpy mountainside. Water dripped from rocks on the edges of cliffs and little birds splashed in puddles along the road. Later in the afternoon, we reached a clearing where we saw a castle and some houses. A man stood by the side of the road watering his horse and waved as we went past. The road we were supposed to take vanished under water. I crossed the river with the doctor's wife while the rider, Monsieur Phlipon and the doctor led the coach and horses. She cried silently as I squeezed her hand.

"This voyage will surely kill me." She gasped for a breath, teeth chattering.

I felt the water creep up my legs and said a prayer for Armande's book to stay dry. Madame Jolycoeur was weak and so I pulled her along with all the force I had in me. The river going fast made me think of the doctor's account of when he cut apart a human. He told it to us very early that morning. *The inner person is the same within each of us. Veins like rivers run through the body. They enable the blood to flow freely from the heart and render the bodily juices to the various regions so they work.* It was hard for me to picture that I too had rivers flowing through my head, arms, fingers, belly, legs and feet. That within us all was water just like in nature, which kept us alive.

We climbed into the carriage on the other side of the water, our skirts soaked to the waist. The doctor's wife sat beside me to share a fur cover. Her eyes were bits of glass and she stroked her icy blue fingers. The doctor and Monsieur Phlipon arrived. Soon the carriage was back on dry road, and, within three or four hours of our torment, we stopped to rest for the night. Monsieur Phlipon reached over to touch my knee through the fur. I went against my instincts and smiled.

"The cold water did you good," said the doctor to his sleeping wife.

I heard when crones suckled the blood of infants they were restored because their blood was young, innocent. Yet men and women of quality had less barbaric ways of crushing fires of the blood, as the doctor was teaching me.

"My wife must drink light wines and eat goat meat, pheasant, borage and lettuce if she is to restore her blood to its original airiness," he said. "Reading light verse and watching flowers dance in the breeze is another way to achieve this end."

His wife's skin, since walking in the water, was greyish in colour. Her eyes opened a little and closed as her husband spoke, yet showed little sign of life, no fire or spark.

The carriage stopped in front of a white inn with green shutters. On one side was a vineyard, on the other a cornfield with dead stalks poking from the scant snow. A tall man who had cheeks like ox bones greeted us. My leg was poorer from sitting. I leaned on Monsieur Phlipon while stepping from the carriage. The ceiling was low in the entranceway and the tall man bent his head down as he led us through the door. The front room of the inn had wood floors and no carpets or pictures on the walls, just a couple of plates and ceramic jugs on high shelves. We sat at a long table and he served us each a bowl of lentil soup then placed a large wheaten loaf and a flagon of wine on the table. Madame Jolycoeur did not wish to eat and so she and the doctor followed the man upstairs to their bedchamber.

As I ate my soup, a black and white spotted dog sat in the corner eyeing me and licking its jowls. Monsieur Phlipon took off his boots and began, under the table, to rub his foot up and down my leg. The man who owned the inn came back downstairs.

"You are Monsieur d'Agenais?" The man eyed him suspiciously.

"Yes, why?"

"A letter has come for you from Versailles."

Monsieur Phlipon looked at the writing on the envelope, thanked the innkeeper, and then tucked it inside his waistcoat.

Who could be corresponding with him from Versailles, I wondered? Was it the man he plotted with to kidnap Armande at the King's instruction? Thinking about it gave me a stomach ache and I could not finish my soup. I tossed and turned all night while Monsieur Phlipon snored. Just when I got up the nerve to sneak away from bed and fumble in the dark to find the letter, he flung a heavy arm over my body. I was trapped there until morning when sun streamed in, almost blinding me.

We would travel all that day and some part of the night if the full moon was in the sky and the road was clear. For the most part, the day passed quickly. I slept on Monsieur Phlipon's shoulder while his head rested on mine. The carriage got so cold driving through the woods I would have snuggled next to the Devil if he promised to warm me. Both of us wore our coats and a fur cover atop our legs. Nobody would ever think we were not married. Still I waited for the right moment to steal the letter he received, at least long enough to read its contents. Soon after dark, we stopped for supper at a tavern where a handful of scrubby men drank ale by the fire. Our chicken and leeks were cold, though the large hearth in the centre of the room made up for it. I had not felt heat like that since Pierre kissed me by the chapel. He was not very smart to have tangled himself in his mother's apron strings the way he did, though he did seem more like a man last time I saw him. Even if he had no learning, I would have taught him what I knew of the world. We might have married, had a child or two.

After travelling close to one week, we reached the city of Orléans at nightfall. Morning crept into our hotel room from a small window, dirty with street swill. The curtains were torn and, in the half-light, the upholstered chair, beds and carpets looked old and tattered. The wall closest to the bed had spots of yellow on it that looked like pea soup. The night before, fire and candlelight made the room and everything in it appear dream-like as a pinkish hue had covered the objects giving them a pleasing look. Monsieur Phlipon's silk breeches were strewn over the foot of the bed and my stockings lay crumpled on the floor. When he was still asleep, I went through his pockets and found, in the smallest inside pocket used for coins, a piece of paper folded in two. By the dim light of day, I was able to make out the words.

Very little boy, very little boy what are we to do?
It was only yesterday you cracked your head falling from the roof.
Valiantly you stood up and were soon as good as new.
After that, you read some books until the day was through.
Never did I see a boy as good and strong as you.
The next time you will not wake up and your mama will be blue.

It was not the letter from Versailles as I hoped. The clumsy rhyme was in Monsieur Phlipon's own handwriting. I could track a person in the woods and could even tell his height from the broken branches above, yet I was no good at riddles. So when Monsieur Phlipon left, saying he was to visit a local garden, I followed him through narrow, winding streets until we reached a church with spires and two rising towers. Three round windows in the centre were like finely stitched lace. He sat on a bench with an older gentleman who wore a shabby coat and hat and carried a cane. Crouched behind a tree I watched but could not hear. Horses nodded and snorted a few steps in front of me. I scrambled behind one of them, its tail swishing my face.

"Still no word about where she went?" Monsieur Phlipon asked the man.

"None." The older man's face screwed up. "When you arrive in Paris see to it you meet him...." He muttered something after that, which I was unable to hear, and the two parted.

The stranger headed for the horses while I dashed into an alley and then into the street before stopping to catch my breath. A shop window displayed perfumes in colourful bottles and all different shapes and sizes such as a light-blue horse and an emerald seashell. Ducks hung in a neighbouring window over baskets of pigs' ears. Then, further on, my attention was taken by a large painting on the side of a building of a man wearing a suit of armour. At first glance, I saw a man wearing a suit, yet when I drew closer, I realized it was in actual fact a woman with long, wavy brown hair, narrow face and small eyes. She held a sword in one hand and a flag in the other, looking full of courage and ready to take on an army. The woman reminded me of Armande at first. Then when I looked more closely at her eyes and mouth, the slightness of her frame, I thought no, it was me up there on the wall. Above her head were a banner with two angels on it, and a man holding something in his outstretched hand. Those at the top of the picture were very small and hazy.

When I looked down the street I noticed the very man Monsieur Phlipon met only moments ago heading straight for me.

"What is this picture?" Fear coursed through my veins.

He stopped and looked at me suspiciously, then said, "Why, that's la pucelle."

His complexion was rough and he had no front teeth. Another thing, he did not look me in the eye, as though I was a gentlewoman, and he merely a peasant. "English troops attacked Orléans and its inhabitants were dropping like flies as no food could enter the city," he explained. "With her army, she marched on Orléans and freed us. She heard voices that told her to rise up. Only a peasant girl, yet she led the march to save France."

The words *only a peasant girl* echoed in my ears. We stood there for a few moments gazing at the portrait. I wanted la pucelle to reach her hand down and cradle me in it.

"Where you off to my lady?" He smiled, finally looked up and winked at me.

"Nowhere in particular." I was stalling. "I am going to Paris."

"To Paris?" He came closer, his breath smelling of cabbage. "Travelling on your own are you?"

"With my mother," I chirped.

"Well, well." He patted the bulge at his middle. "Chaste women go there and disappear. Best to have your wits about you."

Was he referring to Armande? In the park, he spoke of a missing woman. About a man Monsieur Phlipon should see when he got there. When he was almost all the way down the street, he turned back and shouted, "The girl was captured and burned for being a witch."

I gazed once more at the huge canvas before me and my heart sank. The girl was so wise and yet she was punished. I heard voices, though mostly in the form of babies or children who also spoke of rising up. Did that make me mad or possessed? I walked on, sensing the eyes of la pucelle following me down the street. To imagine her with her sword and armour caused me to take a bolder stride. I would seek out Armande and kill her captors, freeing her just as that brave woman did for the people of Orléans. That would be the only way for miserable folk to take what was rightfully theirs.

Hours later, I came to the hospital and decided to wait there for the doctor who was inside. After a few moments he came out of the building with a strange object, curved like tree branches or the jaws of an African beast.

"Do you know what these are?" He approached me with it as if to challenge me to a duel. "Forceps for delivering infants. Have you ever seen such stunning architecture of form?"

I slowly reached out and touched the smooth, hard surface when he suddenly clacked them open and shut, almost snapping my thumb off. I wrenched my fingers away looking to see if there was any blood.

"I am sorry, Céleste. I was toying with you, but these are not to play with. With this tool, I hope to save many infants' lives. The little ones become stuck in the birth canal." With his fist, he demonstrated the head of a baby, his other hand imitating a woman's vessel. "Their craniums are often too big for the mother. I've waited a whole year to have a pair of these."

I wondered why there was a need for these things when midwives could put their hands in and direct the baby out. The doctor and I walked down the street to join his wife and as we went, he clacked the forceps. The sound was like a rusty old cowbell. Before long, we saw her sitting on a bench feeding pigeons. A wind crept up which knocked her hat to the ground. The object then rolled a short distance away, and me after it.

Human Heart

EARLY THAT EVENING, we were moving at a quick pace until there came an enormous thump. The carriage stopped abruptly and tipped to one side. The doctor's wife stayed asleep and I followed the two men outside. The moon was big and orange above the trees. A wheel had come off at the back and I could see the silhouette of the rider holding the busted wheel.

The rags I used that day for my monthlies were bloodied. After entering the woods, I squatted down and pulled the damp cloths out from between my legs. I watched in the low moon's light blood stream out of me like molasses, pushing and forcing like a pregnant woman until the tap finally closed off. The men were making grunting sounds behind the trees and the words *hold it … steady … turn the wheel …* drifted into the night air. Before heading back, I watched the moon and wondered if she was thinking of me at that instant. Armande wrote in her diary that the moon was the mother of all things. Maybe she too looked up at the moon from wherever she was.

"Where have you been Mrs. d'Agenais?" said Monsieur Phlipon as I climbed into the carriage. He gazed on me as though I were his possession.

I swallowed my loathing for him and settled in under the fur cover. The doctor sat by his wife, the two of them arm-in-arm. The rider shouted at the horses and we were away once again, though this time at a much slower pace. The new wheel the rider put on was not the proper size for the carriage, which meant we wouldn't reach Paris until the morning. The cloth between the scoundrel's buttons opened and closed like mouths laughing as he breathed. I imagined opening his waistcoat ever so slowly and slipping the letter from his inside pocket. If I was very careful I might just be able to do it. I reached my hand out, all the while watching his face for signs he stirred. I managed to open one of the buttons on his waistcoat when he turned away from me, still sleeping. My heart pounded in my chest.

I could do nothing for the moment, so I turned to one of my fairy stories. It was old and tattered, the cover bent from water spilling on it. What I really wanted to read was Armande's diary. Last time I read it she was sobbing because she thought her father had died. She was on her way to Master Dogface's estate where she and I first met. I was desperate to find out whether she wrote about me, and what she might have said. I removed the diary from my embroidered pocket, concealing it in my skirt pleats. Then I had an idea. The pages of my fairy book came out with no trouble. I opened the coach window and began casting out the loose pages. One by one, they flew into the night air. Armande's diary fit nicely into the empty book cover like a new skin. The moon was on my side of the coach, which meant I could read her words with little trouble. Yet Robert sat next to me and had only to turn his head to see what I was reading. For the moment, his eyes were shut, his mouth slightly open. If the old couple were to wake up and see me, why, they would think I read fairy stories. How wrong they would be. Somewhere on these pages, inside letters or words, Armande held me close, not letting me go.

June 15, 1786

As I write this, fields of wheat bow and curtsey in the wind. Monsieur Bluche who employs me to nurse his infant also has a daughter and several servants. The house has eighteen rooms and is surrounded by carpets of soft green grass. Cypress trees shelter a road leading to the house, and flowers and shrubbery line the many footpaths. The owner is amicable enough to me though not an amicable man generally speaking. I am sure he feels that he does everything he can to satisfy me, though his efforts lack sincerity. He has a large nose and small, impenetrable eyes.

Monsieur Paradis from the Bureau des Nourrices told me that Monsieur Bluche's wife fell into a vat of wine yet the circumstances surrounding her death remain mysterious. Was it really her husband who drove her to drink or rather landed her in the drink? She must have been a strong woman to suffer the torments of life with him. Was she handsome? How did they meet? Did they become betrothed because their families came together over land and she had no choice in the matter? There are no paintings of her anywhere in the house. Nevertheless, several family portraits line the walls going upstairs. There is even a portrait of somebody's dog: two teeth protrude from his chops as he grins. His paws rest one atop the other as a count or king might rest his hands on a baton.

My milk continues to make an impression. Only this morning, I heard the master of the house in the stables boasting to the groom as he brushed the stallion in preparation for his master to ride.

"Since she has lived under my roof the infant is no longer sickly and the other day he uttered his first word," he said proudly.

For saving his only son, he is obliged to tolerate me, as I am he. Monsieur Bluche pays me handsomely, which is enabling me to accumulate a tidy sum that will be worth the effort of staying here in the end. Of course, he would never commend me to my face for all I have done to bring his child back from death's clutches. The infant has become healthy as any mother could wish her boy to be. His dark eyes are full of life, moving about as flies attacking honey. He wobbles around, pulling himself up onto chairs, hugging the legs of tables. A few words exit his mouth, yet only when he has exhausted every other possible form of expression. Just as some women complain that nursing takes them away from what is most important to them, such as the hurly-burly of societal affairs, I sense that wet-nursing brings me closer to my thoughts or at least makes them clearer to me. This causes my heart and head to align instead of each one flying off in different directions. This gift is preventing me from succumbing to dark thoughts, which cloud my perception. Three months have passed since I heard the awful news of my father's disappearance, and I am still no closer to knowing whether he died on that boat. Yet if he's still alive, why hasn't he tried to reach me? Surely he would be in touch with Monsieur Taranne who would tell him of my whereabouts, unless of course he is in hiding and finds it imprudent to contact us.

A few days ago, I had a brush with Monsieur Bluche's temper when he took it upon himself to ride on horseback with his son. The infant is still too small for such escapades yet he sat him down between his thighs to gallop to where men and women were working that day in the fields. I told him that his son nurses regularly and that, if he is to grow up to be strong then he requires a consistent feeding schedule. I also explained that the jostling of the stallion could hurt his development.

"He is strong enough to ride a horse with me now and I will let him feed when I decide it is time." He studied me from his princely spot on the horse. Then he added to his lopsided science of infants by saying, "It is good to deprive children. It makes them stronger, more rugged of temperament."

His treatment of the servants—particularly a little bit of a thing that recently turned up—is horrid. She is fair-haired and keeps to herself. Just last week, while strolling along the garden path lined with wild rose bushes, I heard screaming, turned around and saw him chasing after her with a stick.

"Come back here, you lazy wench. I told you to make curds and then scrub the kitchen floor. Here you are prancing around outside like you own the place."

"She's with me," I said firmly. "I asked her to help me gather thyme." Of course it was a lie, yet I was not about to tolerate such cruelty.

Monsieur Bluche looked at me, not knowing whether he should yell at me or be polite, as he had managed with some difficulty thus far. "Madame Vivant, perhaps next time you will ask me before you make use of my servant. After all, you don't want me looking like a complete imbecile in front of the likes of her now, do you?"

Paying no attention to him, I gently brought the girl to me. He needed my milk for his son and wouldn't cast me out for anything.

"What is your name?" I asked when the servant girl and I were alone. She tried to free herself from my clutches yet I repeated my question.

"Céleste," she said waving her head in the air like a wild horse, her dirty hair dangling in front of her face.

"You are of the skies, the constellations," I told her, adding that her name meant she was from the stars.

She spoke in quick bursts as she told me her mother sang her name when calling her, though only when her father wasn't around. Then she broke away from me and ran to the house.

A day later, I met her on the stairs. She was like a little bird and I dared not go too close for fear she would flutter away. Her thin frame was bent and her head and neck were stiff like an old woman's. For a brief flash she looked right at me, then turned her head down once again. Since that encounter she has begun to spy on me from behind the paravent in the boy's room while I suckle the infant or write in my diary. I sometimes see one eye peering between the panels. The last time she did this I began to sing very softly while rocking the baby. It looked as though I was singing to the little one when in fact the song was for her.

Yesterday at dusk, I heard her laughing to herself in one of the bedrooms as she tidied. Her lovely, light laugh told me she was not always sorrowful. I peeked around the corner and saw her smoothing out the sheets with her hands. She sat on the bed for a moment, all the worry in her face vanishing as she gazed out the window, and I observed that she took pleasure in her own company. Something about the girl stayed with me. She seemed full of self-loathing, yet even with her wildness I found there was a certain grace about her. Perhaps it was her vulnerability that made her appear that way to me. Whatever it was, she made me want to stay on at the estate to know her better.

Is the human heart merely a muscle, divided into chambers that expel blood through the body or is it something more? When I saw the servant girl that day on the stairs I thought I perceived what was living and dying inside her. She wondered whether to flee or to look into my eyes, and finally she did. Her hands shook and her tongue was caught inside her mouth like a bird clawing the sides of its cage. My mind knows nothing of her struggles, family, or even from whence she came. I am no doctor. Even so, what I read in her eyes allowed me to understand things about her that moved me. My father would say animal spirits produced by the blood are responsible for moving the body like that. All I know is, a flood of emotion welled up inside me as I sensed our hearts aligning. Can science measure such a thing as this?

Holding Armande's loving words to me, I rocked the book as one would a baby. Heat on my face spread to my arms and legs, belly filling with warmth. Monsieur Phlipon asleep beside me in the carriage suddenly opened his eyes and I closed the book so quickly that it made a clapping sound. Doctor Jolycoeur looked at me sternly and placed a finger on his lips. I heard about these animal spirits Armande wrote about in her diary. Monsieur Vivant told me animals abided by the laws of nature, whereas humans were governed by their minds. That is, if their bodies had sense enough to listen. All I knew was my mind told me to rise from bed in spite of my lazy body wishing to stay put. If I did not let my mind win over my body each morning, I would get nothing done. Yet at times my body instructed me to do certain things that stumped my mind, like when my body told me to leave that estate to live with Armande. My mind still suspected she was a witch out to harm me, yet thankfully my body overrode my head's chatter. She wrote, I sensed our hearts aligning. So she had known this from the very start.

The doctor glanced at me once more. Perhaps his eyesight was not very good and he could not see I cried, yet Monsieur Phlipon saw. He half-smiled at me as though my sadness gave him pleasure. Though he did not know my tears were happy ones from reading about Armande's love for me.

Bees

WE ARRIVED IN PARIS on a clear morning. Outside the carriage window, a water carrier lugged two buckets, one on each side. Another man peddled lanterns. An organ player's music drifted through the air and a man carrying an enormous basket at his waist began shouting, "Who'll buy spoons and larding pins?" Horse carts and carriages rattled past women with baskets and children in hand. The ladies I saw were simply dressed with no care for primping. Not like the women Armande told me about who wore ribbons and pearls, hair piled high on their heads.

Monsieur Phlipon opened the carriage door and helped Madame Jolycoeur into the street. The sun was warm on my face and shoulders. People, horses and carriages filled every nook and cranny around me. I felt as though I was still in the carriage and had not yet woken up from a dream. Could we really be in Paris? It seemed so unbelievable to me.

I bid the doctor and his wife adieu and she hugged me to her with more strength than I thought she had. She did not cry as I did, though her hands trembled as she pulled away from me.

"Come visit," she said weakly.

The doctor embraced me, the ostrich fringe on his hat tickling my cheek.

"Please do come by and see my wife when you have a chance. We will be staying at *37* rue Fabrice."

After dropping our baggage at the hotel, we went to eat at a café next door. I instantly felt plain next to the ladies with their silks, oriental caps, beads and feathers. My gown was heavy, almond-coloured, and I had only a simple braid in my hair. My wool cloak was now too warm for the spring weather. The spacious room had a glass ceiling with lush plants throughout. There were marble tables with apricot lamps and an enormous fountain in the middle.

"Armande is no longer at court," said Monsieur Phlipon once we were seated. "She is somewhere in Paris."

"What?" I was stunned and couldn't spot if he was lying.

"I found out just before we left the village," he told me. "That's why I asked you to come. I'll do what I can to investigate further."

I thought to ask him why he had not told me this before, yet then I remembered that he was not who he pretended to be, and so he would surely keep his true motives from me. In the street, he said he had some urgent business to attend to and would meet me later at the hotel. A stranger from the café exited just after we did, turned his head and walked in the other direction. Monsieur Phlipon gave me a kiss on the cheek, waved dumbly and vanished into the crowd of people walking by.

What reason would the King have to let her go? Her motherly liquid would not only make the future king healthy again, but benevolent also. He would see the excesses of those rulers before him and right past wrongs carried out in Almighty God's name. There would be bread for everybody. Bread. Labour. Education. Yet then a flash of terror ran through me as I remembered Margot's words before I left the village. *Wisdom in the wrong hands can drain magic from those that possess it.*

My thoughts were pulled apart by shouting and the beating of drums. A group of women, mothers, children and grandmothers marched through the streets in my direction just like la pucelle going into battle with her army. Carts, carriages, horses and those on foot were forced to the sides to make way for the thunderous cavalcade.

"The rich are taking all the grain with barely a crumb left over for the poor," shouted one woman, the shine of her bluish skirt piercing through the thick cloud of street dust.

Her hat had a colourful ribbon hanging from it and her parasol struck the ground as she marched. Younger ones were arm-in-arm with older ones; some carrying babies while others dragged their small children behind them. Through the dust, I saw the faces of the women, their eyes full of fire, their mouths booming out slogans with the words prejudice, superstition, and lies. Then as if on cue, they sang a song about the flame of truth scattering clouds of folly.

One of the women was about my age, slender and fair, she held a baby in her arms.

"Excuse me Mademoiselle I'm looking for a woman by the name of Armande Vivant. Do you know her?" I asked, half-thinking to see her marching with the angry women.

"I don't recognize that name," she said as she walked past.

I stood in the road and watched the last of them go, fists clenched and waving above their heads, skirts swishing, children running behind yelling, people making fun or shouting in approval as they went. Two skinny dogs barked and tagged along after a hurdy-gurdy player who followed the women. I wanted desperately to march beside them, tell them I knew how to read and write—something to be proud of, as not many women could do that. Many of the marching women could read because they shouted things about changing laws in favour of the poor. Some carried placards with words they surely wrote themselves. Sooner or later, the air in the street cleared. Carts, carriages, and bodies filled the street as before.

I passed two women peddling green walnuts. They were plump, rosy cheeked and looked like sisters. Monsieur Phlipon could be deceiving me about Armande being in Paris, yet there was no harm in seeing if somebody might have spotted her. If she was known in Versailles, then surely all of Paris knew her reputation by now.

"I'm looking for a woman," I said, accidentally knocking over their bucket of walnuts. I began scooping them off the ground when one of the women pushed me aside to finish the job.

"Never heard of her." The other sister coughed and waved her hand to rid her throat of dust.

I then went up to a street porter who wore a cloak the same colour as his dark, thick moustache. "I'll give you quelques sous if you can lead me to a woman named Armande Vivant." I held out my handful of coins.

"Don't know her." He then took my money, turning the corner quickly to blend with the crowd.

What an idiot I was to hold out my money as a pickpocket would see I was naïve and stupid and be after me so fast. I could even be knifed, ending my sorry life in a rubbish bin at the back of some shop. I came upon a man selling rabbit skins. He pulled the skins away when the pleat of my skirt nudged them. Gazing at me, he squinted, his free hand protecting his goods.

"Have any coins?" he asked. "If not then get away from here. I have to make a living."

I wandered away, tail between my legs. At that moment, I longed for our home in the mountains with its creaky stairs and low ceilings, its pleasing gardens and country air. Yet most of all I longed for Armande. If only I was given a sign she was truly in the city, like when I walked through the field in winter and could tell if Pierre passed by that way because he would drag a stick through the snow beside him. Or Margot, who wore a thick skirt that made deeper impressions in the snow or spring mud.

I turned to look behind me at a man selling ink and saw the same person who was in the café earlier and who came out while Monsieur Phlipon and I were saying goodbye. As soon as he saw me staring at him, he vanished behind a building. The idea I was being spied on gave me a chill. What could he possibly want with me? The man was short, wore dark clothes, and had brown hair, a smallish nose and thin face. I began running through the streets in order to lose him. After scurrying along the river, climbing some steep stairs and wandering through several winding streets to another part of the city, I stepped into a bookshop. I looked out the window and, seeing nobody, snuck to the back, took any old book off a shelf, sat myself down on the floor and began thumbing through it. I decided to stay there a while until the man lost my trail completely.

The volume in my hands was The Feminine Monarchie and told some amusing tales of bees throughout the seasons, mainly in the summer months that contained Gemini, Cancer and Leo. My head buried in the book, I brought my knees up to my chest and fell to sleep. It was not clear how long I slept before sensing a figure towering above me. Over the top of the book, I looked down and saw trousers. Shoes were shiny black with silver buckles.

"What do you think you're doing Mademoiselle?" The bookshop owner lowered his hand and snatched the book, which had become my protective shield. He then pulled me up with the other hand. By that time, I was fully awake and hunting for excuses.

All I knew about bees was from Armande's father, and, so I blurted out, "I am looking for a book by Monsieur Vivant on the topic of bees."

No sooner did I say these words than the merchant pulled a thin volume from a shelf in front of us.

"You're very fortunate as this is newly published," he said proudly as he handed it to me.

The cover was buttercup yellow and in uneven capital letters the title read, A STUDY OF SOLITARY BEES AND THEIR PREFERENCES FOR CERTAIN FLOWERS. A crudely drawn bee appeared under the words, and under that, the date: *1789*. On the next page was a dedication. *For my dearest Armande, philosopher and explorer of life.* So he had published it after all. My breath was rapid and I had trouble finding my words. Blood ran to my cheeks, the bee on the cover quivering before my eyes. In my hand was, I felt, a sign not to give up my search for her.

"Will you purchase the book?" He looked curiously at me as if he thought I might steal it.

"Oh, yes," I stammered. "I wish ever so much to learn about bees."

I left the bookshop, bee book in hand. The street was empty except for an old woman knitting by her door. I made my way to the river, constantly checking to make sure nobody followed me. I sat by the water's edge far from street crowds and hawkers and flipped through the book reading phrases here and there. I recognized some of the expressions her father used to describe the bees, and even recalled passages from his notes for the book, left on the desk in his library. *Solitary bees are very selective about what flowers they gather pollen from. Most frequent only a few species of flower and it is not apparent whether this is as a result of a preference for one colour of flower over another or whether it is the unique nectar that draws them.* On the book's last page was a delicate drawing of a lion's head. The creature had a shaggy mane, deep-set eyes and a wide, knowing mouth. Underneath was an inscription that read, Un Vieux Lion. Armande had taught me that such an emblem showed who published the book. I wondered if Monsieur Vivant was the publisher, and if so whether his business was located in Paris. There was no address under the name as I saw with other books. Nobody was watching so I lifted my petticoats and secured the yellow book in my embroidered pocket. It was my very own book now and the first book I ever bought.

Two men were fishing downstream, and one caught a fish and

was reeling it in. The man had strong arms, long blondish hair tied back and a small, feminine nose. His profile was not like Monsieur Vivant's in the least. Before I ever met him, Armande had showed me her locket wherein there were two silhouettes, one of her father and one of her mother. Armande's father had a nose like a Roman emperor and a distinguished chin. The men were shouting as they watched the fish twist and jump, its glassy body slapping against a rock. I was sorry for the poor creature. The fish took a last breath and was dead, and then the man who caught it took out his knife and cut the belly from head to tail, its guts spilling onto the ground. If I saw her father in the streets of Paris, I would of course spot him right away. If Armande were here, then surely she would be looking out for him too.

Along the bank, a woman lounged on a rock reading a book. Every so often, she lifted her hand and brushed away a curl that the wind tousled. Her hair was the same shade as Armande's, yet I knew it was not Armande because the woman's back was bent. It rained earlier and the moist air clawed at my face and neck, its cold breath slid under my skirts. A glint of sun hit the water and then sailed away on a ripple made by some children who were on the other side of the river skipping stones. In my pocket was a piece of cheese from yesterday's supper outside Paris. Gnawing on it, I pulled out the diary.

I imagined Monsieur Vivant wore a big, dark hat and heavy cloak to hide himself from his enemies. Maybe he played the part of a sweeper or billsticker to avoid being noticed. He crept around buildings, choosing to stroll down lesser travelled streets and dimly lit alleys. Armande would surely visit Monsieur Taranne or Madame Rousset to find out where her father was staying. Sifting through the beginning pages of her diary, I learned that the old woman lived at 12 La Rue des Capucines. Just before sundown, I found myself standing outside Madame Rousset's house, an iron staircase framed by a pair of stone horses just as Armande had described it in her diary.

At first, the old woman did not believe my story and did not even invite me to sit down. In the drawing room, she arranged herself on the sofa while I stood awkwardly in front of her. She wore a black gown with a stiff lace collar and a black bonnet on her head.

"You say that you lived with Armande in their mountain village?"

Her lips were small, framed by tiny lines as though her mouth was sewn on. "I lost touch with Armande after she came here to stay back when we thought her father died in that boating accident. She was nursing children of those far inferior to her. It must have been her husband's death that caused her to lose her way, or that of her child, poor dear. I haven't heard from her in a long time."

From her diary I knew Madame Rousset thought Armande's husband had died, when of course he had left her. She drew her lace handkerchief to her face and dabbed the corner of her eyes as old people sometimes do.

"Describe for me her village then, and ... rooms in her house," she said. "My dear husband and I stayed there many years ago when Armande was still only a girl, yet I have a very good memory for such things."

Of course it was a simple exercise for me because I knew the village well just as I did every one of her rooms, except for her father's room, which I only saw a couple times. I knew what floorboards creaked and where cobwebs hung in corners and where there were broken windowpanes. I told her a bird flying overhead would see the shape of the village as a many pointed star with the church in the middle and the footpaths leading to each house from the square, while plots of land for growing grains would resemble squares on an embroidered blanket. I then went on to describe the position of the furniture in each room of our home, and the design on the carpets. Madame Rousset was impressed when I mentioned the plants in the garden and what trees bore fruit and how many pears we picked last summer. Her eyes grew softer and the lines of her puppet mouth widened into a smile.

"It is strange that you should come by at this time. I have only just learned that a mutual friend saw Monsieur Vivant last evening in an unsavoury part of the city. He was in a hurry and when my friend called out to him, he lowered his hat to conceal his face and then sped away into the night. I knew he came back to Paris, though as yet he hasn't paid me a single visit. He can be frightfully unsociable even though he is generous of spirit. Like many who have their hobbyhorses, he prefers solitary time spent with his researches to the hurly-burly of society affairs. Since I no longer hold my famed salons, most of the gens de monde have forgotten I even exist."

Her sad eyes followed the dancing flicker of candles on the table and then settled on the exotic birds flying on the carpet that covered the floor. "One shudders to imagine what he was up to on that filthy street."

Madame Rousset seemed not to care why I was in Paris and did not look surprised when I told her Armande was kidnapped.

All she said was, "I can't believe she never remarried after her husband died as she is a very handsome woman."

Mantua-Maker

AFTER MY VISIT WITH MADAME ROUSSET, I arrived at the Hôtel Bourgogne to find Monsieur Phlipon at the fire. He leaned on a chair with gold-painted arms, which had beside it, a fancy brass poker.

"Céleste, where were you? I've been waiting here for hours." His eyes were cracked and shiny like bits of broken glass. His green-sleeved waistcoat was wet at the front, and he turned away then brought his shirtsleeve to his face as though to dab his eyes. "I met with Comte Buffon today and he read notes for my book on alpine plants. We are to meet again next week to compare research on similar plant findings. Aren't you happy for me?"

I nodded. Though the news of his book cheered him, I could read on his face that he was troubled. There was one bed in the room. Plum curtains covered the windows and a glass chandelier decorated with grapes and leaves hung from the ceiling.

"What have you found out?" He put his arm around me, pushed a piece of hair from my forehead and then planted a kiss on my lips. The scent of his perfume now disgusted me, though I tried not to let on.

"Nothing." I kissed him back.

"Tomorrow I shall help you then. We can go out together."

I forced a smile wondering what game he was playing. Then he said, "Come now, Céleste, let us go to sleep."

Before daybreak, I went through the pockets of his buckskin breeches and waistcoat hoping to find the letter he received at the inn. There was only a pair of leather sock garters, two dried rose petals and a handful of sous. The poem I took from his pocket while we were in Grenoble was important somehow as I knew people often sent letters and poems to one another with secret messages hidden inside. Armande told me her father would embed author names or book titles into his letters when corresponding with booksellers and customers. That way if the letters were intercepted, the information would remain secret. Sometimes every first letter makes the word, sometimes every second, or diagonally like so. I crept into the corridor so Monsieur Phlipon wouldn't see me. Then after rereading the poem over a couple times, I was finally able to see the name, the first letter of each line spelling out V-I-V-A-N-T.

In the early morning, we ventured into the Paris streets. Snot-nosed elves with rags for clothes grabbed my skirts to tell me their troubles.

Mummy died and daddy gone drinking.
Baby sister died and mommy ate poison.
Don't know where I came from; I'm an orphan.

A bell sounded from a nearby church. Then a tinker sped by us clanking his pots. Monsieur Phlipon tried to talk to a beggar, yet he was too busy stuffing his sentences to hear him. Words left his mouth faster than worms from a burning chunk of wood.

"A woman I loved made a cuckold out of me … foolish man, stupid and shy…." Then gazing at the sky, he muttered, "What a flabby derriere the King has. Light and sweet like two cakes." He trailed off.

"We're looking for a woman who was captured, a wet nurse," I announced.

The man stopped, shoved his face up to mine, and then persisted with his exchange for one. "The King does not know me, yet neither does my wife."

We talked to more passersby until Monsieur Phlipon said, "Perhaps we should look for her father. After all, he is in Paris, and surely his daughter would go to him upon her release."

I thought of Monsieur Vivant's book on bees showing the name of a printing house, Un Vieux Lion, yet I would never tell Monsieur Phlipon that. I judged from what he said, and from the name hidden in the rhyme, which was about a boy and not a girl, that Monsieur Phlipon was not only after Armande. I had to somehow get rid of him so I did not put father and daughter in harm's way. I told Monsieur Phlipon I was feeling unwell and needed to lay down. He was surprised, yet said he would carry on without me.

In case he followed me, I went to the hotel as I told him then climbed out the window, which led to a staircase at the back of the building. From there, I walked to the other side of the river where several streets housed artisan ateliers for bookbinding, pottery, glass and painting. There, I reasoned, one might know where to find the proprietor of Un Vieux Lion. I walked for two hours or more, entering shops, asking each person I met if he knew of such an enterprise. Then my heel ripped off one of my dainty shoes and I limped to a fountain to sit down.

Peeling the shoes off, I inspected the bottoms of my feet. To my surprise, my soles were the colour of blood pudding, like the kind my mother used to make. Not only that, three of my toes on the left foot, were fat as sausages. I could hardly touch them for sores. After discarding my broken shoe and the other one, I tore my fichu in half and wrapped it around each of my feet. Yesterday a boy ripped my coat when he pushed into me. My skirts were filthy from passing carriages and my hair had not had a comb through it all day. About to cry over my lot, I thought of la pucelle, the peasant girl who rallied her army to save France. If she had no shoes, surely she would have kept going.

I pushed through the crowds. Market stalls displayed rounds of bread, parsnips, carrots, beets, apples, and carp. Ahead of me, rising from the crowd, was a tall figure with a black hat. Monsieur Phlipon. I could not believe my good fortune. I opened the door he went through to see him mounting a winding staircase, his red heels echoing through the passage. When I could see no more of him, I crept up the steps, the cloth pads on my bruised feet making no sound. I climbed one floor and then another, all the while, looking above me through the iron balustrade to see if he was on the floor above. There was the loud creak of a door opening. Two men were talking as I crept up on hands and knees. My eye caught a lacy cuff and green silk breeches and then, for a brief instant, I saw the man's face. The voices died away as the two stepped inside closing the door behind them.

That evening Monsieur Phlipon came back to the hotel just as I was slipping the diary into my pocket. I studied the grain of wood on the table where we sat and asked him what he found out about Armande. He told me, as he swished down a sizeable piece of mutton with a glass of ale, and ate some Brie and a slice of apple, that his search had led him nowhere. Then he changed topics. "I'll be recording details of plants in my notebook this evening. Specimens I saw while at the Jardin des Plantes."

He took a pinch of snuff and stretched out on the carpet by the fire. He held the delicate notebook in his hand.

"Why don't you read me a fairy tale, Céleste?" He gazed at me from his restful place. "Something to amuse me this evening."

Sweat gathered at the back of my neck and under my arms. There was no such book as its pages went away with the wind. Maybe he knew what was hidden inside the cover and was simply toying with me. My thoughts raced back and forth until I remembered I knew the stories from memory having read them over so many times. Even before learning to read, I could recall word-for-word stories heard at the bakery in my childhood village. So I began my story, looking at the page of the diary and pretending I was reading a fairy tale.

"This is the story of the sentimental woman and her ass," I said clearing my throat and trying with every part of me to stay calm. "It is a short tale, but I think it will delight you."

My heart thumped and my knees shook together.

"That's nice, Céleste, please continue." He clapped his hands, his clown mouth perking up like a freshly watered flower.

The morning after I spied on Monsieur Phlipon, he told me he was going to the countryside to dig up new plants for his collection, and he would be back the following day. Before quitting Paris, he said it was no use me going with him and that I must stay in the city to look for Armande. He kissed me, nibbled my ear, his arms squeezing me tight. I thought of asking him to give me some money for food to fill my belly, as there remained very few sous from what I borrowed from Armande's leather pouch in the library. Then, I recalled how I loathed the man and so said nothing. Instead I saved my remaining coins and wandered the streets looking for bits of bread or other grub. I ran after a cart on the way to market in hopes of catching some fresh scraps that might accidentally fall off. The only thing that came my way was a fishtail a driver tossed at me.

While rummaging through a sack of rotting vegetables at the back of a market stall, I caught sight of a gentleman watching me. Once again I began to run as fast as I could through the streets, having no time to look back to see if he caught up to me. Drops of sweat trickled down my face and my legs trembled. I dipped into a cranny between two buildings. Beggars lay a few steps from me in the excrement and street swill. I turned a corner and two small children ran up to me pulling at my skirts. Their eyes appeared to roll from side to side, so worn down that the soul ceased to cry out from them. When I looked behind me I saw the man gaining on me. He was tall with a square jaw; his appearance could not be mistaken. I crossed the street, passed a cathedral and entered a steep alley where I waited for several minutes until it was clear the stranger had lost me. Slowly, I walked back to the street with market stalls, hoping to further lose myself in the crowd and perhaps steal a bit of food.

I spotted a distinguished gentleman who wore a heavy black hat, yellow embroidered waistcoat, brown silk breeches and a large bow in his hair. What struck me were the gold rings that decorated his fingers, smoky brown and red stones. He stood by a woman who was selling stoneware, her large basket overflowing with pots and jugs. A group of children scuttled by, the one in the lead holding a kitten. When I looked again, I noticed the finely dressed gentleman with someone wearing the long blue coat that was the police uniform for Paris. Yet when the man turned his head, I saw it was no stranger at all but Monsieur Phlipon. He had not gone to the country after all as he told me. Their shoulders bent inwards, heads lowered. The woman who sold stoneware was decorating one of her pots with a brush and paints. Now close to her, I got down on my belly, worming my way to a spot behind her basket. I heard the men as clear as if they whispered in mine own ear, yet I was just far enough away so they couldn't see me.

"Tell me then, what is the news?"

"Still no sign," said Monsieur Phlipon. "I visited his business associate a few days ago, a Monsieur Taranne. He gave me no clue … as closed as a virgin's bedchamber."

The two men chuckled nervously.

"This rapacious and corrupt man has made damn fools of us at the censors' office."

"And of his King and Country," Monsieur Phlipon chimed in.

"How did he get past us? Printing his scatological treatises about the King right under our very noses! If only he was as we thought, dead."

"Ah yes. When I heard the news about the fire, I practically danced in the street with the gypsies."

"How did you discover then that he still...? "

"Can you believe it—he was in hiding all that time and then signed his proper name to a public record, a cahier de doléances circulating in his alpine village! One of the King's delegates spotted his account as being odd, because his words were more poet than peasant. When the delegate looked more closely, he recognized his name as being on a list circulating of wanted men. *Your people are dying of hunger having abandoned cultivating the land. City and countryside are being vacated. Instead of taking more money from these poor people, alms must be given to nourish them. There is so much hopelessness. The whole of France is an enormous desolate hospital without provisions.*

"What a bundle of nonsense." The man clapped his hands startling the woman beside me who painted her pot.

"The deputy made several inquiries until he found out that Monsieur Vivant had been living in his native village, yet recently fled," said the man. "No more than three weeks ago he was seen in Paris exiting a house of ill repute."

"An interesting development ... his daughter is newly arrived in the city from Versailles. She will seek him out," said Monsieur Phlipon.

"How do you know of this woman?" The gentleman looked puzzled.

"It is of no consequence. Suffice it to say, she was escorted to Versailles from her mountain village to assist the Dauphin in his weakened state. The child's life is hanging by a thread. As a wet nurse she is known throughout France for the quality of her milk. Armande Vivant is her name."

My body was cold and numb from lying on the ground, scrunched-up hands paining under me.

"I received a letter from a contact," Monsieur Phlipon continued. "He is a valet de chambre and had daily news of her comings and goings as he bribed the manservant who had personally attended to her every whim. I am told she demanded pure chocolate from the Aztecs to feed her craving and improve her milk supply. He told me she was let go because she refused to nurse the ailing prince."

"I cannot conceive of such impertinence. Can you?"

"From her, yes, I can," replied Monsieur Phlipon. "Nevertheless that's another story altogether." His voice turned grave. "Another source confirmed this for me when I was in Orléans...."

So it was Armande's father he wanted. It was all coming clear to me now like a river in springtime.

"Enfin! We shall have the rogue." The man uttered a high-pitched laugh followed by a snort.

"How did *you* discover that he was still alive?" Monsieur Phlipon asked.

"Ah well." He sighed and then emitted a long, thin laugh from his throat. "A most interesting occurrence. A courtier who fancied himself a poet had penned rhyming couplets about some royal orgies. These bits of paper made their way to the markets where a handful of artisans communicated them to some noblemen. Naturally, the royal chambers in Versailles got wind of it and I tracked down the loathsome courtier responsible. He gloated about how he was now the celebrated author of his very own chronique scandaleuses. He showed me the book of his verses that he came upon by chance the previous evening, and then purchased from a simple bookseller outside the opera. I could tell by the paper that it was printed from Monsieur Vivant's own printing press. He even wrote a preface to the vile work. He used a nom de plume, yet I recognized the style...."

The two men parted. I clumsily curtseyed to the peddler that painted the jug, brushing dirt and straw off my skirts and hair.

My head was spinning. I was hungry, sick, and felt soon I would collapse and not be able to pick myself back up. Even so, I had to act quickly, get to her before Monsieur Phlipon did, and make sure one of his spies did not spot me in the meantime. He said he was only seeking out her father and not her, yet I did not believe that for a moment. I now knew for sure he was a policeman, not a humble tutor as he told me. He ruled the streets, beat up on the poor for their own amusement, taunting wretched orphans with no place to sleep.

A trickster grabbed me by the arm and yanked me into a doorway.

"I have three apples in my hand. Show me where the fourth is and you can have it."

The man was wiry and dressed in a red waistcoat and black breeches.

It was better to play his game than try to shoo him away, and anyway I guessed right away the apple was under his hat. When he handed me the fruit something came over me and tears started flowing.

"I am looking for a woman called Armande Vivant," I blubbered. "She is known for the quality of her milk, was kidnapped and brought to Versailles. Now she roams the streets of Paris." Soon my whole face was a mess of snot and salty tears. Instead of insulting me or taking off like the rest a soft glow took over his eyes.

"Come with me and I'll introduce you to a mantua-maker I know."

The shop was filled with precious cloths of many different shades and textures. A streaming piece of yellow velvet with red stripes caught my eye.

"We're closed," said a woman who came from the back of the shop, separated by a heavy curtain.

Then seeing the trickster she motioned us to come in. Curls were piled on top of her head and her cheeks took up much of her face. She carried a large pair of scissors in one hand, while her other hand held a pole to pull bolts of cloth down from shelves. I told her my story as she took apart a blue silk gown on the wire frame. She stopped her work, opened a drawer and pulled out a cap, which she gave to the wiry man with the apples. His face lit up, he bowed to the woman and bid me adieu.

"I've heard of this woman who nurses children." She set down the pair of scissors and wiped her brow. "She revives babies, frees them from mortal constraints to imagine all that is possible. She makes them alive, yet not just breathing, no—buzzing with life." She waved her arms as an actress on a stage.

"Yes, that's her." My body felt as though it was lifting off the ground.

"A woman who sells brass on the corner told me that this extraordinary woman was captured by the King."

"Yes, yes," I cried again, this time gesturing with my hands just like her.

"Another woman who buys fabric from me for her three fine daughters said she is still not free, though she is no longer at court."

Still not free? I squeezed the apple given to me by the trickster. My hand was so tight and strong around the fruit that it sifted between my fingers making applesauce.

She noticed the fruit gushing onto the floor and said, "I don't know where she is now but if she is harmed in any way I will see the culprit is made to pay."

There was anger in her voice I had not heard in such a fair woman as she. The mantua-maker went about adding a piece of shimmering rose-coloured fabric to the back of the gown for a train. While pinning it in place, the fabric made a swishing sound as it swept over the floor. I thought of Armande making that same sound as she moved gracefully through the rooms of our mountain home, singing as she went.

"Come to the Cercle des femmes tonight," she said to me, her eyes still on the dress she was making. "One of the women there might know where to find your wet nurse."

Prison

NIGHT FELL. I stood in the shadows between two buildings across from the mantua-maker's shop. Two women entered, then one, and two more, so I stepped inside. At the back of the shop were five women sitting at a table stacked high with bolts of fabric, buttons and lace. The mantua-maker was also there and nodded as I approached. Two younger women spoke loudly, laughing and tipping their chairs. Another woman held out a chair for me to sit on. She did not smile at me, yet her gesture made me feel at least that I was welcome among them.

The meeting began.

"The formation of a more liberal divorce law would allow for women to have equal rights to property," said the older woman. She wore a black lace mantelet over her shoulders, was slender and had white hair with a fringe.

"Women are left with nothing after divorce," said another. Her hair was dark, almost black and she spit as she talked. "My cousin has two mouths to feed and her husband is now with a woman half his age. He buys his mistress shawls and hats and perfumes while my cousin stays with us as she can't afford to keep a house."

Sitting there amongst the learned women, I began to feel smaller and smaller. The mantua-maker said nothing about Armande as if she forgot why I was there. Pretty soon I was a useless rag doll that could not even see the top of the table. Only the women's pointed shoes jutting out from beneath their skirts. I did not care about so-and-so's cousin and her husband's mistress or about France's wretched divorce laws. As they spoke, my mind beat out the name A-R-M-A-N-D-E, one letter at a time. She was all I could think about, and it angered me that these women were not helping me find her.

What if Monsieur Phlipon or that frightful man with all the rings had already found her? Then, just as the women were getting up to leave, the mantua-maker told them my name and asked me to describe Armande for them.

After I did so, one woman said, "Of course, we know who she is. Why only the most celebrated wet nurse in the country."

The one who spoke had an ostrich neck. Her head was covered with the hood of her black mantelet, yet her long hair hung down on either side. She laughed in a carefree way, looking at me as if I was a fool. Earlier that day I was seen as a fool for asking the very same question, yet it was because nobody had heard of Armande or cared to know my story. One of the women opened her moneybag.

"She gave me this as thanks for distributing pamphlets for her." It was a comb carved of redwood, exactly like the one Madame Lefèvre gave to Armande as thanks for nursing her son Jacques last winter. The woman continued, "She marched in the streets alongside merchant's wives and young orphan girls to see poor street girls receive an education. If they don't, they'll be forced into prostitution to feed themselves. I could have told you there was something to her, a shiny rock in a heap of shit."

I forgot my manners and grabbed the comb from the woman bringing it to my eyes: a single dark curl was trapped between the teeth. I could have kissed the hair, as the sight of it gave me renewed hope. I passed the comb back to her as it was hers to keep. After the meeting, I quit the mantua-maker's shop, my heart growing bigger with the thought that she was in the city and that I had only to find her.

I went to the street where the woman with the comb said she saw Armande. Every few moments a beggar tugged my arm or skirt and I was almost cut apart by a broken bottle while crossing a bridge where a fight was playing out. I walked into a lodging house. The man on duty had wide shoulders and a fat belly. He slept in a chair, his chin resting on his chest while a skin-and-bones cat napped by his feet.

"Never heard of her." He shook his head, upset at being woken up. "Might try the café on the corner. They know everything about what goes on."

I entered the café and sat down, sick from hunger and feeling as if all was beyond hope. Beside me was a woman my age with light hair and a dark cloak over her shoulders. It was strange, I thought, for a woman to be sitting by herself in a public place at that late hour. Her chemise was open and showed the top of one breast. I thought she must be crazy to wear a gown like that on a cold night. Her skirt was deep red like the roses in Armande's garden.

A girl came to my table. Instead of telling her why I was there, I asked for tea and a pastry, not knowing how I was to pay for it. When it arrived, I forced the whole thing into my mouth to feed my hunger. The woman beside me turned her body in my direction. I was too tired and hungry to care that she saw me. After gobbling up the dessert, I lay my head on my hands and began sobbing.

"Whatever is the matter, Mademoiselle?"

I told her my sad story and she listened patiently.

"She suckles peasants' babies mostly. Her milk is...." I thought of the child's telling words ... *the flames of revolt are catching, little by little*. Unable to hide my secret anymore, I blurted out, "Babies speak of all the troubles to come for the people of France. I must find her to protect her and her milk. She wanders the streets seeking out her father, or she might be in prison." I thought of the contradictory accounts about Armande as told by the mantua-maker and the women from the Cercle des femmes.

The girl from the café stood over me. "Well, are you going to pay up?"

I lowered my head in shame.

Then the woman who had been listening to my story, produced some coins in her hand and said, "I'll take care of hers."

I was so moved by the stranger's kind gesture that I thanked her many times. My belly was content and the sweet pastry flavour still lingered.

Shortly after, a gentleman came to sit with the nice woman yet she shooed him away telling him to wait outside for her.

"Cry as much as you want." Her voice was gentle. She straightened her skirt and moved her chair close to mine. "Why don't you try the prison? Not the common gaols, the Bastille Saint-Antoine where they put those who defy the King? If she has some enemies and is well loved by people, as you say." She put a hand on my shoulder, pressing me gently to her. "I've heard it has its share of booksellers, authors and nobles."

It was almost morning. I asked a man who roasted stale bread at a makeshift fire by the road if he knew where the prison was. Others crouched by him sleeping, moaning or praying. "Take a short-cut down this alleyway until you come to rue Maritime," he told me. "It's quicker than the other road along the water."

Further on, I asked another person who urged me to keep going, and then he named a couple of streets I since passed. From that I knew I was definitely on the right track. A scrawny dog barked at me showing his teeth and his bloodshot eyes crawled over my body as though I was his next meal. The dog's frenzied look made me remember Monsieur Phlipon's eyes that first night in Paris. Even the smell on him was of desperation, and I now knew it was because he had been tracking Armande's father with no success: the wolf was finally narrowing in on its prey. This thought gave me a shiver and made me press on.

I reached rue Saint-Antoine. Many towers rose to the sky, each one bigger and taller than the oldest tree in our mountain forest. Three enormous archways opened as the mouths of great sea monsters and a man on horseback looked like an ant next to the buildings. To my right were trees, apple or some other fruit tree. At the entrance, a man lay on the stone steps. He wore a grey cloak with a kerchief tied around his head.

"Pray, tell me, who are you?" His nose was crooked and long like a finger pointing.

"Céleste," I said, feeling myself shrink with his gaze. "I have come to see Armande Vivant. I am her daughter."

He turned his head, and then gestured for me to go away. I stood there for a few moments until he let out a loud belch and then I walked over to an immense column and sat down. A cloud hugged the face of the moon. Two women stood by an archway wearing cloaks with hoods partly covering their faces. Their bodies were bent together for warmth. One of the women sang or tried to sing yet her words became tangled as they left her mouth. The other one whistled in a half-hearted manner, which made me think about how Armande's voice would fill the house when she sang. Her tone calmed me, settled my stomach as though I was an infant and it was her motherly liquid I was taking in.

"Who are you waiting to see?" A woman—not the one who was singing—asked me.

"A wet nurse."

"Did she kill a child? Is that why she's in prison?" Her eyes were wide with hunger to hear my story. "So many of them do, you know."

I shook my head and closed my eyes, pressing my hands against my ears. Yet I heard her senseless chatter all the same.

"I knew a wet nurse once that killed two babies on account of her milk drying up," she said. "Instead of passing them on to another woman she let the poor things die of hunger."

"To be dry with no fruit and no moisture is bad for the weaker sex," sang the other woman, her voice whining like an out-of-tune violin.

Soon, day cast light through the streets like the colour of pee. The two women went away, and, in their place was a boy tossing stones.

"I sell boot laces," he said with a heavy sigh. "Yet I have only one more to sell. Tonight I'll be eating wood soup." He raised his empty wooden poll but for one bootlace, and then he struck the ground with it.

His lonely lace reminded me of the last year in my childhood home when worms turned my only cane chair to a few strings holding it together. I hung the remains atop the window so angels might see them and bring another one for me to sit on. My mother told me to do that, saying it was our only hope. I emptied my pocket of my last small coins, yet urged him to keep the bootlace. The boy was overjoyed, thanked me and was on his way.

The man outside the prison was not the same as the one from the night before. He was taller, had a crooked back and held a rod that was gnarled. He opened the door to the prison letting in a man and an old woman. One gave him a small brass kettle and the other, a bird in a cage. If I had gold coins or objects to sell, the watchman would let me in, yet all I had with me was Armande's diary and I would not give that up for anything. A young man approached him and the two spoke back and forth about a maiden's flaxen hair, her juicy thighs fresh as cream. The watchman laughed with the man and then swiftly let him through the doors. I was next in line.

"Armande Vivant," I said approaching.

"What've you got for me?"

I shook my head and said her name again. I had no possessions to offer him and could not think of a saucy story to tell. The man laughed, beating his rod on the ground. I thought of the woman at the café the night before who so generously paid for my tea and dessert and told me to check the Bastille Saint-Antoine. She showed some of her skin that evening to an older gentleman who watched her comfort me. As I was leaving he sat down next to her, clasping her waist with his strong arms. With that image in my head, I tapped the man on his crooked back, lifting my skirts.

The ugly creature grinned and moved his hand underneath my skirt. He stroked my ankle then put his hand between my thighs. The sensation was not pleasing in the least and it was all I could do not to raise my arm and cuff him on the head. His hand fumbled under my petticoats, fingers scratching between my legs like a dog after a bone. Before I could stop myself, the last thing I ate—a creamy pastry—came shooting out of my mouth. A thick stream of white liquid landed right between the man's eyes. His wiry grin turned to surprise and then anger. I ran as fast as my legs would carry me, the man cursed and yelled, yet he could not catch up to me due to his limp—worse even than mine. Eventually his cursing grew fainter and I found myself in an orchard. My heart was beating so fast it hurt. I wiped my face and mouth with some leaves.

It was still early in the morning and the sun had not yet lifted coolness from the air. At the river I saw a man feeding his horse some grains, the sound of the animal banging its nose against the bucket as it ate, echoed around me. On the bridge, a monk was fixing his eyes on the water as if waiting for a boat to pass. Then a thought came to me that the bridge was known to me. When we first arrived in Paris, I had stood by that very spot where the man fed his horse as I was saying goodbye to the doctor and his wife.

The number and address the doctor gave me stuck in my mind. 37 rue Fabrice. Why hadn't I thought of it before?

Doctor

WHEN I FIRST MET THE DOCTOR, I did not expect him to be jovial and goodly. He struck me at the time as having a stern character that could not be softened, yet then halfway through our journey by carriage together I found him very agreeable. He cared for his ailing wife, caressed her hands and looked on her lovingly as she slept. He was a man that could be trusted, unlike the scoundrel I pretended was my husband, and who was all along plotting to find and likely murder Monsieur Vivant.

"What in the Devil has happened to you, Céleste?" said the doctor when he saw me at his doorstep.

Warmth filled me as my eyes caught his wrinkled brow and plump middle. The cloth I wrapped around my feet had come off. Blisters formed on my heels and toes from walking the Paris streets. The doctor noticed my pained expression and then saw the sores.

"Where are your shoes?"

"Torn apart."

"And pray where is your devoted husband to let you roam about the city shoeless and in such a bad way?"

I lowered my head knowing that I would have to tell a lie.

He sat me down and came back with a bowl of steaming water and a cloth to wipe the blood from my heels and from between my toes. The pain I felt lessened as my heart filled with affection for the doctor and his care of me. The chair he sat me on was by the front door where the light was dim. The glass doors to different areas of the house such as the drawing room and other rooms were all closed and a wide staircase led to the bedchambers. A silver vase with dead flowers sat on a table under a small window. Brown petals that had fallen onto the table made a circle around the vase.

"Look at yourself." He pointed to my filthy hands, chemise and skirts.

My clothes—once those of a gentlewoman—were streaked with dirt, grease from the pastry I ate the evening before, a cheese stain, along with a powdering of dust from the comings and goings of countless horse carriages. It was not until that moment I saw how untamed I had become. Just like I was before I met Armande.

"The man I called my husband...." I was about to tell him the truth when my courage failed me.

The doctor doused my feet with water from the bowl then dried them off.

"Was he called away?"

"Yes, that's right."

I lied just as I did when I was a child and my mother and father scolded me if I did not tell the story they wanted to hear. I was too ashamed even to tell the wretched, stinking truth to a goodly doctor who squatted down on his hands and knees to wash my feet.

He handed me a jar and said, "Rub this into your feet. It will help take away the soreness."

The ointment stung at first and then soothed before long.

"My dear friend Doctor Poirier and his family are away in Italy and we have been living here in their absence. There is a room that belonged to his oldest daughter before he married her off. It is small, yet has a bed and a window. The maidservant will fix it up for you. Then when your husband returns, he will find you in good health, and we won't mention all this unpleasantness."

He thought me a mad woman, yet still he was kind to me. Armande would want me to tell the truth, I thought, and so I did.

"Monsieur Phlipon is not my husband," I said.

The doctor was cutting thin strips of cloth to make bandages for my feet. He looked up from where he knelt on the floor.

"I am in Paris to seek out Madame Vivant, a wet nurse who vanished from our village," I continued, aware that he might not believe my story. "I ran away from home and she took me in. Her abundant source of milk makes children calmer ... more clever. If France is to be saved ... we have to find her."

The doctor proceeded to wrap bandages around each of my feet and then he tied them in a little bow at the side.

"Monsieur Phlipon is mixed up in a scheme to capture Armande's father," I added.

"Not to worry. I shall buy you some new shoes. Pretty ones just like before."

My words seemed to have made no impression on him. Did he even hear me? The doctor pulled me up from the chair by my hands, and before I knew it was leading me down a corridor. After passing two doors, he opened a third door, which led to a darkened room. In the bed in front of a blazing fire lay his wife. Her lids were crumpled rose petals, her hair sprayed out around her grey-white face. She looked much older than before and I was reminded of poor Sophie. The girl's body had been covered in blood that did not come off easily even after water and soap were applied.

Madame Jolycoeur was slighter than before and I could barely see her shape under the sheets. A little warmth came from her hand as I held it, veins pulsing under the surface. *Veins like rivers run through the body* just as the doctor had taught me. She said hello to me, I guessed, with the slight pressure of her hand on mine.

"I hoped that Doctor Poirier could help her. That is why we left our home to come here." His brow was heavy, his small hands restless in his lap. "Patients have responded well to his treatments and she was doing well at first. Now there's nothing that can be done to save her."

I realized then that he was occupied with his wife's illness, and that was possibly why my story was not so astonishing to his ears.

As offered, the doctor gave me the little room and I was happy to have my own bed, and to have told the doctor the truth about the scoundrel and me, even if he did not seem to hear it. The pain in my feet lessened from the ointment and bandages. The doctor gave me a pair of his wife's shoes, pink with white embroidered flowers, which were a bit big yet stayed on. That night, I dreamed of Monsieur Phlipon dressed in his fitted blue police uniform. Then, turning into a wolf, he came toward me on all fours, his teeth clenched.

The next morning I tried to get the image of the part man, part wolf out of my head. I could not let him find Armande and his father before I did. I opened the curtain and saw a pretty courtyard with trees in large pots and a trellis of climbing vines. In my mind, the words, *marching now, one, two, three, let's all fight together for our liberty* flashed upon a yellowish wall at the far end. Little

Jacques had recited that song while playing with the wooden horse on the stairs. I rushed out the door, hardly giving a wink to Doctor Jolycoeur. The man with the crooked back was at the prison gates. I stood very still beside the door, my breath soft, hiding my face with my hood. The door was open as he talked with another man who waved his arms, the two of them shouting curse words. I edged my way towards them, the smell of shit and sweet hay entering my nose as I stepped over the threshold.

Discovery

THE PASSAGE WAS DARK AND WET. Water droplets fell from the ceiling and onto my shoulders and hair. The only light came from a chain of small, narrow windows. Close to the wall, I looked over my shoulder to make sure nobody trailed me. After walking through a series of passages that veered sometimes right and sometimes left, I came upon a heavy wooden door that opened easily. The echo of my walking sounded through the passage as I climbed heavy stone steps. The woman I saw outside the prison the other day sang a tune that seesawed this way and that. The passages had that same strange and troubled rhythm, I thought, as I wandered through them.

I breathed in the damp. My heart felt cold and heavy while my hand felt the shape of Armande's diary in my pocket, the thickness and weight of it. To know it was still there, gave me comfort. After walking along the passage to a higher floor, I saw a door with a tiny window. Inside was a room with a chair and a table covered in dust and cobwebs. Past that were other doors. The chambers were dark and empty, and I began to feel that there was nobody in that stink-hole but me. Past a large arched door, I found myself in a courtyard overgrown with ivy. In the middle was a statue of a child, its face blackened with moss. After crossing the courtyard, I reached another arched door, which led to another tower where I heard a faint sound like a woman whimpering. I ran up the stairs after the sound but it faded as quickly as it came.

A light appeared at the far end of the passage, and then I saw a figure holding a lantern. His footsteps echoed and grew louder as he approached. Quickly, I dashed to a door nearest me. Once inside the chamber, I crouched under the little opening and waited for the man to pass. The room was no bigger than a store cupboard and had a fancy chair in it of red and gold that seemed out of place next to the dust, stench and cobwebs. In the far corner were tapersticks and a row of books. I sat down in the chair and then realized that my feet hurt, the bandages the doctor applied to them, were coming undone, much like my prospects of finding Armande alive.

I walked along the passage to a different tower. Yet this time, instead of looking in every chamber, I said her name, in a low voice, though high enough so somebody might hear. Perhaps I was going mad just as the doctor suspected when he saw my knotted hair, dirty clothes and feet. "Armande," I called out again. Another voice joined my own. In one of the rooms, a young man sat on the floor, legs spread out in front of him. He wore a white embroidered waistcoat, silk breeches and a black cloak over his shoulders.

"I'm looking for a woman whose name is Armande Vivant. She's a wet nurse," I said between the bars of the window.

"Come Henriette, there's a good girl. Bring me some pheasant and grapes, and, oh yes some of that jasmine-scented chocolate, s'il vous plaît. I do not care one stitch if you have to pawn my carpets from Siam."

His head then collapsed into his chest. I repeated what I said yet he did not budge.

I scurried for hours in the dark corridors like a lowly rat, hearing the echo of my voice saying her name. Tiny stones broke away from the ceiling and landed on my head. My aching feet dragged on the ground and my legs were blocks of wood. The chain of windows along the passageway shook up and down like nighttime fireflies. My legs were not strong enough to walk anymore, especially my bad leg, and so I lay down in the filthy passage. An enormous pang of sorrow cut through me. Then, as I was catching my breath, I heard a woman singing. Dizzy, and still not able to walk, I crawled to the sounds.

Inside the chamber was a figure, sun from a nearby window lighting her hair. Was I dreaming? Her torso was shadowed, yet I knew straight away it was she. Armande's hair was fixed atop her head, two curls cascading down her back. I called out to her, yet my voice, which shook with joyous excitement, was too faint for her to hear me. I rapped desperately on the door, and she turned toward me lighting a lantern. The burst of light in the dark chamber made her appear to me. She pushed her hand through the bars to caress my cheek.

"My darling Céleste," she said, her eyes filling with tears. "Give this to the man in the black hat at the end of the passage to the right." She dropped three coins into my hand.

I grabbed her fingers to make sure what I was experiencing was real, and did not want to let her go.

Yet then she said, "Go now, Céleste ... quickly," and so I took the coins and ran to the end of the passage where a lantern flickered. Behind it sat a man on a block of wood, a wide-rimmed hat concealing his eyes.

"What do you want?" He picked up the lantern and brought it to my face. "I was just tending to an old bugger that by all rights should have died weeks ago. I was told to stop giving him grub, as we're short. I snuck in a bit of oats anyhow because I don't want to go to Hell for doing my job."

"Armande Vivant." I trembled as I held the handful of coins out for him.

Flashes of lantern light waved in front of my eyes and then he took the coins, pulling a bunch of keys from his pocket that were tied together with rope. I followed behind him as he opened her chamber door then locked it just as quickly with an echoing clank. She pressed me to her as I wailed right into her chest, into the place where babies drank her wondrous milk. Where somehow—in a world of both misery and excess—she gave them wisdom. I drank her in not wanting to stray from the precious goodness that might disappear in an instant.

After we embraced, both of us crying and stroking each other's hair, she said, "There, there my angel," her chestnut eyes taking me in. "How did you find me?"

My heart pounded. I tried to speak, yet could not find my words.

She wore no jewelry, no necklace, rings or trimmings. Her gown, which was new to me, was a simple cut, chocolate with a white ruffle at the arms and neck. I sat on a sofa with violet satin cushions while she lit candles and another lantern. The chamber was larger than others I saw in the towers, and even reminded me a little of our drawing room at home. There was a carpet on the floor and a picture hanging on a wall, piles of books on a table and clothing draped over a chair.

She did not press me to tell her how I got to Paris or how by some miracle I found her there. Instead, she told me what became of her since I last saw her on that momentous day. "I was very near home after leaving Margot's house for medicine to help me sleep when I saw two men on horseback. They smiled at me and waved and then one of them asked where the church was. It seemed an odd question as the church spire could be seen from a great distance. Nevertheless, I began to direct him to the village square when the other one jumped from his horse and tossed a sack over my head, tying ropes around my hands and feet." As I listened intently to her story, I lowered my head to her lap, and she gently stroked my hair, the ruffle at her wrist brushing my ear.

"Through one of my kidnappers, I discovered that my husband Robert helped the King's men find our house in the village. Not only that, he almost killed me paying that peasant woman to feed me belladonna," she continued, resting her hand on my shoulder as I lay there. "When they came for me, they moved upon me with such swiftness that I was helpless to stop them, poison or not."

My stomach sank, my throat partly closing off, which made me gasp for air. Heat took over me, burning my skin, my tears wetting her skirt. I sat up to look at her.

"After they kidnapped me, I began to suffer the pain of engorgement. It was a condition I experienced once before when hit with a dreadful bout of milk fever. My breasts were hard and swollen, my nipples stopped up from not nursing. By the time we reached Versailles my milk was all but gone."

A shiver went through me and I thought, Margot was right when she said, *Wisdom in the wrong hands could drain magic from those that possess it.* For the future of France the milk's special qualities had to be protected.

"You are cold, your hair wet. Poor Céleste, what you must have gone through to find me."

She tossed a woollen blanket over my shoulders and began rubbing my legs. She told me how the King's soldiers brought her to a large mirrored room where she was fed partridge, duck, pig and fancy cheeses. They stuffed her, gave her feathery silks to drape over her body and filled her glass to the brim. Wine flowed long into the night, yet she was alone as she drank. The only person she saw during that time was a servant who served her each course and then stood at the door in silence.

"I began to see the meat on the table as crawling with vermin," she said with disgust as she stood up. "The wine suddenly tasted of vinegar as though the Devil himself had invited me to dinner and I just sold him my soul. The mirrored walls and chandeliers gave me the sensation of a bad dream, not a fairy tale. Once they figured out I wouldn't oblige, I was treated in a heartless manner at court and began to wonder whether there was an ounce of compassion among them." She stopped pacing and sat down beside me. "That week, still alone, presents began to flow in from so-called court admirers who knew my reputation as a wet nurse: a bit of lace, a peacock feather, a jade broach from the Orient. In other circumstances, another time in history perhaps, I would have been flattered and might even have powdered my face in anticipation of meeting one of them. Locked away in the luxury of that room put a bad taste in my mouth.

"By the time the King summoned me, my head was all in a whirl, and his face looked like one of those meat courses I picked away at the night before. His eyes were the figs I pulled apart with my fingers and his nose was an apricot I dug into with my teeth.

"'It is because of the bad milk of a wet nurse that my son has been ill since he was born,' said the King. I stood in front of him, averting his gaze, as was custom.

"'What I require is the good milk of another wet nurse to put it right.'"

Armande then raised her head, looked at the King square in the eyes and told him she had no milk whatever, and so did not see how she could possibly nurse the ailing Dauphin.

"Can you imagine what a stir that caused?" she said. "Nobody tells the King news he doesn't wish to hear. Though it wasn't within my control to change the hand Nature dealt me. He then asked me in a lighter tone if I would care for a tour of the locksmith's quarters."

She laughed. "He thought I was being stubborn by refusing to nurse his son as though through sheer will I was able to stop and start my milk like a tap. Perhaps I would change my mind after being shown some Royal hospitality, he must have thought. After refusing to nurse the Dauphin a second time, I was sent back to the large mirrored room. A woman with a stern, unfeeling face came in and she shouted at me to pull down my bodice. When I refused, she promptly called out to a man wearing a mask who then tied my hands behind my back. When I struggled, he hit me over the face with a leather strap doubled and wound around his wrist."

She pointed to a scar, across her right cheek that was shiny and red, and I could feel myself breaking apart inside.

"The sour-faced woman had a basin in her hands, which she placed under my left breast. With her thumb and forefinger, she squeezed my nipple. When no milk came, she went to the other one. A doctor who was hunched over and seemed a kindlier soul entered the room. He told the woman to step aside and then massaged both nipples in a gentler fashion, asked me a few questions about the milk stoppage, and then said that he could see I had no milk. He also said that, although he couldn't tell this to the King, he would do what he could to see I wasn't hurt. The next day, I was accompanied back to Paris as befits the most noble in our midst and was led to believe that I would be set free once we arrived in the city. Yet this never happened, as they then brought me to the Bastille Saint-Antoine where I have been ever since. They told me that I am in prison because I have lost my senses and am a danger to public decency."

The chamber door flung open and in walked the man with the black hat who said, "She must go now, Madame Vivant."

She handed the man a handful of coins wrapped in red silk, which he took and then left the chamber.

"I am a favoured one here," she told me. "People, mostly strangers, bring me desserts and other gifts." She offered me some cake.

Once my belly was full words rushed from my mouth as bees from an upset hive. I told her about coming to Paris with Robert Phlipon and the conversation I overheard between the two men relating to her father.

"That ungrateful man," she said, her face turning plum red, the veins in her neck pulsing. "My father taught him astronomy and botany and this is how he repays him? We must find my father ... warn him of the danger."

"But how?" All I knew of his whereabouts was that friends of Madame Rousset saw him leaving a house of ill repute.

"Monsieur Taranne is my father's old friend and business associate. If you go to him he will tell us where my father is hiding."

"I know where he lives," I said, relieved to be useful in some way. "One day I followed Monsieur Phlipon to the man's lodgings that are close to the river and market."

"You always were the very best at spying. I recall you watching me from afar at that man's estate." Then she paused, and said, "What did you secretly call him?"

"Master Dogface."

"Yes, that was the name," she laughed and then proceeded to tell me about a book she was working on.

"While in prison I have been taking notes for a book dedicated to women," she said. "Margot taught me so many things such as how to boil the leaves and seeds in barley water to improve the quality of my milk, making it wholesome for the child. Increasingly, these lessons are no longer valued, yet if I put them in a book then perhaps they will be."

Two of the tapers burned out, and, in the half-light, the intensity of her beauty caught me off guard. I told her about the woman at the café who suggested I go to the Bastille, and about Armande's redwood comb that another woman gave me at the meeting of the Cercle des femmes.

"Do you mean like this one?" She picked up the very same object the woman showed me.

I nodded my head in disbelief as I saw Armande had her very own comb with her all along. She was curious to know more about the women, and looked surprised when I told her two of them saw her marching in the streets.

"It wasn't me, Céleste. I've been here for two weeks now."

"The women said they saw you. How could they?"

"Perhaps they mistook someone else for me."

She cradled my hands in hers rubbing them gently. I lay my head in her lap once and she stroked my damp hair just like she used to when I came to her crying from a nightmare. Or from fear my father or Master Dogface might come for me, even though they were in my past.

That night we slept together in her narrow bed. "Can I come back to see you?" I asked as I sank into her familiar curves.

"Yes, of course," she answered. "Although I won't be here much longer ... only a couple more days."

The room was dark and a shit smell rose up every so often. Yet then my nose would catch her lavender scent and I would feel calm again. I imagined the tower where we rested stretching into the night, the unknown, and thought of what she said about having no more milk.

Morning came and with it was a sloppy feeling of being undone like a ball of string. The mixed up song by the woman outside the prison came into my head. *To be dry with no fruit and no moisture is bad for the weaker sex.* I knew without a baby to suckle Armande would soon lose her milk for good, and with it, the wisdom.

The man with the black hat brought Armande some bread and a slice of cheese, which she shared with me.

"Come now," he said.

His big green eyes peered from under his hat and scabs on his knuckles were thick and brown. My palms grew wet and warm, and my belly filled with fire to know I would soon be leaving her. To settle myself, or maybe to do something nice, I reached under my skirts, pulling her diary from my embroidered pocket. I sensed her present circumstances would make her less angry with me for having read it.

"This is yours." My cheeks were hot with tears and my heart was in my throat.

"Mine?" She looked surprised, and then her eyes sparkled. "Yes I remember now. I keep it tucked away in the little drawer of my desk."

She opened it up, softly caressed the pages while reading her own words. Was she reading about when she was ill with milk fever, or about when her child died?

"It's yours for now, Céleste," she said. "Keep it for me until I am freed."

I returned the diary to my pocket. "I've been reading it in hopes it would lead me to you."

"Tell me then, did it?"

"Yes," I told her.

We said goodbye, and the man with the black hat pulled me through the dark passage toward blinding sunlight.

Pistol

I ARRIVED AT THE HOTEL to collect my belongings. Monsieur Phlipon's shirt and silk breeches were rumpled on a chair and the half-burned log in the fire was cold. I took Armande's diary from my pocket to make room for some gloves when a sudden noise at the door made me jump.

"There you are, Céleste. Three days is a long time to be away from me." Monsieur Phlipon stood in the doorway, his hands folded at his chest. "You're reading that book of fairy stories again. Have you no other interests besides the fantastical, the far-fetched?"

I hugged the diary.

"You have found Armande, have you not?"

I shook my head as he came closer—my heart in my mouth, arms and legs trembled. He pushed a pile of clothes onto the floor with his pointed shoe then sat on the chair. Before, his clear blue eyes had tempted me. Now gazing upon him I found him too ugly to even look at: a wolf in sheep's clothing.

"You poisoned her, Robert and helped them capture her." I was tired of lying, and, seeing Armande gave me the strength I needed to confront him with the truth.

He was stunned I called him by his real name. After a few moments staring at me, his mouth gaping wide, he said, "It was a soporific, a sleeping potion. No harm came to her."

"She was blinded for several days." My grip on her diary tightened. I thought to hide it in the ruffles of my skirts, yet his eyes never left me.

"I assure you, Céleste, that it was not my intention. The men heard she was a spirited woman and wanted to make sure she didn't give them too much trouble. A valet de chambre confirmed the rumours that the King summoned her to court to revive the ailing

Dauphin. The lettre de cachet sent to her father had produced no result and his Highness was impatient. If I could assist in some way then the poet would see to it I was rewarded. The King and Queen will be presented with a copy of my book on alpine plants when it's completed."

His fingers toyed with his waistcoat buttons and his eyes lingered on my face. "As chance would have it, I was already planning a trip to my village to settle my father's affairs after his death."

Although her diary was hidden inside another book cover, having it in my hands made me feel naked.

He leaned towards me. "Now, tell me, where is she then?"

"I told you I don't know."

"I can see it on your face. You are too honest, Céleste. It doesn't pay to be read so easily like a book."

"Think what you like." I felt like a trapped animal.

"Céleste, you must tell me where she is." His voice was like a toad's rattle. "Her father is engaged in illegal activities and has evaded the authorities on countless occasions. He has quite possibly the largest file of any criminal and naturally she'll seek him out."

"He's a good man," I told him. "What has he ever done to you?"

"It's true he was always kind to me when I was a boy. He would take me into his library where we conversed until the wee hours of the morning about botany, astronomy…. Yet, at the time, I was naïve about his writings." He stood up and began pacing.

"The libelles portray the King as despotic, impotent and indecisive." His voice was loud, enraged. "They fuel this talk of revolution, and mass protests. Villagers are disregarding the game laws and go about killing rabbits, partridges and woodcocks for their sheer amusement. In other districts, they have even shot gamekeepers when they encountered them."

"Their winter crop was destroyed," I said, matching his loudness. "They didn't want the animals to eat all their seeds."

"They only want blood and will stop at nothing to have the King's head on a stick." Then he stared at me, and, in a low voice said, "I know what you have in your hands, Céleste, now give it to me."

I ran for the door and he lunged at me.

"I stole the object from your hot, little hands one day while you were fast asleep. You didn't suspect a thing. I remember that diary very well. It was the one she wrote in when our daughter Rose-Marie...." He stopped and I caught the hurt in his eyes.

He grabbed me by the shoulders, thrusting me onto the bed. I punched him square in the face, and then he touched his nose, a grimace appearing on his face. There was blood all over his fingers, his nose gushing. He twisted and hit my hand, forcing the diary from me. Still wrenching my hand, he opened the book, his eyes wildly hunting.

"Ah yes, listen to this, *At that moment, I let my mind wander to a place where ideas and justice dictate actions. I questioned what it would be like if these women could read and write. I knew that it would mean they would not only be able to teach their own children but also be fit for political life. As it is they have no power that is theirs, just the claim of being so-and-so's wife. Yet they are given the reins to nourish a child, to rock this bit of life back and forth when it cries. They see the child take its first steps and hear it utter words for the very first time. How can it be then that there is no room for their learning?"*

His eyes were crazed, his face streaked with blood. "How can it be indeed?" He closed the diary, finally letting go of me.

"The diary belongs to Armande. You have no right to keep it, Céleste."

He pushed me down on the bed once more, fumbling under my skirts and ripping my embroidered pocket from me.

"Tell me where she is. I won't harm her I promise. It is only him I want."

He retrieved a knife from his trousers, cut the ties from my lovely pocket and then used them to fasten me to the bedposts. I struggled, crying out, yet it was no use, as he was much stronger than me. I screamed and shouted; the bed banged against the wall. He shoved his face up to mine; his river-blue eyes pierced through me, blood from his nose smudging my cheeks. Then, before leaving with the diary, he took a handkerchief from his pocket and stuffed it in my mouth.

In the early morning, the man who ran the hotel heard me banging the bed against the wall, came in and untied me. My hands stung where the ties had been, bloody rings around my wrists. When I tried to stand, my legs almost gave way, yet then a stroke of good fortune befell me. As I was gathering up the rest of my belongings, a skirt, bonnet and books to take with me, I noticed a shiny brass object jutting out from beneath the mattress: a pistol. It was heavy and long, made of wood and had a carved brass handle. The thought that the weapon might be used to murder Monsieur Vivant caused a painful sensation like splinters to pass through me. Too big to fit in my stocking, I wrapped it up in one of my skirts, and then secreted it away in the bottom of my sack.

My apron was soiled with blood, both his and mine. I took a few moments to wash my face in a nearby basin and run a comb through my hair. Then, as I was about to leave the room, I looked out the hotel window and, just as I thought, there was a man across the street. Different than the other one, he stood not moving, his eyes fixed on the hotel door. After trying to climb out a window at the back and seeing another spy—the same tall man as before—waiting in the alley, I snuck into the back of the hotel where they soaped the linens. There I found an apron with a faded flower print and a bed sheet, which I ripped apart to make a shawl and kerchief to cover my head. I bent over, lowering my head like an old beggar woman.

After walking for a few minutes, I turned to see if I was being followed, and was delighted that my disguise had fooled them. Women were walking to market, baskets in hand and children trailing behind. Two men loaded boxes onto a cart, the horse whinnying. A woman and man stepped from a carriage. The man smoked a clay pipe and their laughter pierced the chilly morning air. Outside a bakers' shop, I passed a group of men who shouted and waved their arms. One said, "We are being fined for selling our bread at fifteen sous, yet due to shortages and high flour prices we can't sell it for less or we'll be ruined." The man's fingers were thick and worn down, his fat nose was round like a fresh bun.

At dusk, I walked past empty market stalls, past a cemetery where upturned graves and skulls pushed from the soil like rutabagas. I looked behind me every so often to make sure nobody followed me. Pretty bottles hanging on posts created splashes of light on wet stones in the street. I reckoned Monsieur Phlipon patrolled the area where I first saw him in his blue police uniform with the man from the censors' office. I had to act fast as it would not take long for word to reach him that she was in prison. I sat on the ground, my back resting against a building. The pistol was tucked inside my skirt at the waist. Nearby, beggars crowded around a makeshift fire. A loose woman walked past, her face decorated with powder and splashes of red on her lips and cheeks. My heart beat so fast my chest hurt. I never murdered anybody before. Two children came by, kicked me, laughed and ran away, which made me happy as it meant I played my part of a poor old woman well. When all was quiet, I took out the pistol. I closed my eyes and felt for the trigger so I could find it instantly. I would not have time to stop and reload so would have to get him on the first try.

Heavy rains came with flashes of light and crashing overhead. Log floaters maneuvered their logs towards others lined up and bobbing at the river's shore. Women pulled their cloaks over them and ran for cover. I ran to the nearest building and stood under the roof watching the rain pound down on barges along the Seine.

The rainstorm cleared the street of people and nobody passed my way for at least two hours. Then, just when I started to nod off, I spotted Monsieur Phlipon wearing a police uniform. He carried a rod in his hand and his stride was steady like a soldier. As he got closer, I put the pistol down low so it was out of sight, while aiming it straight for him.

"Old woman have you no home to go to?"

His question caught me off guard. My fingers clenching the weapon were damp with sweat.

"No home sir." I looked up, the kerchief covering my face so just my eyes were visible.

"When morning breaks, you need to be gone from here. You are in front of a solicitor's office. He'll be angry I didn't arrest you."

I nodded dumbly as I watched him turn and walk down the street, his boots clapping on the stones underfoot. The fact he was not cruel took me by surprise, and made me forget what I had been waiting there all that time to do. Quickly, I held the pistol up, cocked it, aimed for his head and pulled the trigger. It took a couple seconds before I realized the pistol was not even loaded. Morning sun edged its way into the street. That day I would load his handsome pistol with bullets and blast him clean to Spain. I snuck into an alley, stripped off the apron, and changed into a fresh, dry petticoat and blue cloak from my sack. There was the sound of children and babies coming from a nearby doorway, and I felt a deep sadness thinking of Armande, and how she had no milk.

Inside the orphan house children ate lentils and bread at a long table. They wore black bonnets each with a white border, fichus at the neck and white aprons. In another room were newborns in baskets and a woman suckling a child in the corner by a window. Radiant delight filled my heart as I was sure God had led me there to help Armande restore her precious milk. "The flames of revolt are catching, little by little," said the small, knowing child shortly after Armande was kidnapped.

"I have come for an orphan," I said to the woman. "It is for a very well regarded wet nurse."

She looked on me curiously and replied, "The wet nurse must come herself. We want to get a look at her to make sure she is fit to nurse the orphan."

I walked out of the room, then waited outside and peeked in the window until I saw the woman leave. Some of the babies cried, some fussed, while others slept. I snatched a sleeping infant from its basket and headed for the door. As I took off in the rain, I pressed the warm bundle to my heart. Blood coursed through my veins and I ran and ran until I was too far away for them to catch me. For the revolt to be a success, these babies had to keep drinking her wondrous milk. The baby was awake, though still, its little eyes searching my face. Barely breathing, I waited by the gate, crouching down to avoid suspicion. A group of men passed by me talking and laughing. Then after a while, only a few people lingered.

"I'm here to see Armande Vivant." I spoke in a delicate manner so he might think I was someone special.

He looked at me as though we were now best friends, tapped my backside with his rod and I was in—just like that. The last time I had counted the number of doors in each passage so I would not get lost, yet now I knew from memory when to veer left or right. As before, I brought the man at the end of the corridor some coins the doctor had given me, and the guard opened her chamber door. Wedged between the bars of her door was a bouquet of lilies, daffodils and pussy willows. No doubt a gift from some admirer. Their soft fragrance cut the stench that lingered in the air as I brought them to her. Armande lay on her bed, curled up. Hair washed over her face and she clutched her hands to her chest.

As I drew closer, she opened her eyes, smiled and said, "Oh, Céleste. How nice to see you. They tell me I will be released tomorrow."

She sat on the edge of the bed smoothing her chemise, underskirt and her red gown with a blue sash at the waist. She then gathered her hair from her face and twisted it, tying the curls on top of her head with a deep red ribbon.

"She's lovely, Céleste," she said when she saw the baby in my arms. I had no time to waste and so came right to the point. "Can you suckle her?" I held the baby out for her to take from me. "If you don't your milk will disappear for good."

"I tried at court, Céleste, remember I told you that. My milk had dried up by then. My life as a wet nurse has come to an end."

"But it can't. Please just try," I said pleading. My wish for her milk to flow as before was so strong that I thought I could will it back.

Tears streamed out of me and I was helpless to stop them. Then, moved by my show of emotion, Armande took the baby into her arms.

"There, there little nut," she said as she unlaced her bodice, offering the screaming orphan her nipple.

The baby's mouth fastened to her and sucked, its tiny fists clenched, eyes moving from side to side under closed lids. I held my breath while marvelling at the spectacle I had seen many times before.

"In the beginning I didn't believe that my thoughts were impressing upon the infants through the milk," she confessed to me. "I showered them with affection and nursed them when they cried." The ruffle of her chemise brushed the baby's cheek. "Stories began in the village about my milk and I added to them, partly for my own amusement, yet also because I did feel that a mother's milk—not only mine—was essential to a child's development. Some women didn't fancy having a baby clinging to them. Others were too poor and had too many mouths to feed to care about one more. I thought perhaps they would draw from their own motherly wisdom if they perceived their children transformed by the milk. Before I knew it, the stories about me were being communicated to people in towns and villages across the country." She gazed down at the little one as the candlelight reflected in the baby's head.

"In the past I thought that this gossip had no weight to it, that the claims about my milk transforming babies were false...."

I hung on her every word. Then, just when I thought she would finally tell me the truth about her milk, she said, "Céleste, it isn't coming." Her loving voice was apologetic. "There is no more milk."

Rumours

THE BABY WAS FLUSHED, face wet with tears, her mouth gaping wide as she howled. On my way back to the Maison de la Couche, I saw traces in the streets that confirmed what the babies were saying. The anger and misery of so many was building up and would soon explode. At the dock, a woman sat slumped over crying. Her heavy grey skirt was soiled, mossy hair hung over her face.

"My husband has gone to dig at the buttes of Montmartre," she said to me as I walked by. "He is a mason, but has had no work for months. I fear he will catch cold and die. Just like so many others."

A sharp wind nipped my cheeks as I ran along the wooden footpath by the river. Surely they would already count the baby missing, yet the sooner I arrived the less chance I had to be caught. The room where I took the baby was empty and I could hear someone playing a piano nearby. I crept in and searched for a spot to lay the child. Thankfully I was able to bring the orphan back and place it in its basket without anybody seeing me.

The next morning, the streets were clear once more and buildings glistened in the sunshine. I was on my way to visit Monsieur Taranne when I entered a café for a glass of water. The place was bright with white countertops and a polished marble floor. A woodstove emanated warmth to those seated at small tables on chairs barely big enough to hold them. A jug of spring flowers sat on the countertop underneath an enormous gilded chandelier with many unlit candles perched on top. The air was sweet smelling, an intoxicating mix of pastries and lilacs. Two gentlemen sat by the window, one on a bench and the other on a chair. I was just close enough to hear their conversation as I sipped my water.

"No more Director of the Book Trade, no more royal censors."
The man who spoke wore a cravat, a pink silk waistcoat, periwig
and cocked hat.

The other man clutched his cup. "They say the King is doing away
with his dreadful lettres de cachet. No more ludicrous, epistolary
demands." He wore a grey jacket with a green collar and his cocked
hat sat crooked on his head.

"Thank God for that!"

"I expect that the thousands of cahiers de doleances he'll be receiving
comprised of grievances from citizens of the realm, the farmer who
can only afford to feed his family meat three times a year and the
coffee-lemonade-and-vinegar sellers who complain about competitors
ruining their business, will only instigate further reform."

"We shall see," said the man in the pink waistcoat. "The cahiers
will be discussed at the time of the Estates-General, which convenes
this May with *double* representation going to the Third Estate."

"The King shall finally be forced to consider the rot oozing from
every corner of his beloved country."

"The times are auspicious mon ami."

"Indeed."

I bolted into the street. A boy was selling pamphlets one block
down. I picked up one, and then another, looking as I did at the titles,
*What Wasn't Said, Confessions of the Comte de * * **, and *Anecdotes
About Madame Du Barry*.

"Formidable," I said to the boy, imitating the fine gentlemen at
the café.

"I don't know Ma'am. I cannot read, but something tells me it's
better not to understand these stories. Take this one." He held up a
pamphlet. "On the first page is an engraving of a woman undressing
a man in his very own bed. What kind of morals does a man have
who would fashion such a book?"

The news of the King stopping the ban on libertine works caused
me to give the peddler a fat kiss on the mouth. Of course I surprised
him, yet I did not care if he thought me a harlot because I was happier
than I could remember. As I was still close by, I decided to return
home and tell the doctor the good news. Monsieur Phlipon would
have no reason to want Monsieur Vivant dead now, as he was free
to publish whatever he wanted without fear of prison or death.

When I arrived, I found the doctor praying at the bedside of his dying wife. The somber mood made it hard for me to disturb him. After holding his hand and his wife's limp one for several minutes in silence I set out again, this time wearing my spring gloves, a birthday present from Armande. With a muslin handkerchief at my neck, I almost looked a gentle lady. Armande would be beside herself with joy when I told her about her father no longer having censors and police chasing after him.

As I made my way, the doctor shouted at me from the front door, "You better not be off to the Bastille Saint-Antoine. Guards have just been summoned to contain rioters in that area. A wallpaper factory owner's house is being sacked along with the house of a saltpeter manufacturer. Rumour has it that the factory owner was going to reduce the workers' salary to fifteen *sous* a day from fifty."

It was beginning. The *flames of revolt were catching* just as the babies had foretold. I thanked the doctor with a wave and continued down the street. I had seen danger many times in my life and was not about to let a group of angry workers stop me from reaching Armande.

Even so, when I finally made it to the district of the Bastille Saint-Antoine I was shaken by what I saw: the spectacle of thousands of out-of-work river men, brewers, tanners and others storming the factory worker's house armed with sticks. Men were tossing furniture, paintings, paint, and paper out of windows and onto immense fires that blazed in the streets below them. The gardes françaises were there with guns, cannons and drums beating. The crazed demonstrators kept their looting and then began to attack the soldiers with roof tiles and stones.

I slipped through the crowds in the direction of the prison.

"You won't find your woman here," the man with the rod said when he saw me. "She was freed earlier today."

"She wasn't supposed to be out until tomorrow? Where did she go?" The smell of paint streaming through the air burned my eyes and nose.

"No idea." He stared at the ground.

In the direction of the fires, I heard the crowd roar, "Death to the rich, death to the aristocrats."

A group of about five hundred carried a mock gallows to which was attached an effigy of the wallpaper manufacturer. "Edict of the Third Estate Which Judges and Condemns the Above Réveillon and Henriot to be Hanged and Burned in a Public Square," read the placard.

I scurried down an alley to escape the din and stench, my plan to reach Armande burning away as the chairs and paintings that lit up the Paris streets.

The doctor's wife died the evening the factory owners' houses were sacked. For two days, he prayed by her body. I joined him and kept vigil at night should Armande come as, when I saw her, she said she would be released the next day. The streets were abuzz with talk about the hundreds who were injured and all those who were killed during the riots. Angry voices talked about a *massacre* referring to how the gardes françaises fired a shot in the air and when that didn't stop the looters, they began to shoot into the crowd.

Three days after the riots, there was still no sign of Armande. I reckoned she would soon turn up at the door, given she knew where to find me. That day the doctor and I went to the cemetery, strolling past upturned graves where part of an arm stuck out of the ground, only two fingers remaining on its shrunken hand. A man with a red cap and a face like a rabbit was fitting the doctor's wife with sackcloth. We arrived just as he was to shovel her body into a grave and douse her with quicklime. Being in that place made me remember the cemetery where my father dug graves. I went there when he was not working and slept behind a grassy mound of earth where bones jutted out among tombstones of angels, lambs and saints.

That same afternoon the streets were quiet for the first time since the riots. Clouds were thick in the sky and the sun seemed lost amongst them. I went out to buy a loaf of bread with the coins the doctor gave me.

A woman was shouting insults at the man who sold the bread. "Thief, dog, dullard, swine…. This is what I'm paying for the bread because that's what it is worth."

"But, Madame, you see how much I'm selling it for. You'll have no bread unless you pay full price."

The woman threw some coins at him, grabbed the loaf and hurried down the street. The man went after her, but then saw me and stopped.

"I suppose you also want some bread for nothing?"

I counted out the right amount and he handed me the bread.

"Thank the Lord. There's one honest woman in the bunch."

I sat by a fountain, broke off an end and before I knew it, the bread was gone. Two boys played with boats in the water fountain beside me. They had dark blonde hair, chubby cheeks and wore matching blue coats.

"She drank from a jug of wine to make her numb to the fire's heat," one boy said watching his boat sink. He looked like an older brother.

"A midwife?" The younger one had a stick that he was using to bring his boat in.

"No, she suckled babies,. She was a learned woman, studied languages of the Ancients."

"What was this woman like?" I interrupted.

"She had dark hair, curly ... light brown eyes."

"I was with my mother and the woman looked into the eyes of all who watched as flames burned the flesh from her bones."

I pressed the boy to tell me more, yet the two began chasing each other around the fountain and then skipped away.

I rushed back to the man who sold the bread. My voice was pulsing, caught in my chest. "Can you tell me what you know of a woman, a wet nurse who was killed?"

"I know about a woman who died by fire. The King's wife would invite her to Versailles where she loved to dine on pheasant and grapes. She was her treasured companion they say. She was there at the time of the factory lootings. A soldier tried to stop them from dragging her away, but it was too late."

"What was her name?"

"All I can tell you is she was celebrated for the wondrous influence her mother's milk had on little ones."

"I heard about this wet nurse and the magical properties of her milk," said a woman who was listening to our exchange. "The Good Lord bestowed on her a special gift ... damn to eternal Hell those that killed her."

Their voices grew distant as my legs carried me from the words they spoke. I entered a small street empty of people and noise. Near a chapel, a patch of grass inside the gate beckoned me. Far-off voices shouted prices for lard pies, parsnips, onions and bread at market, and, two men passed talking about a horse one of them was about to shoot. A little girl screamed as she ran down the street and a boy yelled after her. I dropped to my knees, my face pressed against the ground.

Locket

THE NEXT MORNING, the doctor hired a horseman to take us to the district of Saint-Antoine where the riots took place. The streets were wet with rain, a low fog creeping around the buildings like a pickpocket after his next victim. The coach ceiling was very low and the burgundy-covered seats smelled of stale perfume.

"What do you see, Céleste?" The doctor squinted.

"Towers for prisoners."

Clothed in a thick, white mist only the tops of the towers were visible. It was the same stinking prison where I climbed up all those stairs and the countless dark passages I hurried through to find her. The driver sped up. At my back, the towers were fast dissolving behind a cloud.

"It is here," shouted the driver.

The doctor clung to my arm as we stepped from the carriage. The force of wind tossed rain in our faces. Drops seeped into my coat, wetting my skirts, and landing in my shoes. Over the sensations of dampness and cold, came a burning stink. We stopped behind what we guessed was the factory, which had been reduced to walls sticking up. In the middle of the building were several rolls of wallpaper piled against a long metal table. Under it was a white section of paper with a scene in purple of sailing ships, all kinds of masts, big and small. A man with a spear in one hand held up his hat with the other as if to greet us. Several empty wine bottles were scattered on the floor along with chair legs and drapery. Beyond the burnt building and its contents was the factory owner's house: an empty blackened shell with a few possessions remaining. Paintings and glassware scattered in pieces over the floor.

Behind the house was the garden where rioters drank wine and brandy until they were so drunk they could not see straight. Their discarded bottles lay amidst piles of ashes where the fires had blazed. As I sifted through the remains, I found leather book covers with no pages inside, a woman's looking glass and a globe of the world just like the one in Monsieur Vivant's library. When I walked back to the factory, I noticed a willow tree that was miraculously unharmed by the looters. Past the tree I came to a spot where clay covered the ground, rain creating milky puddles of grey-white around me. I squatted down to look into a puddle and saw my own sad and thin reflection. Only that. There was nothing to confirm what the baker said about Armande being murdered. No bone, teeth, or the kinds of stuff that remain after a body was burned. That gave me hope the dreadful story I heard was made-up.

Then, heading back to join the doctor by the coach, my eye caught sight of a shiny object in one of the puddles. Curlicues ending in flowers were etched into its body. The chain was missing, yet the gold oval piece looked good as new. As though trying to find its little heartbeat, I gently touched her locket to my cheek. Rain poured down mixing with my tears and my heart caught wind of a tune that I had thought I only imagined the child Jacques sang one day while playing on the stairs. *Marching now, one, two, three, let's all fight together for our liberty.* Was all the destruction I saw around me what it meant to be liberated? Slipping the oval piece into my glove, I straightened my cloak and skirt.

The doctor was standing with a woman dressed in black from head to toe. "We met at the mantua-maker's shop remember." She took off her hood, showing me her long tresses. "I was the one with the redwood comb given to me by the wet nurse."

When she said this, I instantly thought of what she told me about Armande. *A shiny rock in a heap of shit.* The gold locket was safely nestled in the palm of my hand.

"I came here to place some flowers at the spot where they murdered her." She held out a bouquet of daffodils. "I'm meeting some women here from the Cercle des femmes."

The woman shed a tear and then dabbed it with a handkerchief.

"This should stay here with her, don't you think?" she said, gazing on the comb.

I turned away from her and caught another whiff of burning remains. Was it cloth, wood, bones ... hair? The very thought made me be sick right in front of the woman and the doctor. Wind splashed the soupy, bitter liquid all over my cloak. The woman retrieved her handkerchief.

"We'll go on without her, won't we, Céleste." She began to wipe up the mess I made. "Though she'll be with us all the same. The alarm bell of reason is making itself heard throughout the land. Women are waking up."

There was no use telling her the redwood comb she held in her hand was not really Armande's as she thought. What did it matter as the wet nurse was gone? The woman placed the comb among the blossoms of the bouquet in her hand and walked towards what used to be a beautiful, stately garden.

That evening, I lay on my bed turning Armande's gold locket over in my hands. Inside, the silhouettes were of her mother and father. The woman's nose was small, delicate and she had a slender face. The picture showed Monsieur Vivant with his hook nose, high cheekbones and manly chin. The artist painted in tiny lines for eyebrows. I held the open locket up close, my eyes playing tricks on me. Both faces mixing, then separating and mixing again. Eventually, the two faces became one: small, delicate nose, oval face with high cheekbones, finely drawn eyebrows. A portrait of Armande was playing out before my eyes. If I had found her in time I might have saved her. I began to sob. My heart was a deep chasm and everything I knew or cared about was slipping into it.

The doctor called to me from the drawing room. I closed the locket, wiped tears from my face and went downstairs where a boy with fat cheeks stood in the doorway. His jacket sleeves hung past his knuckles.

"Monsieur Vivant from rue Martine sent me to fetch you." He was out of breath. "Go to the black door at the end of that street. There you'll see a gold lion. He said to give this to you."

The pamphlet was by Armande's father. My heart pounded, thoughts rushing away from me. How did he know where to find me? For all I knew Monsieur Phlipon bought it from a bookseller or street hawker just to trick me. Then I flipped through the pamphlet coming to a page marked up with words, *Triompher notre liberté*

... selon nos propre passions ... déterminée par nos prejugés, and I recognized Monsieur Vivant's handwriting. This proved that he was the one reaching out to me and not the scoundrel. Before slipping on my cloak, I took one quick look at his silhouette inside the gold piece then tucked the locket into my stocking for safekeeping. I had no time to lose.

The sky was bright with stars and a scraggy crescent moon. I turned the corner and was about to quicken my pace when I noticed a tall figure slumped against a building on the other side of the street.

"How are the doctor and his wife then?" A low, mournful voice echoed through the streets and sent a chill through me. "Keeping well I trust."

As I looked back I could just make out the shape of Monsieur Phlipon's face, shiny mane of hair resting on his shoulders. He had gashes on both his cheeks, and his raised hand glistened with blood in the dim streetlamp.

"What?" I stopped unable to force more words from my trembling lips.

"I almost had him," he said, biting his lower lip. "In time she would be relieved of her wet-nursing duties in Versailles and would journey to Paris to seek him out. There would be no more need to plot his capture as she would make the thing painless for me for once."

His breath was quick, his voice shaky. I handed him the kerchief around my neck, watching as he wiped blood from his wounds. His white cravat and green velvet waistcoat were blood-soaked. One arm wrapped around his chest like a piece of string holding a package together. His police cloak was stained with blood at the collar.

"He can write whatever he wants now," I said drawing closer. "The law is no longer on your side."

"The King will come to regret his decision. Besides that is not why I sought him out all these years."

"What do you mean?"

"Monsieur Vivant put thoughts into Armande's head about the importance of her own ideas. If it weren't for him she wouldn't have been so selfish as to neglect our little girl."

His face was a blur. I tried to squint to see him better.

"You never really knew her, never loved her at all." My words were spilling out of me and into the night air.

"Of course I did." He tried to raise his voice yet was too wounded. "You don't understand," he went on. "The pain of losing a child is too much to bear."

Where had he hidden her diary? Was it in his coat pocket, the pocket of his bloody waistcoat?

"Women who march in the streets speak of sacred rights and want their demands constituted into a national assembly. Pure folly. It's fine to dream of a place where women have the same rights as men, to nurse babies and educate peasants in a village far from Versailles. Yet to write about it ... expect these words will one day be understood, accepted, implemented as law ... nothing less than delusional."

He closed his eyes. Blood gushed from an opening in his chest when he took his arm away. But I had seen death before.

"A woman did this to me, pair of scissors in the chest."

He covered his wound as best he could with his bloody waistcoat, tugging the outer coat across his chest. He was trembling from cold and so I took off my cloak and draped it over him.

"Holding meetings at her shop to arrange demonstrations not sanctioned by the King. I returned this evening to warn her."

Scissors? Could the mantua-maker have stabbed him? She was not a woman to trifle with. From time to time, he looked at me then his eyes would glaze over, and his head slump to one side.

"The Nation has been degraded by these newfangled ideas that incite hatred for the monarchy ... peddled by people like Vivant ... I have tried to fight...."

A group of men passing by looked on us curiously then kept walking, talking and laughing. Monsieur Phlipon lowered his head, grunting in pain.

"Armande is dead," I stammered. "She was killed by rioters. They made a fire around her and burned her." My words, as I said them, cut my throat like knives. I had to tell him even though it was unbearable to do so.

The skin over his brow wrinkled and he let out a whimper. Tears rolled down his cheeks full of cuts and scrapes and he rocked back and forth like a small child. With his head, he motioned for me to open his coat.

"In here," he said faintly.

Her diary was inside his waistcoat. I grabbed it, tightly clutching the book containing her most precious words. He had discarded the fairy tale cover I put over to conceal and protect it. His eyes closed once more and he let go of his chest. Even if I called the good doctor who was only steps away, he could do nothing for him now.

"We were happy once." He took a final breath and then his body slumped forward. For Armande, the women of the Cercle des femmes and myself, I lifted his head to spit on his face then said a prayer for his soul to rest. After I tugged my cloak up to cover his neck and shoulders, I made a sign of the cross on his forehead with my thumb.

Afraid his ghost might come after me, and snatch the diary back, I ran as fast as my legs would take me all the way to the river. The stone I skipped along the surface of the water flew and then disappeared into the gaping darkness in front of me. "I gave death my cloak," I murmured to myself as I skipped another stone. I looked out at what I knew was the river—though I could not see it as it was then too dark, stars and moon now hidden by clouds—and began to cry and laugh until I fell to the ground clutching my body.

Part 4

Father

MONSIEUR VIVANT WORE NO PERIWIG and his long hair, tied at the back, was whiter than I remembered. Though it had not been that long since I saw him last, he looked older and had more lines under his eyes. We embraced and he held me firmly and with much affection, just as a true father holds a long-lost daughter.

The small drawing room was the colour of apricots. Lanterns hung from the ceiling, wine and blue cushions decorated chairs and sofas, and sweeps of heavy cloth covered the windows. In the dim light, the room was like a house in the desert where emperors might live. Armande had told me stories of how these men travelled from place to place with hundreds of wives, servants, baths, long tables, camels and sleeping quarters, all of them in great tents as big as castles. Monsieur Vivant wore black breeches and a blue shirt of fine silk.

I looked to his face for glimmers of Armande; his dancing chestnut eyes, cheeks, and his forehead. He directed me to a chair underneath a painting on cloth of a woman and man in a loving embrace. He then sat in front of me, crossed his legs and rested his hands on his knees.

"You must be wondering how I found you and why I didn't come myself."

At first, he showed me only his lively character, yet on closer inspection I saw his eyes were red and he mostly likely had not slept.

"Did you visit her in prison?"

"Yes, Monsieur."

His eyes took in my body, yet in a way that was friendly, not menacing.

"Not long after I came back to Paris from a voyage to England I heard street gossip that my daughter was in a Paris prison. Of course,

I didn't believe it was true yet went to investigate all the same."

He took a deep breath and said, "It was the day of the riots, utter mayhem in the streets near the Bastille with men shouting and looting, smoke and people everywhere. I witnessed souls trampled to death." He gazed at me, his eyes watering. "A small child lay face down, blood streaming from his head. I was about to run for cover when a group of men and women appeared, dragging a body through the streets. The woman's hair trailed on the ground, her body was limp. I yelled after them to stop, and saw in the same instant that it was my daughter. A man said something about not having any bread, and added that this woman, meaning Armande, dined with the Queen. A woman yanked the gold locket from around Armande's neck and held it up as if this would somehow prove she was a rival.

"I ran towards her attempting to fend them off, yet anger gave them more strength than I had. Our eyes locked and she reached out to grab my arm. During those few moments I felt her womanly strength, her love for me. Then came a blow with a stick to the back of my head."

He covered his face with his hands, his wooden shoes clunking on the ground as he wept. I knelt in front of him, placing my hands on his knees. My grief threatened to overcome me, as did the guilt over my failed promise to keep her safe. I fought hard not to give in only because I knew that's what she would wish.

When I had gained strength to speak once more, I said, "How did you find me?"

"Armande spoke your name before I was knocked unconscious. She told me where you were and that she was on her way to join you there."

He looked away from me to somewhere distant.

I slipped a hand into my stocking and then showed him the locket. He gazed on it in disbelief, and then told me a story about Armande before I knew her.

"When she was a child, she couldn't wait to tell me things. Even before French words came out of her mouth, she conversed in a mysterious language, very intricate and rampant with melody. She wanted to read everything, to understand it all, yet I told her to be patient as children need time to run in the fields and gather what is rightfully theirs. I know that I wasn't a very good father for her these past few years."

"I've been reading her words." I held out the diary.

A red dot in the corner of the book caught my attention—a stain left by the scoundrel.

Monsieur Vivant's eyes darted away from me. His face was full of dread. "Shush. Can you hear?" There was banging and shouting at the front door.

He swept me up, pulling me, and the diary along with him. Then he rested his hand on a wall and the surface moved as if by magic, opening to a little room. The wall shifted back and we were in a cold place as dark as a cave. Men were shouting and knocking things over on the other side where we were only moments before. Monsieur Vivant felt my face, pressing two fingers to my mouth to tell me not to speak. A dull ache started in my bad leg, spreading to the rest of my body. Armande's diary was close to me, my fingers running over the swirling patterns of the soft red cover. After we sat, waited and listened for a long while, the men finally quit the room.

"They sometimes come to steal books for evidence of my conspiring so I leave out only non-political ones—love stories, church hymns," Monsieur Vivant explained. "This reassures them that the person living here is a pious romantic."

"What about the King being rid of censorship?" I heard it with my own ears that he changed the law.

"Oh, yes, yes," he quipped. "It will take a while for that new law to sink into the dim-witted skulls of the police."

I wondered if Monsieur Phlipon's body was still lying in the street. When they found him they would probably accuse a nearby street beggar of the crime. At least that would protect the mantua-maker from suspicion. Monsieur Vivant lit a lamp and a machine magically appeared before my eyes.

"This is the apparatus I use to print pamphlets and books," he said. "No one can find it tucked away behind this wall. This is the lever." He moved it up and down to demonstrate. "And these are the frames or coffins that the blocks of type are placed in. The paper is put under here."

I cautiously ran my fingers over its hard edges. Could that really be how books were made?

He showed me a book he was putting together: a half-sewn object in the throes of becoming. Like a butterfly or snake shedding its old skin. It contained pictures and had a brown and gold binding. I moved my fingers over its body. Not so long ago these objects looked like food to me. All over the pages, I saw black stains, not words. Nor did I know these were even pages. For a short spell, I sensed this again, the not knowing. Then I made use of what Armande taught me and read a few lines. *The horseman combed the countryside looking for a place to bury his bride. Her body was limp and cold and her hair smelled of lavender flowers. She was as beautiful dead as she had been when he first set eyes on her.*

Later that evening, I went home to a meal of chicken pie and tea, and the good doctor announced he would return to Grenoble.

"Could you stay with Armande's father?" He sat at the dining table, his hands clasped atop his belly.

Although I nodded my head, in my heart, I did not know if he would let me. After all, he was in hiding and had lived on his own for a little while now since leaving our mountain village. The doctor gave me his wife's ivory coloured mantelet and a silver pillbox. The lid was ornamented with a basket of flowers. The sides showed a laurel wreath and lute.

"Only a fashionable woman would have such a precious object like a silver pillbox." He winked at me.

The mantelet was silky on my arms and at my neck. I did feel quite the gentlewoman with it.

"I promise to treasure both of these gifts and to think of her when I use them." I embraced him as one would a cherished uncle. "Please take this tortoise snuffbox," I said being generous in my turn. It had belonged to Monsieur Phlipon.

I had kept it thinking I would pawn it for food, yet never did. The doctor graciously accepted.

The next morning, I visited Armande's father and settled the question of whether I could stay with him for the time being. I sensed he wanted to spend time with me and fill the deep hole that Armande made by dying. I knew that to be true because I saw him in the same light. The day after that, the doctor quit Paris and I moved my few possessions to Monsieur Vivant's apartment. News was out about Monsieur Phlipon's death, killed while serving King and Country. They would soon be lining up wretched suspects to pin the murder on. Armande's father told me so far, no rogues returned since last Sunday when we hid in the little room behind the wall. There were only spiders and mice to fight off in the attic where he set up my bed. He said I was safer up there in case they came looking for him again. The attic was filled with books, statues of elegant women and stately men, a lamp with piles of dust on its glass shade, and a portrait of a woman wearing an old-style gown. Spider webs hung from the ceiling like grape vines. There was no moon that evening just a splash of stars in the sky. I climbed out of my skirts and stockings.

My monthlies had not come for a while. There was constant pain around my navel and down by my curly hairs. That night, I fell asleep with a picture in my head of a wild animal growing inside me—sharp whiskers and lots of fur, a long tail like a snake and grey eyes like mine, sweet but with an air of mischief.

Weeks passed and I knew it was no animal, but a little girl God gave me to take the place of mine that had not lived, and the one of Armande's that died. Though not quite a baby, I sensed the being inside me wanting to be born, wanting me to be its mother. It would not be like the first time when a tangle of dark blood and lumps came out. My belly was small and roundish as a gentlewoman's bonnet, yet I knew soon it would overtake me and I would not be able to see my feet.

One morning, Monsieur Vivant was in his little room near the apparatus he called a press with its wooden frames and ink smells. Black ink on his fingertips, he stared proudly at a page he just printed, his bright, yet sad eyes jumping from line to line.

I told him my news, yet not that the father was Monsieur Phlipon.

"I never knew my daughter's little girl." The ends of his mouth turned down and he bowed his head. "At the time, I showed little interest in her offspring, and in her desire to be a mother. My own wife suffered so much on her childbed before she died." He stopped and turned his head away, as men do when they are about to cry. "A few years back I let the authorities believe that I died on a boat sailing the Rhône River in order to protect myself and those close to me," he said. "That day in Lyon, a man chased and almost killed me and I had to burn my tracks. I couldn't even tell my own daughter that I was alive. Now, once again in Paris, I thought the police, the censors and others would have forgotten about me. Yet they did no such thing and I am now once again forced into hiding. With bread prices fluctuating, people are terrified of dying of hunger. More riots will continue to break out here and throughout the nation. The Estates-General shall open in May, yet I fear real reform will not come so easily." He rubbed his eyes, moving fingers through his hair. He then pushed his chair away from his work and took off his wooden shoes.

I too sensed a growing unrest that had become even more palpable than when I first arrived in the city.

"Why would I stay in Paris any longer when I can breathe fresh mountain air and continue to write and print books without the rattle and reek of the city? Besides, I know Armande would want me to go back."

I nodded thinking of her home, which still held winter in its walls. In the village at nightfall, the mountains would cradle me to sleep as their shadows moved over the houses, trees and churches.

"Monsieur Taranne, my very dearest friend and business associate died only a few days ago while taking one of his daily strolls along the river. Not even he is in Paris anymore." Sitting crossed-legged, he held onto one of his feet.

"I should like to help you raise her in our mountain home," he said, his warm eyes meeting mine.

Tears of joy began pouring out of me, yet tears of sadness too, as I knew there would be no more reading by Armande's side in the drawing room while she suckled. Nor laughter or walks with her in the rose garden at sunset. Before her death I thought to stay in Paris and partake in the revolts foretold by the babies. Strong women were needed to fight and claim what was theirs. Like la pucelle, there were few who heard voices telling them the truth of what was coming. Yet without her magical milk, I felt sure the revolts would soon go awry as people lost their way. Their anger at having nothing for so long would overtake any hope of reform. How could a girl feel protected in such a place? Already, their rage had stamped out Armande's precious life and the motherly liquid that would have done them so much good. How could there be liberty without womanly wisdom? In any case, she was murdered here, and for that I did not care if Paris burned to the ground after we left it.

And so, after spending a week packing up her father's books and other belongings, we left one early morning, bound for our alpine village—my only true home.

Growing

THREE WEEKS PASSED since we left Paris, and, as the days went on my belly grew. Monsieur Vivant called what was inside me a "she" because I told him that his daughter, the last time I saw her, before her solemn death, said one day I would be mother to a little girl. Her father never asked how I came to be with child or who made me that way. His questions were more about how I was caring for myself and the baby, and what sensations were running through my body.

"What did you eat for lunch today?" he would ask.

To which I might reply, "A piece of bread with butter and a handful of carrots."

"And what did you feel in your belly?"

"That I would like to eat a little more."

"Bread is good, but you should eat beans also. Anything else?"

"A clawing in my stomach."

He told me that infants make themselves known even before coming into the world. They do this, he said, by moving, kicking, and singing. Then he turned in his chair, shuffling his wooden shoes on the ground. He made me laugh, which was good given all the tears shed between the two of us.

He cared about how I was getting along just as Armande would have, yet they shared other qualities too. I remember once when she was teaching me poetry, I wrote down a few words that pleased me such as brunante, étoile, panier and she asked me to make a poem from them. As I went about doing this, I accidentally spilled ink all over my paper. To my surprise, she did not shout at me or make me sleep outside in the woods, as my parents had me do. After mopping up the black stain, she looked at me and simply said, "Let us find more paper to write on." Even when I did a stupid thing, she thought

I was good, and that is how her father was.

It was evening and we were in the drawing room. Monsieur Vivant added a log to the fire and brought me a blanket to warm my feet. He sat on the floor, a fat cushion under him, and talked about his time in Paris, his hopes for France, and books he wished to publish. At his feet was a map of a city somewhere in the world. He glanced at it from time to time, though I judged from the grave sighs and looks to the fire that his mind couldn't follow the avenues and boulevards of the strange city as too much sadness weighed down his heart. What of his pain could I ease, knowing Armande died so horribly and unjustly?

He quit the room and returned with a book.

"This is for you," he said, handing it to me.

The cover was brown with red and yellow leaves dancing on the inside.

"Where are the words?"

"It is a diary, Céleste, for you to write your thoughts in."

Nobody ever gave me a book like that before. It was so beautiful that it forced my tongue into hiding.

Monsieur Vivant tossed another piece of wood onto the fire and studied his map. I said goodnight and climbed the stairs to my bed-chamber. Lighting a candle, I placed it on the table near my bed. The cover of my diary was soft like hers and cool to the touch. I put my diary next to the other so the two were side by side. Without opening hers, I pictured her words, drawn out in my head, with spaces between them. Tall and shapely, they stood proud and pretty just like her. I gazed through the spaces and into the distance seeing a field of mountain wildflowers as big and wide as the sky. I put out the light and crawled under the blankets.

The next morning, a glimmering sun was easing its way past the window, onto the floorboards, warming my hair. Birds sang outside, and I sensed my baby growing inside me. Maybe it too was waking. I counted out the days and months to the time when my little nut would be born. When all the big and small rivers flowing into the lakes froze and snow clothed the branches of trees. When cold and foul wind would make us stay indoors and gather at the fire then Margot, the midwife, would come. Armande's father would fetch her. In a storm, he must be wise to the snow that swept away tracks of those that went before. Wind pushed us in all directions so his head had to be certain that his legs would take him where he meant to go. As she did with others, Margot would bring over nourishing soup. She would make me drink it after the birth to give my body the goodness that a child must take for itself.

In the wee hours, words would calm her and my milk would have a lasting impression on her heart and mind. Armande told me little ones were sharper and wiser than we were, yet without the experiences, we older bodies had. I wondered if the fact I was becoming learned might in time have a pleasing influence on my baby. Would she surprise me with poems and wise words just like the babies Armande suckled? My own mother was not learned and lived in fear of my father's anger. If I heard she left him then I would want to see her again, and to show her my child. Unlike me at that age, my little one could play in the meadow and make pansy necklaces if she wished it, as Monsieur Vivant said we must be gentle with little ones during these hard times. To give her understanding, I would read pages from Armande's diary, tell her the stories she once told me so they could be passed on and not forgotten. Monsieur Vivant would teach her astronomy, botany and to be strong of character. I would show her how to clap her hands together, count to ten and make silly rhymes too, as it pleased her. Hug her, kiss her, and hold her near. Oh, there would be chores for her to do and lessons to master, yet her heart must all the while stay joyful.

Acknowledgements

Many thanks to all the incredible people who helped me with edits, suggestions, and for their love and encouragement throughout the writing of this book. I really appreciate the fact that you didn't tell me to take a hike. I wouldn't have blamed you one bit.

Thanks to Daphne Marlatt for starting me on this journey several years ago at a writer's retreat at the Banff Centre. Her poetic intuition and gentle encouragement helped me find a voice for my characters.

To Andrea O'Reilly at Demeter Press for her jubilant enthusiasm and support, and to Luciana Ricciutelli, my gifted editor who worked tirelessly to get the job done.

To Jen Sookfong Lee for her friendship and no-nonsense editing advice, and to my dear sister Shannon Cowan who was always there to commiserate with and give me the straight goods.

To Penelope Cowan, my dear mom and trusty editor who was an 'early adopter' of my novel even though there were some naughty bits. To Joanna Stonechapel who was always full of encouragement and hope, and to my writing partners in crime Kim Goodliffe, Leslie Palleson and Dilara Ali who are also crazy enough to love to write. To Elyssa Schmid, dear friend and über-talented designer for her inspired book cover design. To Zool Suleman for his love of language and legal chops.

Special thanks to Sanjay Khanna who stood by me and encouraged me, even when it seemed all was lost.

Although *Milk Fever* is not based on any particular historical character, many of my ideas for the characters and for the historical details came from books written at that time in French and in English. Two books, *The Private Memoirs of Madame Roland* by Madame Roland, and *Declaration of the Rights of Woman*, a pamphlet written in 1791 by Olympe de Gouges, were instrumental in helping me shape my characters Armande and Céleste.

Books that I consulted throughout the writing of *Milk Fever* were *Selling Mother's Milk: The Wet-Nursing Business in France* by George Sussman, Simon Schama's *Citizens, A Chronicle of the French Revolution* and two books by Robert Darnton, *The Literary Underground of the Old Regime* and *The Great Cat Massacre and Other Episodes in French Cultural History*. These remarkable works enabled me to flesh out the novel's historic backdrop and themes.

Lissa M. Cowan is the author of works of non-fiction, is co-translator of *Words that Walk in the Night* by Pierre Morency, one of Québec's most honoured writers, and her writing has appeared in Canadian and U.S. magazines and newspapers. She has received fellowships from the University of Victoria's Writing Department and The Banff Centre. She holds a Master of Arts degree in English Studies from l'Université de Montréal and lives in Toronto. Visit her website at www.lissamcowan.com.